Praise

"*The Ruin* is as much a m........... ....ary
page-turner . . . [A] superior haunting novel of murder, decep-
tion and ethical dilemma."
—*Bookseller + Publisher*

"If you're on the hunt for a crime story that's going to con-
sume every other thought in your head, wring you out like a
wet towel, and then deposit you back in the real world with
your nerves fried to a crisp . . . you're in luck. *The Ruin* is
the kind of book that you will inevitably find yourself recom-
mending to every person you know, and probably also that
lovely person who makes you coffee. It's blisteringly good."
—*Readings*

"A breezily confident debut and promises a bright future for
this new Irish-Australian talent."
—*The Australian*

"A terrific debut and a rare gem: a compelling crime thriller
that delivers depth as well as twists."
—Sara Foster, author of *The Hidden Hours*

"Instantly hauling the reader into its permanently charged at-
mosphere, *The Ruin* is as convincing as it is multilayered, as
compelling as it is complex, and heralds the arrival of Dervla
McTiernan as a future star of the genre."
—Christopher Brookmyre, author of
Country of the Blind

"There are not many books that will keep me reading from
start to finish . . . Began before breakfast and just finished now
after midnight. An excellent story, very well written. This one
was a winner for me."
—Alex Gray, author of the
DCI William Lorimer series

"I tore through *The Ruin*, desperate to unravel the mystery that McTiernan so cleverly lays out. Heartbreaking and heart-stopping in equal measure, it's an incredibly well-crafted, complex tale and yet remarkably easy to read, such is the subtle brilliance of the plotting. . . . McTiernan maintains the suspense all the way through, yet never at the expense of plausibility. She's sure to become one of my go-to authors!"
—Caz Frear, author of *Sweet Little Lies*

"Loved every page. Cormac Reilly is a brilliant new character, so real you can hear his footsteps on the stairs. Utterly gripping, brilliantly executed story. Serious contender for Irish Crime Novel of the Year."
—Sinéad Crowley, author of *One Bad Turn*

PENGUIN BOOKS

THE RUIN

Dervla McTiernan was born in Ireland and now lives with her family in Australia, where she works for the Mental Health Commission. *The Ruin* is her first novel.

THE
RUIN

DERVLA McTIERNAN

PENGUIN BOOKS

PENGUIN BOOKS

An imprint of Penguin Random House LLC
375 Hudson Street
New York, New York 10014
penguinrandomhouse.com

First published in Australia
by HarperCollins*Publishers* Australia Pty Limited 2018
Published in Penguin Books 2018

LIBRARY OF CONGRESS CATALOGING-IN-PUBLICATION DATA
Names: McTiernan, Dervla.
Title: The ruin / Dervla McTiernan.
Description: New York : Penguin Books, 2018.
Identifiers: LCCN 2018002072 (print) I LCCN 2018005883 (ebook) I
ISBN 9780525504894 (ebook) I ISBN 9780143133124 (paperback)
Subjects: LCSH: Murder—Investigation—Fiction. I Detective and mystery
stories. I GSAFD: Suspense fiction I Mystery fiction
Classification: LCC PR9619.4.M45 (ebook) I LCC PR9619.4.M45 R85 2018
(print) I DDC 823/.92—dc23
LC record available at https://lccn.loc.gov/2018002072

Printed in the United States of America
1   3   5   7   9   10   8   6   4   2

To Kenny, my partner in crime. Thank you for the Thursday nights, for the log-lines, and the laughs.

Ní scéal rúin é más fios do thriúr é.
An Irish saying, meaning 'it's not a secret if a third
person knows about it'.
The title of my book can be read in English, or can be
given its Irish meaning. In Irish, Rúin means something
hidden, a mystery, or a secret, but the word also has a
long history as a term of endearment.

Dervla McTiernan

Mayo, Ireland

February 1993

PROLOGUE

Cormac leaned forward to peer through the windscreen, then nearly cracked his head on the steering wheel as the car bounced through another pothole. Shite. There was no sign of the house, and he'd been searching for over an hour. He could barely read house names or numbers in the settling gloom. Maybe the whole thing was some kind of first-week hazing ritual. If it had been Dwyer who'd sent him he would have been sure of it. Dwyer was the sort of bastard who was forever telling jokes, jokes with an edge to them and usually a target. But it had been Marcus Tully who'd called him in off traffic duty, barely looking up from his newspaper as he handed Cormac the post-it note that was now stuck to his dashboard.

Dower House, Monagaraun Road, Kilmore. Maude Blake. Tully's handwriting, unlike the man himself, was tidy and perfectly legible. His muttered instruction had given Cormac the impression that the call was for some sort of minor domestic. Cormac hadn't asked any questions; he'd been concentrating too hard on trying to look like he knew what he was doing. It turned out that Kilmore was a blink-and-you-miss it kind of village, with a church, a mart, a tiny primary school, and two pubs. The Monagaraun Road was forty miles long, and pocked with a bare scattering of farmhouses and bungalows, none of which bore any resemblance to a dower house.

Cormac pulled in at the next gap in the hedgerow, and sat for a moment. He was sweating. The heater was broken – the only settings were off and furnace – and given the temperature outside, he'd chosen furnace. Christ. The car was a nightmare, with a clutch that made threatening sounds every time he changed gear, and a faint but persistent smell of vomit from the back seat. Even the radio was in bits, its wires hanging loose, waiting for a fix.

It could be a piss-take. The whole thing, giving him a phantom address, a squad car that was falling apart. In which case he should give up now. Drive back. Pretend that he'd known all along and had spent the last couple of hours eating his lunch. On the other hand, what if this was a real call and he arrived back without even having found the house? No. He had to find the damn place, or be absolutely sure it didn't exist. His best option might be to try one of the village pubs – there was a fifty-fifty chance he would get real directions that wouldn't send him into the nearest bog. Cormac released the hand-brake and started a slow drive back towards the village. He was about a kilometre out when he spotted two crumbling stone gateposts, almost hidden behind a thick layer of ivy. The gate they'd once supported was long gone. Cormac pulled into the gateway. His headlights illuminated a drive that was little more than mud and weeds. It was lined with mature sycamore trees, overgrown now, their bare branches meshing overhead.

Deep ruts had been dug through the soil by the recent passage of a tractor. He'd seen the drive before, on a previous pass, had taken it to be an access track for farmland and dismissed it. But those sycamores and the gateposts suggested something else. Hundred-year-old trees, planted to offer an elegant entrance to the parkland of some grand estate. An estate meant a dower house, or at least the chance of one.

Cormac moved the car forward another few metres and peered through the windscreen. He couldn't see a house, but the tractor marks petered out halfway down the visible drive. Was there a farm gate there in a break in the trees? Maybe. Beyond that the driveway continued, and curved, and the tree line blocked whatever it might lead to. Cormac put the car into gear and started down the drive. He drove at a steady pace, aiming to keep his tyres out of ruts where he could, and he made it without getting bogged down, following the drive until it swung abruptly to the right and opened out to form a parking area in front of an old Georgian house.

At first glance the house seemed to be in complete darkness, and it was obvious the place was in disrepair. A broken gutter was spewing dirty rainwater down one side of the facade. Paint was peeling and stained and all but one of the windows of the first floor were boarded up. The ground floor windows were in better shape, and Cormac thought he could see a dim glow coming from a room to the left of the front door. He felt only relief that he'd found the bloody place, that he wouldn't have to go back to the station hat-in-hand, looking as clueless as he felt. He got out of the car and walked through the rain to the front door. It opened before he reached it, and was held ajar just enough for him to see that the person behind it was a girl. She was a teenager, fourteen or maybe fifteen. Dark hair. Slight.

'Why are you by yourself?' she asked, before he had a chance to speak.

'Sorry?'

'I thought you always come out in pairs. You know, with a partner.'

'Not always,' was all he could think of to say. He couldn't very well tell her that Marcus Tully would rather sit on his fat arse eating chips and reading the *Daily Star* than get into a squad car and drive out in this weather for a domestic. He took his ID from his pocket and showed it to her. 'I'm Garda Cormac Reilly,' he said.

She looked at his ID, then back at his face. 'You're very young,' she said doubtfully.

'I suppose I am.' He swallowed his smile. Fifteen, and she spoke like his mother.

'Come in out of the rain,' she said after a further pause, during which the water that had pooled on top of his hat started to drip down the back of his neck.

The hall was huge, the pitch pine-panelled ceilings at least four metres high. The other end of the hall held an ornate returning staircase. It must have been grand and beautiful once but what struck Cormac was the smell. Damp hung in the air, there was an underlying hint of something nastier, and the place was bloody freezing. The girl was waiting for him, her face grave.

'Are your mum or dad home?' he asked.

'My little brother is in the drawing room,' she said, gesturing to an open door leading off the hall. Looking past her, Cormac could see that there was a fire lit in the grate, and the small figure of a very young boy sitting on bare wooden floor in front of it, turning the pages of a book.

'Your mum?' he asked again.

'In her room,' she said, and pointed towards the stairs. She turned and took a step towards the drawing room, then spoke to the little boy. 'Jack, stay here. I'm going upstairs with the garda for a minute, but I'll be back really quickly, okay?' The little boy raised his head at her voice, but said nothing. She shut the door and turned and walked up the stairs, leaving Cormac to follow.

As they climbed the smell of damp became stronger. Wallpaper peeled away from the walls in long strips. The upstairs landing was in almost complete darkness, and as they took the last step Cormac reached automatically for the light switch. Nothing happened.

The girl kept walking. 'There's no power,' she said. 'Don't worry. There are candles in Mother's room.'

She led him along the dark corridor to a room where a glimmer of light leaked under the door. She opened the door without knocking and held it for him. He stepped past her.

The room was sparsely furnished, with little more than a double bed and an antique wardrobe. The floorboards were bare. The fireplace was black and empty and the room was very cold, but the woman on the bed had no need of the blankets that were pulled up past her bare feet. She was dead. Very obviously dead, her eyes open and staring at the ceiling.

'Jesus.' Cormac took a stumbling step into the room. He looked back at the girl, then at the woman on the bed. 'Jesus,' he said again. Despite knowing she was dead, he found himself walking to her and checking her neck for a pulse. Her skin was cold to the touch, and he wiped his hand reflexively on his pants, then realised what he was doing and hoped the girl hadn't seen him. 'This is your mum?' he asked.

She was inside the room now, but she stared fixedly away from the tableau on the bed, and nodded stiffly in response to his question.

Cormac looked down at the corpse. Her arms and legs were skeletal, her hair lank and greasy. The top sheet was grubby and thin and through it he could see the outline of her body. There was a dark stain at the apex of her legs where death had caused her bowels to open. The smell of sour body odour and faeces was thick despite the frigid air. Cause of death seemed obvious. An empty vodka bottle stood beside a guttering candle on the bedside table. A shoelace was tied around the woman's left arm, and on the floor lay an empty syringe. There were deep scratches on her arms. Track marks? He'd never seen them before. In the crook of her exposed left elbow was a single pin-prick mark and a smear of dried blood.

Cormac turned from the body and walked in three quick steps to the girl. He took her by the arm. 'Come on,' he said. He pulled the door closed behind them and walked her to the top of the stairs.

'That woman's your mum?'

She nodded again. She had very dark eyes. They dominated her pale, frightened face as she looked up at him.

'There's no one else, no one to take care of you? Who called the police?'

'I did. From the village, this morning. When I brought Jack to school.'

'This morning? You've been here all day?'

She said nothing. He stood, paralysed by indecision, until he noticed that she was shivering. Shock. Or maybe just the cold. She was dressed for it, in jeans, boots and what looked like layers of jumpers, but it was bloody freezing in the house, as cold inside as out.

'Come on downstairs,' he said, and this time she followed him as he led the way down the stairs and back to the drawing room. The little boy climbed carefully to his feet as they entered. When the girl chose a seat he settled himself into her lap, and they turned matching pairs of dark eyes in Cormac's direction. He took a seat himself, and leaned forward to talk to them, trying to look as reassuring as possible.

'What's your name?' he asked. He felt like a fool, felt like the worst possible person to be here in this moment. How were you supposed to handle traumatised children? Two years in Templemore had not equipped him for this.

'I'm Maude, and this is Jack.'

The boy struck him as very young, although he must be five at least if he'd started school. He was sandy haired and solemn faced; Cormac could see the smudge of an old bruise on his cheek. Both children seemed thin, the girl in particular.

'Maude,' Cormac said quietly. 'Do you know how your mum died?'

She dropped her gaze to the floor.

'Okay,' he said. 'That's okay.'

Maude drew the little boy closer and he softened against her, his eyelids drooping a little.

'I'll need to call some people, you understand? People who will come and take care of your mum's body. People who will take care of you and Jack.'

Her face tightened with anxiety and she glanced towards the dark windows. 'But you won't leave us here? It's getting late. I think you should just bring us with you now, you can bring us to the hospital if you like. To Castlebar.'

'The hospital?'

She nodded, her face pinched. 'A doctor should examine Jack.'

The little boy was falling asleep on Maude's lap, his head resting against her shoulder.

'He's sick?' Cormac asked.

'He's hurt.'

'Okay. Okay Maude. I can bring you to a doctor, of course, but I'll need to call a social worker. Do you have a family doctor? Maybe in Kilmore?'

But she was shaking her head violently now, disturbing her little brother. 'Jack needs to see a real doctor, okay? Like in a hospital.' She must have read the doubt in his face. 'You won't get the social in Kilmore at this time. There's no social worker on at night. No one 'til the morning. And then what'll you do with us? If you bring us to Castlebar you'll get them no problem. And Jack can be properly looked after.'

Cormac hesitated. She was afraid, that was obvious. She was only a child, and her mother was dead upstairs. Was that all it was? More than enough for most kids. What was he supposed to do now? He couldn't just pack two children into the back of his squad car, a car that still smelled of vomit due to a half-arsed clean out from a Saturday night arrest. On the other hand, she was probably right that there'd be no social workers in Kilmore at this stage of the evening.

'I'll radio the station,' he said in the end. 'See what my sergeant thinks.'

Maude just stared back at him, real worry in her eyes, and in the same moment Cormac remembered the broken radio. *Shite.* She was looking at him as if all her hopes were pinned to his response and she expected the worst. God she was thin. And very young. She had pulled the sleeves of her jumper so that they were halfway down her hands, and the fingers of her right hand were worrying at a loose strand of wool. He could hardly leave them here.

'Castlebar it is so,' he said.

She didn't smile, didn't say or do anything, but he could see the relief in her eyes, and he felt a little more confident.

'Do you have some things you'd like to bring with you? Have you pyjamas, or maybe a favourite toy for Jack?'

Maude pointed behind him and he turned, noticing for the first time two small schoolbags leaning against the wall beside the door.

'I packed our stuff already,' she said. 'We don't need anything else.'

Jesus. Cormac swallowed hard against a wave of emotion. There was something so utterly pathetic about the two little bags.

'Right so,' he said, rising. 'Can I take the little lad for you?'

She shook her head, then stood and cradled the boy so that his legs were either side of her waist. She was stronger than she looked; she carried him easily. Cormac took an old blanket from the back of his chair, picked up the two bags from their places by the door, then led the way out of the house. He laid the blanket over the smelly back seat, and Maude put Jack down, letting him lie flat before settling in beside him and putting one hand protectively on his back. Cormac drove them carefully down the drive, conscious now of every bump and jolt and afraid that Jack would be hurt by the rough progress.

They didn't speak again for what felt like a long time.

'How is Jack hurt, Maude?'

She had kept her hand against the little boy's back, to prevent him from falling off the back seat in his sleep. Now she stroked his sandy hair back from his face. 'He has some bruises,' she said, after a pause.

'Did someone hurt him? Did someone hurt you?'

'I'm fine. I can take care of myself.'

She didn't say anything more. Should he push her? No. He might fuck it up, say the wrong thing. Scare her or traumatise her. But how the hell had this happened? How had two children been left to rot in a freezing, empty house with someone as far gone as their mother must have been? He looked at Maude in the rear-view mirror.

'Jack doesn't have a dad,' she said, looking very tired as she spoke. 'There's no name on his birth certificate. Can you please tell them? If they know he's an orphan, then he can be adopted. He should have a proper family.'

'I'm sure you'll be kept together,' Cormac said, then cursed himself inwardly. A five-year-old like Jack would have no trouble finding a home. A fifteen-year-old girl was a different prospect. Placing them together? That would take a miracle.

In the rear-view mirror he saw Maude give a slight smile, but the smile was a sad one and she said nothing. She didn't speak again on the long drive to Castlebar. When he pulled into the emergency area she woke Jack, quieting his protests and coaxing him from the car. She picked him up again when he started to cry, and walked with him towards the sliding doors.

The waiting room held the usual mix of the genuinely ill, the drunk, and the stupid. Seats were taken by a trio of teenage boys who looked like they would fit at least two of the three categories. The heaters were on too high, and the muggy warmth was unpleasant. The triage nurse was absorbed in paperwork as Cormac shepherded the children towards her, but a flash of his ID and an edited explanation saw them brought through the A&E double doors and into the assessment area.

Maude followed the nurse to a curtained off bed and gently sat Jack down on it. He clutched at her hand.

'Is there a loo?' Maude asked the nurse.

'Just down the corridor there. First left and it's on your right.'

Jack started crying again as Maude untangled her hand and walked away.

'Now be a good brave boy,' the nurse said. 'Your sister will be back in a minute.' But Jack lowered his head and wept, his tears horribly silent, his small body limp. Cormac took a little hand in his and gave it a gentle squeeze. He tried to distract the boy. Told him stories and talked hurling and superheroes as the nurse took off Jack's clothes and put him in a hospital gown. Tried not to show his horror at the black and blue bruising that ran up Jack's spine, at the swollen contusion above his left hip. Then the doctor came and Cormac had to step back as he examined the little boy. Cormac stood there, his arms folded and his eyes bleak. And all the time, Jack cried his silent tears and ignored them.

It was a long time before Cormac realised that Maude had not come back. And some time later before he thought to check for her. A full two hours passed before an agitated Tully arrived and they did a proper search of the ground floor bathrooms, the café and the public wards, and realised that she probably wasn't in the hospital. In the end, that was the only search that was ever carried out for fifteen-year-old Maude Blake. She was labelled a runaway, and with no family to notice or care that she was gone, the system forgot her. Eventually, Cormac Reilly forgot her too.

Galway, Ireland

Saturday 16 March 2013

CHAPTER ONE

It was two hours into the day shift when Aisling finished her last chart and signed out, which meant she had the dressing room to herself. She took her time in the shower, letting the hot water ease the tension in her shoulders and lower back. She took her time too getting dressed. The solitude was a balm, and for once she was in no hurry to leave the hospital. She was sitting on the bench, dressed, but with her wet hair still wrapped in a towel, when Mary Dooley broke the peace by pushing the door open hard, and entering the room while still calling to someone over her shoulder. When she saw Aisling she let the door swing shut, then turned, and pointed to her back. Her blonde pony-tail was stuck to her top with blood-streaked vomit. An acrid, metallic smell reached Aisling from across the room, and she felt a solid punch of nausea. *Jesus.* The smell of vomit hadn't hit her like that since she was a first-year intern.

'Never turn your back on them,' said Mary. 'I swear.'

She un-peeled her scrubs top carefully, and dropped it into the waiting laundry basket. The long-sleeved top she'd worn underneath went straight into the bin. Every female doctor Aisling knew bought those tops in packets of five from Dunnes Stores. They were cheap and warm, and once you'd been puked on (happened more than you'd think) or a blood bag exploded on you (not common but once was enough), you really didn't want to wear that top again, no matter how well washed.

'Shouldn't have left surgery,' Aisling said. 'You'd be out of that stuff by now.'

'What stuff?' asked Mary. 'You mean actual medicine, looking after people?' She went to her locker, took out her towel and shampoo, and held them in one hand, half-turning to talk to Aisling as she pushed each runner off using the toe of the other foot.

'Exactly.'

'I'm well off out of it. All that obsessing over test scores, assessments; putting socks in my knickers so the consultants forget I'm a woman.' She smiled. 'Now I just have nice relaxing night shifts in A&E to worry about.'

Aisling rolled her shoulders, freeing the remaining tension from her muscles. 'How was it?'

'Shite,' said Mary, as she balled up her scrubs pants and threw them neatly into the laundry basket. She grimaced. 'Apart from the usual, we had two suicide attempts. One of them was only fourteen.'

'Ah God, Mary. I'm sorry.'

Mary nodded. 'He tried to hang himself. Made the rope too short so he didn't break his neck, and he can't have been hanging long or he would be dead. His mother walked in on him, cut him down. He's in a coma now.'

'Brain damage?' Aisling asked.

Mary shrugged. There was a shadow behind her blue eyes. 'I suppose we'll see.'

Aisling made for the mirror and the sole crappy hairdryer. She didn't want to go home, but she couldn't put it off forever. She'd dried her hair, and was pulling on her puffa and boots when Mary emerged from the shower and started to dress.

'Are you coming tonight?' Mary asked. 'You're finished nights now, right?' Her voice was muffled by the T-shirt she was pulling over her head.

It took Aisling a minute to remember, then it came back. Mary's boyfriend, Derek – dental student by day, band member by night – had a gig in the Róisín Dubh every second Saturday night. *Bugger*. 'I'm off for the weekend,' she said. 'We might come. But I think Jack said something about a work thing.' She couldn't face Róisín's; the music, the drink, the shouting to be heard. And she needed to talk to Jack in private. They needed space to think. To figure out what to do.

Mary wagged a finger at her. 'They'll be brilliant,' she said. 'You'll miss out.' But she let it go, and launched instead into a rundown of patients she'd seen and assholes she'd put manners on during her fourteen-hour night shift in Galway University Hospital, Accident & Emergency. Aisling leaned back against her locker and listened, enjoying Mary's delivery, though she'd heard the jokes before.

She should feel good. It had been a hard week – long hours, lots of politics – but she'd done well, and it should have felt good to come out ahead, and to have nothing but Jack to look forward to all weekend.

When she finally left the hospital the sun was fully up. For once the clouds had cleared, and the sky was a bright, hard blue. Some of the puddles were still frozen, and she picked her way around patches of ice as she made her way up University Road towards the city. She was overtaken by a group of students. There was a lot of foot traffic – more than usual for this time on a Saturday morning.

Of course. Sunday was Paddy's Day. She'd forgotten. Town would be packed. This year there was going to be an evening parade. Quay Street pubs would have their doors wide open, and the street would be so full of people that the drinkers – an enthusiastic mix of students and tourists – would almost be able to convince themselves that they weren't semi-hypothermic. Aisling shivered reflexively. She just wanted to get home.

She let herself into their little place in the Claddagh half an hour later. They had been renting the two-storey terrace for nearly two years, and she loved it, despite the dodgy heating and dated décor. It was close to the city, close to the sea and walking distance from work. Best of all, it felt like home. The cosiness of the small rooms felt like an embrace after the sterility of the hospital.

Jack was awake – she could smell coffee, and bacon, and the heating was on.

'Jack?'

'Kitchen,' he called.

He was making breakfast – he had rashers in the pan, and toast in the toaster – and he smiled at her as she came in. 'How was work?'

She leaned against the doorframe and watched him, the words she'd carried around all day growing heavier and heavier in her mouth, until she finally spilled them out on the floor.

'I'm pregnant.'

'Ha ha, funny.' Jack didn't look up from rummaging in the bottom kitchen drawer. 'Have you seen the tinfoil? I think it's fallen down the back.' He got down on his knees, started to lift the drawer out.

'Jack.'

He caught the tone of her voice and turned to her.

'You're pregnant.' Shock widened his eyes, slackened his mouth, so that he looked like a stranger.

Slowly Aisling nodded her head.

He closed his eyes. 'Jesus, Ash.'

Aisling turned and left the room. She walked on autopilot to their bedroom. The bed was still unmade. She started straightening the sheets. He never made the bed. Not ever. Had he ever once, since they moved in together, even washed the bloody sheets?

'Aisling.' He was standing at the door, watching her.

'You didn't make the bed,' she said. 'Again.'

'Aisling, seriously. Just – how did this happen?'

She very deliberately tucked the sheet over, then straightened out a wrinkle, before turning to him. 'I don't know, Jack. How do you think these things happen?'

He wiped his hand across his mouth, looking grey-faced. Then he said, 'But you've been on the pill.'

Aisling walked past him, then pushed the door open into the bathroom. She rummaged in her washbag, taking out her pill packet. Every day of the month so far had been neatly punched out – she was only three days into the next cycle.

She handed the packet to him. 'I threw the other one out. It's in the bathroom bin probably, so you can check if you want. Of course I could have been throwing the pills into the toilet. As you know, it's always been my dream to get pregnant at twenty-five. Isn't that what I've been working for?' She left him at the door and went to the bed, lying down on the sheets she'd just straightened, turning away from him. She wanted to climb under the covers, pull them over her head, and hide from the world.

'For fuck's sake Aisling. I'm not suggesting you got pregnant on purpose. I'm just ... trying to get my head around this. I know you're careful. I mean, we're careful. Ash. Aisling.' He walked over, climbed onto the bed, and pulled her gently towards him.

She resisted, shaking her head, her eyes closed. She thought of all the times she'd worked a long shift, maybe been on call the next day, gone for a few drinks and dinner with friends on the way home. She always took her pill, sure, but how many times had it been forty-eight hours between pills, or more? That made a difference, particularly at the beginning of a cycle. She kept her eyes closed. She couldn't look at him. But he was lying down now, pulling her against him, curling himself around her protectively. His left arm came around her so that her head rested against him; with his right hand he wiped a tear from her face.

'What are we going to do?' she whispered, without opening her eyes.

He hugged her a little tighter, said nothing.

Then, eventually, 'You're sure?'

'I did a test, at the hospital. I never had a period. I just realised this morning that I was three days into the next packet and still no bleed. So I did the test. A urine test first, which was negative. But it was one of the hospital ones; they're not very sensitive. So I did a blood test. Put it through the system under a different name. And it came back positive. I'm pregnant, Jack. I mean, barely, barely pregnant. But I am. What the fuck are we going to do?'

His arms tightened around her again, his lips brushed her hair. 'I suppose we'll just have to make it work, Ash. We're not the first to be in this situation. We won't be the last. At least we love each other.' His voice grew in confidence as he spoke. 'We're not babies. Jesus, Americans get married at twenty-five all the time, the crazy bastards.' There was a laugh in his voice now, that Jack-joy that always made her happy. 'We've got good jobs. The hospital will have to give you maternity leave. We've got this little place. Or we could rent somewhere bigger.' He hugged her closer. 'We can absolutely do this.'

Oh Jesus. 'Jack,' her voice was aching with unshed tears. She turned to him, pushed backwards so there was enough distance between them that they could see each other. 'I don't want to be a mother. At least, I don't want to be a mother now.' His dark eyes held hers; there was a patch of stray stubble on his chin. His left arm was still under her, his jumper warm and scratchy under her cheek. She put her hand against his chest. 'I want to be a surgeon. I have to be a surgeon. If I get pregnant now, then I can forget about it. They'll never, never, never give a training spot to a pregnant girl, to a mother.'

'They can't stop you. You're right up there – what, third in the country at the moment? They can't refuse you.'

'They can. There's the interview. They can just say I'm psychologically unsuited and that will be the end of it.'

'They can't do that. You'd sue them.'

She shook her head. 'Sue a consultant in Ireland and you'll never get another job in a hospital. You know that as well as I do.'

He half rolled away from her, so that he was lying on the flat of his back, his left arm still holding her, his right hand running through his hair. 'Fuck.'

'Yeah.'

They were quiet for a time. Aisling found herself listening to the distant sounds of traffic at the end of their street. If she was standing outside she'd be able to hear the waves crashing, but up here, in their bedroom, she only ever heard the sounds of the city. It was a little cold in their room. She felt it creeping in the gap between her jeans and her top, where her jumper had ridden up. She wanted to curl up to Jack, to pull the quilt up over them, close her eyes, and let all of this disappear.

'We need to talk about options,' she said.

'Yeah.' His voice was flat.

She took a deep breath. 'I can't have a baby and be a surgeon; even if I got a training spot for next year, I wouldn't be able to do it. It's three years of crazy hours, moving every three to six months. You'd have to be alone here with the … the baby, and I'd only be able to get home the odd weekend.' She paused, breathed in again. 'If I gave up on surgery I could try for the GP scheme. They say that can be family friendly. If I got in I could get credit for the hospital time I've already put in; then I'd just need to get a training contract with a GP practice here in Galway, maybe even arrange to do the two years training over three, so I could work part-time.'

He rolled back towards her, his expression quiet, waiting. She felt claustrophobic. The conversation was moving too quickly. She'd gotten here before she was ready.

'Or we could talk about Liverpool.'

'Is that where they do it?' Jack asked.

'Liverpool. Or Manchester. I think that's where most people go.'

'Right.' He stroked a strand of hair back from her face. 'Would it hurt you? I mean, are there risks?'

Aisling closed her eyes. Her head ached with the effort of holding back her tears. She didn't want to be in charge. Didn't want to be the one with all the information. Would she have to make this decision? And if she did, would he ever forgive her?

'It's very early. I'd just have to take a couple of pills probably. Mifepristone. I'd have to stay in the UK overnight, in case there were any complications. Then we could come home. I'd have to have a scan later, to make sure everything was okay.'

'Could we have the scan here, or would we have to go back to Britain?'

'Jesus Jack, I don't know. I haven't thought about all that.'

'Right. Sorry. I'm just trying to …' He let his voice trail off.

He was still holding her, but she rolled away from him, stood up. She took one of his old sweatshirts from the wardrobe and pulled it over her head. It was too big, but it was warm.

'I might make tea.'

'Okay,' he said.

But she didn't go down, just leaned against the door jam, head bowed.

He closed his eyes. Opened them. Looked at her, and she ached at the dearness of him.

'I know what I'm supposed to say. I know that this is supposed to be your decision, and I'm just supposed to support you. Maybe it has to be that way. But it feels wrong. It just feels wrong, Aisling. For me to sit back and leave the hard stuff to you, then pat you on the head and say "I've got your back darlin'," This should be something we decide together.'

She smiled at him then. A small smile. Then let it drop.

Jack being Jack, he knew why. He'd always been able to read her, far better than she could read him. 'What if I want to keep it, and you don't?'

She shook her head, said nothing.

'Yeah. See, then it's your decision again.' A long pause. 'But what does that do to us?'

'I don't know.' Her voice was very quiet, not much more than a whisper.

'Can we wait awhile? Talk about it?'

She nodded. 'A little. We can wait a little.'

They ate breakfast together, and made stuttering small talk. Jack wasn't working – he never worked weekends – so he said he would do the food shop, and when she woke they could just stay in, cook something together. He didn't say he wanted to talk some more, though he obviously did. By the end of the meal she was fighting against sleep, fatigue pulling at her in unfamiliar ways. It was always a struggle getting back to normal after a week of night shifts, and she told herself this time was no different. Jack kissed her before she went upstairs, and gave her a long hug, but said nothing.

Aisling used the bathroom, brushed her teeth and splashed water on her face. She was already half asleep as she stripped, too tired to do anything but leave her clothes where they lay and pull the previous night's t-shirt over her head. And then she slept, long and hard, and woke, disoriented, to a dark bedroom.

'Jack?' No answer.

It was cold. The house was very quiet. She pulled on Jack's old sweatshirt from where it lay at the foot of the bed, and went downstairs. No Jack. The oven clock told her it was nearly nine o'clock. She had slept so late, far later than usual, had missed the whole day. She checked the fridge – nothing, except leftover rashers. Jack must not have shopped after all. Would he want to go out? After almost ten hours of sleep the idea was no more appealing. Aisling took a rasher and ate it cold, standing in the kitchen, then went to put on the heating, and the kettle. She made tea and toast and watched television, but by ten o'clock there was still no Jack.

Aisling turned off the television and sat in the silent living room. Looked at her phone, and picked it up.

Text me to let me know you're all right, ok?

She let her eyes wander around the room, taking in all the paraphernalia of their daily lives, all the little signs that a childless couple lived in this house. There was dirt on the hearth, where Jack had left his hiking boots to dry the day before. The hearth was cold now, and grey with ash. There was no fireguard. The remnants of the previous weekend's newspapers were stacked haphazardly on the coffee table. At the other end of the room they'd pushed an old dining table up against a wall, installed a narrow Ikea bookshelf in the little space that was left. That was where she worked, where she should be working now. Her laptop and the pile of textbooks sat there, waiting for her. She turned away, lay back on the couch and stared at the ceiling. There was no space in this little room for toys. How would they squeeze a buggy into the narrow hall? The spare bedroom had a bed, buried under their ski gear, dumped after their January trip, and two baskets of laundry. What would they do, clear it out, move in a cot? Or move house altogether? Her hand strayed to her stomach. If they did this there would be no chance to try to for a fellowship in the States. No paediatric surgery. No surgery full stop. Never again to feel that clarity and focus as her scalpel pressed down. Aisling sat up abruptly, turned the television on again, stared at it without seeing anything. She didn't want this pregnancy. Guilt rose again at the thought and with it a matching, overwhelming anger. Aisling thought of the years she had spent working towards her goals, of everything she had overcome to get this far, and clenched her fists hard enough that her nails bit into the palms of her hands. If it were possible she would have lit that guilt on fire, burned it out of herself from the inside out. Why shouldn't she put her life first, instead of sacrificing her future for what was nothing more than a scrap of biological material, now busy, cells dividing, inside her?

She gave up at eleven, feeling more tired than she would have thought possible after a day asleep, and climbed the stairs slowly to bed. She would never sleep, not after a week of night shifts. Was Jack that upset, that angry, that he went out and left no note, made no attempt to change their plans? That didn't feel like him. Maybe he'd just met friends, and his phone had died. She stood for a moment in the bathroom, toothbrush in hand, and stared at her reflection. She turned to one side. Her stomach was flat, unassuming. She pushed it out so that it curved, smoothed her t-shirt over the bump. For a moment she could see it; a warm body curled in her lap, a soft hand to her cheek. Later, a laughing Jack with a boy on his shoulders. Aisling closed her eyes. No. Just no.

In bed, she thought again about calling him, then decided against it. If he needed the time to himself, then fine. They had tomorrow to talk, to catch up. He needed space, and she needed rest, and tomorrow they could make a more sensible job of it.

The deep weariness she felt translated only slowly into sleepiness, and she tossed and turned for a couple of hours before sinking into a disturbed sleep. She woke the following morning to an empty bed. It was dark in the bedroom, and it took her a moment to remember that she was at home, and not in the on-call room. She turned and groped across her bedside table toward the glow of her phone's battery light. It was 9.30 a.m. and fingers of weak morning light were starting to creep in at the edges of the curtains. It was very warm in the room; she'd forgotten to turn the heating off before she went to bed, and the timer was broken. Shite. And then she heard the doorbell, followed by a brisk knocking at the door. Still half-asleep, Aisling climbed out of bed, pulling a jumper of Jack's over her head, and pushing her feet into Uggs, before she went down the stairs. She opened the door to two gardaí, standing on the porch in the early morning light. It was another bright day – scudding white clouds buffeted overhead in an otherwise blue sky. Two gardaí, one older, overweight. He looked her up and down as if she were inappropriately dressed for a function. The younger one, a woman, had a nicer face.

Aisling folded her arms. 'Can I help you?'

'Can I ask your name?' the older man asked.

'Um, I'm Aisling Conroy.' She wondered vaguely if she was supposed to just give her name, or if she should have asked to see their ID or something.

He looked down at his notebook. 'And Jack Blake lives at this address?'

'He's not here at the moment,' Aisling said. She felt the first trickle of fear.

'Are you a relation of Jack's?'

The female guard was shivering, but trying to hide it. She stared straight at Aisling, as if she were determined not to break eye contact. Aisling returned her attention to the man.

'I'm his girlfriend. His partner. We live together.' She half-glanced over her shoulder into the house, feeling increasingly uneasy. 'What's this about?'

And now they were silent, both of them, exchanging meaningful glances as if urging the other to take the lead. Finally, the young woman turned back towards her and stepped forward, taking Aisling gently by the upper arm.

'I'm very sorry Aisling, so very sorry,' she said.

Sunday 17 March 2013

CHAPTER TWO

Cormac dropped the heavy box file onto his desk and flipped the lid off. His expression was carefully impassive as he looked into the mess of documents, half-empty files and duplicate and triplicate forms that had been dumped into the box without ceremony over thirty years ago. Thirty years ago, or possibly just yesterday, if someone had taken the box and messed with it before placing it neatly back on a cold-case filing shelf. If he made a big deal he'd look like an asshole. The best option was to act like he didn't know what was going on, until he could find out who was doing it, and put the fucker in his place. That was the way the game was played after all, and he'd known exactly how it would be as soon as he'd been shown to his new desk one month earlier.

Mill Street Garda Station squad room had been carved out of three smaller rooms by the demolition of two dividing walls, and their replacement with steel supporting columns and beams. The intent had been to create one large open-plan space, but it had been only partially successful. The supporting columns effectively segmented the room into three. The section Cormac sat in was occupied almost entirely by uniformed gardaí and the odd sergeant. To Cormac's immediate left sat Garda James Rodgers, who seemed to spend the majority of his time alternating between two favourite activities – slurping foul-smelling pot-noodle as loudly as possible, and picking his nose. The row of desks ended with Cormac's, for which he was thankful. The other end of the room, which had the dual benefit of natural light, and distance from the kitchen, the toilets and the highly-trafficked entrance, was where most of the detectives sat. Cormac's desk, notwithstanding his stellar twenty-year career, the last five as a detective sergeant running complex and high-profile cases, was among the shittiest in the room, far away from the business end of things and right in the middle of the high traffic zone. Desk allocation hadn't been an accident. Nor was the fact that in the four weeks he'd been at Mill Street he'd been assigned only cold cases.

He was also working solo. The National Drugs Unit, which was based in Dublin Castle, was running a temporary task force out of Mill Street, and the gardaí who would make up Cormac's future team were largely seconded to it. A temporary state of affairs, he'd been assured. It was refreshing, actually, to work alone. He'd wondered sometimes if the seniority he'd gained in recent years had been worth the HR headaches, the bureaucratic bullshit, that came with it. So he'd taken the few weeks as a gift, an opportunity to get a read of the station, the gardaí who worked out of it.

Cormac started to lift documents out of the box and into piles on his desk for sorting. This was the third file he'd started. The previous two had been equally messy. He had taken them apart before putting them back together, organised to his meticulous standards, only to find that it had been a complete waste of time. In the first case he found that the physical evidence had long been destroyed; in the second that the key witnesses, including the prime suspect, were long since dead. It had been a lost cause, as this latest file almost certainly would be. They were hospital passes, every one, selected for him especially for their absolute lack of potential.

Cormac reminded himself that he had asked for this transfer, and that he was no longer, if he ever had been, the golden boy of the Special Detective Unit's anti-terrorist section. This was a new job, with a new boss, and a new set of colleagues, most of whom were keen to prove that elite Dublin-based units were seriously overrated. He thought about Emma, who was enjoying every moment of her new project, and told himself that the move was worth it. He lifted a witness statement from the box, and found it stuck together with coffee that hadn't quite dried. He stared at it for a moment, felt sure that he heard a snort of laughter from somewhere in the room, and dropped it back into the box.

Fuck it.

Cormac closed the lid of the box and wandered over to the other side of the room, slowing as he approached Danny McIntyre's desk from behind – Danny was intently studying what looked like football scores on his screen. Cormac put his face up close to Danny's before he spoke.

'Is that what you call work, down here in the bog?'

Danny didn't move an inch. 'It is,' he said. 'What do you call it in the big smoke?'

'We call it inappropriate use of Garda resources and sentence you to twenty lashes. What are you doing here on a Sunday? You're not working the parade?' Cormac checked his watch. It was St. Patrick's Day, but the arts crowd were switching it up this year and running a night parade. The streets would be thronged, alcohol- and rain-soaked, and a lot of overtime would be paid, but he'd assumed that gardaí assigned to the parade wouldn't be on for another few hours.

'Jesus, Dan. Had a late one did you?' Danny had turned his chair around to face Cormac. In the cold morning light he looked stale, his skin had a greasy sheen to it.

'Told you I had a few things going on, didn't I?' Danny winked at him. Something about that wink made Cormac think he was more likely talking about a woman than a stakeout.

Cormac glanced around. The temporary task force had taken on the feel of something more permanent. When

Cormac had arrived a month earlier they'd taken up one double row of desks – enough for eight people. Since then more officers had been assigned and the group had spilled over into other areas of the room. Today however, the place was quiet.

'You're the only one in?' Cormac asked.

Danny shrugged. 'No one took over my other work when I was assigned to the task force. I'd some paperwork to finish so I thought I'd come in.' He stretched, yawned. 'Going home soon though. I told the little lad I'd kick a ball about.'

That might be true but to Cormac it had the feel of an excuse about it. Maybe Danny wanted one day at the station without Healy looking over his shoulder. Detective Sergeant Anthony Healy was the task force commander. Cormac knew him from Dublin – the Drugs Unit and Special Detective Unit reported to the same Assistant Commissioner and worked out of the same building. Healy was old school and old time, and his reputation was shady. He'd brought his second in command from Dublin, but otherwise the gardaí assigned to him were all Galway men and women. Despite his reputation, Healy seemed to be popular enough in Galway. He was affable, liked to keep people close to him, everyone but Danny. Cormac had watched the entire task force troop out together more than once for lunch, and Danny was always the one left to man the phones. Danny hadn't admitted it, but Cormac was beginning to wonder if he'd seen or heard Healy do something he shouldn't have. That would certainly have been enough to put him on the outs.

Voices, two detectives returning from lunch. They took their seats not far from where Danny and Cormac sat, first giving Danny a nod of acknowledgement. There was an energy about them, as they exchanged jibes and took up their work, that Cormac would have recognised from a mile away.

'What's that about?' he asked, nodding in their direction.

'Clarke and Higgins? They picked up a murder this morning.'

'Are you serious?' Shite. Another case not assigned to him. He definitely wasn't top of the pecking order in Galway. He wasn't even supposed to be working; had come in only because it was Paddy's weekend, the night before had been crazy, and he'd been hoping to pick up whatever cases were generated by the drink and that chaotic party energy. So much for that idea.

'Student. She met her friends in town for a few drinks and walked home afterwards. Took a short cut across the park. He grabbed her, raped her, strangled her.'

Cormac shook his head.

'We've a fair idea who did it.'

'What? Already? Was he seen?'

'No, but he's done it before. Raped a girl I mean, in the same park. He lives down the street. Lazy, you see. Doesn't like to stray far from home.' Danny wasn't smiling. 'We got him last time too. He used a condom, left it at the scene.'

'Shit.' Cormac didn't need Danny to tell him what had happened next. State labs were completely backed up. Rape testing did not get priority. It could take six months to get a result. In the meantime, the suspect's lawyer would make a bail application, which would probably be granted. Most people didn't understand that it was unusual for a judge not to grant bail, unless the crime was particularly violent and the evidence very compelling. The absence of a DNA result weakened the prosecution's case in a bail hearing, which essentially meant that backlogs in state lab testing put more rapists on the street.

'You're sure it's him?' Cormac asked.

'The lads got the call at six a.m. Guy walking his dog found her. Scene virtually the same as last time, except this time the girl is dead. Condom thrown in the bushes a few metres away. Higgins and Clarke had a fair idea. They were at his place by seven. They brought him back here, half an hour later they had him. They told him they had DNA. He told them she'd wanted it, that she was all over him in the club.'

'Jesus.'

'Yeah. He's thick as pig shit. His lawyer will probably use that too – claim he's intellectually disabled.'

They fell silent for a moment, then Danny seemed to shake off his mood.

'So what's the story? Are you settled? How's Emma?'

He'd told Danny the whole story of how they met, one night over too many pints. He should have regretted it – they hadn't planned on sharing that with anyone in Galway, certainly not at his work – but didn't. Danny had been good about it, had said all the right things.

'Good. She's good. Busy. I'll be honest with you though, Dan, I'm finding this place a bit slow.' Cormac spread his hands in a 'no offence' gesture.

Danny grimaced. 'Still on the cold cases?'

Suddenly, Cormac didn't want to talk about it. He stood, checked his watch. 'Are you going out for lunch? Madigans? My shout?'

'Grand,' said Danny. He turned back to his computer to log out, but he'd already been automatically booted for inactivity. He stood.

'You don't think you're taking the plain clothes thing a bit far, Dan?' Cormac said, his tone dry. Danny wore a t-shirt with the slogan 'Pigs should not cause Beef' in oversized black letters, and jeans that had seen better days. The bottom of his jeans and his boots were mud-spattered.

'Drug squad, man. Undercover. Gotta look the part.'

They crossed the road in the inevitable silence of two people trying to get to where they are going in the rain. They walked as quickly as the busy footpaths and heavy traffic would allow – Galway was a city of narrow streets and complicated one-way systems. When it rained it sometimes felt like the whole place came to a halt. Danny reached the pub first, and as he joined the queue for food he started a conversation with a pretty brunette who was just ahead of him. Cormac was more focused on food and he kept only half an ear on the banter. Danny hadn't changed.

They'd met in training college; hadn't been close but were in the same class and so part of the same extended group. In Templemore Danny had always had above average results with women, despite the handicap of a goofy-looking pair of sticking out ears. It was his confidence, maybe. You could just tell by looking at him that he didn't give a shit what you thought about him. They were all so young, a bunch of twenty-year-olds working hard to give just that impression, but only Danny'd had it for real.

Cormac had been surprised when Danny's career didn't progress. He'd moved around a bit in the first few years, as they all had, but when Cormac had made Detective Sergeant, Danny had still been a uniformed garda. A few years later Cormac heard that Danny had never made sergeant, but had been assigned to a tiny country station – a two-man-band kind of place within easy drive of his parents' place – and looked like he was staying. And that was how it turned out. Cormac had been ambitious, and dedicated, and (he would acknowledge now) had pursued promotion with an obsessive focus. He'd earned a transfer to the SDU – the Special Detective Unit, an elite unite responsible for counter-terrorism and armed responses to serious incidents – and had moved up the ranks there too, working on larger, more complex operations, eventually running them. His appetite for advancement only eased when he realised promotion to Inspector would take him away from investigative work and further into the realm of people management and politics.

Danny had spent the same years working his small-town beat, getting married and having kids.

The ease with which he and Danny had renewed and improved on their former friendship had been the nicest surprise about Cormac's return to the West. Cormac thought that was probably due to his own reduced intensity about work, and Danny's recent promotion in equal measure. It helped also that Danny didn't report to him, but to Sergeant Melanie Hackett, or at least he did when he wasn't seconded to the task force. Cormac had called Danny on his first weekend in Galway, a weekend that Emma had spent in the lab, feeling slightly embarrassed about getting in touch out of the blue, but hopeful that Danny would be willing to go for a pint and catch Cormac up on local politics. It ended up being a late one. They traded war stories, Cormac avoiding the serious and telling some of the more scurrilous inside gossip from Dublin. Danny had a few stories of his own. His transfer to Galway and to more challenging work had happened the year before, and was a direct result of Danny more or less single-handedly busting a drugs operation run out of a nightclub in Mayo.

'It was a local guy. Had a nightclub he'd opened in the back of beyond. He ran buses to all the local towns and virtually every kid for fifty miles around turned up every Friday night. Name was Jim Kavanagh. Big Jim, he likes to call himself. Fat as fuck.' Danny's lip curled, and he spoke with barely repressed disgust. 'He was selling all sorts. I heard it from more than one source.'

Cormac was a little surprised at Danny's vehemence. He had a sudden image of Danny passing a joint around a party, and that had been at Templemore, if he remembered correctly. But even Danny had to grow up eventually, and he had kids now of course. The oldest, Luke, would be what, six? The little girl two or three.

'I couldn't get much traction,' Danny was saying, 'so I started watching the place myself. I figured out when he was likely to be getting deliveries, and the next time it happened I just walked straight in – he had the stuff spread out over the desk in his office. Stocktake day.' Danny was shaking his head, a vicious grin on his face. 'Ten kilos of coke if you can believe it. For a small country club? He must have been running it all over the place.'

'Fair dues, Danny.' He meant it. 'Any luck getting up the supply line?'

He regretted the question when Dan raised an eyebrow and said, 'Not yet.'

The arrest got Danny his long overdue promotion, and he was transferred to Galway, to work on the drugs squad. The promotion meant seniority, better pay, and a change to plain clothes, which Danny clearly enjoyed. It also meant that he was away from his family a few nights a week, though now that the family had moved to a rental in a family friendly suburb of Galway that should change.

'How's Sarah?' Cormac asked now.

'Grand, she's grand.'

'Any chance we could get out, now that you've moved in? I could check when Emma's free, we could have dinner or something.'

'She'd love that,' said Danny. 'Tricky with the kids, but Sarah's mother might take them.'

'Will we try for Saturday so?' Cormac asked. He'd asked before but the timing had never been quite right. If the wink Danny had tossed him earlier meant what he thought it did, the time would probably never be right. Was Danny cheating on Sarah? If he was Cormac was going to stay well and truly out of the whole thing. The last thing he needed was to get dragged into Danny's marital problems.

Danny didn't answer the question. He was looking over Cormac's shoulder, watching something or someone.

'What?'

Danny shook his head.

Cormac turned to take a look. Someone he thought he recognised was taking a seat at the bar.

'Is that Liam Hearne?' he asked. Cormac started to stand, but Danny put a hand out to stop him.

'He won't thank you for it,' he said.

'What?'

Danny grimaced. 'He's had it rough since he retired. Hit the bottle very hard. Doesn't want to see anyone from the old days. I've heard his wife has asked people to stay away. Makes him worse, apparently.'

Cormac glanced once again, then away, conscious of a sinking feeling in his stomach. Liam looked younger than his, what would it be now? Seventy years? He was dressed well enough, looked put together, his grey hair cut tight to his head in a style that hadn't changed in twenty years.

'I'm sorry to hear that,' he said. The words felt inadequate. Liam Hearne was a man he admired. A detective for almost forty years, he'd taught a class on interview techniques when Cormac and Danny were at Templemore. He'd returned to active duty soon after, and had spent the last ten years of his career dealing with the worst of crimes. He'd been part of a major investigation into a paedophile ring that operated in the West of Ireland for over twenty years. It would have been brutally difficult work, made harder by the fact that most of the victims who came forward to give testimony were now adults, badly damaged by their experiences. Many of them were alcoholics, some had mental health problems. Their testimony was inconsistent and this and the passage of time made it harder to get convictions. Cormac had a friend who'd worked a similar investigation in Cork the year before, and he'd gotten off it as quickly as he could. Even so he'd been haunted by it. Haunted by all the victims, and by the feeling that they were being let down by a system that had already failed them so badly. And Liam had done that work for ten years. What would that do to a man? Cormac looked back in his direction.

Liam was alone at the bar, a pint in one hand.

'Don't,' Danny said again. 'Leave it.'

They finished their food and left the bar in a very different mood.

Thursday 21 March 2013

CHAPTER THREE

Sleet had spattered miserably all day, and the clouds promised more to come. It was an awful day for a burial. The cemetery was at Bohermore, just over a kilometre from the city centre, and traffic had been brutal before the cortege had added to the congestion. There was no pleasure to be taken in the freezing air – it was cold but not fresh. The heavy smell of car exhaust hung in the air from traffic idling at the lights at the top of the hill, and storm drain overflow ran down one side of the street.

The group that followed the hearse into the cemetery was not large. Perhaps thirty mourners clustered loosely around the open grave, breath fogging the air, as the pallbearers took the coffin from the hearse and placed it gently, awkwardly, on the pine supports laid across the grave. The priest said his prayers over the casket. His words gave no insight, answered no questions. He spoke on – prayers and generic condolences, sprinkled with the few useful specifics about the deceased that could be picked up in a hushed five-minute conversation with a bereaved family member. Finally, the obligatory reference to the death itself. An accident – and here the priest stumbled. For in the Catholic Church suicide is still a sin, and a suicide could be denied burial in consecrated ground, unless it could be proven that they were of unsound mind when they took their lives. Easier by far to pretend.

Jack's body was in that coffin. His beautiful body. Every part of him that was hers. He was so precious to her, she wanted to scream out for them to stop, to open up the coffin so that she could hold him, embrace him one last time. To think that she would never hold his hand again, never feel the warmth of his lips on hers, the strength of his arms around her. She wanted to tell them that they didn't understand. Didn't they know that she and Jack were supposed to be together forever? That this body they were burying, as if it was something that could be discarded, was one she knew as well as her own, and was far more precious?

'Eternal rest grant unto them, O Lord, and let perpetual light shine upon them. May the souls of all the faithful departed, through the mercy of God, rest in peace.'

The faithful departed. But what about the souls of the unfaithful? Jack hadn't been Catholic, not really. He'd been baptised by his parents, brought up in the Church, but he'd never been to Mass in her memory and he certainly didn't have much tolerance for the Church's views on homosexuality and a lot more besides. So. A suicide, and not particularly faithful. She felt a wave of dizziness, of disconnection. Was this how she would say goodbye to him? In a muddy graveyard, surrounded by people and some of them strangers, led through a ceremony by a priest of a faith that neither of them believed in?

And yet, as the priest looked towards her, and as she stepped forward to place her single lily on the casket, Aisling felt the hard knot of pain in her chest loosen as her tears came again.

She stepped back and the priest waited a moment before nodding to the gravediggers, who stepped forward. The outer ring of mourners started to drift away, some of them coming forward to shake her hand, or to murmur condolences to Jack's parents. Brendan didn't respond – he'd been wheelchair-bound since his stroke the year before, and he spoke very little. But Aisling saw tears leak and run down his face, and she wished – fiercely and with a sudden shocking anger at Jack – that he'd been spared this.

Mark approached her, hugged her, held her hand, while Fergus hung back. She'd seen Fergus twice since Jack had died, and both times he hadn't been able to talk through the tears.

'We're going across the road, me and Fergus, a few of the lads. We thought we'd have a drink and talk about Jack. Will you come?' Mark said. Jack, Fergus, and Mark had grown up together, had gone to the same country primary school. They were still close … had been close. She liked Mark, Fergus she'd always thought of as a bit self-involved. She watched him bend down to hug Brendan over Mark's shoulder. Maybe she'd been wrong about him. She'd been wrong about so much.

'Aisling?' Mark said.

She refused the invitation, politely, firmly. The thought of sitting in the pub and reminiscing made her feel sick. It would be too much like a wake, make it all too real. She wasn't ready for that.

Her friends were there too – David Murray distracted her from her grief for a moment when he stepped forward and trying to kiss her cheek, kissed her on the side of her mouth instead, then flushed scarlet like a schoolboy. She'd seen David deal with death. He'd lost patients. She'd seen him give the news to bereaved family members; watched him answer questions and hold a hand with professionalism and a sincere, adult, compassion. What was it about this situation that caused all his poise to desert him? Was it that he'd known Jack? Liked him? Or maybe it was because Jack had killed himself, and no one had any idea how to handle that. There was a reason, after all, that there were so few at the graveside. A reason that so many of Jack's friends sought refuge in convention – *I'm sorry for your loss* – and avoided eye contact as they kissed her cheek, and gave her a one-armed hug.

Aisling watched as the priest took his leave of Aggie, then accepted the murmured condolences he offered

her. Aggie squeezed her hand too, before turning back
to Brendan and walking beside his wheelchair out of the
cemetery. That was a good idea. He shouldn't be out in
the cold like this. It wasn't good for him. Their departure
was taken as a cue by everyone who remained, and soon
Aisling was alone with the gravediggers. They waited for
a time, but when she made no move to leave they stepped
forward and started their work, removing the pine supports
and lowering the coffin into the grave, their movements
smooth and unhurried. The coffin in the ground, they
rolled out a length of green felt, securing it in place so that
it covered the gaping hole. All four of them stood with
heads bowed, for a few respectful seconds, before turning
and walking towards a cabin at the back of the cemetery.
Aisling realised that they wouldn't replace the dirt while
she was standing there, but they'd find a warmer place to
wait than the graveside. Somewhere they could get a cup
of tea to warm their hands, and a bit of friendly banter to
lighten their hearts. Was she delaying them? They probably
wanted to get home, and the fact that she was standing
there was making them late. She still couldn't move. She
couldn't leave Jack. Aisling was aware that her body was
shivering, but it felt like an abstract thing. She didn't really
feel the cold. Didn't really feel anything.

The graveyard was empty now, except for another woman
who stood alone at another graveside. She was watching
Aisling. There was something about her. Something familiar.
Maybe a family member of a patient they'd lost? The woman
took a step towards her, and Aisling quickly looked down at
Jack's grave. Not today. Just not today.

Suddenly, she felt someone take her arm, and heard a
familiar voice in her ear.

'I don't know about you but I'm freezing my arse off out
here.' Mary Dooley. 'Will we go to the pub?'

Aisling gave a half-laugh, half-sob, and Mary gave her a hug, then pulled her gently but firmly away from the grave and towards the exit.

'I don't know what the hell I'm doing Mary.' But she allowed herself to be led.

'You're doing great. Honestly. There's nothing left to do now. We just need to get you warm, and get you to eat something, and then ... I suppose we just figure out what comes next.'

What comes next? Her cold house. Their bedroom, with all Jack's clothes in the wardrobe, his toothbrush on the sink. Just this morning she'd found a print-off he'd left for her, stuck to the fridge. It was an ad for a puppy – a disreputable-looking pup someone wanted to offload – Jack'd been mad to get a dog. She'd thought it was a crazy idea because they were never at home. He'd said that he could take the dog to work sometimes, and maybe it'd be company for her on the evenings he wasn't there. She'd laughed at him and it had become a bit of a joke, but he'd still stuck the photo of the puppy to the fridge. Aisling had found herself staring at the picture, milk carton in hand, and wondering if Jack would still be alive if she'd said yes to the pup.

'I'm not sure I want to go home,' Aisling said.

Mary gave her arm another squeeze. 'Grand so,' she said. 'Stay in my place as long as you like.' There was a long pause, and Aisling could almost hear Mary trying to figure out where Aisling would sleep, in the house that Mary had shared with her boyfriend and three other med students since they were in college. Not much had changed in their lifestyle since, except that their hours in the hospital were far longer. The house looked – and smelled – like a student house, and all of the bedrooms were taken.

'Ah no,' said Aisling. 'Thanks. Thanks a million. But I'm just putting it off.'

'No harm in putting it off for a few days. At least a few days.'

They started to walk together towards the city. Aisling's feet were freezing. The toes of her boots were soaked through and water squelched between her toes. There was nothing good about a Galway winter.

'No wake?' Mary asked.

Aisling shook her head. 'Aggie and Brendan didn't want it. I think they would have found it hard in any circumstances, but ... with the suicide.' Aisling swallowed. 'They just couldn't handle the questions.'

There was a pause before Mary said, 'People say stupid shit.' But the unspoken question hung in the air between them.

'I had no clue,' Aisling said. 'Not a clue. I thought he was happy. He never said. I have no idea why he did it.' Except that maybe she did. But if that had been the reason, she didn't think she could handle it, so she wasn't going to think about it. Not yet.

'Your parents couldn't make it?'

'Dad can't fly with his heart, and Mum didn't want to leave him.' Aisling was an only child, born late to parents who'd long since let go of the idea of children, and for whom, she'd sometimes wondered, the unexpected arrival hadn't been entirely welcome. They lived in Toronto, where her mother still lectured at the University, and her father, until his heart attack the previous year, had practiced medicine.

They came to the bottom of the hill and crossed the street into Eyre Square. It wasn't much of a public space, just a postage stamp-sized park with a bit of lawn and a few trees around the margins. The square didn't look like much in winter, but in the short Galway summer it could be pretty enough. People would sit out and eat their lunches on the grass in the chilly sunshine, and there was usually at least one busker to provide a bit of musical atmosphere. Today it was all but deserted; just a few shoppers walking with heads down, making their way as quickly as possible from carpark to shopping and back.

As they crossed the square Aisling felt a sudden wave of nausea and her vision darkened at the edges. She stopped walking and stood still for a moment, putting a hand to her forehead and blinking to try to clear her vision. Her legs felt weak.

'Are you okay?' Mary put an arm around her waist, looked at her more closely. They were only a few metres from the Skeff and after a moment Mary tugged her towards the pub. 'Come on. You need food and drink and somewhere a bit warmer than this.' Aisling allowed herself to be led, grateful that her vision had cleared and that she wasn't about to faint in the street.

The pub was gorgeously, overwhelmingly warm. Mary found a pair of armchairs close to the fire that burned in an ornate grate at the back of the bar. Aisling just about managed to pull off her wet coat before she sank into the chair. The lunchtime rush had passed, and the evening rush hadn't begun, so the place was near empty; just one couple sitting with heads together in a corner and a man reading his newspaper at the bar. It was all so normal. Aisling wanted to pretend, just for a minute, that everything was normal for her too. Mary went straight to the bar and returned a few minutes later with a cup of tea for Aisling and a coffee for herself.

'I thought about something stronger but figured you need food first. It's only toasties, but they'll be here in a minute.'

The tea did make Aisling feel a little better. She felt sick all the time at the moment. Had since the day Jack died. Maybe she wasn't eating enough. She tried to remember what she'd eaten over the past few days and failed – everything was a blur of tears and funeral arrangements. She stretched her feet out to the fire, wishing she could take her boots and wet socks off, then felt embarrassed by the banality of the thought. Was this what grief did to you? She felt disconnected from everything around her, an out of body sensation that came with double shifts and sleep deprivation, except that she was sleeping like the dead.

The sandwiches arrived, and the smell of warm food made her feel sicker at first, then intensely hungry. They ate, and Mary talked. Hospital things. Gossip. There'd been some drama about hours – did she know? Someone in health services had been crossing out hours from timesheets, so that junior doctors were paid less. The union was onto it apparently. Such and such consultant was screwing a nurse in ICU, had she heard? Mary didn't seem to need a response, and listening to her talk was oddly soothing.

Mary finished her sandwich and sat back in her chair. 'Will we get a drink?'

Aisling shook her head. 'Not for me.' She gave another of her awkward-feeling smiles. 'Not 'til I feel a bit more human anyway.' What would drink do to her as she was at the moment? A glass of wine would probably have her sobbing on a stranger's shoulder, and if that started, where would it end? 'I think I just need to sleep, really. The last few days have been endless funeral arrangements and phone calls and cups of coffee.' Her eyes dropped to the empty cup on the table. 'The gardaí have asked me to go to the station tomorrow, for a meeting. For now I just want to go home to my empty house, put on a fire, lie on the couch and watch something stupid and comforting. *Downton Abbey*. Or *X Factor* maybe.'

'*Strictly Come Dancing*,' Mary said.

'Christ, there's no need to go that far.'

Mary smiled. 'Do you want me to come with you?'

Aisling thanked her and said no. The truth was she didn't know what she wanted. She desperately wanted to be alone, to be unobserved by anyone, and at the same time the thought of going back to the empty house and facing her life as it was now appalled her. But being with other people when you felt so vulnerable was tiring too.

'Will you let me know if you need anything?' Mary was asking. 'I know it's too soon, but if you need help with Jack's stuff, or just want a bit of company, you'll call me? I'm on for the next couple of days, but I could call over after work on Sunday, if you fancy a bit of company.'

'I think I'll go back to work.'

'What? When?'

'Maybe the day after tomorrow.'

Mary was staring at her.

'I have assessments. Surgeries. The last thing I need right now is to take time out of the hospital.'

'But surely, you need to take some time. You need to grieve.'

'What I need is to focus on my work.' Aisling tried to remember what had been scheduled at the hospital for this week and couldn't. She saw the appalled look on Mary's face changing quickly to one of concern, and a wave of frustration and loneliness hit her. Jack would have understood.

'Might be best not to rush it though. You know what it's like in there. People will be full of sympathy for about an hour and then you'll be under the pump again.'

'I'm not looking for anyone's sympathy.' Aisling didn't want to talk about it anymore. She was too tired to be polite. Too tired to say the things she was expected to say. She stood, picked up her coat. 'I have to go.' She paused. 'Thanks. Thanks for the tea.'

She didn't wait, just turned and walked quickly to the door. She caught a cab home, and ignoring the piles of dishes, the week's worth of laundry piled on the floor, fell into bed and into another deep and dreamless sleep.

Friday 22 March 2013

CHAPTER FOUR

Cormac spent the week working his way through cases he knew were likely to go nowhere. He could have delegated the work. But in reviewing the cases he'd felt that many of them had gone unsolved because they'd been approached in a half-hearted, haphazard way. It was almost certainly too late for most of them, but he didn't want to close them until he was sure that everything possible had been done. The Hughes case had the most potential. First thing Monday morning Cormac had dropped the file on Peter Fisher's desk, with instructions to clean it up and organise it. He'd spent the rest of the week chasing down tenuous leads on the other cases, expecting nothing but grateful to get out of the station for a few days.

Friday saw him back at his desk, if not brimful of enthusiasm, at least relieved to be able to turn his mind to a fresh puzzle. The reordered Hughes file was waiting for him. Fisher had done a decent job. He must have taken the time to look at the case files Cormac had already been through; the file was now organised exactly as he liked it. The coffee-stained pages had been allowed to dry, and Fisher must have copied them before placing the new sheets into the file, because they were neat and unwrinkled. Fisher was ambitious, and didn't try to hide it. He wanted out of the regions and into a specialist unit. He didn't have much of a poker face, and it was clear he didn't understand Cormac's transfer. He'd all but asked if Cormac had done something to warrant a demotion. Specialist units tended to attract the talent, though the powers that be were trying to shake that up a bit. There was talk of devolution – of breaking up some of the units and resettling expertise back in the regions, keeping smaller, mobile specialist squads in Dublin. Cormac liked to think he was just ahead of the trend.

He settled back in his chair, took a sip of coffee and started to read.

Maura Hughes had been fifteen years old when she had disappeared in 1975. She had attended camogie training with her club, then got on her bike to cycle home. She never made it, and was never heard from again. Maura had been part of a close-knit rural community, she'd been a good student, and a beloved daughter and sister. A full-scale search had been launched less than twenty-four hours after her disappearance. Her body was never found and by 1977 she was declared missing, presumed dead.

Cormac read quickly, skimming through statements from distraught parents and friends and glowing reports from teachers, and skipping over the ragged mess of disproved sightings. He stopped and read more slowly a statement taken four months after Maura's disappearance. Maura's best friend had come forward to say that Maura had been in a secret relationship. An older man; she didn't know who. On the morning of her disappearance Maura had confided in her friend that her period was late, and she thought she might be expecting. She was going to tell her lover and they would run away together. Though Maura had never confessed the name, her friend was sure that the unidentified lover had been Timothy Lanigan, a twenty-two-year-old teacher at their school and the assistant camogie coach.

The rest of the file told the balance of the story through a mix of reports, statements and local newspaper clippings – Cormac was not, it seemed, the first to review this particular cold case. Detectives had looked into Timothy Lanigan, and none too discreetly. They found no evidence of any relationship between Lanigan and Maura – the friend had based her theory on very little evidence. She'd once seen Maura get into Lanigan's car (it wasn't so much the taking of the lift, she said, as it was the fact that Maura never talked about it) and she was sure that Maura looked at Lanigan *that way*. Not much to base an investigation on, and nothing more had ever been found. Lanigan volunteered the fact that he'd once driven Maura home; he could remember time and date and was wholly unembarrassed about it. Other than that one time he claimed to have had no more interaction with Maura than with any of his students, and the gardaí were never able to prove otherwise.

It didn't stop Lanigan from being hounded out of town. An article in the local paper, printed after his departure, lamented the wrongs done to him. Tyres slashed. White paint poured over the driveway of his rented house. Shit through the letterbox. Calls to the house in the middle of the night, abuse shouted down the phone when he answered. The school supported him, but in the end he gave up, handed in his resignation, and left the country. With his departure the investigation effectively ended. The phantom hand that had placed newspaper cuttings on the file must have also followed up on Lanigan in the States – there was a handwritten note to say that he was married, with a child on the way, and settled in Massachusetts. He was teaching English at a local high school.

Cormac took Lanigan's photograph from the file and studied it. It was black and white, not a mug shot – Lanigan had never been arrested – but a photograph taken at some school event. He was outside somewhere, and he was laughing, his hair a little long and tousled by the wind. Another photograph, this time a photo with his rugby team, Lanigan's face circled in black ink. In both photos he looked very young, and very innocent. Cormac put the photographs away and flicked back through the file. No other suspects were ever identified, and for a while the popular theory had been that the friend had been right about the lover, though wrong about Lanigan, and maybe Maura and her secret man had run away together.

Eventually her family would have accepted her death. He wondered how long it had taken. Ten years? Twenty? If Maura had lived she would be fifty-six now. Her parents might still be alive. She'd had a sister. It was clear from the file that they'd stayed in touch with the investigative team for years. Cormac found a photograph of the family, and looked at it for a moment, fixing the image in his mind before closing the file. It helped sometimes, to know who he was working for. He picked up his coffee, realised it was cold, and put it back down on his desk.

Cormac stood, took his phone and left the squad room. He walked the length of the hall to the broad window that overlooked the carpark. It wasn't a particularly attractive view. The river was less than a hundred metres away, but it couldn't be seen from this angle. He sat on the windowsill and dialled Emma's number. When it had rung five times without answer, he ended the call. Emma couldn't bring her phone into the lab. Security protocols required her to leave all her personal belongings, particularly electronics, in a locker before entering the main facility. She usually checked her phone in her breaks, and called him back when she had time. He waited for a few minutes but the phone remained stubbornly silent.

He was distracted by the sight of Danny arguing with a woman in the carpark below. Danny had a crumpled piece of paper, and he was gesticulating with it towards the woman. She was smaller than him, but she was clearly unintimidated. She held her ground, and whatever she said to Danny next seemed to calm him down. Cormac strained to make out who she was, and when she turned in his direction and started walking back into the station he thought he recognised her. From this distance her face was a blur, but her short, dark curly hair was distinctive. It was Carrie O'Halloran. Sergeant Carrie O'Halloran. She worked domestic violence, sometimes vice. Danny didn't like her. He'd once warned Cormac that her looks were misleading. *If she thinks you're even looking in the direction of one of her cases, she'll take your balls off with a pliers.* But O'Halloran didn't work drugs. So what did she and Danny have to argue about?

When Cormac returned to his desk he went to find Fisher at the business end of the room. As he approached he could hear Anthony Healy, in full flow. He was talking to a very young garda reservist, who was standing with her back to Cormac, facing Anthony, and writing down everything he said as fast as she could.

'Don't go to the shitty place you went last time,' Healy was saying. 'I like my coffee hot, and strong. And can we, do you think, maybe find somewhere in this hole that makes a decent fucking sandwich? You're a Galway girl.' He looked her up and down. 'You look like you've eaten a sandwich or two in your time. Do you know what, go to the Bierhaus and get me one of those banh-mi yokes they're making down there. And a coke.'

Cormac had reached the little group. Looking over the reservist's shoulder, he saw she was struggling with the spelling of banh-mi.

'No, no,' Cormac said. He put out his hand and tapped her list. 'There are two "l"s in bollix.'

Cormac let his eyes go straight to Healy, who couldn't hide his flash of anger. The reservist flushed, and laughed. Trevor Murphy smirked, then looked disapproving. Fisher sniggered.

'Reilly,' Healy said. 'Not bored of this place yet?'

Cormac had never worked with Healy, but Cormac's former unit and the Drugs Unit worked out of the same Dublin building, and he knew Healy by reputation. Healy was widely thought of as a bit of a wanker, someone with a bad case of small man syndrome. There were also rumours that he had a little more money than he should, suggestions that he might have taken a backhander or two in exchange for information. And now Healy was here, running a task force out of Galway, with Trevor Murphy as his little sidekick. His go-to man. What made things interesting was that Trevor was also the eldest son of the Superintendent, Brian Murphy himself. What did the Super think of his son's close connection to a man with Healy's reputation?

Cormac raised an eyebrow at Healy, then gave Fisher the nod, and turned back towards his desk.

'Of course,' Healy said, smirk audible in his voice 'You're busy feathering the love nest, aren't you? Must be nice. Has a few quid, I hear. Almost worth giving up your career for that.'

Asshole. His relationship with Emma had started under difficult circumstances. Not many in Dublin knew exactly what those circumstances were, but a few had heard there was *something*. Someone like Healy wouldn't be able to restrain himself from poking at it until he found out more. Cormac's transfer off the Special Detectives Unit and back into regional operations had probably added fuel to whatever rumours were buzzing around.

Cormac wanted to ask about Healy's wife. It would have been an easy score; last he'd heard she'd buggered off to Spain, the day after their youngest left for college. It must surely gall Healy that his wife was enjoying the sun in the Costa del Sol, along with half the drug dealers he was still trying to put away.

Instead he kept walking. Fisher caught up after a moment, and Cormac pretended not to notice his reluctant glance back to the men seated around the drug squad table.

'I want your help on something,' Cormac said, as he led Fisher back to his desk. He gestured to an empty chair and Fisher dropped into it, reassuming his eager-to-learn look.

'It's all right?' Fisher asked, and Cormac blanked for a moment, before realising that Fisher meant the filing.

'It's grand,' he said. If Fisher thought a neat filing job would impress, he had a long way to go. 'I want you to have a go at tracking this guy down,' he said, taking the photographs of Lanigan from the file.

Fisher looked down at the photographs, then back at Cormac, as if checking to see if Cormac saw something he didn't.

'Didn't he go to America?' Fisher asked. So he'd read the file at least. One point in his favour.

'Everything's online these days, Fisher,' Cormac said. 'I doubt if you'll even have to make an official enquiry. I want you to find this guy. Come back to me with a list of places he's lived, schools he's taught in, everything and anything you can find.'

Fisher was nodding slowly, his eyes back on the photograph. 'When do you want it?' he asked.

Cormac checked his watch. Nearly lunchtime. Over Fisher's shoulder he saw Danny approaching, shrugging on his coat. Cormac stood, picked up his own coat.

'Take the weekend,' he said. 'Let's see what you have on Monday morning.'

Danny led the way down the stairs. 'Keeping Fisher from evil influences?' he asked.

'My good deed for the day,' Cormac said.

They reached the ground floor and made their way towards the main exit. As they passed the interview rooms Cormac caught a glimpse of a woman through an open door. Her head was turned away, but something about her jarred him. He stopped walking and tried to take a second look just as Rodgers approached the door from inside the room, gave him a nod of acknowledgement, and shut the door.

Danny had turned. 'Problem?' he asked.

'I thought I recognised someone,' Cormac said. 'A woman.'

Danny was studying him. 'It's important?'

'It's probably nothing.' Cormac followed Danny out through the security door, then the double doors beyond, and into the fresh air.

Cormac waited until they were out on the street, and walking up towards the city.

'What's going on with you and O'Halloran?' he asked. Danny stiffened, looked like he might shrug it off, so Cormac continued, 'I saw the argument in the carpark.'

Danny let out a breath in frustration. 'It's just family drama,' he said. 'My sister Lorna.' They walked on again for a minute or two, then Danny fished into his back pocket and took out an A4 sheet of paper that had been folded until it fit into the palm of his hand. He gave it to Cormac. Cormac unfolded it, and found himself staring at a missing person's poster. A black and white poster with a photograph of a very pretty young woman, long dark hair, big fuck-you smile.

'That's Lorna,' Danny said. He let Cormac study the poster for a moment, then reached out and took it back.

'Mill Street is a bloody cesspool,' Danny said. 'It's all politics, all the time, and I can't get my head around who's an ally and who's an enemy.' He gave Cormac a look. 'If you haven't been on the receiving end of it yet, you will be. They don't like outsiders. I thought Mayo was bad, but Galway … Jesus, it's like bloody *Deliverance* country.'

'What's happened with your sister?' Cormac asked.

'Lorna's gone on a skite,' Danny said. 'She does it all the time. Takes off with friends for days, doesn't let anyone know where she's gone or when she'll be back. I think she likes it when Mam worries.' Danny cast a sideways glance at Cormac. 'It's not that she's a bitch, she just likes a bit of drama. I keep telling Mam to let it go. Lorna's eighteen going on forty. She's well able to look after herself. But Mam worries and the more she tries to keep tabs on what Lorna's up to the bigger the fireworks.'

Danny stepped off the footpath to let a woman pushing a buggy by, then continued. 'Lorna went to college in September, in Dublin. She's been living with my mother's sister. For reasons known only to herself, Lorna set about convincing my aunt that she's been treated badly, and now my aunt and my mother aren't talking.' Danny shook his head. 'It probably didn't take much. Mam and Caroline – that's my aunt – never really got on.'

'And the poster?'

'Dublin was obviously a bit tame for her. She fecked off last weekend to see friends of hers, and didn't come back. She hasn't bothered her arse to call my aunt, or my mother, or anyone else, and Caroline reported her as a missing person.'

It started to drizzle just as they reached the pub. Danny pushed the door open and they paused at the threshold and looked around. The tables were all taken but there was space at the far end of the bar. They took two stools, ordered, then waited for the barman to drift to the other end of the bar before Danny told him the rest. Danny had been tipped off about the missing person's report on Monday, the same day it came in. He'd called home first, then called his aunt. After that he'd made more calls, tracked down a friend who eventually admitted that Lorna had been talking about a music festival in Wales. A gang had taken the ferry over, weren't due back 'til

Monday. Danny'd spent the last three days trying to ensure that Garda resources weren't wasted trying to find his party loving little sister, who would undoubtedly show up when she felt like it and not before. The missing person poster, which he'd discovered hanging in the public area of the station, had been a surprise.

'So what's the story with O'Halloran?' Cormac asked.

'I don't know,' Danny said. 'We don't get on. I can't figure out if it's because I've transferred in and she sees me as a threat, or if it's just because I'm a man.'

Cormac raised an eyebrow.

'Yeah, I know,' Danny said. 'But if you knew the Domestic Violence crowd you wouldn't think it sounded so stupid. They're all man-hating nut-jobs and Carrie O'Halloran is the worst of the lot. I think she did women's studies or some shite before she went to Templemore.'

Cormac was almost sure he had heard someone say that O'Halloran was married. He opened his mouth to say so but Danny anticipated him.

'Can you believe she's married? He's probably a kale-eating, preachy vegan fucker. Every word I said to her about Lorna she threw back at me. I said Lorna liked a drink and she asked me if I thought drinking was unfeminine. I told her that bloody hippy friend of Lorna's *told* me she'd gone to Wales, to that festival, that it wasn't the first time Lorna's gone on a bender and it won't be the last. She said my Aunt Caroline had a very different view of things. She listened to everything I said, then she *escalated* the case instead of calming it down. She'll have them out doing a man hunt before long.'

Something about that idea – maybe the image of O'Halloran out searching a bog while Lorna was living it up at a music festival – finally punctured Danny's frustration and he laughed, in one of those mercurial changes of mood that Cormac had come to expect from him. 'Nothing I can do about it now anyway, at least not until Lorna decides to come home, or answer her bloody phone.'

Cormac thought about the tension he'd seen between Danny and Healy, wondered if there might be something more to O'Halloran's hostility. Station politics maybe.

'What's going on with you and Healy?' Cormac asked.

Danny looked taken aback. 'What? Nothing.'

'It seemed to me like there was some tension there. You don't think there could be a connection between that and this trouble with O'Halloran? Are they friendly?'

Danny hesitated, but looked thoughtful. 'I didn't think so. Maybe I've missed something.'

The barman returned with their sandwiches, and a couple of office workers took the vacant seats to Cormac's right, putting an end to the conversation. But Danny seemed distracted for the rest of lunch, apparently thinking it through.

CHAPTER FIVE

A isling really didn't want to be late, but it was one of those mornings where little things kept going wrong. The water temperature plummeting when she already had shampoo in her hair. A stain on the pants she'd been planning to wear. Then the fuse blew in her hairdryer, and she ended up wasting ten minutes trying to find a hair tie so she could put her half-dry hair up. The bloody things were never to be found when you needed one; then you'd put your hand in your jeans pocket and come out with three. Which was more or less what happened when she gave up on the pants, and pulled on her jeans instead. That made her feel better for a few minutes, particularly when she found one of her favourite jumpers – a pale blue cashmere that Jack had bought her for Christmas – lurking at the back of their wardrobe. But then she had to face the shitty weather, and driving the car.

Driving the car always made her think of Jack. He'd been the one to drive it most days, as she preferred to walk to work. He'd driven it on the night of his death, had parked it only a few streets from their house, down by the water. He must have parked the car, then walked up river until he reached O'Brien's Bridge. The gardaí had found the car a few days after Jack's death, had called her and asked her if she wanted to pick it up. She'd had to find their spare key, then walk over to find the car. And she'd sat in the driver's seat, looked out at the water, and cried and cried. Why hadn't Jack come home? He'd been so close to home. The memory of that day flooded back as she turned the keys in the ignition, saw the warning light, and realised that she'd have to get petrol on the way. Shit. Walking would be faster, but it was pissing rain. Aisling shoved the Jack memory aside, concentrated on getting through the traffic, and was still ten minutes late when she pushed through the double doors into the police station.

There was a queue at both reception points, three people deep, and Aisling's heart sank. She took her place at the end of a queue, and started to flick through web pages on her phone, searching for distraction. What was the point of this meeting? Jack was buried, it was done. Nothing the police could tell her now would change anything. She could be studying, or better yet, at the hospital. The line didn't move. Two Italian girls at the front were trying to explain the theft of their phones in broken English to a clearly uninterested garda in uniform. He kept pushing a form at them, and they kept talking. After the Italians there was a young guy, headphones on, head bent over his phone, and then immediately in front of Aisling a harried mother with a toddler asleep in her arms. Aisling made the mistake of catching the woman's eye as she cast about for someone to complain to.

'Isn't this ridiculous,' the woman said, in a sort of a hiss. 'You'd think they put a few more on. I've only to get a passport application signed, and I've been here for twenty minutes.'

Aisling gave her a nod of sympathy, joined her in an eye-roll at the Italians, and returned her attention to her phone. What could this meeting be about, anyway? Probably paperwork. She'd done nothing but fill in forms since Jack had died.

'Aisling.'

Aisling heard a voice call her name and turned to see a female garda she recognised. Ceri – she'd forgotten her surname – one of the gardaí who'd come to tell her about Jack. She'd sat with Aisling that day, had made her tea and asked a few gentle questions. She'd even come to the funeral,

which, Aisling supposed, was above and beyond the call of
duty.

'Sorry, weren't you told?' Ceri asked. 'There's another
window, for appointments. Come through.' She handed
Aisling a visitor's pass, then swiped them through the security
doors and walked along the corridor beyond.

'Jack's parents not coming today?' Ceri asked.

Aisling shook her head. 'They're not up to it. They asked
me to let them know if you need anything more from them.
And they wanted to know when you're going to release
Jack's personal effects. Aggie would really like to have Jack's
watch.'

Ceri turned her head. 'You don't want it yourself?'

'It was a gift from his parents. It's only right they should
have it.' It was his clothes that Aisling wouldn't be able to give
up. His old shirts, his wool jumpers. She'd taken to wearing
something of his whenever she was home. A T-shirt to bed. One
of his jumpers, sleeves rolled up, over her tank top and jeans.

'Well, I know we have his wallet and his watch. They're
held in evidence at the moment, but I expect they'll be released
as soon as the coroner gives his formal verdict.'

'Not his phone?'

Ceri shook her head. 'It wasn't found, I'm afraid.' She
hesitated. 'Did you know that you won't be the only family
member attending today's meeting? Jack's sister has already
arrived.'

'Jack doesn't have a sister,' Aisling found herself saying;
knowing even as she said it that that wasn't true, exactly, that
Jack had had a sister once.

Ceri was watching her.

'I mean,' Aisling stopped, stuck. Then, after a long pause,
'She's alive?'

Ceri nodded. 'It seems so.' She waited, giving Aisling a
chance to respond, but Aisling had nothing at all to say. It

seemed so improbable. Could this person be some kind of fraudster? But she dismissed the thought. No one in their right mind could think that they would benefit by pretending to be a surviving relative of Jack's. Twenty-five-year-old engineers weren't generally assumed to be rolling in it. Ceri gave up waiting for a response and gave her what might have been intended to be an encouraging smile, then continued on down the corridor.

Aisling barely had time to think before Ceri opened the door to the meeting room and she had her first – or rather her second – look at Jack's sister.

'You were at the cemetery,' Aisling blurted.

The woman nodded.

'God. I should have realised. You look like him.'

The woman flushed, an almost instant spread of colour staining her cheeks. 'Do I?' she asked.

'You didn't know?' It was true. The woman had much darker hair than Jack, who had been a sort of sandy blond, but she had the same very dark eyes, and something else that was more indefinably Jack. Oh God. What was her name? Was it Maeve? No, that wasn't right. Damnit. Something else, something more English sounding.

'Can I get either of you a cup of tea? Coffee?' Ceri asked.

Both women shook their heads, and Ceri told them she'd be five minutes, then shut the door, leaving them alone in the room.

Bloody hell. This was awkward. Worse than awkward. What could she say? Aisling opened her mouth twice to start, and closed it again both times. Eventually she took a seat at the table. The room was too warm, so she unbuttoned her coat, but noticed that Jack's sister — God, what was her name? – kept hers on.

The door opened again before either of them spoke. Ceri held the door for another garda, an older man. He came into the room in an unmistakable bustle of self-importance, without acknowledging Ceri. He carried a thin manila folder in one hand, and when he sat, his stomach pressed against the table.

'Ladies,' he said, opening the folder and giving each of them a nod, before lowering his head to the file. He ran his finger along the text as he read. 'You're Aisling Conroy, and you were the deceased's girlfriend, is that right?'

Aisling nodded. 'His partner,' she said. She felt a surge of irritation. This was definitely the same man who came to the house the day Jack died. Did he really not recognise her? He asked her to confirm her place and date of birth, her home address and telephone number.

'And the deceased's parents aren't joining us today?'

Aisling shook her head. 'Jack's dad isn't well. They've asked me to pass on any information to them.'

'Grand, grand. Well if they'd like a home visit tell them to call Ceri here. We can certainly arrange that.' He wiped at his nose with the palm of his right hand, before rubbing his hand on the leg of his trousers. 'I'm Garda James Rodgers. I'll be your family liaison officer.' He looked at them unsmiling, paused as if waiting for thanks. 'It's my job to explain all the processes and procedures to you, in this situation.' He checked something in his file, frowned and looked at Jack's sister. 'You're a friend of Aisling here?'

Aisling caught a fleeting expression on Ceri's face, and it occurred to her that Rodgers knew very well who Jack's sister was.

'I'm Maude Blake. Jack was my brother.' *Maude.* That was it. How could she have forgotten?

Rodger's frown deepened. He turned a page in his file, turned it back. 'Right. Well, I wasn't expecting you, Maude,' he said. 'But I'm sure you're very welcome. I'll need to confirm your details before we can proceed.' And he started to write, laboriously noting down Maude's name and date of birth. 'Home address?' he asked.

'I'm staying at the Radisson.' Maude's voice was low, a little rasping in a pleasant sort of way. Aisling wondered if she had been crying.

'I need your home address.'

'Do you?' Maude raised an eyebrow. She waited until Rodgers opened his mouth to speak again, then said, 'I don't have a permanent home at the moment. If you need to contact me for any reason you can use email.' And with that Rodgers had to be content, it seemed. He took the email address, turned the page on his file, and cleared his throat.

'As you know Jack Blake was seen entering the River Corrib at O'Brien's Bridge a little after eleven p.m. on Friday night. He was seen by a passer-by who called the gardaí shortly after. A car was dispatched and it reached the bridge approximately eight minutes after the call came in.' He raised his head from the file. 'I think we'd all agree, that's a very fast response time.' He gave a nod, as if both women had agreed with him with enthusiasm, instead of looking at him blankly.

'Garda Michael Smith and Garda Jane Keenan searched the area immediately around the bridge but found nothing. They radioed the station and a call was put out to the coastguard. Four more officers were dispatched and teams searched along the river bank down to the coast. A search and rescue boat reached the area a little after three a.m. The deceased's body was found at seven-thirty a.m. He was declared dead at the scene and brought to the morgue, where he was identified by his girlfriend later that day.' He paused and bowed his head slightly for a few seconds, then closed his file with deliberation.

'There will be an inquest, I'm sorry to say. It will just be a formality in this case, as you know, but it's required in all cases of sudden death. You don't have to attend if you find it bothersome, although the coroner may want to hear from Jack's parents. Family members are sometimes asked to give evidence, but I doubt that will be necessary in this case.' He wiped at his nose again with the back of his hand, then pulled a small booklet from his file. It had a plain navy cover with the garda emblem in the bottom left corner, and an image on a small rainbow on the right. The title read *Inquests – Support after Suicide*. Rodgers pushed the booklet across the table to Aisling, who didn't react.

'This is for you. It explains the whole process.' His expression was that of a man vaguely put out. 'I only have the one, but maybe you can share?' Aisling glanced involuntarily at Ceri, but she was staring fixedly at the table, avoiding eye contact. Rodgers stood up. 'There's no rush now, if you'd like to stay here for a while. I'm sure Ceri can get you a cup of tea. And if you've any questions, Ceri will give you a number you can call. Details of some grief counsellors and such.' He stepped back from the table.

Aisling picked up the sad little booklet, and felt the last of her energy seep through her feet and into the floor. She wanted to go back to bed. That dead tiredness pulled at her. She could sleep again, seemed to have endless capacity for it.

'Wait.' Maude spoke sharply, puncturing Aisling's reverie.

Rodgers stopped and turned towards Maude.

'I have some questions. I have a lot of questions.'

He stared at her, but made no move to return to the table. Aisling looked from Maude to Rodgers and back. Maude's face was set, determined.

'You mentioned an anonymous call. When you say anonymous, do you mean untraceable?'

'I mean that it was anonymous. In that the caller did not give his name.'

'Yes,' said Maude. 'But couldn't you trace it?'

He looked at her blankly. 'No,' he said.

'Why not?'

Rodgers took a step back towards the table. He didn't sit, but rested his hands on the back of the chair he had vacated. His manner was sympathetic, his tone that of a patient teacher reassuring a bright but overly anxious student.

'Maude, I'm very sorry for your loss, but I think it's clear that your brother was a disturbed young man, no fault of his own to be sure. But you know, we've had a lot of suicides this year. Very tragic certainly, but we have men out to the bridges more than we should, and most of the time there's nothing we can do.' He sighed and shook his head. 'I wish the bloody media would stop reporting it, it's only giving these young fellas ideas.'

His manner pissed Aisling off. He hadn't known Jack. He didn't know the first thing about him. 'How do you know he was disturbed?' she asked.

Rodgers straightened and turned a little in her direction, tucking his hands into his pockets. 'Well, I suppose it's obvious after the fact, isn't it? Now you shouldn't blame yourself, Aisling. I've met any number of families that had no idea something like this was coming their way. We all get caught up in life and get so busy and you know these young fellas aren't great at talking about their feelings and the like.'

'No,' Aisling said. 'That's not right.' The whole thing just felt wrong. Jack hadn't been disturbed. He'd never shown any signs of depression. Yes, he had nightmares sometimes, but he was happy. She knew he had been happy. 'Jack was only twenty-five. He had a good job. Good friends. He had me.' She stopped, swallowed. 'We were very happy. He wasn't a bit depressed.'

'Well ...' Rodgers smirked, then shrugged. Aisling wanted to slap him. He said nothing more, just passed the file from one hand to another. Glanced towards the door.

'Right, well, let's get back to this call,' said Maude. 'Was the caller male, or female?'

'I don't know, and I don't think it's relevant.'

'Well, perhaps the answer is in your file,' Maude said. Her tone was very dry, and Aisling felt a surge of fellow feeling towards her.

With a sigh, Rodgers put the file back on the table and slowly turned the pages. He didn't sit, but read from the file where he stood. 'At one-sixteen a.m. on Sunday seventeenth March the garda on the desk at Mill Street received a call from a male caller who did not identify himself. He said that he had witnessed a person jump from O'Brien's Bridge approximately five minutes earlier. Caller terminated the call.' Rodger's tone had changed. The bright but anxious student had taken up too much time and the irritated teacher wanted to move on.

'Sunday seventeenth March. St. Patrick's Day,' Maude said.

'Yes.'

'And that was the only call you got?'

He nodded. He closed the file, and picked it up again from the table.

Maude sat forward. 'Look, could you just sit down for five minutes and answer our questions? That's what this meeting is supposed to be about, isn't it?' Her voice was very controlled, but Rodgers was pissed off now and made no effort to hide it. He said nothing, but pulled back the seat and sat himself into it with exaggerated patience, while colour mounted in his face.

'The pubs would only have been closed for half an hour,' said Maude. 'Paddy's weekend. Half of them would have had late licences too. Don't you think that it's strange? That on a Saturday night in Galway only one person saw this, and he called the station but wouldn't identify himself? Why wouldn't he give his name?'

'Certainly someone else may have seen your brother jump into the river. But there would be no need for them to call the police if they knew someone else had made the call, would there?'

'Right, fine,' said Maude. Her voice was a little louder now. 'But you said that you lot got there in less than ten minutes, right? So there must have been people there, people who saw Jack jump, people who gave statements?'

'There were some statements taken, yes,' said Rodgers. This time he made no move to open his file. He was looking at Maude with poorly hidden irritation, his face more florid by the moment. Maybe he didn't like being questioned by a woman, particularly one who was younger than he was.

'I'm asking you if anyone other than this anonymous caller saw Jack jump into the river.'

When Rodgers responded he spoke in a monotone, listing off facts that he suddenly knew without support from the file. 'When officers reached the bridge there were a number of people in the vicinity. Two couples on the bridge were walking from the Róisín Dubh pub to Supermac's on the corner of Cross Street and Bridge Street. A single male was crossing the bridge from the other side, on his way home from Busker Brownes. There were a number of other people near the bridge. Only brief interviews were taken in the circumstances, and no one had seen a man enter the water.'

Aisling sat forward in her chair. Her head was reeling. Maude put both hands on the table in front of her and then, as if she couldn't help herself, clenched them into fists. 'This whole thing is bullshit,' she said. 'Jack didn't kill himself. I can't believe this. All you have to say it was a suicide is the word of some guy who made an anonymous call. There's not a single other person who saw it happen.' She took a quick gasping breath. 'You should be investigating. You need to start investigating this properly. You've gone about it all wrong. Jack's been dead for a week, and you've done nothing.' Her voice rose at the end – still not a shout but raw and loud.

'She's right,' Aisling said, hearing her own voice as if from a long way away. 'This doesn't make any sense.'

But Rodgers was speaking over her. 'That is not at all the case. The gardaí followed the designated procedures and carried out a thorough search of the area.'

Aisling felt more and more disconnected from the scene in the room. Her head was swimming. Why hadn't she asked any questions before now? 'You need to look into this more. I don't think Jack was depressed. He wasn't depressed. And he was a very strong swimmer.'

Rodgers turned to her. He was louder now, his tone angrily condescending. 'I know it's hard to accept, but people can do dreadful things. Really. I've seen it. You sit on this side of the desk for a while and you'll see what people can do. And do you know, he probably drank a fair bit of alcohol before he jumped. They always do. And the alcohol would be very disorienting and make it harder to deal with the cold.'

'But he didn't drink,' said Aisling. 'He had never touched alcohol in his life. He hated it, and he never took drugs.'

'Well, maybe he made an exception, given what was in his mind.' Rodgers stood up again, this time pushing his chair back hard. It couldn't slide on the lino and so wobbled and nearly toppled backwards. 'I suppose we'll never know,' he muttered.

'What?' Maude said.

But Rodgers didn't respond.

'What do you mean we won't know?' she repeated, but it seemed that Rodgers was in no mood to reply. The patient teacher was long gone, replaced by a sulky schoolboy, halfway between the table and the door.

'We didn't order a toxicology report.' His tone was triumphant.

'And whose decision was that?' Maude asked. Her voice was calm again, her tone pitched low. To Aisling she sounded like the adult in the room; Aisling's own questions those of a hysterical teenager.

The part of Aisling that wasn't dull and dizzy knew that toxicology was not a routine step in every postmortem; that it wasn't ordered without a reason, but she couldn't find the energy to pass this information to Maude.

'It's certainly not yours,' Rodgers was saying.

'I am his next of kin. I would like to know who decided not to test Jack's blood for drugs. I also want some answers about this anonymous caller. Has the call been traced since? There is no call box on or near O'Brien's Bridge.' She looked to Aisling for confirmation. Aisling shook her head and Maude continued. 'No call box, so the call would have to have been made from a mobile phone. And I do not think it unreasonable for the gardaí to take the time to carry out what seem to me to be basic investigative steps.'

Rodgers took hold of the door handle.

'I'm sure it's very hard for you to accept your brother's death. Particularly when you weren't really much of a sister to him during his life, were you really? I'm sure you're feeling a bit guilty about that. And maybe now you're trying to make up for it. That's understandable. But you know, your friend here, she's very sad about her boyfriend and I think you'd respect that and stop trying to get her all riled up.'

'All. Riled. Up.' Aisling repeated. She wasn't trying to be funny, but she couldn't seem to pull her thoughts together.

Rodgers' face darkened. 'Right. I've given you the information I have to give you.' He took two angry steps back to the table and shoved the grieving relatives' booklet across the table at them. 'Have a read of that. You'll soon see that this whole thing was textbook, you know. Most drownings in Ireland are young men in their twenties committing suicide at night with drink taken. I'm afraid I can't help you further today, and this room is needed now so I'll have to ask you to leave.' He stood and walked to the door, holding it open for them.

Maude took her time, but she stood eventually, and turned to Aisling. Aisling couldn't move. She thought she might be sick. Despite the confusion and nausea she felt that a little bit of Jack had been given back to her in this room, and if she left she might lose him all over again. The possibility that Jack hadn't killed himself was suddenly everything. It was the thread she could pick up and follow back to a world and a life where things made sense. She had to remind herself that Jack was still dead. No matter how it had happened, nothing would change the fact that he was gone. For the first time that knowledge truly sank in, and the shock of it made her blurt out the thought that was circling around and around in her head.

'But, I'm pregnant,' she said. She looked at Rodgers, and seemingly involuntarily, Maude turned to look at him also.

He spoke quite deliberately. 'I'm afraid major life change can be a trigger for suicide. You'll read all about it in the booklet.' And he turned and walked out of the room.

Monday 25 March 2013

CHAPTER SIX

'She's here,' said Mary.

'Who's here?' Aisling didn't look up from her charts. She was conscious of Mary coming closer, looking over her shoulder and starting to read.

'Checking up on me?' Aisling asked, still not looking up.

'Nope. Just interested.'

Aisling ignored her. Kept writing. Mary had been so supportive, but since the funeral the support seemed to have an edge to it. As if Mary felt that the fact that Aisling hadn't completely collapsed was in some way letting Jack down. Aisling found she liked the old sarcastic, pissy Mary much more than the new uber-empathetic version. The overt sympathy made her feel claustrophobic.

'I told Sandra to ask her to take a seat in the waiting room.'

'Who?' She wished, fervently, that Mary would go away. She had an hour to get through the charts, and needed two. There was so much to catch up on; she wouldn't have believed she could fall this far behind in a week. She would be doing rounds with Cummins in the morning, and he was unbelievably anal about charting. He was due to mark her for assessment, and she wasn't going to give him any excuses to mark her down.

'What's her name? You know. Jack's sister.'

'What?' Aisling looked up.

'Finally, a reaction. She's sitting in the waiting room. Not much like Jack, is she? Skinny thing.'

Aisling was already standing and moving towards the double doors, charts abandoned. It had been three days since the family liaison meeting. She should have called Maude at her hotel. Bad enough that she'd virtually run from that bloody meeting, hadn't waited long enough to exchange even a polite goodbye. Worse that she'd made no effort to contact her since. Maude wasn't in the seating area. Had she left already? But no. She was standing, arms wrapped around herself, looking out of the window at the dull afternoon. The view of the carpark was not inspiring at the best of times. On a dark winter's day it was a bloody health hazard. If you weren't depressed when you reached the waiting room you probably would be by the time you left it.

'Maude.'

Maude turned. Had she been that thin when Aisling saw her at the police station? She'd seemed strong then. Now she looked pale, depleted.

'That girl they just brought in. The one with all the blood on her face and clothes. Did she try to kill herself?' Maude asked.

'What? No. Nothing like that. She had her tonsils out last week, then got an infection. She had a haemorrhage.' Aisling found herself giving a little laugh. 'It looked dramatic, but she'll be fine.' Why was she telling Maude all of this? And in an open waiting room? So much for patient confidentiality.

Maude nodded. 'Do you have time for coffee?'

Aisling glanced towards the double doors. 'I shouldn't,' she said. 'I'm on for another few hours.' She looked back at Maude. 'We're pretty quiet. I can probably take half an hour, as long as I take the bleep.' She patted the pager tucked inside her scrubs top pocket. 'The canteen will be closed, but there's a café across the road. I can meet you there in half an hour?'

Mary all but pushed Aisling out the door, so she restacked her charts, grabbed her puffa, and walked quickly out of

A&E, across the carpark and University Road, and into the café. It was a functional sort of place, but the coffee was decent and it was in range for the pager. Maude sat at a table, two cups in front of her.

'I ordered you a black coffee, but there's milk on the table.' She gestured towards the milk jug and sugar. 'I thought you'd probably want it strong.'

'Thanks.' Aisling sat, and took the cup. She added sugar and milk with an apologetic smile and then felt awkward. She felt ill at ease in nearly every social interaction at the moment – too conscious of every expression that crossed her face. She was still editing herself, reviewing her expressions, adapting them to something appropriate for someone whose partner had just killed himself.

'You look cold,' she said.

Maude was still wearing her coat and scarf; had her arms wrapped around herself. She looked down in seeming surprise, then released her arms and wrapped her hands around her cup.

'It's autumn at home. But still pretty warm. Nothing like this.'

'Where's home?' Aisling asked.

'Australia,' Maude said. 'The Kimberley.' She checked herself, and shook her head. 'Used to be, I mean, not any more.'

'Did you live there long?' The question felt ridiculous, the smallest of small talk.

Maude shrugged. 'Longer than I lived in Ireland.'

'Right.'

They fell silent for a moment, both taking sips of coffee.

Aisling studied Maude as they sat there. Her dark hair was long, tied in a careless knot at the back of her head. She wore a grey wool coat that looked a size too big. She was very attractive – a middle-aged Audrey Hepburn? Except she must only be in her thirties. What, thirty-five? She looked older.

'I'm sorry I didn't stay,' Aisling said. 'After the meeting. I had to ... I had an appointment,' she finished lamely. 'I'm sure you'd like to talk. And I'd like to too. Could we meet again? When I'm not working. Before you go back to Australia.'

'I'm not going back.' Maude said, surprise in her voice. 'My life in Australia ... things have changed there. I'm going to stay in Ireland.'

'I see.' How tragic, then, that she'd waited too long. If returning to Ireland had been a possibility, why hadn't she come before now? Perhaps Jack hadn't meant that much to her.

'I'd like to know what you think happened,' Maude said.

'To Jack?'

A nod.

'I don't know.'

'But you don't believe that he killed himself.'

'I don't know. It seems crazy to suggest anything else happened, but Jack wasn't depressed. He could get down and out sometimes, like anyone, but he wasn't depressed.'

'So nothing had happened in your lives, nothing that would have upset him in some way?'

Aisling shook her head, stared back at Maude. She wasn't going to mention the pregnancy. If Maude wanted to ask if Jack could have killed himself because she was carrying his child, she could bloody well come out with it herself. Yes, Aisling had spent the best part of the week believing it herself, but she would never say it out loud again.

Maude's face was unreadable. Eventually, she said, 'If Jack didn't kill himself, then what? An accident?' She paused. 'Murder?'

'Jesus, no.'

Maude sat, watching her and waiting.

'There's no way. I mean, Jack didn't have any enemies or anything like that. He was just an ordinary guy.' A stupid thing to say. Jack hadn't been ordinary. He had been so very special.

'You can't think of anyone who might have wanted to hurt him?'

Aisling shook her head again. Tears stung her eyes and she blinked them back, then closed her eyes against a sudden, vivid memory of Jack. They'd been in college, had been dating a few months, it hadn't felt like anything serious. She'd been in the library studying, and had met him afterwards, had seen him walking towards her across the quad. She'd watched his face light up when he saw her, his eyes fill with laughter at some story he had to tell her. Jack had gathered her to him in a great bear hug, then kissed her, put her down and started talking. They'd held hands and walked together through the campus. Such a simple moment, to realise that you love someone.

Something in her recognised how right it was with Jack long before her brain could capture it and analyse it. Trying to explain him made him sound less than he was, she'd found. Describing him as a good man, kind, strong, independent but supportive. It all added up to something far more anaemic than the real thing. So she'd given up on trying to explain it to her friends, to her mostly absent family who thought she was too young to settle down, and just enjoyed it.

He'd told her his story the first time he brought her home to meet his parents – that Aggie and Brendan were his adoptive parents, that his mother was dead, his father unknown. He had a sister, somewhere, but hadn't seen her since he was a little boy and didn't know where she was. All of it delivered matter of factly, with a smile that invited her to treat it lightly, as old pain long put away. She'd asked him about his scars later, the three round burn marks on his left shoulder, and he'd told her, not smiling now, that he didn't remember getting them. Something about the tightness in his shoulders made her wonder if he was lying, but she'd kissed him, and let it go. Had she let too much go? Noticed too little?

Aisling blinked her way back to the present, and found that Maude was watching her.

'You think someone killed him, don't you?' Aisling asked.

Maude nodded slowly.

'Why?'

'You knew him best, Aisling. You know his friends, the people he works with, the places he goes. You need to think about who could have hurt him. Who had reason to want Jack dead.'

'I'll have to go to the police again, push them to take this seriously. That guy Rodgers is a joke, but there must be someone else.' The coffee cup had cooled in Aisling's hand, though it was more than half full. She checked the pager in her pocket, though it had been silent throughout their conversation. So strange to be there, with Jack's sister, talking about his death as the sky darkened outside. Maude's dark eyes, so like Jack's but different too. Maude was less joyful, more cautious, harder to read.

'If you're going to take this further, then it would be better to work together, I think,' Maude said.

At that the pager started to buzz. Aisling muted it. Her head ached. 'Maybe I'm just in denial. I don't want Jack to have killed himself, but murder? There's just no way. But we do need the gardaí to look at this properly, just for peace of mind.' It sounded like a plea. She tried to make her voice stronger, more confident. 'There's a garda ombudsman, I think, that you can go to with complaints.'

Maude shook her head firmly. 'I have evidence,' she said. 'Evidence that I think proves that the story the police gave us is bullshit.'

Aisling felt hot, then cold. 'What sort of evidence?'

Maude smiled for the first time. 'The best kind. Video.'

CHAPTER SEVEN

It was Peter Fisher who first mentioned the case. Cormac was on his way back from a late lunch and met him in the stairwell.

'I hear you've caught one,' said Fisher.

Cormac raised an eyebrow.

'The super wants you in his office. Looks like you've picked one up.'

Cormac tried to hide his relief, but knew he had failed when Fisher gave him an encouraging grin. Fuck's sake. Cormac gave him a brisk nod of acknowledgement and restrained himself from taking the rest of the stairs two at a time. He felt the same rush of excitement and adrenalin he always felt, this time complicated by a need to prove himself that he hadn't experienced in years.

Cormac knocked on the door of Brian Murphy's office. He didn't wait, but opened the door and entered. A pair of cycling shoes and a helmet sat on a shelf. Murphy was ten years older than Cormac, but he was probably in better shape. He was lean, very lean, and fit, and kept his thinning hair cut close to his scalp.

He was sitting behind his desk, and he raised one hand in a *wait* gesture, while he finished reading whatever was on his screen. His desk – oversized, but standard-issue white melamine – was immaculate, and completely free of paper. The computer screen, keyboard and phone were pushed slightly to Murphy's right, and a grey cold-case file box sat on the far left of the desk. Shite. Another bloody cold case. Murphy looked up.

'Reilly,' he said. 'Take a seat.' He opened the cold-case box and took out a thin file. 'Settling in?' he asked, then continued without waiting for a reply. 'Not missing the elite confines of Dublin Castle, are you?'

'No, sir,' said Cormac. Of course he bloody missed it. He'd been the youngest garda ever admitted to the Special Detective Unit, and he'd made a success of it. Requesting the transfer had seemed logical to him at the time. The peace process had been successful. A ceasefire had been in place for years, and the unit was a shadow of its former self. There were new threats, of course, but it was obvious to the dogs on the street that the anti-terrorist unit was about to be restructured, which really meant down-sized.

And then there was Emma. She was a research scientist. A biologist. When she'd won a highly prestigious grant from the European Research Council he'd been there with champagne on ice. When she'd explained that the grant was worth three million a year, and was intended to fund the cost of eight researchers who would work under Emma on a project she had designed, he had been delighted for her. And when she'd explained that the lab was at the university in Galway, he had, he thought, been effective in hiding his dismay. When he'd ultimately decided to look for a transfer out of the Special Detectives Unit to Galway Operations, a step down in the eyes of everyone who knew anything about it, there had been the predictable slagging. Plenty of 'whipped' comments. Cormac didn't give a shit. The fact that the unit would likely be restructured within the year took the pain out of it, but he would have made the decision either way. In the face of Emma's concerns that he would miss Dublin and his job, he'd been unrelentingly optimistic, and reality had taken time to hit. But after a month working on no-hoper cold cases – a month of returning to an empty flat, with Emma working late on some project deadline or other, a month during which the rain pissed down relentlessly every day – regret was beginning to kick in with a vengeance.

'I've heard good things about you, Reilly,' the Super was saying. 'You've done very well.' And that was patronising as fuck. Was the intent to needle him? Or to poke and measure him by his reaction? He didn't know enough about Murphy to be sure. Brian Murphy was more administrator than cop, and that wasn't necessarily a bad thing. Word on the street was that he was good at his job, a straight shooter, or at least as much of one as the job would allow. Cormac still wondered how he handled having his son work out of the same station, while said son hung out of Anthony Healy's pocket. It couldn't be comfortable for him. Under normal circumstances, Trevor would never have been able to work out of a station that was under his father's command, but as the National Drugs Unit reported up to the Assistant Commissioner, Crime and Security, rather than through the Western Region command structure, Trevor wasn't technically under his father's leadership. Murphy Senior had to know about Healy's reputation, but if he felt the pressure of the situation he'd hid it well.

'You know your transfer here is part of a broader effort to decentralise some of our specialist skills, out of elite units, and back into operations. The intent is that you share, particularly with your younger colleagues, some of what you learned in the SDU. But of course, we do things differently in Galway, so you will have to adjust, and learn to follow our processes.' He paused, looked at Cormac as if considering him deeply. 'I've no doubt, with your level of commitment, you'll be one of our top men in no time.'

'Yes sir.' Christ almighty. He'd seen nothing yet that impressed him about Galway's best detectives.

'You're about to get a little busier,' Murphy said, and he opened the file on his desk.

'Sir?'

The file looked old but in good condition. An elastic band had been placed around it at some point, but it had rotted off, leaving only an outline on the cardboard. As Murphy opened the file, Cormac saw that it contained no more than twenty or thirty pages.

'Hilaria Blake,' Murphy said. 'You investigated her death.'

'I ... what?'

'On the twenty-first of February 1993, you went to a house in answer to a call. When you got there you found two children and their dead mother. The dead woman was Hilaria Blake.' Murphy closed the file and pushed it across the desk to Cormac. 'Your notes are unusually complete, given your inexperience at the time. I gather you had suspicions about the death. You thought it may have been something other than an accidental overdose.'

Cormac hesitated, then opened the file. He scanned the first page as memories came flooding back. 'It was a call out for a domestic dispute, or at least, that's what we thought. I wouldn't have been sent out otherwise, I was so green.' He looked up from the file. 'My concerns – I raised those questions with my superior back in '93. He did not agree. The case has been closed for twenty years.' Cormac thought back, remembering the response of ... what was the guy's name? It was gone. He could recall very clearly though the complete lack of interest in carrying out any sort of investigation. If it hadn't been for him a file might not even have been opened. And he'd been directed to bring the thing to an end in no time at all.

In truth there had been nothing to go on. Nothing except Cormac's gut feeling that something worse than the obvious had been going on in that house, and the fact that the postmortem indicated that Hilaria Blake had not been a habitual heroin user.

'I want you to reopen the file,' Murphy said.

Cormac said nothing, but stared at his new boss, waiting. There must be something more.

'Jack Blake, the boy you found that night, is dead. He appears to have committed suicide. But his sister ... ah ... Maude ... has returned to Galway. As I understand it, she ran away on the night of her mother's death. Now she has returned and her brother is dead also, again in suspicious circumstances. I want this looked into. And you are the best man for the job.'

'Sir, I'm flattered ...'

'Are you?' Murphy cut across him. 'This is not a compliment to your abilities, Detective. You are simply in the right place at the right time. You are the only person in this station who was present at the time of Hilaria Blake's death – you worked out of Swinford at the time, is that right?' He didn't wait for Cormac's nod. 'You met the children. You carried out at least some sort of preliminary investigation. You are, after all, an experienced detective. I am reopening this case and I want you to run the investigation.'

Cormac turned the pages on the file, scanning its content, looking for something new, something that could have prompted Murphy to call in a twenty-year-old suspicious death file. He saw forms filled in with his own writing, reports signed by him, hospital records, and postmortem results, but nothing new. And nothing to link what should be a Mayo investigation to Galway, except of course Jack Blake's death.

'Talk to me about this woman, about Maude Blake,' Murphy said. 'What do you know about her?'

'I've nothing to tell you sir. I don't know anything about her,' Cormac said. 'I was with her for about three hours, twenty years ago. She wasn't much more than a child.'

'She's not a child now,' said Murphy. 'She's a woman of some means apparently. She lives somewhere in Australia, or at least, that's where she flew in from. She's staying in an expensive hotel. So the question I have is, how does a fifteen year old with no family and no money flee the country and not just survive but apparently, thrive?'

'I have no idea, but she'd hardly be the first from difficult circumstances to make the most of her life.' Cormac kept his tone cool, though he felt a surge of irritation.

'You recognised her.'

'Sir?'

'You saw her coming out of the family room, and you told Garda McIntyre that you knew her.'

Mystery woman. Of course. He was surprised he had recognised her at all, after twenty years. But that night, and Maude, had stayed with him for a long time. And Danny'd gone off his own bat to find out who she was. Probably thought he was doing him a favour. *Fucking Danny.*

'I didn't recognise her. I thought that she looked familiar. I don't know anything about who she is today. I met her when she was a girl, a teenager. She called the station and I was asked to respond to the call. We weren't expecting to find … what I found. I took her and her little brother to the hospital. That's it really.'

Murphy waited.

'She disappeared from the hospital. Left her brother behind.' Cormac paused, thinking again about the little boy's despair. Had Maude ever come back to see him? 'In the postmortem report the pathologist said that the mother – Hilaria – did not show any signs of using heroin, that that night may have been her first time. She was an alcoholic and had advanced liver disease.'

'You clearly had suspicions of foul play,' Murphy said, gesturing to the file.

'I raised it with my DS at the time,' Cormac said. 'I felt that it was a suspicious death and we should make further enquiries. He disagreed.' Cormac paused. 'The little boy was in a bad state. Hilaria Blake was very obviously not a model mother. There was no appetite for an investigation. Different times.'

They had been, truly, different times. In 1993, Brendan Smyth, a former priest and notorious child abuser, was still on the run in Ireland, the true extent of his crimes not known. The documentaries, *States of Fear* and *Suing the Pope*, which did so much to prompt long overdue government inquiries had not yet been screened, and those inquiries had not yet been held. In the twenty years since the Blake case, Ireland had woken up, but Cormac could remember the days when the welfare of a child was not the first consideration in a child protection case, when investigating the death of an unmarried mother and drug addict would never have been high on the garda agenda.

'Sir, are you suggesting that Maude Blake may have had something to do with her brother's death?'

'I don't believe I said that, detective, and I'm not implying it either. Do you understand?'

Cormac nodded, the only acceptable response in the face of bureaucratic bullshit. None of this made sense and Murphy had to know that as well as he did. Wasn't it Jack's death had prompted this investigation? 'Am I to look into Jack Blake's death?' he asked.

'That investigation is being handled by other officers,' Murphy said. 'And you are to leave that work to them.'

Cormac kept his face blank. Murphy must suspect Maude. Why else would he have started looking into her past? But if that was the case it made no sense to split the investigation.

Murphy was watching him, Cormac realised. Reading him, or trying to.

Murphy slapped one hand on his desk, as if punctuating his decision. 'I want you on this case, Reilly,' he said. 'You are the investigating officer. You decide when to bring Blake in, when to question her. Is that understood?'

The phrasing was odd. Did Murphy think Cormac would shirk the case, try to palm it off on a subordinate? He had no intention of it. Murphy might be an asshole – that remained to be seen – but if he was, he was the asshole Cormac had to impress if he wanted to keep his career.

'Yes, sir.'

Murphy dropped the file back into the box, and pushed it in Cormac's direction.

'Preliminary report by Friday please, Detective Sergeant.'

CHAPTER EIGHT

Cormac walked out of the office, thinking about the little boy he had last seen in a hospital room twenty years before. He'd kept track of Jack for some time and had been relieved when he was told that Jack had gone straight from hospital to a foster family. Relieved, and surprised that a family had been found so quickly. The foster family had gone on to adopt Jack, and it had really seemed that he had every chance of leaving his childhood behind him. If he had killed himself, that was a tragedy. Maybe the abuse he'd suffered had hurt him too much, had come back to destroy him in the end.

Cormac dropped the file on his desk and flipped it open. If Murphy thought there was a chance Jack had been murdered, why hadn't he put Cormac on that case, instead of a twenty-year-old suspicious death that had long since been written off as an accidental overdose? There was an agenda at play here, but whatever it was wasn't clear. Cormac looked towards the other end of the room, then closed the file and walked over. The place was almost empty. The drugs unit must be out on a job, everyone but Danny. Carrie O'Halloran, the man-hater, was seated at a desk in the corner, her head bent over her paperwork.

Danny didn't look up at Cormac's approach. Cormac put one hand on Danny's desk, lowered his voice and spoke almost into his ear.

'I just had an interesting little chat with our friend Murphy.'

Danny jumped. 'Jesus.'

Cormac just looked at him.

'About?'

'About Maude Blake. I think you've dropped me in it. I've got yet another cold case because Murphy thinks I have some sort of inside knowledge.'

Danny's face flushed. 'You're investigating her brother's suicide?'

'I bloody wish. No. Cold cases only for me it seems. I'm looking into Hilaria Blake's death. A twenty-year-old accidental death. Heroin overdose.'

Danny looked confused for a moment, as well he might. The flush faded slowly from his cheeks. 'Sorry mate. All I did was ask Rodgers who he was talking to. He asked who wanted to know, I said you thought you'd recognised her.'

Cormac sat on the desk beside Danny's. 'I'm missing something,' he said. 'Murphy didn't come right out and say it, but he suggested that there's something suspicious about Jack Blake's death. I got the impression that's what prompted Murphy's sudden interest in Hilaria Blake. But if that was it then why am I on the cold case?'

Danny shook his head. 'I heard it was suicide. Pretty cut and dry.'

'You haven't heard anything else?'

'Sorry. Maybe you took Murphy up wrong?'

'Maybe.'

Danny was distracted, Cormac realised. He looked tired, strained.

'Any news on Lorna?'

Danny shook his head. 'Nothing. I've tried calling that friend I spoke to but she's not answering her phone.'

'You're worried?'

Danny shook his head. 'No. Paranoid maybe, because of all the bullshit, but I know she's fine.'

Danny had lowered his voice, and he glanced around the room as he spoke. He didn't want to get into it there, and Cormac couldn't blame him.

'Where's the rest of the task force?' Cormac asked.

Danny checked his watch. 'They're down in the case room, planning an operation. It's the same thing we worked through yesterday, and the day before that,' he said. 'Healy likes to over-prepare.'

'Is there a problem?'

Danny met his eyes. 'If you mean am I not Mr Popular with the unit, nothing new there.'

'Do you want to do something about that?'

'Like what?'

'Like tell me whatever you have on Anthony Healy. Let me do something about it.'

Danny grimaced, shook his head. 'If I did know something, and I'm not saying I do, I'd torpedo my career if I talked about it. Anthony Healy and Trevor Murphy are thick as thieves. I go to Internal Affairs about Healy' – he held up one hand, palm facing Cormac – 'if I had something that is, and apart from getting that reputation so that no cop trusts me again, Trevor goes straight to his daddy. Where would that leave me?'

Cormac hesitated, the squad room not being the best place for this conversation, and then the opportunity passed as Healy, Murphy junior and two of the uniforms temporarily assigned to the task force arrived back.

Healy stared at Cormac as he settled back into his chair. There was a challenge there that Cormac thought he would have to deal with sooner or later.

Cormac looked away, straight into the eyes of Carrie O'Halloran, who was watching the exchange with unembarrassed interest. O'Halloran. He'd asked around about her since his conversation with Danny. She'd worked her entire career in Galway, so it was difficult to get any meaningful information, but she'd once worked a case with a friend of his, Séan Hegarty, who'd come down to provide support on a suspected sex trafficking ring. The friend had said she was competent, efficient, not overly friendly. She was also young for her rank, and there had been rumours that her promotion was political. Not exactly consistent with Danny's view of her, but then Danny'd worked with her longer. Best to make up his own mind. Cormac gave her a civil nod, which she ignored, returning her attention to her computer. Fantastic.

Cormac went back to his desk to find an overtime report from Fisher awaiting his signature. He was claiming six hours at weekend rates for the Lanigan case. Cormac signed it, knowing he'd have to justify the use of overtime on a cold case at the next finance meeting, for which he'd probably get a bollocking. He hadn't even caught up with Fisher yet, had been meaning to all day but somehow it had gotten away from him. He had a pile of paperwork to work through – the price he paid for spending most of the previous week out and about following up on leads. He got to work, became absorbed in it, and when he finally looked up from the files, his concentration broken by a buzzing from his phone, he found that the room had emptied out and twilight was setting in. He had a text from Emma.

Sorry sorry. Late again. Tomorrow night? Xx

Shite. Another evening of TV and cooking for one was suddenly unappealing. It was only Monday. He should go to the gym. Bad habit to get into though. He found Danny.

'Pint?' he asked.

Danny rolled his eyes, then shrugged. 'Yeah. Come on so.'

Cormac returned to his desk and locked the Blake file into the drawer under his desk before putting on his coat. The drawer wasn't remotely secure – it could be picked by a five year old with a fork – but the file was hardly sensitive, and putting it away would at least keep it from the casual curiosity of a contract cleaner. Cormac hesitated, looking down at the locked file drawer. This was certainly the first time he'd walked out of the station without even opening the file on a new case. Was he losing his appetite for the job? Had his willingness to walk away from the SDU been a symptom of burnout on the way? He snorted, turned for the stairs. No. This was just a piece of shit case, and he had no desire to start work on another time waster.

Peter Fisher caught up with them on their way down the stairs. Coat in hand, he was obviously finished for the day.

'So what's the story?' he said. 'Did you get a case?'

Danny gave him a look that clearly said *none of your fucking business,* but Fisher didn't irritate Cormac, despite the fact that he was perpetually cheerful. He was smart, he was motivated, and if he didn't have much respect for hierarchy, Cormac could sympathise with that.

'If you could call it a case,' Cormac said, and continued down the stairs.

'Is it that suicide thing then, the thing Rodgers is on?' Fisher asked.

'Related,' Cormac said. Then, catching the look on Fisher's face, 'Why, what did you hear?'

'You haven't heard the story?' Fisher asked. He looked around, his face a perfect mix of excitement at having something juicy to share, and nervousness at being overheard.

Cormac didn't hesitate. 'We're going for pints,' he said. 'King's Head. Will you join us?'

The pub was quiet. On Friday the place would be packed with office workers celebrating the end of another week of the grind. But on a Monday evening at six o'clock, it had a bare scattering of patrons, and the background music was quiet enough for comfortable conversation. Danny led the way to the back bar, and claimed a table by slinging his jacket over the back of a chair.

'What'll you have?' he asked.

Danny got the pints, and came back with menus.

'Sarah won't expect you home?' Cormac asked, taking a menu and scanning it.

'She'll get over it,' Danny said drily.

Christ. There was definitely a problem there. Danny held Cormac's eye, as if daring him to press the question. Cormac looked away. If he was going to have that conversation – and he was going to do his damnedest to avoid it – it wouldn't be in front of Fisher.

They ordered food, and settled back, Cormac letting his eyes wander around the room. The King's Head was a big place. It wasn't their usual haunt, but he'd wanted somewhere they wouldn't be overheard, where they could get a table a reasonable distance from the next punter.

The table Danny had chosen was just the right distance from the fireplace – close enough to enjoy the heat and the flickering light, not so close that you'd be melting after half an hour. The pints were good and food was on the way. Suddenly Cormac felt very much at home. He sent a text to Emma, told her he was eating out, and got a reply seconds later.

Perfect! Date night tomorrow? xxx

Maybe he'd book somewhere decent.

It didn't take them long to get into it. 'I don't know that much,' Fisher said. 'Someone saw the guy, Jack, take a dive from O'Brien's Bridge. Called it in. Car was out in under eight minutes. No sign of him so they mobilised the search team. They didn't find him until the sun came up after nine the following morning. He had been washed out but the tide was coming back in and he was found at Lough Atalia. Pronounced at the scene and taken to UCHG.'

Cormac nodded, and tried not to think about the little boy whose hand he had held twenty years before. The past twenty years had taught him a lot, including the necessity of keeping his distance from a case. You couldn't carry the emotional load for the victims; if you did you were less effective as a police officer, and you burned out. But he'd been in his first month on the job when he'd met Maude and Jack, and Hilaria Blake's was the first dead body he'd seen. Jack Blake had become a symbol for every neglected and abused child he came across in his career. What had caused Jack to take his own life, if that was what had happened? Maybe it had nothing to do with his early experience.

'So the guy was pretty clean cut, it seems,' Fisher was saying. 'Not a drinker, didn't do drugs. Had a good job and lived with his girlfriend. She's a doctor, works at UCHG.'

Cormac nodded, listening, but his eyes wandered across the room. Carrie O'Halloran had just walked in and taken a seat. She was alone. She hadn't looked at them, but he had a feeling she knew they were there.

Fisher's eyes were bright and he was leaning forward across the table, his voice pitched low. He wasn't hard to read. Something more interesting was coming down the track.

'Anyway, Rodgers, if you'll believe it, was assigned to family liaison. Can you believe that?' Fisher raised both hands in the air in an exaggerated gesture of surprise. 'Fucking Rodgers. Ceri is his second on it. She said the girlfriend is in total shock, so not really making things difficult. The parents are pretty old, the dad in a wheelchair, so they're leaving everything to the girlfriend. So you know, despite Rodgers being about as sensitive as ... Jesus, I don't know, you've met him. He's thick as pig shite.'

Cormac gave a small smile, but shook his head. Rodgers did strike him as a particularly bad choice. Family liaison officers were female more often than not, which he'd always thought was a bit sexist, and they were generally expected to have good interpersonal skills, and to be personally presentable. Rodgers was an old-style guard, and in Cormac's view should never have made sergeant. His personal hygiene was also seriously lacking.

Fisher took another drink from his pint, realised he was finished, and stood up to get a round. Danny hadn't said much since they'd entered the bar, and when Cormac looked across at him he rolled his eyes.

'What?'

'I didn't realise we were babysitting tonight.'

'Dan, if he's got the inside track about my case, I need to hear about it.'

Danny rolled his eyes. 'Maybe Murphy's messing with you. Pulling out an old case you were hung up on. Winding you up and watching you go.'

Cormac raised an eyebrow. 'Bit of a stretch.'

Danny returned his attention to his pint, and Cormac did the same. It wouldn't kill Danny to have a pint with Fisher. They were the same rank after all, though maybe that was part of the problem.

Cormac occupied himself with watching Carrie O'Halloran, while Danny brooded. She'd ordered a glass of red, and was taking her time with it. She had a file open in front of her. The jacket was blue, so it wasn't a murder file. Galway had its own colour coding. What was blue again? Domestic violence?

Danny's gaze followed Cormac's to where O'Halloran sat, and he grimaced. 'Whatever you do don't ask her to join us too.'

'You sure you're not worried?'

'About Lorna?' Then at Cormac's nod, 'I don't know Cormac. A bit, I suppose. I can't get that girl on the phone.'

'Who?'

'The hippy, ditzy one who gave me the story about the music festival.'

'Where is she? Where's she based?'

'Dublin.'

'You should go down. Go tomorrow. Track the girl down, talk to her in person.'

Danny blew out a breath. 'I should, I know. Maybe I will.' He looked away. 'It's just ... I'm trying to make something of this job, you know? I just know I'm going to trek all the way to Dublin, screw up my work, then find that little idiot laughing it up with her friends.'

'Danny ...'

'I know, I know.' Danny drank from his pint, refusing to look at Cormac.

Cormac let his eyes drift over to O'Halloran again. She was sipping her wine, reading her file as if totally engrossed. She hadn't looked their way once, which was enough to tell Cormac that she knew they were there.

Fisher returned with pints from the bar at the same time as the waitress arrived with their food. They ate, and by unspoken agreement conversation was restricted to small talk until the last forkful had been eaten, and another round had been ordered at the bar.

'So Rodgers is family liaison then,' Cormac said, eventually.

Fisher nodded. 'It was at the last meeting that the sister showed up. No one was expecting her, by all accounts, not even the girlfriend. She lives in Australia or something, hadn't been in touch with her brother for years. But she showed up for this meeting, full of attitude and questions. She doesn't believe her brother did it. Killed himself.'

Danny rolled his eyes again, but Cormac, thinking of a fifteen-year-old Maude carrying her little brother from their home, said, 'Not unusual. Lot of family members are in denial in those circumstances. Hard thing to accept.'

Fisher nodded again, leaned forward across the table and dropped his voice. It was so melodramatic that Cormac had to restrain himself from joining Danny in yet another eye-roll, but what Fisher had to say next caught his attention. 'Yeah. But I hear she had good questions. And she wasn't very happy that Rodgers had no answers.' He paused. 'She showed up at the station again this afternoon, this time with a memory stick loaded with CCTV footage of the bridge.'

'She did what?' Cormac asked. Danny didn't look surprised, he must have heard the story before.

Fisher sat back in his seat, a smile on his face, satisfied with the reaction he was getting. 'She walked both sides of the bridge, found everywhere that had a camera up, and somehow talked them into giving her copies. Anyway, she got it, watched it, and found that there was no sign of her brother coming from either direction for two hours before he was supposed to have gone into the water. And the phone call reporting the jump? No sign of the caller either, but plenty of other people on camera just before the call was made. Some of them were still there when our people arrived and took statements. They all said that they saw nothing.'

'Jesus. She got that in, what, twenty-four hours?' Cormac asked.

'Yeah. Got it, viewed it, edited it into one film. When she wasn't happy with Rodgers' reaction, she said she'd send it directly to the coroner's office, then to the press. You can imagine Murphy had a fucking coronary.' Fisher was laughing now.

'Jesus,' said Cormac again, imagining the scene. He'd had the briefest glance of Maude in the family room, and his memory of her as a girl kept superimposing itself over the more recent memory of the woman in the police station. 'She's not messing around.'

Fisher shrugged, grinned.

'Rodgers didn't tell you all that,' Cormac said.

Fisher shook his head emphatically. 'No way. Ceri was there. She filled me in.'

'She's still on the job?'

Fisher shrugged. 'Just part of the liaison team, with Rodgers. But she said Rodgers was pretty clear that there won't be an investigation, even with the CCTV.'

'Fuck's sake,' said Danny. 'Why would there be? Chances are the guy jumped from another bridge, and whoever called it in got the name of the bridge wrong. I said as much to Rodgers.' He checked his watch. 'Mountain out of a molehill.'

Cormac watched Danny drain his glass. 'Think so?' Cormac asked.

Danny shrugged, and stood. 'Nothing to me either way mate.' He cut a not-very-subtle sideways glance at Fisher. 'I'm off. I've an early one tomorrow.'

Cormac nodded, watched him leave, made a mental note to tackle him again on the Healy issue sooner rather than later. He turned to Fisher. 'So, what's your take? You think we should investigate?'

Fisher spoke in the direction of his empty glass, avoiding Cormac's eye. 'Not going to happen,' he said. 'If Rodgers is saying there'll be no investigation, that's coming from upstairs. Even with the CCTV, I don't think they're taking this very seriously.' And with that Fisher perhaps felt he'd said enough. The conversation wrapped up, and neither of them showed any sign of wanting to stay for another one. When Cormac looked across the room, Carrie O'Halloran was already gone.

CHAPTER NINE

Aisling's shift ended at 8 p.m. and by half past she was in the lift at the Radisson Hotel, heading up to the fifth floor. She felt shaky. Hunger was the main culprit – her only break had been the twenty minutes she had taken with Maude, and that hadn't been the moment to wolf her usual sandwich – but she was nervous too. Her concentration had been shot to pieces for the afternoon, and it had been a relief when her shift ended. When she reached the door she paused to take a breath before knocking.

Maude opened the door, a glass of wine in her hand. She wore a soft navy cardigan, open over a pristine white fitted T-shirt and skinny jeans. Her feet were bare.

'You're a little earlier than I was expecting,' she said. Not the warmest of greetings, but she stepped aside to invite Aisling into the room. It was a small suite, with wooden floors, a grey velvet couch, and two blue, uncomfortable looking armchairs. Aisling walked across thick soft carpet to the window. The hotel backed onto Lough Atalia. During the day this room would have a view out over the water, which wasn't a lake at all, but a tidal inlet. The Corrib, which ran deep and fast through the centre of the city, emptied into the bay just west of the inlet. Aisling stared out of the window, past the dull glow of the streetlamps below to the dark unseen water beyond. The water that Jack had died in. Was that what Maude thought about, when she woke here every morning and looked out of her window?

A gust of wind lashed rain against the window and Aisling turned away.

'There's wine, if you'd like it, or water, if you'd prefer,' Maude said. The armchairs had been set up to face a small round table, and she sat and waited for Aisling to join her. Maude's laptop was open on the table, and the arrangement felt curiously like a business meeting. Aisling folded her coat over the back of her chair – there was a small gas fireplace in the room, switched on – and poured a glass of water from a full pitcher. As she took her seat it occurred to her that Maude had said nothing yet about her pregnancy.

'You said something about video?' she asked, and then felt gauche. She just couldn't bring herself to make small talk.

But Maude was nodding. She took a sip from her wine glass, turned the laptop so they could both see the screen, then smoothed her hair nervously with one hand.

'After that meeting I was angry. I went for coffee, and started to think it all through. The story didn't sound right to me. Jack died on the Saturday night of St. Patrick's weekend. It would have been incredibly busy in town. Packed with tourists. Don't you think it sounded odd, that Jack could have jumped into the water, and just a few minutes later not a single person on the bridge had seen him jump? If you saw someone jump into the river, would you just shrug and keep walking? Or would you stay, lean over the wall, try to spot them, direct the rescuers?' Maude didn't wait for an answer. 'It was all I could think about, once I left the meeting.'

Aisling nodded slowly. 'It can be busy at night. And it would have been busier than usual that weekend. But the police aren't claiming no one was there. They interviewed people, took statements.'

'Not from anyone who saw Jack jump. Anyway, I started to look around, and I found some cameras. I got the CCTV footage, and went through it all.' Maude opened the laptop, and hit a key to wake it up.

'How did you …' But Aisling let her voice trail off as she watched Maude log in to the computer and open a screen that showed grainy black and white images of people walking on a city street.

'This is the camera in front of the newsagent's – the one at the very end of Bridge Street, just before the bridge itself starts,' Maude was saying. 'This is the clearest of them.'

The camera was focused on the area immediately outside the shop's door and window – most of the image was filled with a stretch of footpath – but the angle allowed Aisling a view of the faces of the passers-by. She watched people in groups of twos and threes, walking in either direction. Most of them were young. The picture was unbelievably clear, and Aisling could see faces laughing, talking, even arguing as they passed, oblivious, under the camera.

'I have footage showing three of the four approaches to the bridge. I've watched two hours of film from 10.30 p.m. to 12.30 a.m., that is, the hour before and after the phone call was made. There's nothing. I couldn't see anyone who looks like Jack. You should look at everything too, of course. I don't think I could have missed him, but it would be better if we could say that you checked the videos. I can give it all to you on a stick. Anyway, if you keep watching, the videos show the gardaí arriving and leaving.'

Maude clicked a button and the screen split in two. Aisling watched as on one side of the picture, two police cars rushed in and out of view, and on the other a group of three people turned and looked back in the direction of the bridge – a reaction to the police sirens maybe? There was no sound, but it seemed like Maude had synced the videos perfectly.

'Do you remember Rodgers said there were two couples on the bridge, coming from Dominick Street? From the Roisín

Dubh?' Maude didn't wait for a reply but clicked again and the screen shifted. 'Look, you can see them arriving. And here.' Another click. 'That's the single guy he mentioned, coming from the other direction.'

She sat back and looked up. 'Jack is not there, Aisling. There's no sign of him. And where's the guy who made the supposed phone call? No sign of him at all.'

On the screen the video came to an end, and another automatically started, showing the street again, this time from the other side.

'How on earth did you get all this?'

Maude shrugged. 'I started looking for cameras. The newsagents had one. The bank across the road had one over the ATM. And the Bridge Mills had one. There were others further up and down the streets and they're useful too but not as close to the bridge.'

'So, what, you just asked and they handed them over?'

'Some of them did. The newsagent's. The girl there was very helpful. Iraqi girl. Her parents were asylum seekers. Came over after the coup. Her brother owns the place but he was away. She had to call him to find out how to make a copy of the footage for me.' Maude was shaking her head again.

'Maude. What?'

'Sorry. Yes. Well, the newsagent girl gave me her footage, which was encouraging. The bank was a bit more challenging but I got there in the end, and the Bridge Mills uses a security firm. The guy there was happy enough to give me a copy of their film for a few quid.'

'Christ almighty. I can't believe this.' Aisling pressed the palms of her hands into her face. She sat like that for what felt like a long time. She felt nauseous. The room was too hot. She needed to take off her jumper.

Maude leaned towards Aisling across the table. Her hair fell around her face again as she spoke. It made her look younger. 'Aisling, he's not there. There's just no way it happened the way they say.' She clicked a button on her laptop and replayed the video. They both watched the faces. Happy couples holding hands. Three girls, who looked like they were shivering, walked with arms linked, one of them holding out an arm to hail a taxi as they walked. A group of students, probably a bit the worse for wear, looked like they were singing a song as they walked out of the frame.

Aisling felt herself shaking. She clasped both hands together, and pressed her feet into the carpet. Maude was looking at her. 'Are you okay?' she asked.

Aisling wanted to say that she wasn't okay. That she didn't know how she felt about anything except that she knew she'd fucked up. Jack had been hers, she'd loved him with everything she had, had known him better than anyone else, and yet she'd believed the story the police gave her with barely a question raised. She felt shame that she'd believed the suicide story. Relief that it wasn't true. Release from the guilt she'd felt at failing him so badly – at missing signs she now thought hadn't been there to miss. Anger, because he was still dead, and she was still alone.

'How could I have been so fucking stupid?'

Maude shook her head slowly, but didn't say anything. She looked down for a long moment and took another sip from her wine glass, then closed the laptop. Aisling stood up and walked back to the window, pressed her forehead to the cool glass, and closed her eyes for a long moment. Jack. Oh Jack.

Maude spoke from behind her. 'You should know that this doesn't prove anything for sure. One side of the street only has a camera at one end, so strictly speaking it is possible that Jack could have entered that end, and that the guy who made the call could have come in and left the same way.'

Aisling turned to face Maude, pulled a face and gestured towards the computer. 'There's no way,' she said. 'There's no time. The police can't ignore this. They'll have to open an investigation.'

But Maude was shaking her head. 'I already brought this to them. This afternoon. As far as they're concerned this changes nothing.'

It was like Maude had hit her. She was ten steps behind, and reeling. She felt slow and stupid. Since Jack's death she had been in a bad dream, and she wanted desperately to wake up.

'What?' she said.

'I saw Rodgers. He didn't say very much, just took copies of the videos. He called me an hour later to say he'd looked them over, that they proved nothing, and Jack probably jumped from one of the other bridges and the guy who made the call got the name wrong.'

'Jesus.'

'I don't believe that,' Maude said hurriedly. 'I mean, I don't know if there are cameras, but we could look into it. I'm just trying to tell you that the police are not on our side. That guy, Rodgers. He's the kind who gets an idea in his head and won't let go. It's all about him and his ego and he's not likely to turn around and acknowledge that he was probably wrong. We're going to have to push hard. This footage is a beginning, but we'll need as much evidence as we can to contradict their conclusions, and we have to be willing to stir things up. Go to the media maybe, if we can make the story sound compelling enough.'

Aisling nodded slowly. 'You think it was definitely a fake call then? Not a mistake?'

'Who makes a mistake about someone jumping into the river on the same night that a body is found in it? No way.'

'I know it's unlikely.' Ludicrous even, when it was put like that. 'But, you're saying, I mean – the alternative is that someone killed him. Murdered him.'

Maude was watching her carefully, and Aisling, aware that her hands were still shaking, tucked them under her arms.

'I don't know, Aisling,' Maude said. 'You were his partner. Is there anything you can tell me? Anything at all in Jack's life that could lead to something like that?' As she spoke she stood and walked to the bed, picked up the phone and dialled.

'Soup all right?'

'I ... I'm not hungry,' Aisling said, automatically.

'You don't look well,' Maude said. 'Like you might faint. Your call, but it might be better to eat.'

She waited for Aisling's nod, then placed an order for two. There was an assurance about Maude that made Aisling feel graceless, like an awkward schoolgirl playing at grownups.

They talked about Jack while they waited. Not in a catching up sort of a way, but a conversation about his typical movements, who his friends were, where he worked, what sort of work he did. Aisling was conscious that she was volunteering less and less as time wore on, until the conversation deteriorated into a question and answer session that made her feel like she was being interrogated, and was making a shoddy witness.

The food arrived and the smell made her stomach clench in sudden hunger. She wasn't eating enough. Maude cleared the laptop and papers from the table and set out the bowls, glasses and cutlery. She handed Aisling a napkin, put one in her own lap, and they ate in uncomfortable silence. The soup was exactly what Aisling needed. She felt her stomach settle, and her energy return.

When they'd finished, Maude set her bowl aside and waited.

'I've been thinking about what you asked,' said Aisling. 'About Jack. About whether there was anything in his life that could have brought him into contact with someone who would hurt him.' She spread her hands in a helpless gesture.

'There's nothing. I can't think of anything. I mean, I'm not saying that Jack was perfect. No one is perfect. But he was just Jack. Just an ordinary guy.' Jack was a civil engineer, for God's sake; he designed roads and bridges. He liked to be outside, loved to hike and climb. She could think of at least four other guys in their social circle alone that could fit that broad description. 'He never got into any kind of trouble. Neither one of us did drugs. Jack didn't even drink.'

'You have to think harder, Aisling. There must have been something.'

'I can't make something up. People liked Jack. He never got into any kind of trouble.'

'When did you last see him?'

'In the morning. I had worked a night shift. We had breakfast together, then I went to bed. When I woke up, he was gone. We were supposed to have dinner together that evening, but Jack never came home. And the next morning the gardaí showed up at our door.'

'But you talked at breakfast.'

'Yes.'

'And?'

Aisling rubbed her forehead with her hands. 'We talked about the pregnancy. About our options. That's all. Then I went to bed.' Her tone told Maude to let it go. That conversation was private, and anyway, there was nothing in it that could have gotten Jack killed. Not if he hadn't done it himself.

'Aisling, there must be something else.' Maude was leaning forward now, dark eyes gleaming. She was so intense; her energy almost frenetic.

Aisling pushed her chair away from the table. 'I can't tell you something I don't know. Honestly, I can't imagine that there is anything to tell. Maybe it was just an accident; the phone call a prank that was just a coincidence. Maybe Jack did drink that night, maybe he fell into the river. We're never going to know, and even if we did know, it's not going to bring him back.' She forced back tears she didn't want to shed. 'Jack is dead, Maude, and nothing you or I do now will change that.'

'Well,' said Maude. She sat back. Her energy didn't dissipate. If anything, she seemed to gather it back in, to control it and to refocus herself. 'You might be able to live with that, but I can't.'

They sat in silence, the moments ticking by.

'What about his messages?' Maude asked.

'Sorry?'

'Did the police trace Jack's calls? His messages? If he had an arrangement to meet someone that day, something he hadn't told you about, maybe they called each other.'

'I ... I don't know.' It hadn't occurred to her to ask.

'We need to follow up on that. And if they haven't done it, maybe the telephone company will release them to you, as his next of kin?'

'Do they do that? Am I even his next of kin? We weren't married. Maybe they'd consider his parents.' Aisling couldn't see a phone company releasing someone's private messages to their bereaved parents, even a wife. Surely there'd be privacy considerations. And if they did release to next of kin, Maude could probably get them more easily than she could. The thought of Maude reading through Jack's messages made her distinctly uncomfortable. 'Don't you think this is something for the police?' She raised her hands in a warding off gesture. 'I don't mean that Rodgers guy, obviously. But there are other police officers. They're not all incompetent, surely.'

Maude shrugged. 'The gardaí have made their minds up about Jack. They won't do anything. They're just the same as social workers. If you push them, they'll go through the motions, file some forms, push some paper. They'll waste your time. They won't waste mine.'

Aisling sat in silence for a moment, unsure what was left to say. 'Of course I want to help,' she said in the end. 'I'll do anything I can to help. I'm just not sure ...' She picked up her coat.

'You're a doctor. You must have connections at the coroner's office. Can you get the postmortem results?' There was an unspoken *at least* in that sentence, and a hint of coldness, of distance, in Maude's gaze.

'I'll do what I can,' said Aisling. For Jack. Though she couldn't see what it would achieve. It would be a distraction from her grief, and from the decision she now had to make alone.

Tuesday 26 March 2013

By the following morning Cormac had decided to attack the Blake case. If there was an agenda within the gardaí, he didn't need to know what it was, at least not for now. He would work this case the way he would any other – follow the evidence wherever it led him.

He started with the case file, and was amused and a little embarrassed to read his own preliminary reports, written as a twenty-year-old rookie in 1993. Reading them with the benefit of two decades' experience, he could see his uncertainty all over the page. Everything was couched in possibilities and maybes, and his recommendation that a further investigation be carried out was tentative at best. Unfortunately, there was as little to work with as he had expected. The file contained only his report from the night he'd found the kids and Hilaria Blake's body, the postmortem report, and interviews that were carried out with the neighbours and at the children's schools.

He read the postmortem carefully. In the pathologist's opinion, which was heavily couched with provisos, Hilaria Blake had not been a habitual heroin user. Testing had been less advanced in the nineties of course, and hair analysis, which would have answered the question conclusively, would have been too expensive. Hilaria Blake had had advanced liver cirrhosis, and severe alcoholic hepatitis, but she had not been a heroin addict. She was jaundiced, had fluid build-up in her abdomen and legs. The marks he had seen on her arms had not been track marks, but almost certainly self-inflicted scratches. Cirrhosis had led to an increased level of bile in her body, which would have made her skin intensely itchy. The pathologist was very clear on one thing – Hilaria Blake had had end-stage liver disease. It would have killed her, if the heroin hadn't got there first.

Heroin overdoses were rare in 1993. The Blakes' house was less than a mile from Kilmore village, which had no known drug problem, and even in 1993 heroin was not a commonly used drug outside of Dublin and parts of Limerick. How had Hilaria Blake, an alcoholic, bedbound with advanced liver disease, procured just enough heroin to kill herself?

Interviews in the village had not provided an answer. Hilaria had not been seen at the local pub or off-licence in a year and a half, or longer. Maude was known to shop at the local convenience place for food, but made no attempt to buy alcohol. In those days the fact that she was under-age wouldn't necessarily have prevented a sale. She wouldn't have been the first child sent to the village to buy a bottle of whiskey and bring it home to a parent. But the off-licence owner had been adamant that he wouldn't have sold to her if she had asked, and she never did. Cormac had spoken to him himself, and had believed him. The village knew that Hilaria was a drunk, and they seemed to see Maude as a good, hard-working girl. They did nothing to help her, as far as Cormac could determine, but they drew a line at supplying the alcohol that was the root of the problem.

He wondered if that minor act of civic responsibility had been a village-wide sop. Something that freed them from the obligation to take any meaningful action to help the children. They wouldn't sell the family alcohol, and every now and again a teacher would make a token effort to get Maude to school. Other than that the family was totally isolated. The only person known to spend time with the family was a local religious do-gooder, a woman who was not terribly popular, but was hardly likely to be a supplier of alcohol or heroin.

When Cormac had tentatively raised his concerns with his boss he had been ignored. There had been no desire to investigate the death of a woman who was widely known to be an alcoholic who abused her children. Having seen the results of her abuse on poor Jack Blake's little body, Cormac himself had little sympathy for the woman, but the hypocrisy of it galled him. Now, twenty years later, the obvious questions were still unanswered.

He turned to the statements from the schools. They'd interviewed the principal of the primary school and Jack's teacher, and the statements were consistent. Jack had been in junior infants, and had only been at the school for a couple of months. Jack's mother never came to the school; his sister dropped him off every morning and collected him at the end of the day. Although he had a reasonable lunch with him most days, and he was generally clean and tidy, his teacher at the time had suspected that his mother was negligent. She'd seen a bruise on his wrist once, and another on his cheek, and had called social services. She'd heard nothing from them and had expected nothing. Similar bruises on Maude had been reported more than once, and as far as the school was aware, nothing had been done. The principal of the secondary school had said that Maude had a very poor attendance record, and a report had also been made to social services about her continual absences. Again, nothing more had been heard and Maude had continued to miss school until she turned fifteen, when she'd stopped attending entirely. Some of her teachers had said she was a bright girl, but she wasn't a mixer, and seemed to have few friends. Hilaria Blake had been seen by the school only at Maude's enrolment meeting, and never after that.

There was nothing in the file to help him. He flicked through again, from the beginning to the end. Nothing from the social workers. Hadn't he requested the file? He thought back. Yes. He was sure he had, but he couldn't remember it coming in. He hadn't had long with the case – within a few weeks of Hilaria's death he'd been told to close it and move on. Cormac made a note to request the file again now.

Cormac turned to Jack's discharge report from the hospital. He skimmed through the description of Jack's injuries. The last page had the treating doctor's recommendations for follow up treatment, which included counselling as well as a special diet to address nutritional deficiencies. Cormac was about to give up on the file when he saw that the hospital had kept track of Jack's visitors. Hospital protocol at the time? Perhaps just for children unaccompanied by a parent. The list was short – only two names. His own, and that of a Tom Collins. Cormac had come each of the four days that Jack was in hospital. Tom, whoever he was, had come twice; early on the first morning after Jack's admission, and again on the last day before he was discharged. The records were detailed – arrival and departure times were noted.

Cormac sat back in his chair, and thought. Tom Collins had reached the hospital before 9 a.m. the morning after Jack's admission. If Maude had been telling the truth that night, she had called only the police, after she had found her mother dead. Which meant that Cormac had been the only person in the world, other than the children, who knew about Hilaria Blake's death until they'd reached the hospital and Cormac had called it in to the station. And that had been late evening. So how had this Tom Collins known he would find five-year-old Jack Blake in Castlebar General Hospital at 9 a.m. the following morning?

Cormac stood and walked to the coffee station, rescued a teaspoon from the sink, made himself a coffee. Could be

Collins was a friend of the family, with a connection to the gardaí? If that was the case he'd have heard the story fairly quickly. But that didn't feel right. If someone like that, someone with connections, had had a relationship with the family, surely something would have been done about the children. Cormac tried to think of other circumstances that could have led to such an immediate visit, and they all seemed a stretch. It wasn't much but it was an inconsistency and it was something to work with while he was waiting on the social worker file. He spooned sugar into his cup, looked around for biscuits to raid. Nothing. He was getting hungry.

He took his coffee back to his desk, closed the paper file, logged in to PULSE and typed in a basic search – Tom Collins, Kilmore. He didn't expect to get a hit and was surprised when the system kicked out a long list of results. He scanned them quickly. He hadn't limited his search in any way, and the system had found a series of criminal cases where the defending solicitor was a man named Thomas Collins, with addresses in Kilmore and Galway. The entries didn't give a date of birth. Cormac turned to Google, which gave him very little information. Thomas Collins, it seemed, was a relatively private person. No public Facebook profile for him. A little poking about led to a short profile piece in an industry magazine – apparently Thomas had been chair of the Free Legal Advice Centre in Galway two years before. He was quoted in the piece as saying that he himself had grown up in less than affluent circumstances – he'd been in and out of foster homes as a child, he said – and that he was a firm believer in giving back. The piece had a little sidebar which listed the schools and university he had attended, as well as his age. Thomas Collins was thirty-five, the same age as Maude Blake. He'd also attended Kilmore Secondary School. It seemed more likely than not, then, that Tom Collins had been a friend of Maude's. Had she called him that night? Asked him to visit Jack?

As Cormac stared at his computer screen, lost in thought, Rodgers heaved himself into the chair to his left and opened a family-sized packet of cheese and onion Taytos. That was enough. Cormac stood, grabbed his coat, and left. An interview with Tom Collins would have to be his start.

CHAPTER ELEVEN

The practice – Collins, Barber and Associates – was on Abbeygate Street, right in the middle of the city and a short walk from the courthouse. Cormac walked there from Mill Street, and had no difficulty finding the place. The offices were on the first floor, directly above a café that advertised toasted cheese and ham sandwiches with coffee for ten euro, on a blackboard placed on the path. His stomach growled. Maybe on the way back out if he got what he came for. The door opened directly onto an uneven staircase that looked circa 1900 and probably needed some structural work. The steps were canted oddly, and creaked alarmingly when Cormac climbed them two at a time. They led to a small reception area, a pleasant sort of place, despite the general shabbiness. The reception desk had seen better days and there was a musty smell that might have been coming from an open filing cabinet that ran from floor to ceiling and covered the entire wall behind the reception desk. The mustiness was almost masked by the smell of coffee from the café downstairs, and every surface in the small room was exceptionally neat.

The receptionist was a young guy in his early twenties. He had an earpiece in one ear and was typing furiously. He gave Cormac a tortured-looking nod, which Cormac took to mean he had been seen and would be dealt with in a moment. After another full minute of furious typing, the receptionist let out a sigh and looked up.

'Sorry,' he said. 'The rewind button is broken so if I don't get it all down first time I have to listen to it all again from the beginning.' He spoke with a strong Cork accent.

'Right,' said Cormac, bemused. 'Is Thomas Collins available? I'm Detective Sergeant Reilly. I'd appreciate a few minutes of his time.'

The young man picked up the phone and pressed a button. 'Tom? There's a DS here for you.' He paused. 'Well, yeah. First go. But I have to go through now and fix the typos.' He hung up and smiled at Cormac. 'He'll be with you in five,' he said.

Cormac had barely sat down when an office door opened and a tall man in a shirt and tie walked towards him, a coffee cup in one hand, and holding out the other hand to be shaken. 'Detective?' he asked. At Cormac's nod, he gestured to a door just off the reception area. 'I haven't much time unfortunately. Case conference in fifteen minutes. But perhaps we can be brief?' He waited for Cormac to open the door, which led to a meeting room, and then followed him in.

The room felt cluttered, the table too big for it, and the chairs not quite fitting comfortably. Collins shut the door behind him, but neither man sat, which left them both standing awkwardly in the uncomfortably small space.

'I'd like to speak with you about your friend, Maude Blake.'

Collins's expression, until then a mask of professional civility, registered surprise. 'What? Maude? Is she okay?'

'You're still in touch?' Cormac asked.

'I thought this was about a case …' He let his voice trail off. 'Never mind.' He pulled out a chair, and gestured to Cormac to sit. 'Take a seat, detective.'

Cormac sat. The conference table was an antique, and not very practical. It was too low for comfort and one of the table legs was directly in front of the seat he had taken.

'You're still in touch with Maude?' Cormac asked again.

'From time to time,' Collins said. 'An occasional email.'

'Recently?'

Collins had recovered his composure. 'I called her a week or so ago to let her know that her brother, Jack, had died. I couldn't reach her, so I sent an email. I haven't heard from her since, so I don't know whether or not she got my message.'

As Collins spoke, Cormac reached into his pocket and took out a notebook. He turned to a blank page and started taking notes, Collins watching him all the while.

'So you knew Jack Blake?' Cormac asked, the question delivered as casually as possible, not looking up from his notebook.

'I knew him as a child,' said Collins. 'I haven't kept in touch.'

'But you knew he had passed away?'

Collins shrugged. 'It was reported in the newspapers. The *Galway Advertiser* ran a feature on the front page, if I recall correctly. We've had a spate of suicides by young men recently, more than one in the river.'

'And you were sure, just from the name in the paper, that it wasn't another Jack Blake? Sure enough to call his sister?'

Collins raised one eyebrow. 'Not from around here then, detective?' he asked. His tone was gently chiding. 'Galway may be a city of eighty thousand, but everyone knows everyone. I wasn't in touch with Jack, but I had a vague idea of where he was living, and I knew that he was in a relationship. A friend of a friend knows his girlfriend.'

Cormac nodded, and resumed taking notes, slowly and methodically. It was an old habit when interviewing witnesses. Most people felt a certain anxiety during the silence. Sometimes they felt compelled to fill it. Collins didn't, but Cormac hadn't really expected it of him. A defence lawyer with his kind of experience would certainly be more self-controlled.

'So you haven't seen Maude then? Recently?' Cormac asked.

Collins shook his head. 'She's back in Ireland? She got my message?'

'She's back in Galway. I don't know if she got your message.' Then, turning a new page in his notebook, 'Did you know Jack well?'

'As I told you, detective, I knew Jack only as a child, and knew a little about him through friends.' Collins's tone was cool but betrayed no irritation at the repeated question. 'What is this about?'

Cormac looked up from his notebook, his expression bland. 'A death in suspicious circumstances, Mr Collins. We would be remiss if we did not investigate before the inquest. In case there is any suggestion that it was something other than a suicide.' After his initial surprise, Collins had become difficult to read. He didn't react to Cormac's statement, but Cormac had to assume he was too smart to accept it at face value.

'Jack Blake was adopted, Mr Collins, you were aware?'

Collins nodded.

Cormac made a show of consulting his notebook. 'His mother died when he was five, as I understand it, and other than his sister, he had no family. There has been a suggestion, too, that his mother may have been neglectful of Jack and his sister. Perhaps even physically abusive. Do you know anything about that?'

Collins laughed, but the sound was constrained, not natural. 'I know that Hilaria Blake was very beautiful, and very damaged, when she moved to Kilmore. She had a problem with the drink even then, but things accelerated, very fast, once they moved into that house. She was a terrible mother.'

'In what way?'

'Neglectful. She got lost in her own pain. Had nothing left for her children.'

'She was violent?'

A hesitation. 'To the children? No.' Tom shook his head.

'She didn't hit them?'

'No.' Simple. Firm.

Would Tom have known about the abuse? Perhaps Maude had wanted to protect her mother, keep it a secret.

'But she was neglectful?'

'In the last couple of years she stopped pretending to provide any kind of care at all. Maude did everything.'

'What about Family Services? They weren't involved?'

'Depends on what you mean by involved. They might have kept a file open, but by the time Maude and I were close they had stopped visiting. No care visits, no case reviews. They abandoned the family entirely.'

Cormac said nothing, but raised an eyebrow.

Collins sighed. He leaned forward, putting his elbows on the table and looked directly at Cormac. He spoke deliberately. 'As I've said, in the early years it wasn't as bad. But in the last year or so before Hilaria's death, Maude stopped feeling like she could leave Jack alone with her mother. She walked him to school in the morning, and she was waiting at the gate when school finished. Maude fed him, washed him, read to him. You know she was only ten when he was born?'

Cormac shook his head, meaning, he supposed, that of course he knew but he hadn't really considered it.

Collins continued. 'I suppose Hilaria was able to manage to some degree when Jack was a baby, but by the time he was three Maude started missing school. The following year – Maude would have been fourteen – she barely went at all. The day she turned fifteen she stopped coming entirely. By then she had a job working for a neighbour, doing a bit of cleaning, gardening, that sort of thing. She was paid next to nothing but she needed the money to feed herself and Jack. As I said, her mother had pretty much given up any pretence of trying during those last couple of years.'

Cormac put his notebook down. 'Look, there were social workers available. If it was that obvious to everyone that Maude and Jack were neglected, why didn't they step in?'

Collins leaned back. 'You'd have to ask them. I was too young to know better at the time. To know that something should have been done. We none of us had reason to respect or trust the authorities at that stage of our lives.'

Cormac thought about asking about the magazine piece, the foster homes, but he didn't want to lose the train of his questioning. He was already straying off track. He opened his mouth to ask another question but the door opened and the receptionist stuck his head in.

'Broderick's running late,' he said. 'Will be another fifteen at least.' Without waiting for acknowledgement he disappeared again and shut the door.

'He has an unconventional manner, your assistant.' Cormac couldn't quite hold back the comment, but Collins was unruffled.

'He's an apprentice. Has a first-class law degree from Trinity. Not sure if he'll make it as a lawyer, to tell you the truth. Too honest.' The look Collins gave Cormac told him that he knew that Cormac hadn't told him the truth, that he knew that Cormac was playing a game, and that unlike his apprentice, Collins knew the rules of this game and could play it as hard as anyone. Cormac liked him for it, despite himself. Defence lawyers were generally not his favourite people.

'Do you know if the Blakes had any other family in the area, or any that would come and visit?'

Collins shook his head, took a careful sip of his coffee. 'Not that I'm aware of. Maude had a father, some sort of artist or writer her mother had lived with for a time, I think in London, although I might have that wrong. Maude never met him. I don't think anyone knew who Jack's father was. Their grandparents on their mother's side were dead. I never heard of any aunts or uncles.'

'Any close family friends?' Cormac asked.

Collins twisted his lips in a semblance of a smile. 'Not within the normal meaning of the word, no,' he said.

'By which you mean?' Cormac asked, but Collins shook his head, sipped his coffee.

After a long pause Collins said, 'Hilaria didn't have friends. She didn't socialise. I don't know what sent her over the edge. Certainly she had been abusing alcohol for years, but when she came to Kilmore she attacked drink with complete single-mindedness. Maude told me she hadn't always been like that, but by the time I knew her ...' Collins paused, his lip curling in unconscious disgust. 'By the last six months she rarely got out of bed. She looked like she was rotting there.'

So he had seen her. Had been in the house. 'If Hilaria Blake wasn't capable of moving about, how did she continue to buy alcohol, collect her dole money? She must have been able to get about from time to time. At least every couple of weeks,' Cormac said. He paused. 'Unless Maude got it for her?'

'Maude would never have bought alcohol for her,' Collins said. 'And Maude never got her hands on the dole money, at least not directly.'

Cormac raised an eyebrow, and lifted his notebook in one hand, as if to refer Collins to everything that had been said so far. 'Then who?' he asked.

Tom Collins was watching him carefully, weighing him up, it seemed, as he considered his answer. In the end, he tilted his head slightly to the left, and spoke. 'You haven't read the file, have you, detective?' he asked.

Cormac thought for a second he was referring to the police file, and the confusion must have shown in his eyes.

'The social worker file,' Collins said.

Cormac hesitated, but decided there was no advantage in hiding the truth from Collins. 'If you could tell me about it from your perspective, that would be helpful,' he said.

'So you haven't read it.' There was no judgement in Collins's voice. 'You should, you know. You might gain a little understanding. Although you probably don't need to read it to guess what had happened.'

'It would be helpful if you could ...'

Collins cut him off. 'Consider, detective. So far in this lovely story we have alcohol abuse, and apathetic social workers. There's only one thing missing, isn't there, to round out the classic Irish trinity?' Collins sat back in his chair, knitting his fingers behind his head.

'I'm afraid you'll have to enlighten me.'

Collins spoke deliberately, enunciating each word slowly. 'The Holy Catholic Church, detective, what else?'

'I'm sorry?'

'A version of it. A cultish little offshoot led by a woman called Domenica Keane.' Collins must have seen recognition in Cormac's eyes. 'Yes, the lovely Mrs Keane. I see you've heard of her.'

Cormac searched his memory. The name was familiar but he couldn't recall why.

Collins helped him out. 'She was a religious nut. Crazy about Catholicism. Or at least her version of it.'

'I don't understand,' said Cormac. 'This woman, Keane, she looked after the children? Hilaria Blake?'

'No,' said Collins. 'She didn't look after the children, though Maude worked for her. Domenica had a small dairy farm. She hired casual farm labourers when she needed them, but she took Maude too. '

From the reception area Cormac heard a sudden burst of noise. A deep bass voice, introducing himself in a tone of self-importance that carried through the wall, the assistant's response, then conversation. Collins checked his watch.

'That's probably my postponed case conference,' he said. 'I can't put it back. The barrister's in court again after lunch.'

'Mr Collins, are you suggesting that Mrs Keane supplied alcohol to Hilaria Blake?'

Collins shrugged. 'I'm not suggesting it, I'm stating it. She kept Hilaria Blake stocked with enough booze to float a boat.'

'Why would she do that?'

Collins glanced towards the reception area, then back at Cormac. 'You'd have to ask her. And I'm sorry, detective, but I have an appointment now.' He stood, hovering expectantly, waiting for Cormac to get up and leave.

Cormac took his time closing his notebook. 'I'd like to talk to you again, Mr Collins.'

Collins looked like he was considering it, his head tilted to the side once again. 'What's this really about, detective?'

'I'm sorry?'

'Why are you asking me questions about Hilaria Blake? She's been dead for twenty years.'

Cormac said nothing. He knew Collins wouldn't believe that he was looking into Jack's background in this level of detail because of the suicide. There was no reason for police to want to understand every aspect of Jack's past. As his childhood was well documented, it didn't really warrant further investigation. An inquiry into Jack's suicide would have focused on any signs of depression or other issues in his adult life.

'Just one more question, Mr Collins, if you can spare the time.' Cormac didn't wait for Collins to respond. 'You're sure that Hilaria Blake could not, did not, leave her home in the last months of her life?'

'You're not here about Jack,' said Collins flatly.

'Questions have been raised about Jack Blake's death. Specifically, as to whether it was suicide, or something else.'

'Questions have been raised. By whom, exactly?'

'That information is not your concern, Mr Collins.'

'Okay. So there are questions about Jack's death. That doesn't explain what you are doing here, asking me questions about his family life twenty years ago.'

'Questions about Jack Blake's death inevitably lead us to look into his family background.'

'Right.' Collins was not convinced. 'Well, I've answered your questions, detective, and I'm out of time.' He put his hand on the door handle, waited for Cormac to stand.

'Just one more question, Mr Collins,' Cormac said. 'The morning after Hilaria Blake's death you visited Jack Blake in the hospital in Castlebar.' He watched Collins's face intently. 'You were there by nine a.m. that morning.'

Collins's face was impassive.

'How did you know that Jack Blake would be in hospital that morning? How did you know where to find him?'

Collins waited a beat, but no more. 'Really detective, it was twenty years ago, and I was fifteen years old. I can hardly be expected to remember.' And with that he turned and walked out of the room.

CHAPTER TWELVE

Three people had been in the house the night that Hilaria Blake died. Two of them were dead, and the third, it seemed, was the suspect. But if Jack had spoken to anyone about his mother and sister, it would surely have been his girlfriend. Jack Blake's last known address was in the system. He'd start there. A house in the Claddagh, walking distance. Cormac was hungry, but not in the mood now to stop for food. He bought coffee from a place on Dominick Street and drank it as he walked. Tom Collins had told him very little that he didn't already know, or at least should have known. He needed those social worker files. He put a call through to Children and Family Services, dialling one handed. He got a receptionist, who asked for his name, before taking what felt like ten minutes to come back and tell him that no one was available to speak with him.

'We're amalgamating,' she said. 'With the Family Support Agency and the National Educational Welfare Board. Everyone's at a workshop.' Her tone was upbeat, almost chattily helpful.

He left a request for an urgent call back, was irritated and chided himself for his impatience. He would have to wait for the information he wanted. Workshop or no workshop, a request for a twenty-year-old file was never going to take priority with a bunch of over-extended social workers.

He'd certainly requested the file back in the day. Cormac tried to remember. He'd been moved onto other work – traffic duty and pub raids mostly – but he'd been working in the same station. If the files had come in, wouldn't he have known? If they had come in there would have been copies, and they should still be on the file. If they hadn't come in, someone should have followed up, and a note of that action should be on the file also. Instead there was nothing.

He should have tried harder to continue working on the case. It wasn't as though Jack Blake had been easy to forget. That night in the hospital had been the first time Cormac had come face to face with a child who had been badly hurt by someone they should have been able to trust. How a mother could hurt her child like that was beyond him. Some of the things he'd seen since should perhaps have made Jack Blake's circumstances seem less appalling, but it didn't work like that. There was no grade curve for child abuse. The more time Cormac spent with this case, the more convinced he was that there were questions to answer. Even as a rookie, instinct had told him that there were layers that he wasn't seeing, that there was a story he hadn't heard. Maybe he'd get to the truth this time. Maybe he owed that much to Jack.

Jack's address brought him to a terraced, two-storey house in the Claddagh. The terraces had been labourers' cottages once, but their proximity to town and the sea had made them fashionable, and many had been renovated. Most were painted pastel colours that were a little sickly up close, but from a distance had a cheerful, seaside appearance. Number 43 was painted a deep blue, in pleasing contrast to the pastel shades. The blinds in the ground floor window were drawn. Cormac searched for a doorbell, rang, then knocked loudly. He waited for a minute or two before trying again.

The front door was glass, and through it could be seen a little enclosed front porch, with a second, solid wooden door inside that led into the rest of the house. Cormac could see two pairs of well-worn runners inside the porch – they must have been Jack's, they were too big to be his girlfriend's – and an umbrella, propped in the corner.

He stepped back. There was no sign of life at the first floor either. The curtains in the windows were open, but the rooms were dark. The policeman in him was distracted by the way the little porch roof provided perfect access to the first floor window above it, which was slightly ajar. If she wasn't home, her approach to home security left a lot to be desired.

'You looking for Aisling?'

He turned to see a woman at the neighbouring terrace, paused in the act of locking her front door. She was examining him carefully, perhaps warily.

He nodded. 'Yes.'

'She'd be at work.' The woman leaned down to take the hand of her little boy and turned to go.

'Can you tell me where, exactly?' Cormac asked.

She hesitated.

'I'm a garda. A detective. I'm acting as a liaison of sorts in relation to her partner's death. I'd like to speak with Aisling but our file doesn't seem to have up-to-date contact information.' Cormac gave the woman a rueful smile that invited her to join him in a critique of bureaucratic ineptitude.

'Have you ID?' She wasn't impressed. She held her hand out.

Each terrace had a tiny walled front garden. The wall came to knee height only – just enough to give a suggestion of privacy between the front windows and the public footpath. The wall was low enough to step over, but Cormac stayed on his side as he moved closer, holding out his badge for her to see. She looked it over carefully, taking her time. At last, seemingly satisfied, she stepped back.

'She's works at UCHG, at the hospital. If you ask for her at the A&E reception they'll send her out to you. If she's not too busy.'

'Thanks. Appreciate your help.'

She nodded, but didn't return his smile and he wondered if she'd had a bad experience with police. He watched her walk towards the seaside for a moment, holding tightly to her little boy's hand. He trailed behind her, and after a moment his mother scooped him up and carried him on her hip. The little boy slung his hand around the back of her neck and rested his head against her shoulder. Cormac watched them for a long moment before turning to walk back towards town. He would pick up his car before heading to the hospital.

Twenty minutes later he was regretting his impulse to drive. The hospital carpark was full, the entrance ramp already clogged with cars waiting for others to leave. He cursed and drove a hundred metres or so from the entrance, parking in a fifteen-minute bay. A ticket at least he could take care of.

It was a Tuesday afternoon, and Accident and Emergency was, as usual, busy. He walked over to reception and took out his ID.

'Aisling Conroy, please. Is she here?'

The nurse was completing a form, and after a brief glance at him she returned to it, ticking boxes until she reached the end of the page. Finally, without making eye contact, she gave the ID a cursory once-over.

'She's with patients. Take a seat and I'll let her know you're here.'

He sat for forty minutes before Aisling finally appeared. Her hair was tied back and she wore a white long sleeved T-shirt under her pale green scrubs. She looked tired – there was a sickly tinge to her skin – and far too young to be a doctor.

She glanced around distractedly for a moment, then the receptionist gestured in Cormac's direction and she walked over to him.

'I'm Dr Conroy,' she said. 'You're a garda?'

'Yes. Detective Sergeant Cormac Reilly.'

'This is about Jack?'

He nodded.

'Okay,' she said. She looked at the the waiting room, visibly rejected the idea. 'There's a canteen, if you'd like to get some coffee?'

He nodded his assent, and she led the way to a small canteen in the basement. She offered to order, but he insisted, and she found a table for them while he bought two cappuccinos and carried them over.

'Thanks for this,' he said. 'For taking the time.'

She shrugged. 'Of course.'

'Is your shift over?'

'No.' She checked her watch. 'I'm afraid I only have ten minutes.'

It was odd that she was working again so soon after her partner's death. It had barely been, what, a week and a half?

'I'm following up on a few things, and I wanted to speak to you particularly.'

She waited.

'I understand that Maude Blake has some concerns about the investigation into Jack's death. That she doesn't believe it was accidental, or that he committed suicide. I'm sorry, I know this must be very difficult to talk about, but I wanted to speak to you, to get your thoughts.'

She stared at him. When she finally spoke it was with a slow, measured tone.

'I think what anyone would think, given what Maude has discovered. I think that there is a very good chance that someone killed Jack, and dropped his body into the river. The murderer then called the police and reported a jumper, to make it seem like Jack killed himself.'

'I can understand why you might think that,' Cormac said, speaking carefully and worrying that he sounded condescending. 'But there is more than one explanation for the confusion around the telephone call. The call didn't come in on the emergency line, and it wasn't recorded. It is possible that the person who made the call, or the person who took the call, mixed up the names of the bridges. It is possible that they were reporting a jump from a bridge further up the Corrib and they confused themselves.'

He was interrupted by a loud beeping noise. Aisling took a pager from her pocket and checked the number, then silenced it. He was reconsidering his initial impression of her. She was young, but there was an unusual self-assurance about her, here on her home turf.

'And have you checked the CCTV footage for the other bridges?'

'I'm sure my colleagues are on that.'

'Are you? I'm not. Maude told me that guy Rodgers made it very clear that you are not going to investigate, that you're not going to ask any questions or check the other bridges, or do anything at all in fact.' Her eyes were guarded.

Cormac was silent for a long moment. He couldn't and shouldn't make a commitment to her about any further investigation. It wasn't his case, and besides, Danny was probably right. Jack had almost certainly committed suicide. Raising expectations of a different conclusion would only lead to pain in the long run. And in the short term, for that matter. Who had ever hoped that their loved one had been murdered, after all?

'I wanted to ask you about Jack's sister.'

'About Maude.'

'Yes. Do you know her well?'

She sighed and rubbed tired eyes with the back of one hand. 'I only met her a week ago. I don't know her at all.'

'You hadn't met her before?'

'No.'

'She and Jack weren't close?'

'As far as I know she disappeared the day after their mother died, and she never called him or saw him again. He never spoke to her. In all honesty, I think he thought she was dead, although he didn't speak about her much.'

Cormac saw that she had tears in her eyes, and he looked at his notebook as he asked his next questions. 'Did she tell you why she left? Why she didn't come back?'

'No.'

'She didn't talk about her childhood, about Jack?'

Aisling looked impatient. 'We spoke about his death. About the manner of his death. It wasn't the time for happy reminiscence.'

'But you know that Jack was abused as a child?' Cormac asked the question bluntly – he wanted to cut to the chase, and he was forming the impression that she might be more comfortable with straight talk.

She nodded slowly.

'He told you?'

'He had scars on his body. From cigarette burns. Other ... incidents.'

'You never talked about it?'

'Once only. A long time ago. Jack had left it behind him. He barely remembered those years. He was only five when his birth mother died. He had nightmares for the first year, then that got better, then Jack got happy, and he didn't look back.'

'He told you about the nightmares?'

She shook her head, took a sip from her coffee. 'No. His mother, his adoptive mother that is. Aggie told me.'

'Aggie ...?' He asked for her name and address, and got it.

'Aisling,' Cormac said. 'What did Jack tell you about Maude? Were they close, as children?' As he asked the question, Cormac flashed back to the night twenty years before, to the pale girl holding tightly to her little brother's hand. He thought of the way she had carried him to the squad car. How she had put on his seat belt for him, how she had held his hand all the way to the hospital. Every instinct told him that Maude would never have hurt Jack. But instinct had been wrong before, so he would ask the question.

'He had very few memories of her. Just vague feelings, really.'

'Positive? Or negative?'

Aisling's eyes went to his. 'Positive. He loved her, and she loved him.'

'You sound very sure of that. But if Jack didn't remember much …'

Before she could answer, the beeper went off again. Again she checked the number, again silenced it.

'I don't know. Jack had very few memories of his early childhood. But he remembered being afraid, and he remembered how it felt to be hungry all day. He said he used to climb into Maude's bed to feel safe at night, and she would let him stay. He had a pair of Spiderman pyjamas. They were the only thing he brought to his new family and he held onto them for years, he said. He said that Maude had bought them for him – someone must have told him I suppose, or he just remembered. God knows where she got the money.' Tears had filled her eyes as she spoke. One rolled down her cheek and she brushed it away absently. 'Poor Jack.'

Cormac handed her the napkin that had come with his coffee, and that he hadn't yet touched. He looked away for a few seconds, giving her a moment to compose herself.

'Jack's memories of the abuse, were they specific?'

'Specific?'

'I mean, did he remember any detail, where he was when it happened, who he was with?'

Aisling shook her head. 'He was only five when he was adopted. And his adoptive parents were wonderful. As I've said, Jack didn't dwell on the past.'

'I understand,' Cormac said. 'But he was clear that it was his mother who hurt him? No one else?'

Aisling took a moment to react, then a look of understanding spread across her face. 'Are you asking me if Maude hurt him?' she asked. Her voice was cool, but there was no mistaking her hostility. He felt slightly off balance.

'I'm not suggesting that,' he said. 'Just trying to understand all of the background.'

'I'm not sure how what happened to Jack when he was five years old has bearing on his death at the age of twenty-five,' she said.

Cormac sipped from his coffee, grasping for something he could use to redirect the conversation.

'Don't try to tell me that the abuse Jack suffered in his childhood caused him to commit suicide. Jack wasn't depressed. He wasn't suicidal. You're just looking for an easy label.'

'I assure you, Aisling, that is not the ...'

She cut him off. 'You can call me Dr Conroy.' She snapped the words out. 'Why is it so bloody difficult to do a bit of work? To get up and do the bloody investigation, to find out what happened? Why are you lot putting so much time and effort in to avoid time and effort? I was sure Maude was wrong – that you would investigate properly once you saw the CCTV. But you've no intention of it, have you?' She stood up, her chair scraping along the floor.

He made an attempt to hold her attention. 'It's impossible to know at the beginning of an investigation which details are relevant and which are not. Sometimes it's the smallest hint of information that can lead you to answers.'

She looked down at him, hesitated. But then her eyes hardened and she shook her head. 'You know what, detective? I think you're full of shit.'

She started to move away. He needed to hold her, needed her to trust him.

'I was there, that night,' he said.

She turned.

'The night Hilaria Blake died. I was wet behind the ears, first week on the job. They weren't expecting a body, there was some sort of mix-up. So they sent me.'

She was holding on to the back of the chair, her eyes fixed on his.

'I found Maude, found Jack, in a house with no electricity, damp everywhere, the place basically rotting around them. Their mother was dead. I brought them to the hospital. I saw what had been done to Jack. I never forgot him, Aisling.' And that, at least, was true. 'I cared about Jack. I care about him now. If there's something suspicious about his death, I'll find out. But I need you to talk to me. If you hear something, know something, come and find me. I won't let you down.'

Her eyes were still on his, weighing up his words, sifting them for truth. She gave him a single reluctant nod before walking away.

CHAPTER THIRTEEN

Aisling's hands were shaking as she walked away from the canteen. She pushed them deep into her pockets and lengthened her stride. She was working an A&E shift. The missed bleeps were from the surgical floor, which she wasn't even covering. This would be the third time they'd bleeped her today, all for innocuous queries that should have been dealt with by whoever was on surgical rotation. But this was a burden of her own making, wasn't it? She'd actively encouraged the nurses to seek her out, wanted them to trust her judgement and think her reliable. She'd wanted to be the one that consultants looked for on their service, because if they brought her in for a surgery they knew that she would double-check the consents, the blood tests. That she would follow up on every patient, stay through the night if necessary.

For the first time she felt that she might have created expectations that she couldn't meet. Maybe Mary had been right. Maybe she had come back too early. Missing even a week meant that she had no context for half the patients on the wards. Surgeons seemed to forget, or not be aware, that she hadn't been present for recent surgeries. And her memory wasn't performing the way it should and always had. The neat little rows of numbers and connections she usually maintained in her head were a fragmented mess. Worst of all, and so terrifying that she couldn't bring herself to think about it, was the shake in her hands.

Mary was working on charts when Aisling reached the A&E desk. Aisling went straight to the phone and dialled surgery. She was conscious of Mary watching her as she spoke to a surgical nurse. Cummins had called in. He wanted bloods on a patient for the morning rounds. They hadn't been done and the patient wasn't fasting. The patient didn't want to fast. Could Aisling come? Yes, she would be there in five, if A&E could spare her. She hung up, turned to Mary, who had heard enough to get the gist.

'I won't be long,' Aisling said. 'You'll beep me, if something comes in?'

'What did the garda want?' Mary asked. 'Was it about Jack?' Aisling didn't need to ask how Mary knew about the meeting. Gossip was a welcome distraction and a popular pastime all over the hospital but particularly in A&E.

'I don't know,' Aisling said.

Mary raised an eyebrow.

'He said it was, but he was asking questions about Jack's sister. He wanted to know what I knew about Maude, about their childhood. He all but asked me straight out if Maude was violent, if she had ever hurt Jack when they were kids.'

'Jesus. What did you say?'

'I told him the truth. That Jack loved Maude. There's no reason to think she'd ever hurt him.'

'That you know of at least,' Mary said. 'But he must have had a reason for asking.

'Maybe,' Aisling said. 'But the gardaí have been pretty useless so far. I told you about the meeting, about the questions Maude asked. They didn't have any answers. It wouldn't exactly fill you with confidence.' Aisling hesitated, then blurted the rest out. 'Maude doesn't believe Jack killed himself. She thinks he was murdered, and she doesn't trust the gardaí. She wants to take things further. I was thinking we could go to the ombudsman.' Aisling stopped talking when she realised Mary was looking at her with something like pity in her eyes.

'What?' Aisling asked.

Mary reached into her pocket, took out a folded piece of paper. She sat there looking at it for a moment, then handed it over slowly. 'I wasn't trying to pry,' she said. 'You dropped it. When you were rushing the other day, to meet Maude. I picked it up. Meant to file it for you. I couldn't find the file, then I figured it out.'

Aisling unfolded the paper. It was a test result. Her test result. The one she'd submitted under a false name.

'It's none of my business, I know,' Mary said, looking away from Aisling and down the corridor to where a cleaner was pushing a low-humming floor polisher, the machine gliding from side to side in a steady arc.

'No. It really isn't.' Aisling paused.

'Do you want to talk about it?'

'No.' Definitely not. But she didn't move.

'Aisling, you can tell me to fuck off if you want to,' Mary said. 'I'm not going to be offended, and we can pretend we never had this conversation if that's what you want. But, I'm just listening to you talk about this mad theory Maude has come up with, and I'm watching you working like a dog and honestly, it seems to me that you're looking every direction but where you should be looking. I get it, of course I get it. You're in an impossible position, but Jesus, you have a lot to lose. Anyway, I just thought I'd offer, in case you need someone to talk to about your options.' Mary lowered her head to her charts again, as if wanting to give Aisling privacy to consider her offer.

'What sort of person kills their dead boyfriend's baby?' The words were out before she had a chance to recall them, and when Mary looked up her expression was so kind that Aisling couldn't bear it, had to look away.

'Is that what you really think?' Mary asked. 'That an abortion would be killing Jack's baby?'

Aisling shook her head, her lips compressed.

'You're what, no more than six, seven weeks?'

'You know as well as I do,' Aisling said, with a gesture towards the test result.

Mary took a slow breath in. 'At seven weeks, you know that that foetus has a long way to go before it becomes a baby.'

'I know that,' said Aisling, her voice low, but cracking with suppressed anger, fear and frustration. 'I keep telling myself that it's nothing more than a little scrap of raw material. Smaller than a coffee bean. But that's not helping me.' She glanced around. This was not the place to have this conversation. 'Even if it's just a bundle of cells, it's more than nothing, right? It's the last bit of Jack left in the world. If I leave it alone, just do nothing, then that thing, that little bit of potential, it'll grow to be Jack's baby, won't it? So if I have an abortion, how is that not the same thing?' The words were muddled, her thinking confused, but it was still the closest she'd come to articulating how she had been feeling for the past two weeks.

'You're calling it Jack's baby,' Mary said. 'Not yours. Not yours and Jack's.'

Aisling said nothing, and Mary chewed her bottom lip. There was a little smear of make-up on her collar. She was wearing more than usual, and she looked tired under the heavy layer of foundation.

'If Jack was alive, would you be going ahead with this pregnancy?'

The answer – a clear, unhesitating *No* – was in Aisling's head before she had a chance to consciously consider the question. No way would she be considering having a baby if Jack was still with her. She'd had a moment, a wobble, on the night before he died, but that was to be expected, wasn't it? Normal, to try to consider all of the options. It did not mean that she wanted to be a mother. Even though they hadn't had a chance to work it out, she thought he would have supported that decision, in the end. And if he hadn't? Would she have risked their relationship rather than have a baby now, at twenty-five, before she'd realised even one of her ambitions?

Mary read the answer in her face. 'Aisling, this is your decision, but for God's sake, don't have a baby out of some sort of misplaced survivor's guilt.' She placed a pointed index finger right in the middle of the chart Aisling had been working on. 'You'll lose this,' Mary said, and she sounded angry, had raised her voice. 'You'll lose everything you've worked for. So you'll have to choose another path.' She paused, took her finger back from the chart, and continued in a softer voice. 'You could try for GP, although they won't be thrilled about being your second choice. If you show you're committed, you'll get in, and in a year or two you'll be out of the hospital and in a practice, seeing thirty patients a day, most of whom aren't really sick. They just want someone who'll listen to them for a while, and you'll be able to give them exactly twelve and a half minutes, because you'll need the last two and half minutes of the fifteen-minute appointment to complete the paperwork.'

Aisling felt cold and hot at the same time. A clammy nausea gripped her stomach. 'I know all this. I know all of this.'

'Well.' Mary fell silent, looked back at her paperwork.

'You did it,' Aisling said. 'You left surgery for general medicine. You can't feel that way about it.'

'I don't, not exactly.' Mary grimaced, looked up at Aisling with a return of her frustration. 'The truth is that I don't I have what you have, Aisling. Jesus, you're … you never give up. Do you remember, when we were interns, and we both worked that awful week? Everyone had flu but us, if felt like, and we worked something like a hundred and twenty hours?'

Aisling nodded slowly, though she didn't remember, exactly. There had been a lot of long weeks. Everything sort of ran into everything else when you worked that hard, on that little sleep.

'We left together that Saturday morning, walked out of the place and went for breakfast across the road. I went home afterwards and I slept until Monday morning, basically. Only got up to eat and use the loo.'

Aisling nodded.

Mary shook her head. 'That Monday was the deadline for the Wylie Medal. Which you won. Jack told me later that you wrote your essay that weekend. You stayed up all night Sunday to finish it. But we worked on Monday morning and you came in and did a fourteen-hour shift with me as if it was nothing. The Wylie Medal is awarded by the fucking Association of *Anaesthetists,* for Christ's sake. You wanted to be a surgeon.'

'There was prize money,' Aisling said, folding her arms across her chest.

Mary snorted, rolled her eyes. Aisling had to fight the urge to just walk away.

'You always win. Not just the medal. You won the Henry Hutch twice. You're what, second, third, in the country right now? How do you do that?'

Aisling wanted to say that second or third wasn't first. Wasn't winning. It was on the tip of her tongue. 'There's no secret Mary. I just work bloody hard.'

'I work hard,' Mary snapped back. 'Harder than almost anyone. But you're fucking superhuman.' She looked back down at her paperwork, face flushed. Was she embarrassed? Or just angry? The conversation had spiraled from its starting point. Whatever Mary had set out to say, it wasn't this. How long had she been feeling like this? It was too much to deal with, on top of everything else. No one would blame Aisling if she told her to fuck off, if she just walked away right now. But Mary was a friend, a real friend. Aisling thought about that hand on her shoulder at the cemetery, when she'd needed it most.

'My mother used to apologise to my teachers,' Aisling said.

'What?'

'At the start of every year, she would come to my school to meet the teachers and apologise for me. *I'm very sorry about Aisling. I'm afraid she has very little ability, though I'm sure she does her best.* She started doing that when I was eight.'

Mary looked back at her, fascinated, horrified.

'It didn't really matter what my teachers said. If they said something positive about me my mother would cock her head to one side and smile in a grateful sort of a way. Then afterwards she would explain to me that my teachers were being kind, and they only did that for the kids who couldn't hack it.' Aisling paused.

'But that's crazy.'

Aisling shrugged. 'I think she believed it. She felt the same way about herself, you know? I suppose now I would label it, maybe low self-esteem and transference. But at the time I just accepted it. For a long time I accepted everything she said. But eventually I noticed that she was that way only about me, and she was that way no matter how well I did at anything. I won a prize once at school, just this little art competition thing, and she tried to convince me that they gave it to me out of pity. After that I started to get angry.'

'I'll bet you did,' said Mary.

'I started working harder. I worked my ass off, to be honest. I was absolutely determined that my mother would finally see I was good enough. The day my leaving cert results came in my mother had this puzzled look on her face. She said congratulations. Then that night, after I went to bed, I heard her ask my dad if there could have been some sort of mix up, if maybe they should do the right thing and let the exam board know.'

Mary laughed, a horrified gasp of laughter that escaped and was bitten back. But the laugh was good, it loosened something in Aisling, and she smiled back.

'I'd like to say I got over it then, but I didn't really. For a long, long time after that I was still trying to prove something. Things got better after I met Jack, but by then ... I don't know. Maybe working that hard is a habit now. Or maybe I am still trying to please her. Christ, that's pathetic.'

'You're the furthest thing from pathetic I know,' Mary said, her tone warm and firm. 'And the truth is it's not just hard work that's gotten you here. I know you've got talent. In spades. You're going to make an incredible surgeon. You're going to save a lot of lives.' She stopped, stumbling over her last words, and silence fell between them. Aisling wanted to say something but nothing came out. The two women regarded each other for a long moment.

'Just be sure you make a plan, Aisling. A plan for the next step, and the next one, and then the one after that, okay? And remember that you've got a friend here if you need one.' Mary squeezed Aisling's shoulder in what was becoming a familiar gesture, then hopped lightly from the desk and walked away down the corridor.

Aisling stood still. A plan. She needed to make a plan. The pager beeped again.

CHAPTER FOURTEEN

Cormac made his way back to the station, irritated that he'd brought the car and had to sit in traffic instead of walking. He hadn't made much progress on the case, but for the first time thought that there was progress to be made. Collins was definitely hiding something. And he was loyal to Maude, or at least wanted Cormac to think so. He needed to think through what that might mean. Cormac's stomach growled as he parked outside the station and he checked his watch. It was nearly three, and he hadn't eaten since breakfast. The few pints he'd had the night before had left him with a heavy head, and he'd been drinking coffee all day. Food was definitely in order. He took a detour to the fourth floor and the somewhat limited canteen.

The place was usually deserted at this time of day because the hot food finished at two, but when Cormac entered in search of a sandwich, he found Anthony Healy occupying one corner table, a file spread out in front of him, two empty coffee cups at his elbow. Cormac ignored him, walked to the fridge and examined the meagre pickings. Egg salad. Beetroot salad. Who the fuck ate beetroot salad? He took a limp ham sandwich – a sliver of processed meat stuck between two thin white slices of bread. Ireland had come a long way over the past ten years, but the food revolution had not broached the garda canteen.

'Reilly.'

Cormac took his time pressing buttons on the coffee machine before turning to Healy as his cup filled.

'How long do you think you'll last, down here?'

Cormac said nothing, waited.

'Come on. No bullshit. This lot don't know their arse from their elbow. What are you doing here? Is it really all about a woman? That's a bit out of character, isn't it?'

Cormac added a leisurely two spoons of sugar to his coffee, stirred. 'Is it?' he said.

Healy laughed as if Cormac had made a joke. 'Seriously man, isn't it a bit slow for you? You've been here what, a month? Two? Are you really going to stick it?'

'I haven't noticed much difference. Same bullshit. Same politics.' Cormac paused. 'But you'd know the place better than me. Task force seems to like Galway. Third visit in three years, isn't it? Is it the weather that brings you back?' The rain was lashing against the windows in one of those sudden violent flurries that added variety to the otherwise near-constant drizzle.

Healy laughed again, shook his head. 'I'd tell you Cormac,' he said, 'but then I'd have to shoot you.' He patted the gun at his side.

Cormac raised an eyebrow, nodded in the direction of the gun. 'Careful with that, Anthony. Are you sure you remember which is the dangerous end?'

Healy shook his head, still smiling. 'We can't all be heroes, can we Reilly?'

Cormac had turned for the door when Healy spoke again.

'You're very friendly with Danny McIntyre. Knew him before you transferred?'

Cormac turned back and stared Healy down. This whole conversation had been an inept attempt to warm Cormac up. And when that showed no signs of working, Healy'd just blurted out what was really on his mind. What was it about Danny that had Healy going? That he wasn't one of Healy's little minions? That he had a degree of independence and a mind of his own? Surely Healy was capable of keeping one temporary assignee under control. No, Danny had to have seen something, and Healy was worried that he might have talked.

As Cormac hesitated, Healy broke eye contact, and started gathering up his files. At the same moment, a trio of uniforms came in, one of them almost taking out Cormac's rapidly cooling coffee. The moment had passed, and Cormac wasn't even sure what it had been. He left the room before Healy, returned to his desk and made short work of the sandwich. He was finishing his coffee when Fisher appeared at his desk, some printed pages in his hands.

'I found him,' Fisher said, without preamble. 'Timothy Lanigan. He did go to Massachusetts, but he didn't stay there. He moved to New York State. Taught in ...' Fisher paused to look at his notes. 'St. Boniface Catholic Academy. Private school. He taught English and coached soccer. He married one of the other teachers, had two kids, and stayed there for ten years. In 1985 his marriage broke down and he moved away. His wife – ex-wife – still works at the school.'

'And?' Cormac said.

'And, it looks like he's pretty clean, don't you think? Taught for ten years, no scandals. He got divorced in 1985 and left the area soon after.' Fisher shrugged. 'Law-abiding citizen. Not much to work with.'

'Where is he now?' Cormac asked.

Fisher made a helpless gesture. 'I don't know,' he said. 'I found him online, some old soccer reports, photos. Called the school, got the secretary talking.' His expression said he thought he'd done well. 'I didn't take it any further.'

'I asked you to find him. Don't stop until you do.' Cormac made a mental note to make a phone call or two to his own contacts. Fisher was good, and he wanted to push him, but getting information from the States quickly would require a bit of pull.

Fisher opened his mouth to speak, then stopped himself.

'Ask,' Cormac said.

'It's just, what's the point of it?' Fisher asked. To his credit there was no complaint in his voice, just honest curiosity. 'There's no DNA, no new evidence. Isn't this a waste of time?'

Cormac smiled, and the smile turned into a yawn, which he smothered with one hand. 'If you start thinking like that all you're doing is shutting yourself down. When you're investigating, you follow the questions until you have answers.' He picked up the Blake file. Fisher took the hint and left.

Cormac's little lecture to the younger man had been a timely reminder. He needed to press on. He found the number for Child and Family Services in Castlebar and picked up the phone.

CHAPTER FIFTEEN

Aisling didn't get home that night until after eight o'clock. After her conversation with Mary she'd turned her tired mind from the questions she'd raised and refocused on her work. After her A&E shift she'd made a round of every surgical ward on her floor. She'd read the charts of eighteen patients, spoken to those who were awake, had a chat with family members, and caught up with colleagues, until she finally felt that everything was as it should be. Her finger was back on the pulse of the hospital, and for the first time since Jack died she felt a little in control. She was also exhausted. Her feet hurt; the pad of her right foot ached like a bruise every time she took a step. Her back was tight and her eyes were burning. Her stomach felt hard and raw with hunger. She hadn't had a chance to eat since breakfast, thirteen hours earlier. She was struggling with the lock on her door – trying to see the keyhole in the dark – when a voice spoke from behind her.

'Aisling.'

Aisling knew who it was before she turned, and she closed her eyes briefly. Shit. She didn't have the energy. Then she turned, and found a smile from somewhere.

'Aggie.' Aisling hugged the smaller woman. 'Have you been waiting? You should have called. I would have come home earlier.'

'I knew you were working.' Aggie gave Aisling a searching look. 'You're tired, and I'll bet you haven't eaten. Well, I can solve one problem.' She raised the carrier bag she held in one hand, and looked beyond Aisling to the front door.

They sat in the kitchen and ate together. The contents of the carrier bag turned out to be two lunch boxes filled with brown stew and mashed potato. Aisling plated them, nuked them, and offered Aggie a glass of wine, which she refused.

'I'll have water, love. I'm driving.'

They ate in silence for the first few minutes, Aisling with an urgency that she knew Aggie wouldn't miss. She slowed herself down after the first few mouthfuls, became conscious of the dirty dishes stacked in the sink, the single brown banana in the fruit bowl, the clothes still hanging on the clotheshorse, which included two of Jack's T-shirts. She hadn't done any laundry since the day he died. Aisling glanced at Aggie, half-expecting to see those grey eyes taking in the mess, or watching her, measuring the degree to which she was falling apart. Except that she wasn't falling apart, or no more than should be expected. She was just bloody busy.

But Aggie's eyes were on her own plate, and it was Aisling who started doing the noticing, the measuring. Aggie had been crying. And recently – her eyes were still puffy. Her soft grey hair was tidy, and her blouse and cardigan had been neatly pressed, but there was a little stain on the lapel that was very un-Aggie, and she looked tired.

Aggie finished her food, then reached out a hand and softly squeezed Aisling's.

'I'm sorry we left it to you,' she said. 'The guards. Unforgivable. But I wasn't thinking straight, Aisling. I hope you'll forgive me.'

'Not at all ...' Aisling started to rattle off an automatic denial, but a second squeeze of her hand and the expression on Aggie's face stopped her.

'I'm sorry for it,' Aggie said. 'If I could have the time over I'd do it differently. But I felt Brendan needed me and I used it as an excuse to turn away.'

Aisling stood and went to the kettle. She filled it, turned it on, then started to clear the plates. 'I don't blame you for anything,' she said. 'Losing Jack. I know it broke your heart. You're doing the best you can.' When she looked back at Aggie she saw eyes filled with unshed tears, and wanted to cry herself. Aggie was the warmest of women. Utterly practical, hard-working, she'd loved Jack fiercely and welcomed Aisling with a kind word and a warm hand when he'd first brought her to the house. They were such different women on the surface, and Aisling had wondered if Aggie would have preferred a different kind of woman for her son. But Jack had only laughed when she'd said this to him.

'She's not that sort of person,' was all he had said, and in time Aisling had come to see that Aggie had wanted only happiness for Jack, and if Aisling made him happy that was good enough for her. Now Aggie blinked back her tears and took a cup, poured tea for them both.

'How are you doing?' she asked. 'Working hard, I know. But are you looking after yourself? Have you seen much of Mark and Fergus? Have they been around?' Jack's friends. They'd both called, Fergus more than once. She hadn't answered the phone, hadn't called them back, hadn't seen them since the funeral.

'Maude was there. At the garda meeting.' Aisling blurted the words out. 'She came back. She's been in Australia, all this time.'

Aggie put her cup down on the table. 'Maude? Jack's sister Maude?'

Aisling nodded, and took a seat opposite Aggie. She held her cup in her hands, wrapped her fingers around its warmth. 'She looks like him.' Did she? Not at all really. Not when Aisling thought about it. Maude was small, slight, where Jack had been tall and athletic. Maude was older, and there was nothing of Jack's laughing eyes about her. But it was in her eyes that Aisling saw Jack. Something about the set of them, the stillness of her expression. That had been Jack too, in a moment of distraction, when his mind was far away.

'She came home? When?'

Aisling shook her head. 'I don't know. She must have heard about Jack, come for the funeral. She was there, you know? On Prospect Hill. But I didn't recognise her.'

It was Aggie's turn to shake her head. 'Poor, poor girl,' she said. 'She finally came home, and Jack is gone.' There were no tears in Aggie's eyes now. Her face was grey, her lips bloodless. She took a sip from her cup, closed her eyes for a moment. 'Will she meet us, do you think? I'd like to see her. I want to show her the photographs. She should know that Jack had a happy life. That coming to us was a good thing for him. That it wasn't all a waste.' Confusion crossed her face, and tears welled again. She blinked against them. 'Well, I always thought it wasn't. But perhaps ... perhaps we were wrong about that.' She turned eyes filled with pain to Aisling. 'Did he talk to you, Aisling? Do you know why he would do this terrible thing?'

'Aggie,' Aisling said. She pushed back her chair and stood, glanced to the kitchen. She wanted to be doing something, felt an urge to wash up the dishes – anything to break the tension of the moment. What should she say? Would it be wrong to give false hope? Mary thought it was all a sort of mad denial, but she hadn't been in the meeting, she hadn't seen the CCTV footage. And how could it be false hope, to tell someone that maybe their son hadn't killed himself after all, maybe he'd just been murdered? Jesus. She sat again, took her cup in both hands, held it and looked down, concentrated on the grip of her fingers, the lightening of her flesh as she tightened her grip, the encroaching pink as she loosened it. 'Aggie,' she said again. 'Maude doesn't think, I mean, I'm not sure.' She forced herself to look up. 'I'm not certain that Jack did kill himself.'

Aggie stared back at her, mouth slightly open as if she were about to ask a question. 'Tell me,' she said in the end.

So Aisling told her the story, starting with the CCTV footage, then doubling back to the meeting with Rodgers, then back again to her conversation with Maude in the hotel room. In the end the story was so muddled she didn't think that Aggie would be able to make anything out of it. When she finished, Aggie sat back, cup of tea forgotten, her cheeks flushed. She said nothing for what felt like a long time, and when she spoke she blurted the words out.

'I want to meet her,' Aggie said.

'What?'

'Maude. I'd like to meet her. I always wanted to meet her. Can you call her? Bring her for lunch. On Saturday. Or Sunday if you're working.'

Aisling wondered for a second if she should start again, make a better effort of it this time. But Aggie reached over and took her hand.

'I want to believe he didn't do it,' she said. 'The world would make sense again. Even though that means someone else hurt him. Killed him. But it's all too much. I don't know where to start with it. But I know I want to see Maude. So I'll start with that, and see where to go from there.'

Aisling found herself agreeing, promising to call Maude in the morning, try to set up the lunch, whenever it suited the older woman. And after that Aggie insisted on washing up, tidying the kitchen, folding the clothes. She was flooded with a sudden energy, and sent Aisling, protesting, to the shower. By the time Aisling came downstairs again, dressed in her last pair of clean pyjamas and her hair wrapped in a towel, the kitchen was cleaner than it had been in weeks, and Aggie was packed up and ready to go. She kissed Aisling briskly on the cheek.

'I'll see you on Saturday,' she said. 'Don't be late, or be late. It doesn't matter.' She laughed an uncharacteristically nervous laugh, then cut it abruptly short. It occurred to Aisling that maybe Aggie had had those moments too. Those moments of horrible self-consciousness, of guilt, of self-censorship, as if outward grief were a borrowed suit that never quite fit. But she was too tired to follow the thought through. Too tired to do anything more than hug Aggie goodbye, and shut the door. She was too tired even to climb the stairs and face her empty bed. She went to the living room and lay down on the couch, pulled a blanket over herself and fell asleep there, wet hair and all.

Wednesday 27 March 2013

CHAPTER SIXTEEN

Children and Family Services didn't return Cormac's call on Tuesday, and his second call on Tuesday evening had gotten him nowhere. His third call, on Wednesday morning, got him an answer, if not the one he was looking for. The voice on the other end of the phone was still chirpy, efficient.

'Oh hi, Detective Reilly, I was about to call you. Yeah, there's no file I'm afraid. I mean there was one but it was in the flood.'

'The flood?'

'Yeah. In Castlebar. 2009. The storage facility was out by the river and it burst its banks, flooded the place. They did try to recover the files, but then there was some sort of problem with mould, so they had to be destroyed.'

'You don't have copies, scans?'

'Not of stuff going that far back I'm afraid.' There was distraction in her voice, and he could hear conversation in the background. A moment later she apologised briefly again, and hung up.

Cursing, Cormac left the station and walked into Galway, waiting until he had crossed the bridge and found a doorway that offered enough shelter from the wind for a phone call. He dialled a number he hadn't called in nearly five years. She answered after two rings.

'Cormac?' Surprise in her voice, a hint of concern. 'Everything all right?' She'd recognised his number. But then, he would have recognised hers.

'Tara. How are you?'

'Grand. I'm grand.'

He'd heard through the grapevine that she was married now, to a guy who worked in banking. The marriage hadn't surprised him, the banking part had, a bit. Tara'd never been a big fan of suits. She was bloody good at her job, but as she'd advanced up the ranks she'd never let go of the fact that she'd started in the trenches, while so many of the middle and upper management types she encountered had no clue what it was like on the front line. Maybe she'd gotten over her aversion, now that so many of them worked for her. Her last promotion had made her Director of Policy and Strategy at the Child and Family Agency.

'I heard you got married?' Cormac said.

'Yes. Paul. Lovely guy. I think you'd like him.' She spoke a little awkwardly, then rushed out with, 'We're expecting.'

'Congrats, Tara. That's great news.' He was genuinely happy for her. It was what she'd wanted, from the beginning really. She'd never pretended otherwise, and he'd always felt guilty that it had taken him so long to realise he didn't feel the same way.

'And you?' she asked.

He really didn't want to get into it. 'Tara, I'm sorry to call you out of the blue like this. But I'm working a case, and I'm hoping you can do me a favour.'

'Yes?' There was caution in her tone, but she wasn't pissed off.

So he told her about the case. That he'd put in a request for a file, an old one, from twenty years back, but it had been destroyed. Did she have access to any information from Dublin that she could pass to him?

Silence for a moment from the other end of the phone. 'Cormac, you should be able to get that information through the proper channels. You don't need to come through the back door.'

Meaning that the back door was now closed? 'It's important. I know it seems like it shouldn't be, with a twenty-year-old file, but I think there's urgency here. The boy is dead, and something from his past may be relevant.'

'Cormac …'

He cut her off. 'Tara, there's something off here. I have a feeling.' He cursed himself inwardly. His *feelings* had been the cause of more than one argument when they prompted his early departure from one special occasion or another. But instead of hanging up on him, she paused for a long moment, then asked for a name.

He heard the click of keys on a keyboard, then silence as Tara read whatever she saw. 'You're telling me that this boy is dead?'

'Yes.'

'Death doesn't bring an end to our confidentiality obligations,' Tara said. 'I'm not going to give you anything that would cross that line.'

'Of course,' Cormac said. She had once before, when a child went missing and Cormac hadn't wanted to wait on a court order. But that was a different case, and those were different times.

Tara went silent again. More reading, or second thoughts?

'There was a file,' Tara said. 'According to the system it's in storage in Castlebar.'

'I was told there was a flood. In 2009. That the file was destroyed along with others.'

More keyboard clicking down the phone. 'There was a flood all right,' Tara said. 'The file is probably gone. But I think they did manage to scan at least some of them before the originals were destroyed. There's a reference number here. You could put in a request through Dublin. I'll keep an eye on it for you, see what comes up.'

It would take at least a week, maybe more. 'Is there anything you can tell me now?' Cormac asked. 'Was anything scanned into the system? Or if there's a name, a social worker I can track down locally?'

Another pause. 'There are a lot of names here. A lot of different case workers. I can give you the most recent.'

Cormac blew out the breath he hadn't known he was holding. 'Thanks Tara. I appreciate it, very much. I'll owe you one.'

She gave him the name. 'You were always a good cop, Cormac. If you're asking, I'm sure it's for good reason.' He was surprised how good it felt to hear her say this. They said their goodbyes and he hung up, then immediately dialled again.

Thirty minutes later he pulled in outside a neat detached house in Knocknacarra, the heart of suburbia. Identikit houses stretched away in either direction. There was a small, landscaped park opposite the house. Someone had installed a swing set and a miniature set of plastic goals. He knocked on the door and a moment later it was opened by a woman who was in the process of shrugging on a coat.

'Katherine Shelley?' he asked.

She nodded.

'Detective Sergeant Cormac Reilly,' he said. 'I'd like to talk to you about a case you were involved in when you worked out of Castlebar.'

Her face stayed blank for a long moment. 'I'm not a social worker anymore,' she said. 'I haven't been one for a long time. You should call the office. Someone there will speak to you.'

'I need to speak to someone who met these children back in the early nineties. I'm told you worked the case. Really I'm just looking for background. Your impressions of the family.

Whether or not you can remember any associates. That sort of thing.'

'I really don't think ... I wouldn't remember any details. Particularly without the files. I don't think I can help you.' She started to close the door.

Cormac took a step forward. He didn't smile, but lowered his voice and spoke very seriously. 'Look, some questions have been asked about a suspicious death that took place in 1993. I'd like to speak to you now, informally, if that's possible.' The implication was obvious, and intentional, and she caught it. She hesitated.

'Do you have identification?'

He showed her, and she opened the door wider after a cursory glance.

He followed her through the hall into the kitchen beyond. The house was warm and inviting, the hall tidy except for a bundle of coats slung over the bottom of the bannisters. The kitchen was a welcoming room too, bigger than the front of the house had led Cormac to expect. There was an oversized kitchen table, some good-looking if dated cabinetry, and glass doors that led into a small garden, which was dominated by a kids' trampoline that had seen better days.

Katherine took off her coat as she entered the kitchen, and hung it on the back of a chair. She was wearing jeans and an old college sweater underneath. Her fair hair was in a careless ponytail. She had to be in her mid-forties, but there was something youthful and outdoorsy about her.

'My girls are playing in a hockey tournament,' she said. 'I was going to watch them. I don't have too long.'

Cormac nodded, but said nothing, and after hovering awkwardly for a moment, manners or habit kicked in, and Katherine gestured to him to take a seat, and went to put on the kettle.

'When did you move to Galway?' he asked.

She added teabags to a teapot. 'I met my husband when I was twenty-four. He's from Galway. After we got married I moved here. I gave up work after I got pregnant. I was glad to give it up. I was burned out.' She looked at him sharply, as if expecting criticism. 'That's not unusual,' she said.

The kettle started to whistle, and she leaned back against the counter, her arms crossed. 'Which case is it?' she asked.

'Blake,' said Cormac. 'Maude and Jack Blake.'

There was uncertainty in her eyes for a moment, and then her face cleared as recognition hit. She said nothing, but added hot water to the teapot, brought it to the table, then returned to the cabinets for teacups and sugar, and to the fridge for milk.

'It was him then, in the paper. I saw his name, and wondered if it was the same Jack Blake I'd known.' She sat at the table, her expression wary. 'What do you want to know?'

Cormac held her gaze. 'Why weren't the kids taken into care?' he asked. It wasn't the question he'd been intending to ask, but it was what came out.

Katherine shook her head. 'You're a cop. I would have thought you'd know better.'

Cormac raised an eyebrow.

'Since 1996 there've been four public inquiries into child welfare in Ireland.' She held up her hands. 'I'm not saying they weren't needed, and I'm not saying they didn't expose terrible things. But the media. Jesus. They apply today's thinking to things that happened twenty, thirty years ago, and they just stoke up outrage. And it's all the fault of the social workers.' Her face was flushed. 'We didn't even have the Child Care Act until 1991. And how long did it take them to implement that? Years. And the Children's Referendum was only last year. That barely passed. People *know*. They know that we didn't have the power. Before the referendum, the constitution put the family first. The best interests of the child came second. We couldn't take the children out unless we had done everything possible to keep the family together. And even then half the time we'd get knocked back in the courts.'

He'd jumped in too fast and now she was defensive. Still, Cormac didn't soften his tone. 'Is that why Maude and Jack stayed with their mother? Because of the Constitution?'

She stared back at him, still flushed, breathing a little fast. 'No,' she said at last, then shook her head. 'Maybe.'

She still held the handle of the teapot in one hand, though she hadn't poured. She stared at it now. Cormac reached over and took the pot from her, poured for them both.

'Their mother wasn't married,' Katherine said. 'Only marital families were protected under the Constitution, according to the Supreme Court. An unmarried mother – it should have been much, much easier to remove the children.'

'But it wasn't?' Cormac offered her milk and sugar as he spoke, added it according to her direction, passed her the cup.

She took it. Her phone, which she'd placed on the table, buzzed, and she glanced at it distractedly, then back at him.

'The children were obviously neglected. I was the third social worker to see the family. The others had attended the family when they'd lived in Dublin, and later in Galway, but those visits were to do with helping the family with money – dealing with rent and electricity arrears, that sort of thing. The notes on the file make it obvious that the neglect had been going on for a while – *mother advised about hygiene*. That sort of thing.'

'But neglect wasn't enough to remove the children.'

She shook her head. 'Nowhere near enough. I've seen much, much worse cases of neglect where we continued to support the family.'

'What was different about your visit?'

'A teacher at the school called the office. Maude had a bruise on her arm, her forearm. It was a nasty one, and the teacher – her name was Carey, or Carew, something like that – she suspected abuse and called it in. The case was assigned to me and I called to the house.'

Cormac waited. Katherine took a sip of tea, then continued.

'As I've said, it could have been worse. The little boy, Jack, was okay. There was some food for him. It was the young girl, Maude. She looked after him, though she tried to deny it at first, claimed her mother did most of it. When I got there Hilaria was asleep in bed. I tried to wake her and couldn't.' Katherine wrinkled her nose. 'She was in a state. That sour smell, of old sweat and stale vomit. God, it was awful. She had urinated on herself. Probably wasn't the first time. There was an empty vodka bottle beside the bed, another on the floor. God knows how much she was drinking a day. I gather that's where most of the dole money went. Eventually Maude admitted that she cared for Jack after school, did the food shopping, cooking, cleaning. Everything really. She claimed that Hilaria stayed off the booze during the day, that she minded Jack while Maude was at school. But I'd say the poor little fella fended for himself. He was so small, only a toddler really. Later I found out that Maude had been a good student, but had started to miss more and more school. I suppose she'd begun to realise that she couldn't leave Jack at home alone with her mother. I suppose she would have been twelve, maybe thirteen?'

'When was this?' Cormac asked. He took his notebook out.

She thought for a moment. 'I think towards the end of 1990.'

'Twelve, then,' Cormac said.

Katherine nodded. 'She was such a serious child. She didn't trust me, or distrust me. She was just ... indifferent. But she held that boy's hand every minute I was there. And when I asked about him she was intent on showing me that he was well taken care of. She showed me his few clothes, and the bits of food she had put away for him. It nearly broke my heart.'

'Did you talk to her about the bruises?'

Katherine's brow was furrowed. 'Is she all right, Maude? Have you seen her?'

Cormac nodded slowly. 'She's all right.' He said nothing more, and after a moment Katherine continued.

'I asked her about the bruise, made her show me. The bruise was nasty, but she told me she helped out a neighbour with the milking sometimes, and she'd had a kick from a cow. She was adamant that it was an accident, that no one had hurt her.'

'Did you believe her?'

'No. She had that look about her. I wasn't very experienced, but I was experienced enough to know what I was seeing. And the little boy was afraid of me. Not just shy. Genuinely afraid.'

'Did you … you left them?' Cormac asked in as neutral a tone as he could manage.

'I didn't have a mobile and there was no phone in the house. I took the kids back with me to the office. Put them in the family room. I went to my desk to call the doctor for Hilaria, for the kids too. My boss was there. Someone had called him, told him where I'd been. He had a shit fit. Said removing the children was totally over the top. Unwarranted interference. Something like that.' She rubbed at her forehead, smoothing her left eyebrow hard with the index finger of her left hand, again and again. 'I tried to tell him, I really did. He wouldn't listen. Said whether or not the mother was ill we had no legal right to intervene. He said that the children were in good shape, and that there was a neighbour, a good Christian woman, who was heavily involved with the family and was providing adequate supervision.'

'Who?'

'He didn't tell me but I found out later. Her name was Keane, I think. Mrs Keane. I think she must have called him, must have known somehow that I had taken the children.'

Cormac shook his head. It didn't make sense. Even in the context of the times, surely temporarily removing two young children from a house where there was no responsible adult was the necessary thing to do. Not to mention seeking medical help for Hilaria.

'Why?' he asked.

'I don't know. My boss was very involved with the church, and Mrs Keane seemed to have a lot of influence with him. But they were all like that. There were three others in that office and none of them would even discuss the case. They just blocked those kids out. You have to understand, we were all so overworked. And there was this mindset that the standard of proof the courts required was so high. So we focused on keeping families together, even when the children might have been better off in care.'

'What happened then?' Cormac asked.

'He told me to bring them home to their mother.' She wiped a tear away with the back of her hand.

'Did you?'

She shook her head. Then nodded.

'I promised them I'd be back. Swore I would. Said I would be back before it got dark. That I would bring them food. McDonald's, I think I said. Maude wouldn't even look at me. They just sat in the back seat, holding hands. The little boy was so scared.'

'But you didn't go back.'

'No.'

He said nothing.

'I called Dublin the next day. Left the office to do it because I was too afraid, didn't want to be overheard. But I called head office. They said that they would send someone down, probably the next day, maybe the day after. I felt sick, thinking of those kids in that house, alone with their mother. I called again a few weeks later. But no one ever went. And by then I had twenty cases and more on the way. I was overwhelmed. So I ... did nothing.'

She couldn't meet his eyes. He wondered how often she had woken in the night, how often she had held her own children to her and had thought about the two she left behind.

'Did you see any sign of drugs in the house, any heroin?'

'No. Nothing like that. I was surprised when I heard. But I suppose I was mostly relieved. And I heard that Jack was fostered almost immediately, which was very good.'

'You kept track of the children?' he asked.

But she looked away. 'Not really. Just heard a few things from an old colleague.' After a moment she stood and walked to the sink, taking her cup with her. 'I'm sorry, but I have to go,' she said.

'The neighbour, Mrs Keane. Did she stay involved with the family?'

'I believe so. I heard that she collected Hilaria's dole – I suppose it was the unmarried mother's allowance, in those days. You could do that then. Hilaria was getting disability allowance as well, so she probably picked that up too.'

Cormac didn't close his notebook. 'Do you think Keane would have bought alcohol for Hilaria Blake? She must have had a source, once she reached the point where she couldn't, or wouldn't, get to the village herself.'

Katherine hesitated. 'I can't imagine she would have. She was supposed to be very religious.' She picked up her handbag from the countertop. 'I'm sorry. I really do have to go.'

Cormac stood. As he followed her to the front door he asked, 'Did you know much about heroin use in the town back then? Was it much of a problem?'

'Not that I can remember. Most of our problems were alcohol-related.'

He followed her into the bright spring sunshine. It was still cold, but he welcomed the fresh air and sight of blue sky. The rain in Galway was so much more constant than in Dublin; it was hard to believe the cities were only a few hours apart. Suddenly he wished he were back in Dublin, in the grotty but familiar surroundings of Dublin Castle.

'I'm so sorry,' she said. 'Will you tell her that?'

'You mean Maude?'

'Yes.'

'I will,' he said. But he didn't mean it. Whatever else he had to say to Maude, he had no urge to remind her of another person who had failed her.

CHAPTER SEVENTEEN

Cormac went for a run immediately after the Katherine Shelley interview. He needed to move, to push his body, to sweat out his frustration and anger. There was nothing he could do about what had happened to Maude and Jack. That was a twenty-year-old story, and he knew better than most that the system was still failing today. He also knew better than to let this sort of shit get to him. Getting emotional helped no one. It didn't make you a better cop. It meant clouded judgement, it meant that you looked for evidence to justify your feelings, instead of pursuing the facts. But this case got to him. Maybe it was because it was a case from his past. At twenty years old he'd had no tough outer skin.

His gear bag was in the boot of the car – he'd put it there on Monday morning but had gone to the pub after work instead of the gym. He didn't feel like the gym now either – it was in the basement of the station at Mill Street, and the last thing he needed was to encounter Brian Murphy – but he used its changing room, then took his frustration outside. Cormac cut down Dominick Street and over the canal, its water murky in the heavy weather. Then down Father Griffin Road and onwards until he reached the sea. It started raining as he ran along the prom, and the ever-present walkers thinned out. Cormac kept his pace up until his heart thundered and his breath was tight in his lungs. It was about four kilometres to Blackrock Diving Tower, and he pushed hard until he got there, then turned and took a slower pace back to the station. His knees were complaining, but otherwise he felt good. Better.

A quick shower and change at the station and he was back in the car, heading for home. His phone rang just as he pulled in and parked outside the little terraced house on Canal Road that he shared with Emma. The number was blocked.

'Reilly,' he said.

There was a bustle of conversation from the other end of the phone. Background noise of a phone ringing.

'Cormac?' a voice said. 'Hang on.' The background noise retreated as the voice changed locations. 'Cormac, you still there?' It was Matt, an old friend and colleague. He worked International Liaison – essentially Interpol – and had contacts in the United States. He owed Cormac a favour or two.

'Yeah. Still here, Matt.'

'I have something for you.'

'That was quick,' Cormac said.

'Yeah, well. It's getting harder to get information from that side of the world, since 9/11, but what you're looking for is pretty straightforward. Plain old uncomplicated murder.'

'Tell me.'

'You asked for anything that fit the profile between '75 and '85. There was a murder in 1983. Sixteen-year-old student, attended the St. Boniface School. She went to soccer practice as usual, never made it home. Body was found the next day. She'd been raped and strangled. Her boyfriend was the chief suspect – she'd told a friend she was planning on breaking it off – but he was cleared eventually. Wrong blood type.'

'Her body wasn't hidden?'

'I didn't ask,' Matt said. 'Does it matter?'

'Check something else for me?' Cormac asked.

Matt had no problem with that, and Cormac asked him to check if a Timothy Lanigan had been questioned in the disappearance. He almost rang off then, but something occurred to him.

'Matt, what's the word on the ground about Anthony Healy? Anything new?'

A pause. 'Why are you asking?' Was there caution in Matt's tone?

'He's working out of Galway, on the task force.'

'And?'

'And nothing. Something feels a little off there, that's all.'

'I haven't heard anything, Cormac, at least nothing more than the usual.' The usual was the stuff that had been floating around Healy for years. That Healy might be inclined to take the odd short cut, might have a fondness for pavement hostesses, as Cormac's old boss had called the working girls. That wasn't great. Apart from the fact that prostitution was illegal, there was an inequality about that relationship that turned Cormac's stomach.

'You sure?'

'Yeah. Cormac, sorry mate, I have to go.' And a moment later Cormac had dial tone in his ear.

By the time Cormac made his way to the house, he'd cooled down and started to feel stiff. He was hungry, and pleasantly surprised to open the door to the smell of dinner cooking.

'Em?' he called.

'Kitchen,' she called back, and he found her there, cheeks flushed, the room warm from the heat of the oven. She came forward for a hug and a kiss. Her hair was still damp from the shower. He held her close for a moment, breathed her in. When he let her go she turned back to the food she was preparing. Cormac sat and unlaced his boots.

'That smells fantastic,' he said. It did. Emma liked to cook, when she had time.

'It's my standard special, I'm afraid,' she said. 'You'll be sick of it, but I wanted to make something nice, and my imagination deserted me.'

'I wasn't expecting you.'

'Three late nights in a row is enough,' she said. Cormac got a wine glass from the cupboard, poured himself a glass from the bottle open on the kitchen table, then returned to his seat and watched her work. She was turning a lamb rack in the pan, browning it. She had already put potatoes in the oven, had herbed breadcrumbs ready. He watched her press the crust to the rack, every movement neat and precise, before putting the lot in the oven.

'Ta-daa!' she said, turning to him, picking up her own wine glass from the counter. 'Twenty minutes and we can eat.' She sat opposite him, reached one socked foot under the kitchen table and rested it on his lap.

'Work's going well?' he asked.

'Getting there. Lab's good to go. Interviews for the last two researcher positions start tomorrow. And I am taking the whole weekend off.' She made a face. 'I know I've been a bit useless lately. Total workaholic. But I promise things will settle down.' She kept talking, suggesting possible plans for the weekend ahead. Go to Dublin Friday evening, see some friends. There was a rugby match, if he fancied it he should go while she got some shopping in and they could meet for an early, boozy dinner after. Or if he didn't feel like the trip, maybe they'd just hang out in Galway? Do a bit more exploring.

Cormac was distracted, his mind wandering back to the Katherine Shelley interview as she spoke.

'What about Danny?' she asked. 'Did you ask him for dinner? We could have them here, if you like. Or just meet in town.'

'Not sure about that,' he said. 'I've asked him again, but he hasn't said whether or not he can do it.'

'Maybe Sarah doesn't want to. She doesn't know us. Maybe she'd rather just stay at home with her kids.'

'Maybe,' said Cormac. He wasn't going to tell her that he suspected Danny was cheating. He didn't want that image in her head, that cliché of the cheating cop using the job as an excuse every time he had to work nights.

Emma got up to check on the food, and the conversation died. Was she pissed off?

'I can ask him again,' he said.

'It doesn't matter,' she said. She started to put plates together, and he got up to help. He almost told her about Lorna McIntyre and the possibility that she was missing, but she'd already changed the subject and he didn't want to bring the mood down on what might be their only night in together this week. When they sat down to eat they talked about incidentals. They finished the first bottle, and Cormac took a second from the wine rack without really thinking about it. When he had sat down and poured for them both, he turned the conversation to the Blake case and Emma listened, her grey eyes serious.

'It was hard to listen to. Not that she didn't have a point. Worse things happen today, where something gets missed, or a child slips through the cracks. And this was twenty years ago. It's easy to forget how much has changed.'

'But,' Emma said.

Cormac grimaced. 'I don't know. It's hard to listen to from someone who was part of it, you know? She was too quick with the excuses.' They fell quiet for some time then, Cormac lost in his thoughts, Emma watching him. Eventually, she spoke.

'You don't usually talk about your cases,' she said. There was empathy in her eyes, and sadness. 'This one is different for you, isn't it?'

'Christ, Em,' he said. He got up and poured a glass of water from the tap, drank and turned to her. 'Sorry.' He smiled at her. 'Very dramatic.' So much for his plan to keep the mood upbeat.

She hesitated, then shrugged. 'I'd much rather know than not, if there's something on your mind. We don't have to talk about it. But it's better for me if you can tell me enough so that I understand at least a bit of what's going on with you, when things are difficult.'

If he told her a quarter of the shit he saw it would break her heart. She'd grown up in a house of privilege, and though she'd had her own trauma, it was different. One shocking, even horrific, incident did not undo a lifetime of love and care and plenty. Cormac reminded himself that he'd had more than his fair share of love and care himself, if not so much of the plenty.

'It's Jack,' he said. 'So many of the kids we see, even the ones who go into care – what they go through before we get to them. They never fully recover. Jack was one of the few kids to get out intact.' He stopped talking. Didn't want to finish the sentence.

'But if he committed suicide, even years later, it means none of them are safe,' she finished for him.

'Yeah.'

She nodded, then changed the subject. It shocked him sometimes, how well she knew him. She could delve straight into him, right to the centre, then pull back and move on before he realised she was there. They talked for a little longer, then went to bed. Emma turned to him with a warmth and desire that easily matched his own, and for a short time, the Blake case and station politics were washed clear from his mind. She fell asleep quickly afterwards, lying on her side with her face turned away from him, her body utterly limp and relaxed. He ran a hand down her back, her warm velvet-soft skin, and she sighed in her sleep. His eyes traced the scar that ran along her jaw. She'd had to have surgery to reset it. A fainter, spider-like scar started at the very edge of her forehead, and ran back under her hairline.

Emma shifted in the bed beside him, then sighed again and seemed to settle back into a deeper sleep. Cormac lay down on his back, one hand behind his head, and stared up at the ceiling. He had to find a way to make Galway work. He would take these shitty cases and make them shine. He was dropping off to sleep when his phone buzzed. A message from Matt, with a link. No subject, no text. He clicked on the link, and it brought him to the website of the *Independent*. Seconds later, he was looking at Healy's grinning face. In the photograph Healy was wearing a reflective garda vest and a hard hat, as he stood beside a front-loader that was pushing plastic-wrapped bags of something into the teeth of an incinerator. Cormac scrolled down to read the caption. *Gardaí destroy more than €2 million worth of drugs.* Scrolled down further to the article, which was dated 11 March 2012.

Detective Sergeant Anthony Healy watches as cannabis, crack cocaine and heroin, valued at more than 2 million euro, is incinerated. This enormous haul had been recovered from the North Dublin area by gardaí over the last six months. It was taken to a local incinerator by officers and destroyed today. 'Seizing these drugs has meant that we have stopped them getting onto the streets of Dublin,' said Detective Sergeant Anthony Healy. 'Today is the culmination of months of work. We need the help of the public if we are to continue to have this level of success. I urge people to use the confidential tip line if they have any suspicions about drug activity.'

Cormac turned off the screen and put his phone down, then lay back on his pillow and stared again at the ceiling. Matt had sent that for a reason, and it wasn't so that Cormac could admire Healy's sterling work. This was confirmation. Healy was up to something, and whatever it was had something to do with that drug haul. It was equally clear that Matt wasn't in a position to give him any more. Maybe there was an ongoing operation. No, if Cormac was going to do anything about Healy, he was going to have to do it alone.

Thursday 28 March 2013

CHAPTER EIGHTEEN

Cormac sat at his desk, typing up his meeting with Katherine Shelley and thinking about the text message he'd just received from Emma. She wanted to know if he was on for going to Dublin or not. He didn't want to go, and wasn't sure why. Maybe it was just that he didn't want to head back and see friends until he had stuff sorted out in Galway. The Blake case was moving forward, but he was following the slimmest of threads, which might snap at any moment. Going to Dublin would mean leaving early on Friday, and he didn't want to be out of the station right now. Something was going on with Healy, and whatever he was involved in had him under pressure.

There was a burst of laughter from the other side of the room. Healy was Mr Happy today, one joke after another. But his tension was evident in the set of his shoulders, and the glances he kept sending Danny's way.

Danny was sitting at his desk, head bent over his work, ignoring the craic and the messing around him. He hadn't been around at all for the last two days – Cormac had looked for him a couple of times, and when he hadn't found him had assumed that he'd gone to Dublin after all, to track down Lorna's elusive friend. The fact that he was back at his desk suggested that whatever he'd found in Dublin was good news. Cormac would drag him out for pints that evening, without Fisher, and check that all was okay, maybe push a bit more about Healy. In the meantime, he had work to do.

The meeting with Katherine Shelley hadn't brought much new information, once he'd had a chance to sit down and analyse it, but in a backwards sort of a way that was helpful. She had given him a different take on Mrs Keane, now the helpful neighbour, according to Katherine Shelley. Why had she wanted the children to stay with a mother who abused them? If she was that close, that present, she must have known what was going on. Tom Collins had been very sure that Keane was the one supplying the alcohol. It should have been counterintuitive, that whole story – that a religious woman would have interfered with social workers trying to care for those children, that she would have plied an alcoholic with booze. Somehow it wasn't. Somehow, it was utterly predictable. How much of his views about Catholic Ireland had been formed by the outpouring of stories of abuse over the past ten years, from the Magdalene Laundries to Brendan Smyth? Had he felt the same way – suspicious of all things religious – back in the nineties? He honestly couldn't remember.

He was still mulling this over when his phone buzzed, and a voice he didn't recognise told him that he was to report to Chief Inspector Murphy's office as soon as possible. Cormac gathered the file and his notebook, and left the room, climbing the stairs to Murphy's office. Murphy's aide, a female officer, waved him directly in.

Murphy listened politely enough while Cormac walked him through his work so far. It was premature for a briefing; he'd only had the case a few days. A review meeting this early smacked of micromanagement. What happened to 'preliminary report by Friday'? Murphy leaned back in his chair, allowing it to swivel slightly from side to side as he listened to Cormac. He had a pen in one hand, which he wiggled between two fingers, occasionally bringing it down on the desk and letting it play against the surface in a drumming motion that punctuated Cormac's report. It was distracting, as was the tension on Murphy's face. He waited until Cormac had gone through it all, right up to the social worker interview, Cormac's planned next steps, and his view that the investigation was, so far, not showing any signs that it would yield a suspect, let alone an arrest.

When he finished speaking, Murphy paused for effect, then sighed. 'That's it?'

'Yes sir,' said Cormac. 'There's not much there. I suppose, after twenty years, it's inevitable to some degree.'

But Murphy was shaking his head. 'And Detective Hackett hasn't spoken to you about the evidence her team's been able to uncover?'

Cormac had nothing to say. Melanie Hackett? Danny's boss? Danny reported to her when he wasn't seconded to the drugs unit. She was young, she was ambitious, and as far as he knew, she had nothing whatsoever to do with his case.

'I'll admit to being disappointed, Detective. I'd heard good things about you. But perhaps I expected too much.' Before Cormac had a chance to respond, Murphy pressed the intercom button. 'Send them in,' was all he said.

Cormac turned as the door opened, and watched as Danny and Melanie Hackett walked into the room. Murphy gestured for them to take the two remaining chairs, which necessitated an awkward shuffle over from Cormac, to allow Mel access to the chair in the middle. Mel gave him a nod, then ignored him, but Danny, who appeared for once both rested and reasonably well dressed – he was wearing slacks and a dark blue shirt with a navy Ralph Lauren pony on the left breast – looked at him and tried and failed to communicate a silent message. Cormac had no idea what was going on, but the signs weren't good.

Murphy nodded to Mel Hackett. 'Mel, perhaps you should fill Detective Reilly in on the assistance you can offer him with his case?'

When she spoke, Hackett addressed herself to Murphy. 'As you know sir, McIntyre has been seconded to Operation Sparrow.' She turned her attention to Cormac and spoke briefly. 'You may be aware that the task force is focused on possible drug-running routes into Europe from landings on the west coast of Ireland. Early on in the operation it focused on gathering information from our local lower level informants, in an attempt to confirm information provided by MAOC.' MAOC was the Lisbon-based Maritime Analysis and Operations Centre, staffed with law-enforcement personnel from European countries including Ireland. 'Garda McIntyre was aware of some of the details of DS Reilly's case. He knew that DS Reilly was searching for a source for heroin in Kilmore in 1993. McIntyre ran a search through PULSE, and came up with a name. A young woman from Kilmore was taken into custody in 1994. She was found in the company of a drug dealer in Castlebar, and was thought to be under age, so someone took her in, took her details. That was the first time she was picked up, but it wasn't the last.'

'And this woman's in prison now?' Murphy asked. 'Looking for early release in exchange for information?'

'Yes, sir.'

Murphy nodded, and gestured for Hackett to continue.

'I encourage everyone who reports to me to use their initiative,' Hackett said. 'And that is exactly what Garda McIntyre did. He ran her name through our database and found that she had provided information to Operation Sparrow in the past, though that information hadn't been useful. He decided that there was a chance she would have information that would be relevant to DS Reilly's operation. As it was something of a long shot he thought he would interview the informant himself before bringing any possible information to DS Reilly. His hunch paid off far better than he expected.'

'I was going to Dublin anyway,' Danny said hurriedly. 'Really, I didn't expect anything to come of it, or I would have brought it straight to DS Reilly. But I ...'

Hackett gave him a look that said 'shut the fuck up' as clearly as if she'd said the words aloud.

'So you brought that information to me,' Murphy said to Hackett. His tone was on the dry side of neutral, and she flushed slightly. 'You didn't think this information would be best provided directly to DS Reilly?'

'I ... DS Reilly wasn't at his desk, sir, when the information came to me, and I thought it best that I provide it to you without delay.'

Cormac kept his expression bland, uninterested, but inside he was cursing himself. He'd underestimated the hostility towards him in the station, and he was about to pay for that mistake.

'Well, he's here now,' Murphy said.

Hackett hesitated, then turned to Cormac. 'The informant's name is Hannah Collins. She grew up in Kilmore. Her younger brother was, as I understand it, very close to your suspect.'

'You're talking about Thomas Collins,' said Cormac, his voice flat.

'Hannah Collins was arrested last year. She's an addict, her boyfriend's a dealer. The boyfriend beat up another addict who owed him money. Hannah was involved. She was convicted of conspiracy to commit GBH, and sentenced to five years. She's served just under a year. McIntyre, will you please report the substance of your interview with Hannah Collins?'

Danny cleared his throat. He didn't look at Cormac. 'Uh ... I was aware from conversations with DS Reilly that he was investigating a suspicious death in Kilmore in the nineties. The victim died from a heroin overdose. As DS Hackett said,

I found Hannah's name on PULSE, figured that if she was doing drugs in Kilmore in '94, there was a reasonable chance that she might know where DS Reilly's suspect could have bought heroin in 1993. I saw she was in prison, I ran her name through the Operation Sparrow database, and found she'd been an informant once before.' Danny shrugged. He looked miserable. 'I thought it would be worth visiting her while I was there, see if she had any idea who would have been supplying heroin locally back in the day.' Danny shifted his weight awkwardly. 'I would have spoken to DS Reilly first, but as DS Hackett said, I thought it was a bit of a long shot.'

'A long shot worth taking, it seems,' Murphy said.

'Yes sir.'

Shit. There was nothing Cormac could do but sit back and watch it coming.

Danny continued. 'Hannah's given a statement. She says that Maude Blake came to her directly to ask her to procure heroin for her. Hannah introduced Maude to her boyfriend at the time, who sold heroin to Maude. Two days later, Hilaria Blake died of an overdose.'

Cormac finally escaped the office fifteen minutes later. It was agreed that Hannah Collins's statement would be passed to him by Danny and Mel. He was to get full copies of Hilaria Blake's medical records, assuming that they hadn't been destroyed. And then he was to bring Maude in for questioning. He didn't go far, just walked to the end of the corridor and waited at the corner. As he'd suspected, Danny got the boot shortly afterwards. Murphy wanted to speak with Melanie Hackett alone. Cormac gave Danny a jerk of the head, then turned and walked down the stairs and out of the station, not looking to see if Danny would follow. He turned left at the steps and walked into the carpark, waited.

'Hannah Collins,' Cormac said when Danny reached him. 'Is this bullshit, Dan? Why is it this smells of bullshit to me?'

'Christ, Cormac, I'm sorry.'

'I don't want to hear about sorry. You could have called me forty times since yesterday, and you chose not to.'

'It wasn't like that. I couldn't call you last night because my phone died. By the time I got out of Dóchas it was dead as a doornail. And I got back too late. I wasn't bothered about it because I figured I'd see you this morning and I'd tell you then.'

'Danny, you were sitting at your desk all morning. You could have given me a heads up at any time.'

Danny grimaced. 'Hackett was waiting for me when I got in. I'd told Healy that I had to go to Dublin to work on something for her. Look, I've no holidays left. I had to take the time, Lorna's friend hadn't called me back all week, and no one who knows her knew anything about a music festival. They all thought Lorna was coming home for the weekend.'

Christ. Cormac blew out a long breath.

'Hackett was all over me, she was going to put me on report. I can't afford to have her pissed off with me too. You know I'm on the outs with the task force. If Hackett won't work with me I'm fucked. And I just moved the family to Galway. So I told her about the Collins thing, to get her off my back.'

'Did you find her?'

'Lorna's friend? Yes.' Danny's face was grim. 'I found her and it was all bullshit. Lorna never said anything about a music festival. She just said she had because when she saw on social media that Lorna's family were looking for her, she assumed Lorna was up to something she didn't want to share with us. She lied, stupid bitch, because she thought Lorna would appreciate a bit of cover. It was only when Lorna never called her back, never answered her messages, that she realised something more might be going on, and then she started to freak out. Went to ground.'

Cormac said nothing. He was still angry with Danny for throwing him under the bus, but at the same time what Danny was dealing with was far more serious than a career ... what? Blip? Danny should have told Hackett the truth about what was going on.

Cormac felt an overwhelming urge to hit someone, and it wasn't just because of the politics.

'Hannah Collins, she's motivated?'

'What?'

'Hackett said she'd tried to peddle information before, but it wasn't useful. Now she's selling out an old friend. What's her motivation?'

Danny had the grace to look embarrassed. 'She's had a baby. While she's been inside. Baby's ten months old.'

'Jesus, Dan.'

'I know. But Cormac, I'm telling you, she just came out with all of this stuff. It was too detailed, too fast. It has to be true.'

'And you offered her the deal?'

'I didn't commit, but I hinted at it.'

Dóchas, the women's prison attached to Mountjoy, was overcrowded and underfunded. Drug abuse was rampant. Women who came to Dóchas pregnant, or with a young infant, were allowed to keep their babies with them until they were twelve months old. Then the baby had to be taken from the prison, into the care of a family member, or if that wasn't possible, to foster care. If Hannah Collins had a baby, and wanted to keep it, she could not have better motivation to lie about what had happened twenty years before.

'Danny, this information is shaky at best. I don't care how fast she came up with the story.' Hannah Collins had read Danny, and had played him, Cormac was sure of it. 'Hackett going straight to Murphy with this was out of line. It was fucking unprofessional.'

Danny glanced back towards the station. 'She would never have come to you. I should have copped that from the beginning.'

There was a sudden bustle at the station door, voices in conversation. It was a group of young uniforms coming off shift. Cormac became aware of his stance, and his expression, and he consciously relaxed his posture. If the uniforms were curious about the conversation they didn't show it, studiously keeping their attention on each other as they walked to the other end of the carpark.

'Why?' asked Cormac. 'Why wouldn't Hackett come to me?'

Danny shook his head slowly, looked at him watchfully. 'There's a rumour going around,' Danny said. 'About you and Maude Blake. Someone saw you leaving her hotel room on Tuesday morning. Very early.'

Cormac's mouth fell open. He stood there, gaping, for what felt like minutes. Then the fury barrelled through him.

'Are you fucking kidding me?' he hissed. 'I got the case on Monday. Went to the pub with you and Fisher, in case you've forgotten. But somehow I end up in bed with Maude Blake, someone I first met as a victim, as a *child* – my fucking suspect – a couple of hours later.'

Danny shrugged, looked away. 'I went home early,' he said. 'Left you to it.'

Jesus Christ. Cormac had never wanted to hit someone as much as he wanted to hit Danny in that moment. He shoved his hands in his pockets.

'I'm not saying anything happened,' Danny said. 'Personally, I don't believe it, and I told them that. But people know about you and Emma. They're saying you have form.'

Cormac felt the rage burn up through him, a flash of fury so intense that for a moment his vision darkened. He hid it all behind a gentle shake of his head, a sardonic smile.

'Jesus, you must be shy of something to talk about in this part of the world.' He rocked back on his heels. 'Where did the rumour start, Dan?' he asked.

Danny shook his head unhappily. 'I don't know. By the time I heard it half the squad was talking about it.'

'And Emma? Our history? That isn't common knowledge.'

But now Danny's eyes were impatient. 'Cormac, it's the bloody Garda Síochána. Half the country probably knew about that after your first date.'

Cormac's phone started to ring and he took it from his pocket, checked the screen. It was Matt, calling him back. Maybe with information about Anthony Healy. Cormac muted the call.

'Tell me, Dan,' he said, keeping his tone conversational. 'What's the story with Healy?'

'What?' Danny looked confused, wrongfooted by the turn in the conversation.

'Don't bullshit me. I know there's something going on. Healy's worried about you. I want to know why.'

Danny stared back at him. His face was completely blank. 'Nothing's happened. He doesn't like me, I don't like him. It's a personality clash, that's all.'

'That's not what you said last time we spoke about this. You said you couldn't talk then for fear of the backlash. But I'm telling you Dan, if you know something, now's the time to come out with it.'

Danny grimaced, a tight twist of his mouth. 'I'm on the outs because Healy has no respect for anyone outside the unit. He doesn't want locals on the team, doesn't want us screwing up his good work. That's it.'

Danny's expression oozed sincerity. He was a good liar.

If Healy hadn't been so obvious, Cormac might even have believed him.

Danny checked his watch. 'I have to go,' he said. 'I have to meet my parents. Fill them in on what's being done to find Lorna.' His expression was bleak. 'I don't know if they'll ever forgive me for getting it so wrong.'

Christ. Cormac felt completely off balance. He was having a go when Danny was trying to process the fact that the sister he'd thought was on the tear had in fact been missing for nearly two weeks now, was in God only knew what sort of trouble, while he'd been running around doing everything possible to slow the work of the team looking for her. 'I'm sorry, Danny. If there's anything I can do, you'll ask me?'

Danny shook his head. 'Do one thing for me, Cormac. Just take another look at your case, will you? The look on your face in there, when you heard about Hannah's statement. I'm worried that you have blinders on about this woman. Maybe she's not the innocent victim she was when you met her. Maybe she was never the innocent victim.'

Cormac said nothing, and Danny shook his head in exasperation.

'Do you know when she came back to Ireland?' Danny asked. 'It wasn't for the funeral. Her flight landed in Ireland on the thirteenth of March, three days before her brother died.'

And that hit Cormac, hard. For the first time he realised how badly he wanted Maude to be innocent. How convinced of her innocence he was.

'Just think about it, Cormac, okay?' Danny said. Then he turned, and walked back into the station. Cormac followed a moment later, returned to his desk just long enough to grab his coat and his notebook, and got out of there.

He was dialling Emma's number before he'd gone ten metres from the station.

'Em?'

'Hi. Yeah, hang on just two seconds.' Then, a moment later, 'So, what do you think? Will we go?'

It took him a moment to remember what she was talking about, another to realise that he had called her without thinking, to pour out the story to her, to find reassurance and comfort in her support. Christ. Emma couldn't fix this, and dumping it all on her would be a shitty thing to do.

'Cormac?'

'Yeah, Em, sorry. I can't go away this weekend. Just rang to tell you. Things are picking up at the station, I may have to work.'

'Oh. But that's good, isn't it? Something's happening on the case?'

Cormac was crossing over the bridge, the wind whipped her words away. He cupped the bottom of his phone with his other hand, pressed it to his ear.

'Yeah, lots happening. We'll go next weekend, all right?'

Even with the wind he could pick up the relief in her voice, the lightness in her tone when she agreed, and suggested alternative plans for their weekend. A late breakfast together on Saturday, before he started work. If he was going to work then maybe she would too, and then perhaps they could go out to eat afterwards. He agreed with everything, his mind already elsewhere. He said his goodbyes and was about to hang up when she spoke again.

'Corm? Is everything all right, really?'

He hesitated. 'Everything's fine, Em. Got to run.'

Cormac hung up, and put his phone back in his pocket. It was the first time he had lied to her. Well, the first time about anything that mattered. Was that true? Hadn't he lied to her about the move to Galway? No. He'd been okay with that, genuinely. Convinced that he'd be able to make it work. How wrong he had been. Someone in the station wanted to take him down, and it went beyond petty professional jealousy, didn't it? That rumour about Maude Blake, that was dangerous. That was a career killer. And there was fuck all he could do about it. If he responded to it he gave it life, legitimacy. And if he ignored it, it would fester. Cormac stopped, realising that he had walked halfway up Shop Street with no destination in mind. He wasn't ready to return to the station, not until he'd had a chance to think everything through. He was standing directly outside Elles Cafe. Food might help. Coffee definitely would.

He went inside, ignoring the queue at the take-away counter. He ordered coffee and a sandwich, and found a seat at the back of the room. The tables were small, the chairs delicate. He settled himself gingerly into a chair not designed for a six-foot-three, one-hundred-and-ninety-pound man. His legs barely fit under the table. The café was busy. Background music and the chatter of multiple conversations blocking out individual voices. Cormac took out his notebook, flicked back through the pages. He thought best with a pen in his hand, a piece of paper in front of him. He had orders to bring Maude Blake in for questioning. But he wasn't ready. It was too soon.

Was there a chance that Danny was right? Did he have blinkers on when it came to this case? He flicked back through his notes, following the logic of his investigation so far. No. It was bullshit. If Danny, or anyone else for that matter, thought that he was missing or ignoring evidence because he was convinced of Maude's innocence, they were wrong.

'How ya.'

He looked up. 'Detective O'Halloran.'

She took the seat opposite him without waiting for an invitation. She was wearing a black rain jacket. Her curly hair was damp and tousled by the wind. She was eating an apple; she took a small bite, chewed and swallowed. 'I worked with a friend of yours last year, on a sex-trafficking thing. Séan Hegarty. You know him, right?' She didn't wait for his response. 'I called him up, asked about you. He said you're good at your job.' The expression on Carrie's face said she had trouble believing it.

'I'll have to thank Séan, next time I see him,' said Cormac. He didn't say that Séan had said the same about her.

She took another bite of her apple, chewed, waited for him to fill the silence. Cormac took a bite from his sandwich, chewed and washed it down with coffee. Said nothing.

'You're good friends with McIntyre, aren't you?' Carrie said, eventually. Cormac raised an eyebrow.

'Known him a long time, have you? Old school friends, is that the story?'

'We were in Templemore at the same time,' Cormac said.

'Stayed in touch over the years? Meet up regularly with the wives, the kids, that sort of thing?' Her eyes strayed to Cormac's left hand, where she clocked the absence of a wedding ring.

'I wouldn't say that, no,' said Cormac. Her questions had the rhythm of an interrogation. He could tell her to fuck off, but he was curious to see where she was going. She was interesting, too. Something about the brightness of her eyes, the birdlike cock of her head.

'He's had a bit of a hard time lately, your friend.'

Cormac laughed. 'Fair to say you've had something to do with that.'

'He's told you she's at a music festival, hasn't he? In Wales.'

'That's what he thought. Not anymore.'

'Because of the mystery friend, right? The mystery friend that no one else has spoken to, that no one else has ever heard of.'

Cormac had his sandwich halfway to his mouth. He put it down. 'What are you saying?'

'Only that I tried the number Danny gave me. It was a pay as you go mobile, and it hasn't been switched on in two weeks. Not a single ping. How many twenty-year-olds do you know who can do without their phone that long?'

'You think Danny made her up. Why?'

'To stop the search for his sister.'

Cormac shook his head. 'That's ridiculous. Why would Danny do that? Even if he ... there'd be no point to it. The best he would achieve is to delay the search, not stop it.'

'I know.' She spread her hands wide. 'It's a mystery.'

Cormac sat back in his chair. 'What exactly do you think happened to her?'

'Lorna's been living with an aunt in Dublin. She went home for a weekend visit, for Paddy's Day, never came back. I know Lorna, from an incident last year. When the aunt reported her as a missing person the case came to me.'

'And you've run with it.'

A flash of anger crossed her face and was gone. She placed her apple core neatly on the table, balanced on one end.

'Maybe you should ask him about it yourself,' she said.

'Ask him what? Danny went to Dublin, he found the friend. Who wasn't calling him back either, by the way. He found her and she finally told him the truth. Now Danny's doing everything he can to make things right.'

She smiled. A quick, happy smile, incongruous to the situation.

'He does seem to be, doesn't he? Still, he could probably use a friend. Might be best to stay close to him. Might take your mind off your own problems.' She stood, slapped the table briskly. 'Enjoy your lunch, detective. And best of luck with your case.'

'O'Halloran.'

She'd taken a few steps away, but stopped when she heard her name, turned inquiring eyes towards him. She wasn't what he had been expecting. He wanted to ask her why she'd come to him, what she expected him to do. She obviously had a theory, and he wanted to push her to share it. He wanted to ask too about the tension he'd felt at the station, if she knew what was going on with Anthony Healy. But all of that would take trust, and he barely knew her. He shook his head, returned his attention to his meal.

'I didn't believe it, if that's what you're wondering,' she said.

And she was gone.

Friday 29 March 2013

CHAPTER NINETEEN

He had his orders and the clock was ticking. He wasn't ready to bring Maude in for formal questioning, but he wanted to take her temperature, get a read. First thing Friday morning he called to the hotel, asked for her at the front desk, but there was no answer from her room. He left a message and his mobile number. She might call him. If not he would call back at the end of the day. After that he went to the office, caught up on messages, tried to find Danny, but he wasn't at his desk and he wasn't answering his phone. After what he'd found in Dublin he might have taken some time off, might be with his family.

Cormac drove out of Galway on the Moycullen Road, in the direction of Kilmore. It was a two-hour drive, but there was one person he hadn't spoken to yet who might be able to provide some answers. Domenica Keane was still alive. Still alive and living in the same house, a bungalow no more than a kilometre from the driveway that led to the old Dower House. In Cormac's memory, the old house was totally isolated. But then memory played tricks, and perhaps over time his mind had forgotten some details, dramatised others. Based on Katherine Shelley's description, Cormac thought Keane must be in her seventies at least, and possibly older. A phone call to the local post office – despite the digital age, still one of the best ways of getting information in rural areas – had confirmed that Domenica Keane was still receiving letters at her old address. The postmistress had not been particularly garrulous, and subtle and not so subtle questioning had yielded no more information than that. He didn't like going in raw, with so little preparation.

It was after three before he left Galway. He called Danny's mobile twice along the way, but it went to voicemail. Carrie O'Halloran had started something. He was aware that the part of his mind that wasn't occupied with the Blake case was nagging away at him, demanding that he give more attention to what O'Halloran had said. She hadn't hidden her dislike of Danny, but she still hadn't struck him at all as the woman Danny had described, as someone motivated by personal dislike. He needed to think about that, about what it might mean.

As Cormac pulled up outside the Keane house he saw a woman leaving, pulling the door shut behind her. She was too young to be Domenica Keane, in her mid-thirties if he had to hazard a guess. She was dressed comfortably in jeans and a fleece jacket. Her dark hair was escaping from a ponytail, the wind blowing it about her face.

'Hello,' he said, as he shut the car door behind him.

'Hello yourself,' she said, and waited near the door for his approach.

'I wanted to see Domenica. Is she in?'

The woman nodded. 'She's in the kitchen.' A pause, during which she gave him a friendly look over. 'She didn't mention that she was expecting visitors.'

'Is that the kind of thing she would mention?' Cormac asked.

The woman laughed, a warm and genuine sound. 'You'd better believe it,' she said. 'Are you a relative?'

Her eyes were still assessing, and Cormac thought she knew already that he wasn't. He shook his head. 'I'm not. I'm a guard. I need to ask Domenica a few questions. Nothing to worry anyone, just a bit of ancient history.'

She nodded slowly, her eyes still considering.

'Are you a friend of hers?' he asked. 'Do you think she'd be up to a few questions?'

The woman extended her hand for a shake. 'I'm Caoimhe O'Neill,' she said. 'Public health nurse. I'm here most days.'

'She's not well?'

'Just dressing changes. Leg ulcer. Not unusual for a woman her age.'

'Right,' Cormac said. 'She'll be all right for a few questions?'

Caoimhe blew out her breath. 'If you mean is she senile, then no she's not. If you mean will she tell you the truth, I wouldn't count on it.'

Cormac laughed himself now. 'A garda can never count on that one.'

She rolled her eyes. 'My husband's a guard. I never get tired of hearing about it.'

The wind was a little higher now, and a light drizzle had started. Cormac would have moved forward but she continued.

'I'm not joking,' she said. 'You'd want to watch yourself with her.'

'Sorry?'

'I'm telling you to watch yourself with her. She's dangerous.'

Cormac was smiling now, waiting for the punchline. 'Does she keep a pistol under her cushion?' he asked.

The woman, Caoimhe, rolled her eyes again. She took a phone from the pocket of her jacket, and held up the screen so he could see it. 'See this?' she asked. 'It's set to record. It's always set to record while I'm in that house. I'm not the first public health nurse to be assigned to Miss Keane. The last one ended up being transferred because she made a complaint.'

'Which was?'

'She went to the guards claiming that the girl assaulted her. Keane had a black eye and a split lip. The girl, she was only a young one. A midwife really, not a public health nurse, and just out of training college. It's hard to get fully trained public health nurses out here. But she was a nice girl. Loved her job, very enthusiastic.'

Cormac glanced towards the house. It was early evening, but so overcast that the light had been sucked out of the day. The windows were dark, hostile. The house looked empty, but he knew it wasn't, and he was conscious that the conversation they were having would be better had elsewhere. He didn't have time. He wasn't going to drag this thing out any more than he absolutely had to. He wanted it done.

'You don't think she did it.'

'Not a chance.'

'Was the girl charged?'

'Yes, but in the end Domenica dropped the charges. Afterwards the girl was suspended, and she went home to her parents.'

'Why would she make it up, if the girl did nothing wrong? And where did she get the black eye?'

Caoimhe shook her head, glanced back over her shoulder at the house. 'Honestly? I think she did it to herself. It would have been worth it to her. She would have seen it as taking the girl down a peg or two. Domenica doesn't like happy people. I think what she wanted was to damage that girl's confidence, to poison her enthusiasm for helping people.' Caoimhe walked to her car and opened the passenger door to put her bag inside.

'If you're right, she sounds like a lovely person,' Cormac said.

She turned to him. 'I think she's a sociopath,' she said, matter of factly. 'So remember that, and watch yourself.' She held her phone up again and wiggled it at him.

He nodded. 'Thanks for your help,' he said.

She was walking around her car to the driver's door. 'Not a bother.' She smiled at him. 'Good luck with whatever you're after.' A last smile, and a wave, and as she reversed down the drive he felt absurdly bereft. As he approached the front door he wasn't thinking about the interview ahead, but that Caoimhe O'Neill's husband, whoever he was, was doing all right for himself.

He rang the doorbell and waited. Rang a second time. He could hear movement from within the house, but it was a full ten minutes before the door opened slowly to a gap of a couple of inches, as wide as permitted by a security chain firmly in place. The woman standing inside the door peered through the gap, but said nothing. She was a little stooped with age, but tall nevertheless. Very tall for a woman, not quite his six foot three but she wouldn't have been far off it. Cormac held his ID up to her.

'Mrs Keane, I'm Detective Sergeant Cormac Reilly. I'd like to speak with you about something if you can spare a few minutes.'

'You'll have to wait while I get my glasses. I can't read anything without them.' She closed the door. The minutes ticked by, and he began to feel the cold. Cormac checked his watch. He wanted to get back to Galway in time to have a late dinner with Emma. He would interview Maude the next day, but not before speaking with a police doctor about the postmortem report. He wanted to get a clearer picture of what condition Hilaria had been in, given the advanced stage of her disease. And maybe the Keane interview – if she ever came back and opened the bloody door – would give him something to work with, an angle to take with the questioning. He had to keep a momentum going, or this case would slip out of his hands. Murphy wanted an arrest. If Maude had murdered her mother, Murphy would have to get it. But there would be no arrest without evidence to support a prosecution, at least not while it was his case and his decision to make. If he hoped to find evidence to prove Maude's innocence, that wouldn't stop him asking the right questions.

He stamped his feet to warm them and tucked his hands into his armpits. She'd probably lost her glasses, or maybe even forgotten he was there. He knocked again, twice, but it was another five minutes before she opened the door again, glasses on this time, and held out her hand for his ID. He held it up for her, and she took his wrist and pulled it towards her through the crack in the door, with more strength than he would have expected.

'Special Detective Unit,' she read slowly. He still had his old badge; hadn't made the effort to get it changed. He'd kept his gun too, had never returned it when he left the SDU. More detectives were carrying now, even outside the units, and he'd assumed he'd be one of them. Either the powers that be felt the same way, or they'd simply forgotten to ask. Keane hadn't released his wrist, and he didn't like to pull away, for fear he would unbalance her. Her lips were red and unpleasantly wet, and his eyes were drawn to them as she spoke. 'And what are the likes of you doing down here?'

'I'd like to speak with you about something that happened a number of years ago. The death of Hilaria Blake. Do you remember her?'

Domenica Keane's eyes were still sharp under drooping upper lids. They brightened on hearing Hilaria's name. 'Of course I remember her. Poor, poor dear.'

Cormac pulled his wrist slowly, but firmly, away from her. She resisted the pressure for a moment, then released him. She pushed the door closed, slid the security chain aside, and opened it.

'Come in, detective,' she said. He entered a hall carpeted in pale peach, the carpet thinning in the centre. The walls were papered in a flowered pattern up to a low timber dado rail, and painted a paler peach above the rail. The décor was so like that of his grandparents' old home in West Cork that it was disconcerting. But this house, for all its superficial similarities, had none of the warmth of his grandparents' place. It smelled stale and unused. Domenica Keane gestured towards a door at the end of the hall, and he turned and walked towards it, only to stop and wait for her as he realised that her progress was slow. She walked with a shuffling gait, hands clasped in front of her and eyes downcast, as if she was in a state of permanent worry. He waited for her to draw almost level with him, then he opened the door and stepped inside the room, holding the door open for her.

The kitchen was unpleasantly hot and stuffy. There was an old-fashioned three-bar gas heater at the other end of the room. He hadn't seen one like it in years, but the thing obviously still worked, it was blasting out enough heat for a room three times the size.

Domenica Keane settled herself into an armchair that had been placed at the side of the kitchen table, facing the door. She gestured for him to take a seat, and he pulled out a kitchen chair and turned it so that he could face her.

'It's Miss,' she said, as he took his notebook from his pocket.

'I'm sorry?' he said.

'You said Mrs Keane. At the door. But I've never married. I think accuracy is important, don't you? Certainly to a detective, I would have thought.'

'That's right, Miss Keane. My apologies.'

'I expect you think that all ladies of my generation married at some point or the other. Unless of course they were utterly unmarriageable. Which I was not. But that wouldn't be accurate, detective. There were plenty of women of my generation who made their own way in the world. Some of them foolishly and wantonly, it should be said. But some of us had a higher calling, and marriage would have been a distraction.' She spoke very slowly and deliberately, but her voice was clear and strong and held no quaver. As she spoke she let her eyes drift to a framed photograph hung on the wall. It was a close up of a woman in her thirties, with strong features and a muscular jaw line, dressed in what looked like a wimple.

'You were a member of a religious order?'

She inclined her head. She must have been very strong when she was younger. The hands she clasped lightly together in her lap were unusually large for a woman, and although she must have lost body weight and muscle tone as she'd aged, he could see hints of her former self in the shape of her shoulders.

'Miss Keane, I'd like to ask you some questions about Hilaria Blake. You've said that you remember her.'

She tilted her head to one side. 'I do remember her. Poor dear woman. Such a terrible waste.'

'You mean her alcoholism.'

'Do I?' Domenica Keane was smiling gently at him.

Cormac suppressed a flair of irritation and smiled back at her. 'You were aware that Hilaria Blake was an alcoholic?'

'Oh, I wouldn't say that, detective. I'd say she liked a little drink, but who could blame her. She was lonely I'm sure. Her husband left her to raise two children alone. Terribly difficult thing to do in that day and age.'

'Hilaria Blake was not married, Miss Keane. And her children had two different fathers.'

'Oh dear. It seems she misled me.' But Domenica Keane kept smiling. Her mouth was wet, her lips slightly parted.

'I understand that you were quite close to Hilaria. That you visited her. That you provided support to the family.'

'My Christian duty.'

'Did you object when Children and Family Services wanted to take Maude and Jack into care?'

'A disgrace.'

'I'm sorry?'

'Taking children from their natural mother. That is an action against God. If God had intended Hilaria to be childless, he wouldn't have sent her those two beautiful children.' She stretched the word out ... beeee–yoooo–tiful. From her mouth it sounded obscene.

'But you do understand that the children were abused?'

'Abuse. What nonsense. They may have had to wait for a meal or two from time to time. I can tell you when I grew up that was just a normal day. Hilaria loved her children. She cared for them well. If they didn't have hundreds of toys ... Well. That is hardly abuse.'

'It was quite a bit worse than that, Miss Keane. Jack Blake was beaten, his sister too. They were badly neglected. Jack was malnourished. I would think that is the result of something more serious than a few late meals.'

She gave him another slow, deliberate smile. 'Well, you're certainly entitled to your opinion, detective.'

'You spent time with the family?'

'Yes. Hilaria and I used to pray together.'

'You were at the house regularly then?' And at her nod, 'You never saw signs of abuse?'

'I remember that the little boy was forever falling down. Clumsy little thing. But no, no abuse at all.'

'How often did you visit the family?'

She tilted her head to one side. On her it was the most artificial gesture – as if she'd seen other people do it and had chosen to imitate. 'Almost every day. Except Monday when I did the church flowers.'

Cormac turned back some pages in his notebook.

'Jack Blake was examined at the hospital after his mother's death. He was found to have numerous healed fractures. Three ribs had been fractured at least once. He'd suffered a broken tibia, and fibula. Two fingers on his left hand had also been broken. He had burns to his left shoulder.' Cormac looked up at her. 'In all your daily visits to the house you never saw any evidence of these injuries?'

She tutted. 'Clumsy. Little. Boy.' She enunciated each word clearly, but it was her smile that made his anger roar. He was careful to show nothing. He wouldn't give the bitch the satisfaction.

'You were aware of course that Hilaria Blake died of a heroin overdose?'

'Did she indeed? Well isn't that shocking?'

'Yes. Although she was dying in any case. You must have known that she had very advanced liver failure.'

'Are you quite sure you are supposed to be sharing all this information with me, detective? I must say, it seems very indiscreet.' She made a show of looking at her watch, then distractedly around the room. 'Did you have a question for me at all?'

'Nearly finished, Miss Keane. Just another question or two and I'll leave you in peace.' Cormac paused. He was working on instinct now. The truism that a lawyer should never ask a question to which he did not already know the answer did not apply to detectives. If anything the opposite rule applied. You had a plan going into every interrogation, but sometimes it was best to follow your instinct, and his instinct was screaming at him that Domenica Keane knew something. 'There is one question I'd very much like your help on. I understand that there may have been other visitors to the house. Members of your prayer group, perhaps?'

Domenica Keane snickered, as if he had told her an off-colour joke. 'Of course. Hilaria was someone who had strayed from God's side. She knew that, and our little group was always willing to do whatever hard work was required to bring someone back to God's loving arms.'

'Who, exactly?'

'I'm sorry?'

'Other than yourself, which members of your prayer group visited the Blake home?'

'Well, let me think,' the old woman said, again tilting her head to the side. 'Do you know, I think I'm having some trouble recalling the details. It was all such a very long time ago.'

Cormac made a show of looking back to an earlier page of his notebook, of taking a further note. 'I must say I'm surprised, Miss Keane.' She didn't respond. 'Your memory has been very clear so far. But perhaps you just need some time to think? To remember?' He looked at her with cool dispassion. She was old, and she was evil, but she wasn't so different from a hundred others he'd sat opposite in an interview room. People like Domenica Keane were too clever. They lied when they should stay quiet. They thought ahead, saw the risks, and moved to tie them off. They could never quite see how the slow setting down of questions and noting of answers could drive them into a trap of their own making.

She was waiting. Watching. Her eyes still amused but a little careful.

'There wasn't someone in particular? Someone other than yourself who developed a friendship with Hilaria Blake?'

'Well now, let me think.' She made a show of putting a finger to her lips. Tap. Tap. Tap. 'I suppose there was Simon ... what was his name again? Smith? No, a German name. Most unusual. Schmidt. Something like that, perhaps.'

'Schmidt,' Cormac said, his tone flat. He tried the notebook trick again, turning back a page and making a show of checking something.

'I think that was it, but I'm such a very old lady, detective. I really can't be sure of anything.'

'Tell me about him.'

'I don't recall much, I'm afraid. Simon was part of our group for only a short time. He was a teacher, if I remember correctly. Taught at the primary school I believe.'

Cormac's confidence that he had found something dropped. Hard to see a primary school teacher as a drug dealer. But there was definitely something here. She was watchful now. 'Did he move on?'

'I'm sorry?'

'You said he wasn't with your group very long. Why did he leave?'

Domenica shook her head. 'Who can say what tempts people from the arms of the Lord, detective? It's not something I've ever understood.'

'Right. You introduced Simon to the family?'

'I really don't recall.'

'But you knew him?'

'We had similar interests, certainly, while he was a member of our little group. I believe he was very involved in charitable causes. Such a good man. So very caring. Particularly good with children.'

Cormac thought back to the night he had taken the children from the house. He thought of the cold, the squalor, their pinched little faces. There had been no evidence of care there.

'How long had Simon been helping the family?'

'I really can't recall, detective.'

'What help exactly did he provide?'

'It's such a long time ago. And really, I can't be sure I ever knew. Simon was very much his own man.'

'I see. Can you recall which charities, exactly, Mr Schmidt was involved with?'

'Something to do with children. Possibly a food drive?' She yawned, making no attempt to cover her mouth. 'Oh dear. I'm really feeling quite, quite tired. It seems you have worn me out, detective.'

He got no further after that. Her answers got vaguer, and started to wander into old memories that had little relevance to the Blakes. He felt sure that her sudden senility was an act, but equally didn't know what else, if anything, he could hope to get from her. He also had a sudden and raging headache. She was lying about Simon Schmidt, that much was obvious. About his name at least, if not about more. Why? What was she hiding? He would need to find the man. Someone in the village might remember him, or at the school. A primary school teacher with a German-sounding surname should be remembered. Cormac stopped asking questions and let the silence sit while he took a moment to finish his notes. When he glanced up Domenica Keane's eyes were half closed, as if she were drifting off to sleep. He closed his notebook and stood, speaking loudly.

'I'll say goodbye so, Miss Keane.'

She gave what he was sure was a faked start of surprise, putting a large hand to her chest.

'Oh, detective, I was nearly asleep. I always have a nice little nap at this time of day. I'm sure you can see yourself out?' She smiled her unpleasant smile, dragging her thin lips over teeth that were too big for her mouth. Cormac wondered what she had looked like when Maude and Jack knew her. He thought she would have been a frightening sight for a child.

The interview with Keane left a bad taste in Cormac's mouth, and there wasn't much he could do about it. He breathed in fresh air outside the house, and felt his headache ease. He had a two-hour drive back to Galway ahead of him. It would be after eight before he got back. He felt more confident after the Keane interview. There was a story here. He had a hold on this case now and he wasn't going to let it go.

Keane knew something. Collins knew something. He'd worked with less in the past. The next step was to track down the German. What had really been going on between Hilaria, Keane and that mystery man? It sure as hell hadn't been prayer. He felt more confident in Maude's innocence. There was a bigger story here, and he meant to get to the bottom of it. Hannah Collins was not a reliable witness. And he'd been there that night himself, was the closest thing to a real witness there was, perhaps. There'd been no anger in Maude, no fear. She had just been sad, sad to the bone. Her disappearance added something to the picture, that was true, but Cormac was inclined to put that down to trauma, or, it occurred to him as he drove, her instinct to protect Jack. She'd wanted him adopted, hadn't she? She had known that the chances were much smaller if she was in the picture. He thought of that sad smile he'd seen in the rear-view mirror all those years before, and a piece of the puzzle clicked into place. Why hadn't he seen it then? Maybe he had, maybe it had occurred to him and he'd filed the idea away, and it had gotten buried under a thousand other ideas, other memories, over the years.

Cormac was driving into Oughterard when his phone rang. He flipped the phone to speaker, hit accept, and balanced the phone in his lap as he drove. Fisher's voice came from the speakers, a little tinny but clear enough to be heard. His voice had the tone of a teenager handing in an assignment that had kept him from playing football all weekend – relieved that it was done, but knowing that it would never get him to the FA Cup. He'd found Timothy Lanigan.

'He's not teaching anymore,' Fisher said. 'He owns a bar at Strandhill, in Sligo. He came back to Ireland after his divorce. Must have given up teaching. He's been in Strandhill for the past fifteen years, and before that worked at a bar in Dublin. No criminal record. Not even a speeding ticket.'

Cormac had news for Fisher as well. He had spoken to Matt the night before. 'You said he divorced when, 1985? So he's been back in Ireland for twenty-eight years? I want to know every address he lived at, every job he worked since he came back to this country.'

Fisher's silence spoke for him.

'There was another murder,' Cormac said. 'In 1983. A fifteen-year-old student at the school – St. Whatever's Catholic Academy. Lanigan was her soccer coach. She disappeared after practice one day; her body was found two days later. She'd been raped and strangled. Lanigan was interviewed, but his wife alibied him and he was never a serious suspect. Girl's boyfriend was charged – she'd been planning to dump him. Boy spent a few months in jail before blood tests came back and exonerated him.'

'Jesus. They got DNA?' Fisher's tone had changed completely.

'They have the samples,' Cormac said. 'They didn't test for DNA in those days. But if we can get a sample they'll test it now.'

'Will I start the warrant application? I can do it now, have it ready for you in the morning.'

'No warrant,' Cormac said. 'You issue Lanigan with a warrant and he'll disappear. Irish passport, he'll jump on a cheap flight to France and have the whole of Europe to hide in.'

A moment's silence on the phone. 'Covert DNA?' Fisher asked.

'That's the plan,' said Cormac. 'Find out what you can about his movements, but do it without scaring him off. Get us something to work with and we'll go up there this weekend.' Cormac made a silent apology to Emma, but knew she'd understand.

Fisher agreed, and thanked him. He was smart enough to know that Cormac didn't need to bring him along for the ride, that a case like this, if they could break it, could make his career. He was probably also conscious that his lack of enthusiasm for the earlier work hadn't been difficult to read. Fisher was all right. He was ambitious, but that was okay if it showed itself in the right way – hard bloody work and good instincts for making a case.

'Oh, and Fisher? Run a search for me, will you? Simon Schmidt. Had an address somewhere near Kilmore in the 1990s. Text me if you find anything.'

'Will do.'

Cormac was about to hang up when Fisher spoke again. His voice was indistinct, and with the noise of the car and the shitty phone speakers, Cormac almost missed it.

Until Fisher said it again. 'They've brought her in for questioning. Maude Blake. Thought you should know.' Then he hung up, leaving Cormac with an hour's drive ahead and a burning anger that he could do nothing to express. He changed the radio to a station playing hard rock, and turned the music up.

CHAPTER TWENTY

Aisling sat on a bench in the hospital locker room, pulling on her boots. Her shift was over, and she was due to meet Maude in an hour, a prospect she was dreading. She hadn't seen her since Monday, hadn't called her to pass on Aggie's invitation, hadn't even called the police to ask about Jack's phone. She had managed to get a copy of the postmortem report, through a friend who had made it clear he thought reading it would be (a) weird, and (b) a very bad idea. And she had called a friend who worked in a London hospital and asked her to send her some mifepristone and misoprostol through the post. It was a huge ask. Though abortion was legal in the UK, posting pills to a patient you hadn't seen was not. But Claire hadn't hesitated. The drugs weren't monitored as carefully as drugs commonly abused, like opiates or tranquilisers, and she'd managed to lift some extras without being noticed.

They'd arrived that morning, those innocent-looking white tablets, and now they were burning a hole in the bottom of her bag. Aisling didn't know yet what she was going to do, but she was going to make a decision this weekend, one way or the other. She wasn't going to sleepwalk into nine weeks, then onwards until the foetus really was a baby and it was too late.

Aisling reached the Quays bar and started to push her way through the crowd. It was busy, but it wasn't heaving yet, though it would be in an hour or so. She made her way to the bar and ordered a Coke, carried it with her as she scanned the place for Maude. She found her at one of the small tables on the narrow mezzanine floor that overlooked the bar.

Maude had a notebook open on the table and was writing something. She had a glass of wine beside her, which she'd made some progress on. She looked up as Aisling approached, and smiled, pushing out the other chair so Aisling could sit.

Defensiveness made Aisling abrupt. 'I looked into the postmortem results.'

'You got the report?'

Aisling nodded. Maude looked as if she expected her to pull the report out of her pocket and hand it over. That wasn't going to happen. Reading it had been difficult enough for her; she wasn't going to inflict those photographs, that horribly specific language, on Jack's sister. 'Through a friend. He broke the rules to get me a copy. We can't tell anyone we've seen it until it's formally released.'

'What does it say?' Maude asked. She leaned forward across the table, so eager.

'He had a basilar skull fracture. Very severe. It probably would have killed him. But he had aspirated a small amount of water, so the official cause of death is drowning.'

'Okay.' Maude swallowed, paused. Her pen hovered above her notebook.

'It doesn't give us any answers, Maude. The fracture could have happened as he entered the water. He could have hit his head on the bridge supports on the way down, or on a rock submerged under the water.'

'What do you think happened?' Maude asked.

'I don't know. The fracture was very low, at the base of his skull. I've seen that sort of injury once before, that time it was a golf club to the back of the head. Someone could have hit Jack, could have knocked him unconscious, then dumped his body into the river.' The image of Jack, tumbling into the freezing black water, came to her, and she pushed it resolutely away. 'But equally, he could have fallen into the water somehow, hit his head on the way down. There's no way to know for sure what happened, at least from the postmortem.'

Aisling looked at the hand she'd placed on top of the table and clenched it into a fist. Surgeons had steady hands.

'You're just tired,' Maude said. She had noticed. 'That's all. It will pass.'

Aisling nodded.

'Did you get his messages?'

'No.' She didn't admit that she'd never asked for them – the way Maude was looking at her, so eager, so intense, made that admission impossible. But there'd been no time.

'Damn.' Maude said. She paused. 'It's a pity the postmortem isn't clear, but I think we have enough to go on. I think we need to start escalating things. Make a bit of a splash. Go to the press. Get some attention. I've already made a few phone calls. Can you do an interview? Tomorrow?' She caught the expression on Aisling's face. 'It doesn't have to be tomorrow.'

'You've been speaking with journalists?'

'We need to put pressure on the police. Media coverage will do that. They won't be able to brush off a journalist in the same way they can with you or me. This way we might get somewhere.'

'What did you tell them? About me? About Jack? Jesus, Maude.' The exhaustion and nausea Aisling had felt earlier in the day burst over her again in a roll of feverish heat.

'I haven't said much yet. Just enough to get them interested.'

'I don't want this. I don't want to do any interviews. I don't want to talk to journalists.'

'Okay.' Some of the animation dropped from Maude's face, and caution took its place. 'I can talk to them. You don't have to be involved if you don't want to be.'

Aisling shook her head. Christ, it was getting loud in here. 'Look, I think we're out of our depth here. I understand. I mean, I get why you want to keep asking questions. But we should bring this stuff to the police. Should trust them to do their job.'

The caution on Maude's face changed to something harder. Something like dislike. She stared down at her open notebook, covered in her own handwriting. Slowly, she started to gather up the papers.

Aisling put out an impulsive hand to stop her. 'Wait,' she said, but when Maude looked up she found she had nothing to say.

'I don't know what makes you think you can trust the police,' Maude said. 'They've made it very clear that they have no interest in investigating Jack's death.'

'You don't know that,' said Aisling. 'Just because they aren't talking to you, that doesn't mean that they aren't doing anything.' Her words rang hollow. Hadn't she told that detective she thought he was full of shit? She didn't even know whose side she was on. And she hadn't told Maude yet about that conversation, about the questions he had asked.

Maude pulled her notebook out from underneath Aisling's outstretched hand. She pushed it into the backpack resting at her feet under the table, then straightened.

'You want to bury your head in the sand, pretend that none of this is happening. Something rotten, something stinking and fetid, has found its way into your life, but you think if you don't look too closely at it, if you turn your other cheek just so, it won't really affect you. It's already taken Jack. You say you loved him, but you're not willing to take the smallest risk to find out who murdered him.'

The words were a punch in the gut, a twisted knife in an open wound, but they woke Aisling up. Anger burned through the fog of grief that had dulled her since Jack's death, and she welcomed it, fed it. She clenched her fists.

'I did love him. We were partners. We shared a life. That's what love is, Maude. It's not a series of dramatic gestures. It's not abandoning a five-year-old boy to strangers, then crashing back after his death spouting conspiracy theories.'

Maude shook her head. 'I never abandoned Jack. I gave him up, for his own good. And it broke my heart.'

'How could that be for his good? He'd just lost his mother. He loved you, Maude. How could his only sister abandoning him have made things better?'

'You don't understand. It was complicated. If I'd stayed ...'

'That's bullshit,' Aisling hissed. '*It's complicated* is what people say when it's not complicated at all. It's what people say when they are only thinking about themselves but don't want to look selfish.'

'Jesus,' Maude said. 'Your arrogance. You think you know everything, and you know nothing.'

'I know enough. I know that this bloody quest of yours is about you, not about Jack. You're trying to redeem yourself. Trying to make up for all the years you wasted. Well, you can't do that Maude. There's no going back. And nothing you do, nothing I do, will change the fact that Jack is dead.'

Maude looked stricken. She opened her mouth to speak but nothing came out. Aisling felt a pang of regret.

'I don't know what you expect from me Maude.' She'd meant it as an apology, but she was still angry and it came out like an accusation.

Maude shook her head slowly. 'I don't expect anything from you Aisling,' she said. 'I don't expect anything from anyone. Maybe that's the difference between us.' She moved to stand, but as she did so someone placed a firm hand on her shoulder. A woman with spiky blonde hair and a serious expression on her face. She wasn't alone, a man lurked over the woman's left shoulder. Aisling didn't need to look at the ID the woman held out to know they were police.

'Maude Blake, I'm Detective Sergeant Hackett.' She put the badge into her back pocket, not removing her hand from Maude's shoulder. 'You are under arrest for the murder of Hilaria Blake, on the night of the twenty-first of February, 1993. You are not obliged to say anything, but whatever you say will be taken down in writing and may be given in evidence.'

Maude had flinched when the detective took hold of her shoulder, and gave the ID held out to her only a cursory glance. Now her eyes held Aisling's, pleading. Pleading, but for what? They were all four of them frozen for a moment in time. Maude, half-standing, Hackett's hand still on her shoulder. The unnamed garda. And Aisling, still sitting at the table, her Coke untouched. Then movement started again, as if someone had pressed play on a video. Hackett reached down and took Maude's handbag, which was slung on the back of her chair. As Hackett turned to hand it to the other garda, Maude turned too, taking a step towards them. She stumbled, recovered, and in that stumble her foot pushed her backpack under the table until it rested, heavy, against Aisling's foot. Aisling stared but Maude didn't look at her again. The gardaí walked her out of the pub, keeping her between them, tiny and vulnerable.

CHAPTER TWENTY-ONE

Melanie Hackett was perfectly civil. Maude sat in the back of the garda car for the short drive to Mill Street, and shoved her hands between her knees to keep them from shaking. How much danger was she in? Her mother had been dead for twenty years and her death had never been looked at as anything other than an accidental overdose. Nobody kept secrets in the village in 1993. If they'd suspected murder back then, Tom would have heard and therefore so would she. Maude racked her brains, trying to think of something, any reason the gardaí would have to suddenly suspect her of this crime.

When they got to the interview room Hackett busied herself setting up the tapes, but the male police officer sat still as a snake in his chair, silently watching Maude. He was trying to intimidate her and he could fuck right off. Maude raised her chin and stared back into his eyes. Hackett pressed a switch and spoke for the benefit of the tape.

'Maude Blake you have been arrested under Section 30 of the Offences against the State Act, 1939. You are not obliged to say anything unless you wish to do so, but whatever you say will be taken down in writing and may be given in evidence. Do you understand?'

Maude assented, quietly, and Hackett nodded. 'Present in the interview room are DS Melanie Hackett, and Garda Daniel McIntyre.'

'Can I get you coffee or tea? Glass of water?' Hackett asked.

Maude shook her head, thought of all the cop shows she'd seen where police got DNA from a coffee cup. But DNA was hardly an issue here, surely? And anyway, she'd been arrested, couldn't they compel her to give a sample? She had no idea. Something to ask a lawyer, if she had one. She would ask for a lawyer, she should call Tom, but not yet. Not until she knew more.

'I'd like to ask you some questions about your mother's death,' Hackett said.

'My mother,' Maude said.

Hackett waited.

'My mother died twenty years ago. She was an alcoholic. She died from a drug overdose, though she was dying in any case and I expect that the drugs only brought her death forward by a few months, if that. I have no idea why anyone would think that I killed her.'

'Perhaps you'd like to tell me in your own words how your mother died.'

'I'm sure you have the coroner's report.'

Hackett inclined her head. 'I do. But I'd like to hear about it from you.'

Maude hesitated. 'I wasn't in the room when she died,' she said at last.

'Tell me what you do remember.'

'It was twenty years ago. I was very young.'

'You were fifteen.' This from McIntyre.

'I remember quite a bit from when I was fifteen,' Hackett said. 'Mostly things I'd rather forget.'

'I don't remember anything because, as far as I recall, that night was the same as every other night. Nothing strange happened. Nothing out of the ordinary. I didn't even realise my mother had died until the following morning.'

Hackett shifted her weight in her chair, turned a page in the file she had in front of her. 'Describe an ordinary night in your home for us, so,' she said. She spoke so casually, just a chilled-out conversation between friends.

Maude shrugged. 'I had a job, milking at a dairy farm down the road, some cleaning in their kitchen. I'd work until two, then I'd walk into the village and pick Jack up, walk him home. I'd make him dinner, make dinner for my mother. We'd play or read for a while, then I'd get him ready for bed.'

'What about your mother?' asked McIntyre. 'She didn't look after you or your little brother?'

Maude shook her head. 'My mother wasn't well. She would have cared for us if she'd been able.' Maude caught a flash of amusement in McIntyre's eyes as she spoke.

'Did you bring dinner to your mother on the evening she died?' Hackett asked.

'I suppose I must have. I don't remember specifically, but I did that every night so I suppose I must have done.'

'It sounds like you had a lot of responsibility for someone so young. You didn't resent it? That your mother left so much for you to do?' McIntyre asked.

Maude shook her head, said nothing. He was making her uncomfortable. There was something behind his eyes, something in the way he looked at her. Her mouth was dry, and she swallowed. Realised she had shifted her weight backwards in her chair, an unsuccessful effort to put distance between them.

'Did you talk to your mother that night?' Hackett asked.

'I don't remember. I'm sorry.'

'What would you have done on a standard night? Did you sit with her while she ate? Did you talk?'

Maude shrugged again. 'I ... mostly just gave her dinner, then went down to Jack.'

'No conversation?'

'My mother was very sick. She slept all the time. When she was awake she was confused. I ... we didn't chat,' Maude said.

'Shouldn't she have been in hospital? Getting medical care?' Hackett's voice was gentle, oh so sincere.

'I'd tried. More than once. She wouldn't go, and the couple of times I got her there, she wouldn't stay.' Maude closed her eyes for a moment, opened them again. 'Looking back as an adult I can see things more clearly. My mother made it very clear though that she didn't want medical treatment. The last time she was in hospital she signed a DNR, then called a cab to bring her home.' With no money to pay for it, all the way from Castlebar. The cabbie had lost his shit, screaming and roaring at Maude, Hilaria having already disappeared inside the house. Until Jack came out, and took Maude's hand protectively. The cabbie had looked at Jack, with his badly cut hair, his little boy chest out but his lower lip wobbling, then looked at Maude, then at the house behind them, with its boarded-up windows and leaking gutters. He'd uttered one last *fuck* and left.

'I think my mother had had enough. She was in a lot of pain. The doctors had told her she didn't have much time left. I think she was ready to die.'

'Are you suggesting she committed suicide?' McIntyre asked.

'No. Just that ... it might have been a release,' said Maude.

McIntyre spoke up. 'Have you been telling yourself that, for all these years?'

Maude didn't miss the flash of amusement in his eyes. She could see, though she thought that Hackett did not, that McIntyre was entertained by the situation. He took pleasure in her interrogation, in the prompting of her painful memories, in an idle sort of way. With that recognition, she realised why she was afraid of him. She had known someone like him once, when she was young.

'Tell me about finding her body,' Hackett said, before Maude had a chance to respond.

'It was the next morning,' Maude said. 'I went into her

room to see her, before I brought Jack to school. It was still dark, but I had a candle. She was lying on the bed, but she didn't move when I called her. When I got close enough, I realised why.' Maude could almost feel the cold clamminess of her mother's forehead, as it had felt that morning when she'd finally been brave enough to reach out and touch her.

'How did you know?' Hackett asked. 'You said it was obvious. How did you know she was dead?'

'I touched her, and her skin was cold. There was blood at the corners of her mouth. Her eyes were open, but they … weren't right. And she had a shoelace tied around her arm. There was a needle still in her arm. I pulled it out.'

'What did you do next?'

'I left the room. I found my brother and I brought him to school. Then I went to the post office and used the payphone to call the police.'

'And then?'

'I waited.'

'You didn't tell anyone else? Didn't call a family friend, or a relative?' Hackett asked.

Maude looked at him blankly. They'd had no relatives, no family friends. Wasn't that obvious?

'You just went back to the house, and waited there by yourself?'

Maude nodded.

'Your mother was dead upstairs; you weren't afraid?'

Maude laughed despite herself. 'It's not the dead you need to be afraid of.'

'What were you afraid of, Maude?' Hackett was smooth. She got the tone just right, a perfect mix of sympathy and solidarity.

Maude shook her head, said nothing. Reminded herself to be careful. Hackett wasn't stupid. And McIntyre. He was something else.

Hackett turned some pages in her file, appeared to check something. 'When Garda Reilly came to the house that night, you were alone with your little brother. You went back to the school to collect him?'

Maude nodded again.

'And you told no one at his school, not a teacher, not one of the mothers, that your own mother was dead at home.' This from McIntyre. A statement rather than a question.

'No.'

'You weren't upset. I suppose no one could blame you.'

'I think I was in shock.'

He waited, but she said nothing more.

'Your brother was hurt. He had bruises,' Hackett said.

'Yes.'

'On examination at hospital he was found to have a fracture to his right arm. And a number of other injuries. Fractured ribs, partially healed. A healed fracture to his left arm. Some burn scars.'

Maude said nothing but memories came flooding back. Memories of pain, of desperate worry. Memories of a small and trusting hand in hers.

'Did your mother hurt him, Maude?' Hackett asked quietly.

Maude shook her head, said nothing.

'She hurt Jack, and she hurt you, didn't she? That's why you had to kill her, to make the beatings stop.'

Maude met Hackett's gaze straight on. 'My mother never hit me in her life. Never hit Jack. That's not the way she was made. She was an alcoholic. She made a lot of mistakes. But she never once raised a hand to us.'

Hackett put her hand on a manila file sitting on the table in front of her. 'A colleague recently interviewed a social worker who was involved in your case. She was very clear that you and your brother were afraid of your mother. It was her view that you were both physically abused by your mother. You're telling me that she got it wrong?'

Maude shook her head. 'Our mother never hurt us.'

'So your brother's injuries were all accidents. He just tripped and fell on the cigarettes, did he? More than once?' There was sudden dislike in Hackett's voice, as if Maude's defense of her mother had offended the detective.

Hackett opened her mouth to speak again but was interrupted by McIntyre. 'Detective Sergeant Cormac Reilly, you know him?'

Hackett stirred uneasily at the question, looked at the tape recorder.

'I'm sorry?' Maude asked.

'Cormac Reilly, the garda who came to your house the night your mother died. You met with him earlier this week. He visited you in your hotel room.'

What? McIntyre's expression was bland again. His face gave nothing away.

'I ... no. I haven't seen Garda Reilly in twenty years.' And somehow that simple truth sounded more like a lie than anything else. Maude glanced towards Hackett, who gave McIntyre a look of her own.

'Let's get back on track,' Hackett said. 'Were you taken into care?'

'No.'

'Your brother's injuries were very severe. If he had been beaten that badly in the past it seems strange that he was not put into care.'

Maude said nothing, waited for the question. She wanted to bring the interview to an end, but she still didn't know why she'd been brought here.

Hackett paused, turned a page in the file. She seemed to have lost her sense of direction. 'Blake. Not a particularly Irish name.'

'My mother's family were Anglo-Irish.'

'Wealthy?' McIntyre asked.

'At one time, certainly.'

'What happened?' Hackett asked.

'An old story. I come from a long line of alcoholics and wastrels. By the time my mother was born the money was gone, except for a small trust fund.'

'Your mother didn't work?'

'She taught English. She was a writer. But I was born in 1978. My mother wasn't married, so after that she couldn't get teaching jobs. By the time Jack was born the money had run out. Not long after that we moved to Galway. The house was an old family house. I don't even know if my mother owned it. Probably the land and house had long since been sold, but as the house was abandoned, my mother just reclaimed it.'

'No other family?'

'No.'

'And you've said your mother was an alcoholic?'

'Yes.'

'And a drug addict?'

Maude shrugged.

Danny broke in, his voice unnecessarily loud. 'The coroner's report showed no evidence of previous drug use.'

'I never knew her to use drugs.' Maude turned her gaze from Hackett to Danny. 'I didn't say she was a drug addict.'

'You didn't say she wasn't,' McIntyre said, then glanced at Hackett.

'She didn't use drugs?' Hackett asked.

'Other than alcohol, not that I was aware of.'

'Other than the day she died.' McIntyre's tone was an accusation.

Maude said nothing. She stared into Hackett's eyes. They were a cool, calm blue. There was no ally to be found there.

'Where do you think she got the heroin?' Hackett asked.

'I don't know.'

'She had friends? People who visited the house?'

Maude shifted slightly in her chair. She checked her watch. 'Yes. Of sorts.'

'Of sorts?' said Hackett. 'Where did they meet?'

'I don't know.'

'Can you recall their names?'

'I'm afraid not.' Maude took a breath. 'Look, I've answered all your questions, though this whole thing is bloody ridiculous. And I have a question I'd like to ask now.'

Hackett raised an eyebrow, waited.

'My brother Jack. Your investigation into his death. I've been asking questions since I got to Galway, and no one is answering them. I've given you proof that Jack didn't kill himself as you say he did, and you've done nothing. I've made a formal complaint; requested that the investigation be reopened. A week later and it seems that you have done nothing at all to find my brother's murderer, but you are instead focusing on the death of my mother. A death that took place twenty years ago, and that for no reason at all that I can see, you have chosen to lay at my door.'

'At the risk of sounding clichéd, Maude, I have to remind you that we are the ones who ask the questions. Although you haven't asked a question yet.'

'What I want to know is what all of this has to do with my brother's death. I want to know if you are ever going to investigate his murder, and if not, why not.'

Mel Hackett shook her head slowly. 'We're not here to talk about your brother's death,' she said.

'Although perhaps we should be,' McIntyre said.

His gaze was almost feverish now. The implication of his statement was obvious. There it was.

'I'd like to see my solicitor now,' Maude said.

CHAPTER TWENTY-TWO

It was half eight before Cormac reached the station. The carpark was almost empty, but he recognised Hackett's little red hatchback. He asked himself what he would do if she and Danny were still interviewing Maude Blake. Interrupt? Take the interview over? Just observe, and let them fuck it up? Cormac forced himself to walk up the stairs, instead of taking them three at a time and at speed, which is what he really wanted to do. He wanted to burst into the squad room, to rant and rage at whoever was present. Instead he compressed his rage into a white-hot ball and told himself he would use it as fuel.

The squad room was quiet. No sign of Danny, but Melanie Hackett was working at her desk. He replayed everything he knew about her. She was short, no more than five foot five. Spikey blonde hair intended to convey … something. He'd heard she was ambitious. That was it. Fuck.

He stood over her. 'What is it that you think you're doing?' Cormac asked, very calmly.

She looked up, took off her glasses, pushed her chair away, putting a little distance between them. 'I'm doing my job, detective, how about you?'

'I'm certainly doing my job, Detective Hackett. In fact, I was interviewing a witness this afternoon, at the same time, as I understand it, that you were arresting my suspect. Where is she?' he asked.

'In the cells.' There was a little pink in her cheeks now, but she was otherwise admirably cool.

'So you've charged her.' It wasn't a question, but Hackett nodded.

'On what evidence?'

For a moment, it seemed as if she wasn't going to answer him.

'On the strength of Hannah Collins's statement,' she said.

Cormac gave a grim smile. 'So you got nothing out of the interview. Because you went in completely unprepared. A twenty-year-old case, no forensics, no motive, and of the three people who were in the house that night, two are dead. But you think you're going to get the DPP to bring this to court based on the word of a junkie who wants to get out of prison. A junkie with a history of providing inaccurate information to the gardaí.'

She stared back at him, poker face intact.

'I don't arrest suspects where there is no evidence, Mel. Do you know why? Because if I arrest someone, they are going to jail. That's the way it works. I take them in when I've got them. This is not a drugs case. This is murder. And you have just fucked up royally.'

Melanie glanced around the room. There was only one garda within hearing distance, a uniform who was keeping his attention on his computer screen. She turned away from him, back to her own computer, and put a hand on her mouse, signalling an end to their conversation.

Not happening. Cormac grabbed the closest empty chair and pulled it towards him, then sat facing her, a little too close for comfort. He leaned in.

'I want to know if this is how you do business here, because it sure as hell isn't how we work in Dublin. This is my case. I was interviewing a witness when you arrested my suspect without my consent, without even as much as a phone call. Where I come from that would be a firing offence. Except it would never fucking happen, because no self-respecting detective would ever do it. So my question is this – are you incompetent? Do you want to get fired? Or is something else going on here?'

She turned her face to him. 'Listen, Murphy ordered it, all right? You were not getting the job done, for reasons I'm not going to speculate about.' She looked him up and down. 'You have a problem, take it up with Murphy.'

She turned again to her computer.

Jesus Christ. Had Murphy decided to pull the case? It was less than a day since their last meeting. 'Maybe I'll do that,' Cormac said. He pushed his chair back.

'You won't get him now,' Hackett said to her computer screen. 'He left for Dublin this afternoon. Won't be back until Tuesday.'

Fuck.

'Melanie.' He put conciliation in his voice, waited until she turned to face him again. 'What changed? I left Murphy's office yesterday just before lunch and I was the lead on this case. Twenty-four hours later he leaves for Dublin, but not before he puts the case in your hands, no phone call, no notice to me. What am I missing?'

He watched her try to take his measure. When she spoke her expression was unsympathetic. 'Look, I didn't speak to Murphy. But I think his reasons are obvious. You know what I'm talking about.'

'You think I slept with Maude Blake.'

She shrugged.

'I'm not sleeping with her, Mel. I shouldn't have to say this. I'm in a long-term relationship, but even if I wasn't I wouldn't sleep with a key suspect in a murder case.' His tone was matter of fact, and seemed to hold her attention. 'It's a bullshit rumour, and I'd like to know where you heard it.'

He could see her think about telling him, then decide against it. But she was listening. It was a start.

'I've heard you have history. Maude Blake wouldn't be the first,' she said.

'That's bullshit too.' He could have said more. Could have explained that his relationship with Emma began after she had been cleared, after the case was closed. That his superiors in Dublin knew about it as soon as they started dating. But fuck her.

'Maude denied killing her mother?'

'Yes.'

'Did she mention anything about a neighbour, a Miss Keane? Or a Simon Schmidt?'

Hackett shook her head.

'Okay.' He stood up, started to walk away, then turned back as something occurred to him.

'If you didn't speak to Murphy, who did?'

She hesitated, then shrugged. 'Daniel McIntyre.'

He stared at her. 'Danny McIntyre told you that Murphy wanted you to arrest Maude Blake?'

'Yes.'

Danny again. And again no call to give him a heads up. Cormac looked around. 'Where is he?'

'He's gone.' For a moment it looked like she wasn't going to say any more, then she relented. 'Danny went home to his parents. I think he's going to take some time off.'

It was an explanation of sorts, giving Cormac a heads up would hardly have been a priority for him under the circumstances. But Cormac had the strongest feeling that with Danny, it wasn't that simple.

'The bail hearing's on Monday,' Hackett was saying. 'In the morning. I'm working on the file now, if you have anything you want to add?'

But it was her arrest. Her file. Her cock-up to defend. She wasn't his enemy, but they weren't on the same side either, and whatever else happened he wasn't going to stand over this arrest. Cormac left the squad room. He made for the exit. It was hard to believe that he'd only had the case for five days. Two days ago he'd interviewed Katherine Shelley, and felt he had a handle on it. How had he lost control so completely? Where could he go with things from here? For the moment, at least, he had no idea. He shoved his hands into his pockets and made for home.

He didn't get far. Carrie O'Halloran was coming up the stairs, stripping off a high-vis jacket, and looking exhausted. They saw each other at the same time and stopped.

'It's official now,' Carrie said. 'Danny's finally caved. Search parties are out, near her parents' place in Ballintober. Only two fucking weeks too late.'

'Search called off for the night?' he asked.

'No. Now that the family has finally copped on, they've gone into overdrive. All the neighbours are out with torches, people from the school.'

'You're not with them?' he asked. That surprised him. She seemed like the type to worry at an investigation until it was done.

'I'm working something else, a domestic violence case. Wife denies the abuse, though it's been reported more than once by others. They have two young children.'

Her tone caught his attention. Her tiredness was less evident as she focused on him and her expression sharpened. She had something to tell him, he could feel it. She was trying to decide if he was trustworthy, if telling him whatever was on her mind would help or hinder her. He opened his mouth to speak, and her phone rang, loud in the echoing quiet of the stairwell. She answered the phone, listened for a moment.

'Where?' she asked.

Whatever she heard in reply got her moving. She turned on her heel and was gone, phone still pressed to her ear.

CHAPTER TWENTY-THREE

It had definitely been deliberate, that slight stumble of Maude's that pushed the backpack under the shadow of the table. Aisling felt its weight against her ankle. She kept absolutely still, as if moving a muscle would bring the gardaí back. People were turning to look at her as the story spread through the pub to those who had missed the action. The noisy buzz had dropped to an unnatural hush and now it picked up and redoubled. Aisling stood, as casually as she could manage, picked up the backpack and slung it over her shoulder. She took a drink from her glass, but nervousness made her hasty, and she ended up coughing. She left the rest behind and walked from the pub.

Sleet was coming down sideways. She zipped her jacket against the cold, took her hat from her pocket and pulled it low over her forehead and ears. She turned her face to the wind and rain, and walked down Quay Street, crossing at the Wolfe Tone Bridge, where the river started to widen before it emptied into the sea. The wind buffeted her and the rain turned to icy needles on her face, but she welcomed it. She wanted to lift her head to the sky and scream out her frustration, her anger, and her loss. Instead, calm, ever outwardly calm, she made her way home, let herself into the house, and put the kettle on for tea. She leaned against the counter, head resting on her hands, listening to the whistle of the kettle on its way to boiling. Then she took a mug from its stand on the counter, turned, and threw it as hard as she could against the wall.

Fuck. Fuck fuck fuck.

She put her face in her hands, closed her eyes, felt the thunder of her pulse in her ears. Then she took out her phone, called Mary Dooley, and asked her to let the hospital know that she would not be in the next day. She was taking some time off. Sorry for the lack of notice, but she needed at least a week. She cut short Mary's expression of concern and support, ended the call, then went to put on a fire in the living room. She showered – a blessedly long, hot shower that leached her pain and distress away – and dressed again in pyjamas and an old jumper of Jack's. Finally, she gathered the backpack, a bottle of wine, an open packet of supermarket hummus and the end of a loaf of bread, and settled herself into the living room couch. The room was lit only by the flickering of the firelight, and she switched on a reading lamp.

She poured herself a glass of wine, took a drink, then rested her head against the couch and closed her eyes. She let everything stop. Jack's death. Maude's quest for vengeance or answers or forgiveness. The constant brutal competition she engaged in at her job. The pregnancy. Everything. She sat very quietly for five, everlasting minutes, then she turned and picked up the backpack.

It was new. A plain navy canvas bag, with a separate cushioned section to protect the newish-looking laptop that sat inside. She took that out first and turned it on, but it was password protected. Besides the computer there was an A4 lined notebook, with additional loose printed pages tucked inside.

Aisling opened the notebook. Maude's handwriting was a soft, rounded cursive. She had written out everything that had happened, what little she had discovered, and a range of possible theories, all in a tidy blue ink that made the whole thing look like a child's project. Aisling turned the pages slowly, reading the notes with deliberation. Was this the work of someone obsessed? The work of a sister overcome with guilt and looking for someone to blame? Or was it the work of someone who simply loved her brother, albeit from a distance of years and kilometres, believed with good reason that he had been killed, and desperately wanted justice for him?

Aisling turned another page and came across the stub of a boarding card for a flight from Perth to Dublin, and two photographs that had been tucked inside the notebook. The date on the card was Tuesday 12 March. Aisling looked at it for a moment, feeling unsettled. She'd assumed that Maude had booked her flight to Ireland on hearing of Jack's death. Now it seemed she'd come back earlier. Aisling tried to remember if she had ever spoken to Maude about her return to Ireland, and couldn't. She set the boarding card down, and picked up the photographs. They were dog-eared and dirty. The first showed a girl, maybe twelve or so, with a baby sitting on her lap. The girl was smiling. The baby, rounded and sandy-haired, cuddled protectively in her arms. The other photograph showed the same girl, but older now, and the little boy was standing beside her, holding her hand. In this one neither of them smiled, but stared back at the camera with a sort of blank distrust that Aisling found disturbing. Aisling drank from her wineglass, then took the photographs and sat back on the couch. She crossed her legs and held the photographs out on her knees. Jack and Maude. Maude and Jack. It felt like she was prying ... getting a glimpse into a life Jack himself had not remembered. The face of the little boy in the second photograph was haunting. Surely that child carried within him memories enough to scar him for the rest of his life? Looking at the photograph, at the lost look in his eyes, at the clasp of their hands, she wondered what the children had lived through. Could Jack have remembered more than he pretended? Maybe he carried the scars of those years in his subconscious. She put the photographs away, tucking them back into the notebook and turning a page so she could no longer see them.

Christ. Maude was probably being questioned right now. Could she have done it? Jack had been told that his mother died from a heroin overdose. It was hard to see how the gardaí could have changed their minds about that. Hilaria was dead twenty years, it wasn't as if new forensic evidence could have suddenly come to light. And if she had died from a heroin overdose it was hard to see how a fifteen-year-old girl could be held accountable for it. The whole thing seemed far-fetched. On the other hand, she'd had motive enough. And if she was guilty, it would explain why she was so wary of police. Aisling lay back on the couch, the notebook held to her chest in an unconscious embrace. Her mind clear of distraction and distress for the first time in weeks, she considered. She did not believe that Jack had killed himself. On the other hand, she found it hard to believe he had been murdered. So perhaps an accident. Maybe even an accident involving a friend, who had panicked, and in guilt and fear made a stupid phone call to try to hide the truth. Did she need answers? Did she need every specific about how and why Jack had died? No. She believed now that Jack had not killed himself and that was enough. She wished she could leave it at that. Maude was so fearless. Aisling didn't know if she wanted to know the details, to know if Jack had suffered, been afraid, before he died. She didn't know if she could carry that pain too, with all the rest. But Maude had been right about something. She owed Jack more than the turning of her cheek. She owed him her best attempt at getting to the truth.

What could she do? What was within her reach? She'd gotten the postmortem report, and that hadn't helped. She hadn't done anything about his phone messages, and she would have to wait until Monday to do anything about it now. She could call the police, find out if they had traced any of Jack's calls that day. Rodgers wasn't the only garda in Galway. Reilly. Could she trust him? Maybe. If she talked to him, properly this time, would the CCTV and the postmortem report be enough to prompt him to get a warrant for the phone records, if Rodgers hadn't already done it? Her phone buzzed and a long apologetic text came in from Mary. She was really sorry, but Cummins had requested a formal handover of her patients before Aisling could take leave. Could she come in on Sunday evening? Cummins would meet her at 8.00 p.m. on the ward. Aisling sent back a quick yes, and tried not to think about how Cummins and the other consultants might react to her sudden absence.

Aisling rubbed at her eyes. If someone had contacted Jack, had asked to meet that day, it would have been by phone or email. Jack didn't use social media, or at least none of the big platforms. She took a second sip of wine, then pulled her own laptop over from the coffee table. She knew Jack's email password. She could start there. A moment later and she was skimming through seventy unopened emails. She didn't need to click on any of them – they were promotional, mostly, one or two from friends sent in the first few days after his death, before the story got around. The little blue 'New' boxes started to disappear from beside the emails, and she felt a wave of grief that Jack would never see these messages. Then she felt an equally strong sense of the ridiculous, and hiccupped out something resembling a laugh. Jack wouldn't be too bothered about missing a buy-one-get-one-free coupon from the pizzeria down the street.

God. This felt weird. There were a lot of emails from hiking friends – someone had sent a group photograph from their last trip and everyone had replied with a comment or a joke. A couple of iTunes receipts. A few new linked-in requests. Nothing much else. Nothing helpful. She rested her fingers on the keyboard, and looked at the neat list of emails on the screen. Something was nagging at her. She didn't use Gmail herself, and had been glad of it recently. Because of something Mary had told her. About a friend who'd used her boyfriend's Gmail account to figure out that he had not, in fact, stopped seeing his ex, but was going around to hers for a shag every Friday like clockwork, when Mary's friend worked a late shift. The cheating boyfriend had been so careful – no emails, no text messages. Because he'd cheated before, and been caught, he'd taken to leaving his phone out where his girlfriend could look at it whenever she wanted, even shared his email password. But the girlfriend had managed to catch him anyway, by tracing his phone.

Aisling picked up her phone and dialled Mary's number. It rang six times before she answered, and then it was with the roar of music in the background. She'd obviously finished work for the day.

'Hang on,' Mary said, as she took herself to a quieter spot. Then, 'Aisling? You all right? Do you need me to come round?'

'That friend of yours. The one with the shitty boyfriend. How did she trace his phone?'

Mary was silent for a moment, but she didn't ask any questions. That was good. Aisling couldn't have answered them. 'He had a Google account – Gmail. He used Gmail on his phone. Didn't realise that when he put his email account on his phone he accepted all sorts of shit. Google keep a record of everywhere you go, how long you spend there; they keep it for, like, years. He gave her his email password, to prove how straight down the line he was. Didn't realise that all she had to do was click on Timeline and she could see exactly how often and how long he was spending at his ex's place.'

'Timeline.'

'Yep. It's in Maps or something.'

'Okay, thanks.'

'Aisling, what's going on? Are you saying … was Jack cheating on you?'

The thought had honestly never occurred to her. It did then, for just a moment, before she dismissed it.

'Not Jack,' she said, 'not his style.' She got off the phone by promising to call Mary the next day, hung up and turned back to her laptop, and Jack's email account.

CHAPTER TWENTY-FOUR

Hackett had ended the interview as soon as Maude asked for a lawyer, and brought her straight down to the holding cells. The custody sergeant took her details, her handbag, the contents of her pockets. His matter of factness was reassuring, but maybe it shouldn't have been. The place smelled strongly of disinfectant. Someone in a cell was singing rebel songs, tunefully enough, although he kept losing his place and starting again. She was put in a cell by herself, and told that she would be brought to Limerick Prison in the morning, until her bail hearing which would be on Monday. She asked again for her lawyer and was told he'd been called, then the cell door was closed and she was alone. Maude was grateful, at least, that she had that privilege.

She sat on the bunk. The sheets were clean. Lights were turned down low, but then it was late now, wasn't it? She'd met Aisling at about six o'clock. Maude lay down and closed her eyes. She could pretend to be somewhere else, while she waited, and thought. In her hotel room, or better yet, back on the station in the Kimberley, before it had been sold. She'd heard *Nancy Spain* sung there too, more than once. She might have drifted off. She was woken by the custody sergeant, who opened her door without warning or ceremony.

'Your solicitor's here,' the sergeant said. He'd spilled something on his uniform; a dark splodge that might have been ketchup stained his trousers right up near his crotch. His eyes followed hers, then he frowned. She opened her mouth to explain and he cut across her.

'I don't have all night.'

He showed her to an interview room, then shut the door. She took a seat at the table, wondering at the fact that her hands were free. Probably the door was locked. She didn't check it. Five minutes later, it opened, and a man walked into the room.

Tom Collins, but so different now, and it wasn't just the width of his shoulders, the grey at his temples. The difference was in his manner, his self-possession. As he walked in his eyes were on her, assessing, examining. He gave a friendly nod of dismissal to the guard, and took a seat opposite her.

'Maude,' he said.

Maude felt the distance between them, felt his caution. She couldn't miss his reserve and it should have prompted her to be careful, but a smile came to her lips unbidden. She pressed her fingers to her lips but the smile grew until it took over her face. It came from somewhere inside, from the part of her that was still a girl and knew that Tom was her true friend. And perhaps it was fed by her adult self too, which understood how rare and precious that sort of love is. Tears blurred her vision and she blinked them away.

'Maude,' Tom said again, but this time was different. He reached out a hand to her and stroked a tear from her cheek. 'Don't cry.'

But she caught her breath and fresh tears fell at the touch of his hand. The Tom she'd known would never have done that. He had hated to be touched. She caught his hand before he could take it away and squeezed it hard before releasing him.

'I'm so sorry about Jack,' he said.

She nodded, scrubbed her cheeks dry with the sleeve of her cardigan. Tom found a folded tissue in his pocket and handed it to her.

'I tried to get in touch, to let you know, but I couldn't reach you.'

'The station is gone,' Maude said. 'Lawton died, and his son wanted to sell.'

The sale had broken her heart, had very nearly broken her. The station had been her refuge for eighteen years. John Lawton had been her employer, and her friend. But now, only a handful of months later, Jack's death had put the loss of her adopted home into perspective. The reasons she'd had for staying away from Jack even after he'd been safely adopted seemed so stupid now – an attempt to put logic around her fear and her deep reluctance to ever return to Ireland. The trauma of her childhood and the loss of Jack had clung to her like a stain, and it had taken years to build a semblance of a life. She'd gone to London first, on the ferry, and spent six horrific, lonely, desperate months working in an East London pub shitty enough to turn a blind eye to the fact that she was under age. When the opportunity came to go to Australia – opportunity in the form of a new job as a nanny for a wealthy family – she'd jumped at it. But caring for children had been too painful, and she'd moved on, taking one job after the other until she'd ended up in the Kimberley, as camp cook on a remote station. The Kimberley was so different from home, it felt sometimes like she had been transported to another world. For half of the year the grass was bleached to a white straw that cracked and bristled under her feet. During the wet season the rain came accompanied by violent thunder and lightning storms. The humidity was intense; the few bits of clothes she'd brought had rotted in the wardrobe. Life was a battle those first few years, a struggle she could throw herself into and forget about Ireland and Jack. By the time things got easier she had fallen into a routine. It had been enough for her. She'd told herself it was all she wanted. But looking back now it seemed like a scraping of a life. She'd been too afraid to want more.

'I'm sorry for that too,' Tom said. 'I wish you'd come

home sooner.' Then, grimacing, 'Maude I'm sorry, I didn't mean ...'

'I ... tried. But I was too late.'

They heard a distant shout, the sound of someone banging on a metal door.

Tom took a deep breath. 'I can't be your lawyer. I came when I got your call, of course I did, but I can't represent you.'

Maude hesitated. 'Why?'

'Hannah is the reason you're in here.'

'I don't understand.'

His eyes held hers. 'Hannah's in prison. She's been in prison the best part of a year. She desperately wants to get out. She's given a statement to the gardaí, Maude, about you.' Tom opened his briefcase, took out a file, tapped it with one finger. 'I think she's trying to make a deal, information in exchange for early release.'

'I see.' Except she didn't really, and the pain of the blow surprised her. She hadn't seen Hannah for twenty years, but she would have laid odds that Hannah would never betray her.

'Her life hasn't been easy. I'm not making excuses. She made plenty of shitty decisions, and Hannah never met a drug she didn't like. But.' He hesitated. 'You know what Hannah was like. There was always a man, and every single one of them a bigger shit than the last.' He swallowed. 'I lost track of her a couple of years back. It wasn't the first time. She never wanted to see me when she was in bad shape. But then she called me. The Christmas before last. She asked to meet. I was so glad to hear from her, but afraid too. It had been more than two years, by then. I'd looked for her, but ...' He shook his head. 'We met in Dublin, in a little café off St. Stephen's Green. She was very thin, seemed very tired, but she was clean.'

Maude waited, sure she was about to hear a story of an attempted recovery, followed by another relapse.

'She was pregnant, Maude. And she was so happy. She was determined to stay off drugs and give the baby a proper home. She came to live with me in Galway, kept getting treatment. There's a rehab place on Eglinton Street – day therapy, you know? But it was working for her. She stayed clean. She even got a job; only two days a week in the local deli, but it was the first job she'd had in years. Her ex tried to get in touch, and she told him where to go. It was the pregnancy. I don't know. It just lit her up.' He stopped then, shook his head.

'What happened?' Maude asked gently.

'They arrested her in June.' Tom's eyes hardened. 'Hannah's ex was a dealer. It happened before they broke up. He had Hann call a guy, ask him over to their flat. When he got there Hannah's ex beat the shit out of him – almost killed him. He owed money over drugs. Hannah hadn't a clue, I swear, Maude. You know her. But they charged her with conspiracy to commit GBH. She got three years.'

'Oh shit, Tom. Shit.'

'She didn't do it. She had no idea that the guy was in debt, had no idea what her ex had planned. But she's been in prison since June of last year.'

'What about the baby?'

'Saoirse was born in July. Hannah's in Dóchas, the women's prison attached to Mountjoy. Women there are allowed to keep their babies until the baby turns one. Then the kids are taken away and put into care unless a relative steps forward.'

'You?'

'Apparently not. It seems Family Services think that a single man who works full time is not a suitable foster parent for a one year old, even if he is her uncle. In three or four months they're going to take Hannah's baby from her and put her into care.'

Maude raised her hands, elbows still on the table, and pressed her fingers against her closed eyes.

'Hannah's been going crazy. She can't give her baby up, Maude. If I was taking her that would be one thing. But Hannah could never tolerate a stranger looking after her child. She knows firsthand how bad the system can be. She sees the whole thing starting again, just the way it was with us, when Mam was sick.'

Maude opened her eyes and stared at him, willing him to tell her the rest.

Tom splayed an open hand across the file on the table. 'I've told them I'm your lawyer. They gave me the file. There's a statement in there. From Hannah. She says that you asked her for heroin. That she introduced you to Rick, and the next day your mother was dead.'

And just like that she was back in Ireland. Fifteen years old and hurrying as fast as she could to the secondary school, wanting to catch Tom before he reached it. She was wearing the old army surplus parka she'd bought in a charity shop – it was waterproof but had a weird acrid smell so she only wore it when the weather was really bad. She was hungry, but she'd dropped Jack to school with food in his belly and a full lunch box, so it was a good morning. She hadn't seen Tom for a few weeks. She sat on the school wall and waited for him. At fifteen it was legal for her not to attend school, so she ignored the looks of the few teachers who recognised her. She spotted Tom when he was half a mile away and jumped from the wall, hurrying towards him.

He looked happy to see her, and despite everything she felt a little less alone, a little comforted.

'I need to talk to you,' she said, and he followed her as she led the way back down the street.

'What's the story? I've a maths test.'

'Come on,' she said. She turned into Main Street, knowing he would follow, then off it into a small park and the little playground that had been funded by the European Union. The sign with the blue EU stars was almost as big as the slide. She sat on the bottom of the slide and started chewing a thumb nail. Tom stood for a moment, then slid his backpack from his back and took a seat on one of the swings, pushing idly into the sand with one foot.

'So?'

'Miss Keane told Mother she thinks I should go back to school.'

'She didn't.' Tom looked confused. 'Maude, that's brilliant. But then, who'd mind Jack after school? He finishes at two, doesn't he?'

Maude tasted a metallic tang in her mouth, took her thumb out, and wiped the welling blood on her jeans.

'She's got a new friend,' she said.

Tom looked confused. 'Who does?'

'Miss Keane came over to the house yesterday. I'd picked Jack up from school. Was making a bit of dinner, and she just came in through the back door. She'd a man with her.'

Tom was watching her. Had he tensed? Did he know what was coming?

'He said he was a teacher, but he's not from our school. They went upstairs to talk to Mother. And when they came down Miss Keane said I was to go back to school. That I shouldn't be missing out on my education. She said the man would bring Jack home from school every day. Stay with mother until I get home.'

'What about the money?' Tom asked.

'Miss Keane said that I can work on weekends, that she won't stop the money.' She didn't need to tell Tom that this made no sense, that it conflicted with everything they knew of Domenica Keane, who made her work for every penny until her hands were raw and her body shook from tiredness and hunger. 'I don't think the money is going to come from Miss Keane, Tom.' The fear rose up in her again then, and she bit down on it hard, before it could choke her. Blood again, in her mouth. She took her thumb out, and watched the swift rivulet run.

Tom's hands were gripping the chains of the swing, hard, his knuckles white from the pressure. His eyes were locked on Maude, but his thoughts were far away, and his face was haunted.

She wanted to stop the conversation there. Go to him, comfort him. 'He said his name was Mr Schiller. Simon Schiller. You never told me who it was, Tom, and I promised I would never, never talk about it again. But I have to ask you now.'

'You have to stop him.' Tom's voice came out in a rasping whisper. He coughed, wiped his mouth. 'Tell your mother. If you tell her she won't let him in the house.'

Maude put her face in her hands, leaning her elbows against her knees. She felt her grief rise, and pressed her palms so hard to her eyes that they hurt. Crying wouldn't stop Simon Schiller. Crying wouldn't change what her mother had become.

'She already knows.'

They sat in silence for a long moment, until Tom stood abruptly and walked away, stopping at the edge of the playground to vomit.

'Sorry,' he said. 'I'm sorry.'

Maude wanted to tell him it didn't matter, that he had nothing to say sorry for, but she couldn't find the words.

'Mother says I have to go to school on Monday.'

Tom swallowed. 'I'll tell the police,' he said. 'We'll go to the social workers.'

Maude was shaking her head. 'They won't believe you. They didn't believe you when you tried to tell them before, did they? What am I going to do, Tom?'

'You'll have to run away. I'll help.'

'I can't run away with Jack. He's only five. How would I take care of him? How would I feed him, get him to school? No one would believe I'm old enough to be his mother. They'd have us back here in less than a week.'

'What makes you think your mother knows?'

Maude looked away. She shook her head. Hilaria was so much worse. There were long red furrows in her skin from the scratching. There'd been blood in her vomit the other night, blood in her urine. And she was confused a lot of the time. But after Keane and Schiller had left, Maude had gone upstairs, had seen the extra vodka bottles, the roll of pound notes on the bedside table.

'I need to talk to Hannah,' she said.

Tom looked confused.

'I need her to get something for me.'

'What?'

Maude took a deep breath. Clenched her fists. 'As long as my mother is alive there's no way out for me and Jack. They'll never take us away from her, and I can't run away and keep Jack safe. He needs a family. He needs a normal family. Parents who'll feed him every day, and bring him to school, and keep him safe. My mother's dying. Do you know there's blood in her pee every day? Her skin is yellow. Sometimes she doesn't know where she is. She's going to die, Tom, but not fast enough to save Jack.'

Tom was staring at her now, understanding as well as horror and pity growing in his eyes.

'Not fast enough unless I do something,' Maude said quietly.

Tom didn't say anything, breathing quickly as if he had just run up a hill.

'So.' She took a deep breath. 'I need to talk to Hannah. I need her help.' Knowing as she spoke what she was asking of him. How terrified he was for his sister. He'd confided his worries to Maude – that Hannah was in over her head with someone older. He was a drug dealer, and maybe he'd started Hannah on some of what he sold. She knew what she was asking of him – to be complicit in this thing, to make his sister complicit in it.

'He might end up in a group home.' Tom's voice was hoarse. 'Or with shitty foster parents.' It had happened to him and Hannah, more than once. They had parents, but their mother had bipolar disorder, and every time she'd had to be hospitalised, they'd been taken into care. Their father said he couldn't cope.

'They weren't all bad,' Maude said.

He paused for a long moment, then bent down to pick up his backpack, slung it over his shoulder. 'Come on,' he said. 'She'll be at the flat.'

She'd followed him down the street, her eyes on his back, terrified and grateful. And as they walked, her dread and her determination had grown. She would do whatever it took to save Jack.

Now, in the interview room, Maude said, 'Hannah didn't say anything else?'

Tom shook his head, looked down at the statement. 'She says she assumed you bought it from Rick to use it yourself, and your mother got hold of it somehow. That she never asked questions before or after.'

They both knew that wasn't true. Hannah had shown her what to do – given her the syringe and shown her how to cook it up, how to inject. She hadn't been expert, not then at any rate. But she'd observed the process more than once and that had been enough.

'Right,' said Maude slowly. 'You think she's trying to make a deal?'

'I'm sure of it. She's not eligible for early release until she's served two years. But they have broad discretion on temporary release – they could release her early and call it temporary release until the end of her sentence. I know that Hannah tried to do deals before, tried to get out any way she could, but it wasn't happening. She had nothing to bargain with.' Tom tapped the file folder again. 'This statement. This was her bait. What else could it be?'

Maude nodded.

'I'm sorry, Maude. But I can't be your lawyer. I can refer you, get you the very best counsel.'

'You can't represent me because you're already Hannah's lawyer. And you think there's a conflict.'

'There's obviously a conflict. You'll have to pull her apart in your defence. And I ... I'm so sorry, Maude, but I have to do what I can to protect her. I'm not saying I'll push her testimony forward but ... Christ, what the hell am I supposed to do?'

Maude was quiet for a long time. When she spoke, her voice was husky, from tiredness or emotion or both. 'They must have asked you too.'

'What?'

'They must have asked you what you knew. We were best friends. Hannah was your sister.'

'They asked me. I told them I didn't know anything.'

'Okay.' She should get another lawyer. A lawyer who would get her bail so she could find out what the hell had happened to Jack. A lawyer who could question Hannah Collins and destroy her credibility so that Maude could be cleared of these charges and get back to her life, wherever that would be.

'I want you,' she said.

He said nothing, just looked at her across the battered old table.

'I want you to be my lawyer, and I want you to be Hannah's lawyer.'

'Maude, I don't think you understand. I can't represent both of you. The only way I could do that would be if you didn't dispute Hannah's evidence, if you accepted it. I can't represent two clients whose interests conflict in this way.'

'I understand better than you do, Tom. Hannah's not my enemy. She wasn't then, and she isn't now.' Maude felt a heavy certainty settle into place. 'Hannah did what she could to help me save Jack. Now it's my turn.'

'What are you talking about?'

'I won't try to disprove Hannah's statement. I'll accept it, just as you said.'

'Jesus, Maude. I'm not telling you to do that. You'd have to be mad. The gardaí have nothing, nothing at all on you, and Hannah's a terrible witness. Any decent lawyer could destroy her credibility in about thirty seconds. Do you not see? You'd be handing them a chunk of the puzzle for no reason.'

'It's not for no reason. I've every reason. It'll get Hannah out of prison. With her baby. It'll give her a chance.' Her eyes searched his. 'You said she's stayed clean, all this time, in prison, with drugs everywhere. If she can do that in prison she'll do it outside, and you'll help her.'

Tom brought his hands up over his eyes, pressed hard. 'Fuuuuuck. Fuck, Maude. This isn't right.' He took his hands away. 'What about you? Are you happy to sit in jail for twenty years?'

He was asking her if she'd given up. She shook her head slowly. 'Do you think Hannah's evidence is enough to convict me? If I say I bought the stuff for personal use, and Mother must have seen it and taken it? Who is there to contradict me?'

Tom's gaze held hers.

'It's such a risk, Maude. Such a monstrous risk.'

'A risk worth taking.'

It took Aisling less than five minutes to find it, once she knew what she was looking for. She logged back into Jack's Google account, fooled about with the settings until she found the Timeline button. She clicked, and a box opened up on the screen with a graphic of a globe, covered with little red location markers. Aisling clicked Next, then Next again, and a map of the world opened up in front of her. Again there were little red dots scattered here and there. This time most of them were in Ireland. Almost all of Galway was covered in a large red disk, then a scattering of red dots appeared in Dublin and elsewhere. A handful more over the European cities they'd visited together, or that Jack had visited for rugby weekends – London, Edinburgh, Paris, Rome. There was a dot over Northern Italy, where they'd holidayed with friends the previous summer. How much could this thing tell her?

She clicked on the mass of red around Galway; the map zoomed in and the red splodge resolved into hundreds of red dots. There were larger circles around their home, Jack's work, his gym, their local pub – places where Jack spent a lot of time. It took her another few minutes of poking about to figure out that the information could be searched by date. Feeling uneasy, she typed in the date, the last day she had seen Jack alive – *16 March 2013* – and Jack's last day opened up before her.

Not just the places he'd been but the routes he taken – the red dots were now linked by thin blue lines. She could hover over a dot or line and the app told her what time Jack left a location, a swoop of the cursor across the screen and she could see what time he arrived at his destination. Jesus. His whole life was in this thing. Everywhere they had been together, everywhere he had been when they were apart, all recorded on some Google database in Dublin. Had he known? That he was effectively carrying a personal tracking device in his pocket? Aisling looked at her own phone, at her laptop. She used a different email provider, but she had Google Maps and for all she knew it recorded her movements in just the same way. And she'd probably agreed to it, clicking to accept every time there was a terms update, never ever reading the fine print.

It was messed up, but she was grateful for it. Someday when she was ready she could sit down and go through the Timeline. It was a record of Jack's life, or at least some of it, and it seemed right that there should be at least this trace of him left behind. For now though, she needed to put grief aside and think.

Jack's last day. She knew as soon as she saw the Timeline that Jack had not been meeting anyone. According to Google, Jack and his phone had left the house just after ten o'clock, not long after she'd fallen asleep. He'd driven to Salthill, where he parked outside a deli they liked, then drove on exactly seventeen minutes later. He drove out of Galway, past Headford – an hour and twenty minutes north in fact, to Castlebar, then north again, to Lough Mask.

Which was where Jack went when he needed to think. There were hiking trails that snaked through forest and mountainside, tough hikes and technical climbs. If Jack had something on his mind that was where he went to work it out, and almost always alone. He'd brought Aisling once, but it was challenging terrain, and after that they'd chosen easier, shorter hikes when they went together. If Jack had been meeting someone they would have met in Galway, in a coffee shop, or Jack would have brought them home.

No, Jack had gone to Lough Mask to think about the pregnancy. He'd gone there because he was upset, and worried, and he needed to think. The possibility of suicide suggested itself again and Aisling shoved it away. She looked instead at Timeline.

Jack had arrived at the trail head at noon. He'd started the hike, but the record of his movements cut off twenty minutes later, on the trail. Aisling sat up straighter, stared at the screen. Clicked again but nothing changed. Jack's trace ended at Lough Mask, right on the quarry trail. That was weird. Either his battery had died, or Jack had turned his phone off. The latter didn't seem likely – she'd never known him to do it, even in the cinema he just muted the thing. And Jack plugged his phone in every night. It should have been fully charged when he set off that morning. Aisling stared at the screen for another moment, then pushed it away. She sat back on the couch again, took a drink. Did it matter? He hadn't gone to Lough Mask to meet anyone, that was the point.

Aisling put down her glass and walked quickly around the room. Then she leaned two hands and her forehead against the mantelpiece and rested for a long moment. This was head-wrecking. Who did she think she was fooling? She was not an investigator. She looked back at the table, at Maude's laptop, her photographs, her boarding card, her notes about Jack's death. What did it all add up to, in the end? Aisling resisted an urge to lift one side of the coffee table with her foot – for a second she could almost see the whole thing tipping, the computer and documents sliding to the floor, the wine bottle toppling and spilling. If she did it, she would leave the lot there.

She didn't know what to do. There were so many questions. Aisling sat again, picked up her phone. She stared at the number for a long time, thinking it all through, before she dialled.

Aggie's voice was hushed, but not sleepy. 'Aisling? Are you all right? Hold on.' A muffled sound, as Aggie left what was probably her bedroom, and closed the door behind her. 'Sorry dear, Brendan's sleeping. Are you all right?'

'I'm sorry to call you so late, Aggie. I'm fine. Just. Maude won't be able to visit this weekend.'

Silence for a moment. 'Oh?'

Aisling took a breath. 'She's been arrested. The guards think she killed her mother. Back in ninety-three.'

Aisling closed her eyes as she listened to Aggie breathe out, a sudden shocked exhalation. Oh God. This wasn't the way to tell her. She could almost see the colour drain from Aggie's face.

The other end of the phone was quiet. 'Aggie? Aggie, are you all right?'

'That poor girl,' Aggie said. 'That poor, poor girl.' There was deep pity in her voice, but no surprise.

'Aggie. You knew, didn't you?'

Aggie didn't speak for a long time, so long that it began to seem like she wouldn't speak again.

'Tell me,' Aisling said.

Aggie's voice sounded like it was coming from a long way away. 'We couldn't have children of our own, me and Brendan. We never knew why. It was just the way it was. We fostered children instead. So many children. Some of them we had for just a few days, a weekend maybe, some for months and months. And some came back again and again.'

Aisling heard the creaking of a door opening and closing. She imagined Aggie going to the kitchen, finding her chair near the warmth of the Aga, seeking comfort.

'Some of those children had been through hell by the time they got to us, Aisling. And eventually, every time, we sent them back to it. You'll never know what that was like. To hold a child in your arms, to soothe his pain, to heal his injuries, to show him what love is, maybe for the first time in his little life, only to have him taken away, and sent back to what brought him to you in the first place.'

'But you kept going,' Aisling said.

'Brendan wanted to stop. It was breaking my heart. It was breaking both of us. But all I could think was that there'd be a child somewhere, in some terrible place, and a social worker deciding that she'd have to leave him there, because there was nowhere better to go. We did stop, for a while, but I had such nightmares.' Her voice was drifting away, getting lost in the memories.

'What happened with Jack?'

'There was a boy before Jack. His name was Tom. He came to us for a few months, when his mother was admitted to hospital. But before us, he had been to other places. I found him one day, in the bathroom, scrubbing himself raw. He didn't tell me what happened, not then anyway.'

Aisling waited.

'Two years later Tom came to our door. He was back with his family, things were going better for them. Tom told me that there was a little boy in danger. That what had happened to Tom would happen to this child, unless I was willing to step in and take him.'

'Jack.'

'Yes, that was Jack. I said I would do whatever I could, pressed Tom to give me names, let me call the guards, call in social workers straight away. But Tom wouldn't say anything more. He told me I needed to wait two more days, and he would be back. And he did come back. Two mornings later he showed up at the back door, and told me that Jack was at the hospital. That he needed me.'

'Tom came to you before Hilaria died.'

'Yes.'

Aisling turned it all over in her head. This meant Maude was guilty. She'd known her mother was going to die, known that Jack would need a home, had worked with Tom to make sure he had one. Christ almighty. It was so cold, so *planned*. What sort of person could do that?

'You never told anyone,' Aisling said.

'It was weeks before I figured it out. I didn't know about the heroin, not in the beginning. By the time I realised what must have happened, I had Jack. I was afraid I would lose him.'

Aisling made reassuring noises, but the truth was that she didn't understand. None of this made sense to her. It was like she had strayed into a nightmare, where no one and nothing was as it seemed. Jack, lovely Jack, dead by suicide, or murdered because of some secret life he had never shared with her? And Aggie, lovely, motherly Aggie, hiding secrets of her own. She must have pulled every string she had to get Jack fostered with her, to adopt him.

Aggie was still talking. 'When Jack was seven we applied to adopt him. We didn't change his surname though. He was a Blake, and he stayed a Blake. That was for Maude, in case she ever came back.'

Aisling got off the phone as quickly as she could, promised Aggie whatever she wanted to hear. She didn't want to talk to her, didn't want to hear her talking about Maude the murderer, with that note of what in her voice ... Empathy? Gratitude? As soon as she hung up she started to gather everything up, to repack Maude's backpack, to shut her own computer down. It was Friday night. She would go to work the next day after all. She'd been scheduled for an early shift. She would do that, then do the handover with Cummins on Sunday evening, since that was all arranged. Then take some time off, try to get her head straight. On Monday she would go to the police, bring them Maude's boarding card and her laptop, and ask them if they would review Jack's call and message history. This was – it always had been – a matter for the gardaí, and she had other things to worry about. She was finished playing detective.

When the room was tidy she found Jack's jumper where she had left it on the back of the couch, and pulled it on. She sat and thought about the future she was fighting to hold on to. A future that suddenly seemed leached of colour, of warmth, of humanity. It was the story of her life. She strove for perfection, and the closer she got the emptier she felt. Aisling had never felt more alone, less worthy, than she did in that moment. She laid her aching, tired head down on the arm of the couch, curled into a ball, and cried.

Saturday 30 March 2013

CHAPTER TWENTY-SIX

'I've lost control of the thing completely,' Cormac said. He was lying in bed, his arms folded behind his head on the pillow, so he could watch Emma as she moved around the room. She was wrapped in a towel, her hair still wet from the shower.

'And she's been arrested, this woman?'

Cormac nodded. Emma took a pair of knickers from her underwear drawer and pulled them on under her towel. She dropped the towel to put on a bra, then pulled a grey T-shirt over her head. It was old and well loved, and it moulded itself to her soft curves in a way that made him want to pull her down into the bed beside him and restart what they had just finished. She flipped her hair forwards and wrapped her towel around it, twisting it so that it formed a neat turban, then came and sat on the bed facing him, tucking her bare legs back under the covers.

'Do you think she did it?'

'I don't know.'

Her grey eyes were assessing. 'I think you do know, Corm.'

He grimaced, closed his eyes. 'She may have. Her mother was abusive. Maude loved her little brother; she could have done it to protect him. But the abuse had been going on for years. And the mother was on her way out. According to the postmortem she didn't have more than a few months, maybe six at the outside. End-stage liver disease. Maude would have known. So why do it then? Why take the risk? I can't see it.'

Emma had pushed her feet up against his thigh – they were cold and he reached down to rub some warmth into them.

'Maybe she didn't know, didn't realise. She was very young, after all. And I'm not sure I would recognise end-stage liver disease. So, a teenager? Used to her mother being sick?' Emma shrugged. 'Maybe she'd had enough, just lost it after years of abuse. Isn't that what happens, sometimes?'

Cormac was shaking his head slowly. 'She was fifteen years old. She would have had to source heroin, needle, everything. Then learn how to inject it, all of which would have taken planning, premeditation. This wasn't a situation where someone finally lost it and retaliated.'

'And Danny thinks he knows where she got the heroin.'

Cormac couldn't prevent his face from stiffening, and Emma, watching him, said, 'Do you really think he would do that? Solicit someone to give false evidence, I mean?'

'Jesus, I don't know, Em. I'm beginning to think I don't know Danny at all. And everything about this case has been off from the beginning. The fact that this investigation was prioritised, when there was nothing new to go on at the time. There wasn't a cop in the station who didn't know the case was intended to put pressure on Maude Blake, to get her off our backs about her brother's suicide. Which makes no sense. And then suddenly Danny's up to his knees in my case, bringing me a junkie mother's statement, and Murphy's singing his praises like he just caught Osama bin Laden.' Cormac snorted.

'I suppose it's just as well we never met them for dinner then,' Emma said, and curled her toes around his leg, smiling slightly, probably trying to cheer him up. He forced a smile in return and she abandoned her spot at the end of the bed, climbing back under the covers and laying her head on his chest. She took one of his hands in hers, slid her fingers through his and squeezed, as if engaging in a gentle game of mercy. 'What's in it for him though?' she asked.

'Maybe he thinks he'll get another promotion if he keeps the boss happy.'

'But then what's in it for the boss? What does it matter if she asks questions about her brother's suicide? I don't understand why that's a big deal.'

Cormac was beginning to think it was a very big deal. Something was going on here. Something much bigger than garda embarrassment over a shoddy investigation. He just couldn't see the connection, not yet.

'Danny's sister is missing. She's been gone for two weeks, and they've only just started searching for her.'

'What? Why? I mean, why the delay?'

He shook his head. 'Her aunt reported her missing, her parents said no, that she was probably with friends.'

'What does Danny say?'

'He thought it was nothing, initially. He's realised now I think that there really is a problem. I haven't spoken to him since Thursday. I tried to call, yesterday, last night, but no answer.'

Emma was quiet for a moment. 'Do you regret coming back?' she asked softly.

He squeezed her hand, then brought it to his lips in a quick kiss. 'Same bullshit, different location,' he said, his tone lighter. They were both quiet, listening to the rain outside. It was early Saturday morning. Cormac wasn't sure if there was much point in going in to the station, with Murphy in Dublin until Tuesday, and the case effectively out of his hands. He'd spend the day with Emma, think about how to handle Murphy when he saw him. How could he respond to that rumour, if that was the root of the trouble? Pull a Maude on it and look for CCTV footage from the hotel? A hotel like the Radisson might have cameras in the hallways, would certainly have them in the lobby. He'd need to send someone else to get it though; once he put his hands on that evidence it would be tainted. Christ, if Murphy was taking the rumour seriously, things could get messy very quickly. He'd have to get out in front. He needed his job. Needed to be in Galway. Mostly because this was where Emma would be for at least the next couple of years, but partly because he'd never failed at anything, and he didn't want to start here.

Cormac tried to put the job out of his mind. He'd send Fisher for the security footage when he came in from Strandhill. Get him to log it into evidence. Beyond that there was no point in obsessing about the station all weekend. If the weather improved Emma would want to go for a walk on the prom, which would be freezing but packed with people taking their morning stroll to the crash of the grey Atlantic waves. They'd get lunch somewhere warm and busy, and come home afterwards with the newspapers to sit in front of the fire for the rest of the day. Cormac kissed Emma, then pushed himself out of bed and headed for the shower, moving like an old man. He knew he had what he wanted, that he should be happy, but at best he'd just screwed up his first case in a new job, and at worst half the Galway police force were corrupt as fuck.

CHAPTER TWENTY-SEVEN

Tom left Galway at 7 a.m. on Saturday morning, and got to the Mountjoy security gate by ten. Visiting hours were 10 to 12, and he'd had a booking before the Maude situation had blown up, before he'd known about Hannah's statement.

The Dóchas Centre was a special-purpose block built within the confines of Mountjoy Prison, and it was operating at one hundred and forty per cent capacity. Rooms intended for single occupants had been fitted out with pairs of bunk beds and were occupied by up to five. Thirty per cent of the inmates were on methadone replacement. It was medium security, but some of the inmates should have been in solitary. It was not the place for a child.

Hannah was already waiting for him, seated at a table with Saoirse asleep in her arms. The room was like a particularly soulless university canteen, without the buffet, furnished with formica tables and plastic chairs. It filled up slowly, families taking their places around tables. A little girl with an anxious expression on her face was drawn into a hug, where she started to cry. Tom looked away. Visits were only half an hour, a pitiful period of time for children to catch up with a mother they got to see only once a week.

Hannah sat at a table pushed up against the far wall, alone if you didn't count the baby on her lap. She looked tired and strained, pale-faced with grey circles under her eyes. Her dark hair was unwashed, and tied back from her face in the same loose plait she'd worn at fifteen. Despite everything, she was still beautiful. Hannah acknowledged him with a brief flick of her eyes and an attempt at a smile, before she dropped her gaze again to her daughter. Tom looked at his sleeping niece. She was a round, happy little baby. He desperately wanted her to stay that way.

'I already know the appeal was refused,' Hannah said, her head still bowed.

'How did you ...?'

'Cellmate has a cousin who's a social worker. She was delighted to give me the good news.'

Bitch. 'When did she tell you?'

'Week ago.'

Jesus. He'd wanted to keep it from her, hoping that he'd find a solution. He'd known the likely outcome when he'd visited the week before, but he'd had to tell her about Jack, and that seemed enough tragedy for one day. Besides, he'd still been hoping to pull a rabbit out of the hat, had even thought about asking Aggie, but she was too old to foster now. She couldn't be the rescuer this time, and even if he'd had a guardian angel to call on, these days the system was much more regulated.

'I tried, Hannah. But I'm not married. I work long hours. I told them I'd hire a full-time nanny, but they insisted that they want a foster parent who'll be at home all day.'

'Bastards,' she said, but she was distracted, her tone without rancour. She stroked a stray lock of wispy hair back from Saoirse's forehead. She'd been avoiding eye contact since he sat down.

'How is she?' he asked.

'She's grand. She doesn't know where she is. She doesn't know what normal is.'

Tom said nothing. They'd talked so many times about the situation she was in. The overcrowding. The drugs. Her fears for Saoirse. Hannah was terrified for her baby. He'd tried and tried to reassure her. When his first application to foster the baby had been refused he'd told her that the system was better now, that the families were properly vetted, that he'd visit Saoirse every week, as much as they'd let him. She'd looked at him with despairing blue eyes and said, 'You won't be there at night though, will you, Tom? You won't be there when they come into her room at night.'

'Hannah,' Tom said quietly.

She still wouldn't look at him.

'Hann, I know.'

'What do you know?'

'I spoke to Maude.'

She went absolutely still. The remaining colour deserted her face, and for a moment he thought she was going to faint. She cradled the baby closer, raised her eyes to his.

'Have they arrested her?'

He nodded, and her eyes filled with tears.

'Tom. I feel like there's nothing left of me. I keep trying. I keep saying I'll do anything, anything at all to keep Saoirse safe. And every time I take another step everything gets worse. I'm running out of choices. And every choice I make is a bad one.'

'Listen to me, Hannah. You're doing the best you can.'

'Do you remember when we were kids, Tom? Do you remember how we used to be together? You and Maude so serious. And the way she would mind little Jack. Do you remember when she came to Kilmore first? She used to push him around everywhere, in that knackered old pram. And the way she'd run, I mean just *run* home after school? And when he got bigger she never left him alone, except at school.'

'I remember,' said Tom. He waited, but she said nothing, her eyes lost in memories. 'Hannah, tell me the whole story. How did you know Maude was home? Who did you call to set this up?'

Her eyes came to his, confused. 'I didn't know,' she said. 'And I didn't call anyone. He came to me.'

'Who?'

'The guard. He said he knew I grew up in Kilmore, that I had a drug history. He said he could get me early release if I gave evidence against a woman from back in the day. I didn't know he was talking about Maude, not at first.'

Tom sat still. 'You didn't call anyone? Didn't mention Maude by name to anyone?'

'No,' Hannah said. 'Not to a sinner. Why would I? Maude's been gone twenty years, or at least I thought she was. Why would I think the guards would give a shit about something that happened twenty years ago?'

'Tell me exactly what he said.'

Hannah shook her head. 'They brought me out of my cell to an interview room. This guy – McIntyre is his name – he was waiting for me. He took Saoirse out of my arms the moment I came into the room. He held her, gave her a cuddle, and I just knew, Tom. He would have knocked her against the wall as soon as look at her. Holding her was a threat, you know?' Her grip on the baby had tightened as she spoke, her voice grew louder, and Saoirse shifted and made a soft sound in her sleep.

Tom reached across and held Hannah's hand, and she loosened her grip.

'After Saoirse was born and I knew I couldn't lose her, I went to the governor. Told him I would give evidence to the gardaí if it would get me a remittance on my sentence. He set me up with a detective. I told her everything I knew about the trade, gave her names. Stuff that would get me killed probably, if anyone was to know about it. But she told me my information was no good to them. That they knew it all already. That the people I knew were too low level to be any use to them.'

'You never told me,' Tom said.

'I was ashamed of myself,' Hannah said. 'The people I talked about, they were the dregs, mostly, but I still felt like the worst kind of shit.'

'And McIntyre?'

'I don't know. He must have gotten my name from somewhere. He knew enough to look me up anyway, check my record. I was still living at home in Kilmore the first time I was picked up by police. He said they were very interested in someone called Maude Blake, and if I was in a position to say I knew Maude had bought or tried to buy heroin back in 1993, that he could get my sentence remitted.'

'Christ.' Tom held Hannah's gaze, wondered for a moment if she could be shading the truth. But the look she gave him was open and clear, and Hannah had always been a useless liar. 'Hannah, are you telling me that he didn't know? That he just stumbled onto the truth?'

Hannah shook her head slowly. 'It sounds crazy, I know it sounds crazy, but that's what happened. I told him I would go along with it. Told him I'd say that I knew Maude, that I knew she had been looking for someone who sold heroin. But that's it.' She locked eyes with him then, pleading with him to understand, and he had a momentary flashback to the morning when he and Maude had found Hannah at the apartment. The morning when they'd sat with her and explained everything, and she'd made no protest, asked no questions, just got them what they needed and explained exactly what to do. He remembered the sick feeling in his stomach as he realised just how familiar she was with the process. Remembered the moment before he and Maude had left, how the three of them had sat there, in silent solidarity. Three damaged kids, determined to save a fourth.

'This was a set-up,' Tom said. 'Maude was right. They are trying to set her up. This isn't about Hilaria. They're after her because of Jack.'

'Jack? I don't understand,' Hannah said.

'Hann, did McIntyre realise that he'd stumbled onto the truth?'

'I don't think so. I didn't tell him. I wouldn't have gone along with it at all except that he told me that if I didn't give the statement, he could charge me with conspiracy to commit murder. He would say that I was in on it. Either way, Maude was going down, and I could go down with her. But if I gave the statement, he'd get my sentence remitted and me out of here before the end of the month. I'd get to keep Saoirse.'

'Why didn't you call me?'

'He told me I had to make a decision there and then. If I agreed he would take a statement from me, then he'd get a deal signed off.'

Tom hesitated. 'Did you get the deal in writing?'

She snorted. 'Of course I bloody did. You can't spend a year in this place and learn nothing. Are you going to ask me to withdraw it? But the thing is, Tom, apart from Saoirse, this guy McIntyre? I'm afraid of him. He's a garda, but I think he's the type who'd kill you if you crossed him.'

Hannah had good instincts for everyone but her boyfriends. 'No Hann, no. I'm not going to ask you to withdraw it. Jesus. I'm your brother. And it's not just me. Maude wants you to stand over your statement. She's not going to contradict you. She wants you and the baby out.'

She held his gaze, fear and hope in her eyes.

'She thinks she can beat the case regardless of your statement. She's willing to take the risk, because she owes you.'

'Jesus.' A breath of hope, of air, an exhalation.

'I think she should be right. There's not enough evidence against her for a murder case, nowhere near enough. But I'm worried.'

'Tell me,' she said. And her eyes were dry now, and steady.

'I'm worried. This guy McIntyre is out to get her. Maybe more gardaí, too. Why? This all has to come back to Jack, doesn't it? Someone killed Jack, and Maude wouldn't let it go, so now they're after her too.'

'And if they were willing to kill Jack …' she let her voice trail off. 'Tell me what you want me to do.'

He shook his head. 'Let's get you out first, then figure out what to do next. Maude's bail hearing is on Monday. The full trial won't be for months. What does your deal say? When do you get out?'

She pulled a folded sheet of paper from her pocket. Handed it across to him and he read it. 'Jesus,' he said. 'We might be able to get you out after the bail hearing, the way this thing is written, and with Saoirse and everything.'

'Really? On Monday? That can't be … he never said.'

'He'd want you here as long as possible, to keep an eye on you, but the deal is done, remittance of sentence in exchange for testimony. You've given a written statement. I'll bring this to the governor. See if I can arrange release for Monday.'

She reached across the table and gripped his hand hard, tears brimming in her eyes. She couldn't speak. She swallowed. 'Do what you can, Tom,' she said. 'And tell Maude thank you. Tell her I'll see her soon.'

CHAPTER TWENTY-EIGHT

They went out on Saturday night. It was the last thing Cormac wanted to do, but Emma pulled a rare veto. If they sat in and watched TV he would only brood over everything, and end up in worse humour than he'd started. Better to go out, have a few drinks, talk to friends about everything and anything else for a while. Let his subconscious mind work at the problem while the rest of him got on with living. She knew him well, and she might have been right, if it wasn't for the fact that most of his friends were in Dublin, and none of them were here, in the pub, providing the required distraction. Instead they had met most of Emma's team. Emma's second in command had young children and hadn't come. The others – three women and two men, all under thirty – were happy with their new jobs, happy with the progress of the last few weeks, and ready to celebrate both. In other circumstances he might have enjoyed their company, but tonight they seemed too young, and in spite of their undoubtedly vast intellects, too insubstantial. Cormac could feel Emma's eyes on him as he allowed himself to withdraw from the conversation. He gave her a wink, and was relieved when the buzzing phone in his pocket gave him a reason to excuse himself and go outside.

It was Fisher, calling from Strandhill.

'Anything?' Cormac asked.

'I've been watching him since four,' Fisher said. Cormac checked his watch. Nine o'clock. Fisher continued, 'It's busy. Other than himself there's just a young one working the bar.

A student I'd say. When she arrived Lanigan disappeared into the back for a while. He might have eaten but if he did there's no opportunity in it for us. Since then he's been working. He's not touching the drink, just a plastic bottle of water he keeps behind the bar – he's taken a few swigs out of that. But I don't see how we could reach it.'

'And?' Cormac asked. Fisher's tone told him there was something else.

'I think he's a smoker. He served me himself, and his fingers are stained. Every thirty minutes or so he's disappearing out the back. Has to be to have a smoke. Can't be inside. Smoking ban.'

Cormac thought for a moment. 'Can you get around back? Without being seen?'

'It's a carpark. It's full, and mine's out on the street. I could wait for the next person to go. Take their place, and wait and see.'

It was a mark of Fisher's ambition, or maybe his youth, that he sounded enthusiastic at the prospect.

'Do that,' Cormac said. 'Text me when you have something.'

When he returned to the bar a full pint stood next to his last one, which he hadn't finished. There was talk of going on to a nightclub. Cormac caught Emma's eye. Not a fucking chance. She smiled, a quick flash of amusement, noticed by no one but him. God he loved that smile. That sudden dimple in her cheek, the arch of her eyebrow. He felt his mood lighten, and took a drink from his pint. Then he turned to his neighbour and joined a debate about Galway football.

They walked home together, hand in hand. It was cold, but the rain held off and there was such simple pleasure in that.

'What will you do?' she asked.

He shook his head. 'I don't know. If Murphy ordered that arrest, then he's taken the case out of my hands. If he didn't order it, if Mel Hackett just saw an opportunity and went for it, that might be just as bad.'

'Why? Because Murphy won't undo it?'

'Exactly. She must have thought – they must have thought – that Murphy would at least condone it.' He shook his head. He had bigger problems, but he wasn't telling Emma about the rumour, not until he had dealt with it and it was in the rear-view mirror. He couldn't wrap his head around how quickly things had gone wrong, how fast the ground had slipped from under his feet. The first few weeks had been nothing more than he'd expected – a testing period. He hadn't thought much of the hazing – messing around with cold case files was unprofessional, in his opinion – but it had been within the realm of normal. But the looks, the not-so-subtle cold shoulders he'd received from other detectives this week, was something different. It was the rumour of his involvement with Maude Blake that was doing the damage. And if Murphy suspected him of that then taking him off the case was the necessary next step.

It could be Healy. Healy saw him as a threat to whatever he had going on, and perhaps he had decided that he was going to take Cormac down before Cormac could get to him. But Cormac had a nagging feeling that Danny was in this thing too.

As they turned into Canal Walk, his phone buzzed in his pocket. A text from Fisher.

He smokes at the back door. Drops his butts. Probably a hundred of them there. Take some?

'What is it?' Emma asked.

Cormac replied. *Leave it. Find a place to stay. I'll meet you tomorrow, four o'clock. Bring some rubbish bags and a brush.*

'I might have to work tomorrow,' he said to Emma.

Her eyes searched his face in the dim light of the street lamp. 'Another case?' At his nod, she shrugged. 'If you have to, you have to.'

She didn't ask him anymore about the Blake case. About what he was going to do on Monday. She must have known that he didn't have any answers. Instead, they went home, went to bed, and did what they could to forget about everything but each other.

Sunday 31 March 2013

CHAPTER TWENTY-NINE

Despite all her resolution, by mid-morning on Sunday Aisling found herself driving out to Lough Mask, Jack's smaller backpack keeping her company in the passenger seat. She'd traced his every step so far, including the deli stop, and the backpack held a sandwich and a thermos of soup, as well as the mini-first aid kit, her water, and the basics that usually took up space at the bottom of the bag.

She reached the trail at 2 p.m., two hours later than Jack would have. The small parking area was just off the road but hidden by trees – if you didn't know it, it would have been easy to pass it by. The place was deserted, despite the fact that the weather was good for the time of year. No rain, beyond a bit of drizzle, and the sun had won the battle with the clouds so far that day. Aisling parked, and grabbed the backpack and her jacket. She pulled everything on as she stood beside the car. Would she really find answers here? What was she looking for – signs of a struggle? She felt ridiculous, a grown-up playing at Veronica Mars. She excused it by telling herself that this was where Jack came to figure things out. Maybe it would work for her.

She zipped up her jacket and started to walk. The advantage of the cold weather was of course that the mud was frozen. She was able to balance her way through the worst of the tussocks and ruts that made up the first few hundred metres of the track. Once she'd passed the last farm gate the track narrowed very quickly, and the trees drew in overhead, splintering and fracturing the feeble winter sunlight.

She reached the point where Jack's trail stopped, and looked about her. It was shaded under the canopy, the air frigid, the ground covered in a blanket of wet leaves. There was nothing to see. She turned, stared back down the trail, then turned again. Nothing. The place was innocent, and deserted, and there was no sign that Jack had ever been here. Aisling told herself she hadn't been expecting anything anyway, and pressed on.

The track split in two and she chose the right fork. The left would have been an easier route – out towards the quarry – but she wasn't looking for easy that day, and she wanted to be out from under the canopy, wanted the warmth of the sun on her face. She pushed hard, and it didn't take long for her breath to feel tight in her chest, for her hamstrings to complain. She ignored it and pushed harder. When she was out she would slow her pace; would need to anyway once she hit the steeper incline. The hike was harder than she'd remembered, and she wasn't as fit as she should be, but she was strong enough. She stopped thinking about everything, about Jack, about the future; switched everything off except her focus on the next step, the next breath.

Aisling stopped to eat two hours into the hike. She hadn't made it to the halfway point, but her breath was coming in hard gasps, and she was high enough that she had a view out over the quarry. She found a place, a little protected from the buffeting wind by a scrubby tree, and sat. The cold settled about her like a cloak, chilling the sweat on her brow and stiffening her hands. The sun was still out, but it was a winter sun – all show and no substance – and clouds were gathering. She was grateful for the warmth of the soup in her thermos as she ate and took in the view.

The water below was ice-cold perfection, reflecting the sky overhead. When they had come in summer the water had looked so inviting that she'd suggested a detour, and a swim, but Jack had told her that what she was admiring was a flooded quarry, and the water was toxic.

'If you were closer you'd be able to see,' he'd said. 'There are warning signs all around it, because people did come here to swim. There are fences too. There's a farm down there, and the fences keep the livestock from drinking the water.' He made a face. 'You'd never think it was toxic. Up close the water is bright blue and incredibly clear. Clear enough to see the car wrecks and mattresses that have been dumped in it.' He'd grinned at her. 'Looks great from here though, doesn't it?'

Now Aisling sat far above the quarry, and enjoyed the illusion. She let herself relax, felt the lightening of the weight on her shoulders, the first loosening of the tension she'd carried in her muscles since Jack had died. She felt so close to him here. She smiled through eyes that were suddenly filled with tears, and drank again from her thermos.

All at once, Aisling was distracted by movement from the treeline at the far side of the quarry. She squinted. Leaned forward. It was a car, must be a four-wheel drive, making its bumping way towards the quarry. Another followed a little behind. Both vehicles stopped, and people got out. They walked towards the water, seemed to consult, then two of the figures returned to the cars.

Curiosity got the better of her. She pulled Jack's backpack towards her and looked through it for the mini-binoculars he'd carried. He'd had two pairs, but the small set that she'd bought him for Christmas two years before was usually in this bag. Yes. She pulled them out and unfolded them, put them to her eyes and adjusted the focus. The figures swam into view. They were gardaí – two in uniform – and they were unloading diving equipment from the cars. She watched as two men put on drysuits, then one of them tied a rope around his waist and they both approached the water.

The taller of them walked straight in, took a moment to adjust his mask, then started to swim. The other followed a few metres into the water, and stood there, paying out the rope until there was about twenty metres between them. The swimmer gave a thumbs up, then went under. They were searching for something. The diver swam a full arc, using the rope to control his position. He resurfaced, another thumbs up, the rope was payed out again, and down he went. Aisling's sandwich was abandoned, her soup rapidly cooling. She was utterly absorbed in watching them, and might have stayed longer if the sun hadn't disappeared behind a cloud, and she'd suddenly become aware that she was shivering.

Aisling checked her watch. Shit. It was almost four-thirty. If she didn't hurry she wouldn't get back to the car before dark. She took a bite from her sandwich, one last swallow of cold soup, then stowed everything and started back down the trail.

What could they be searching for? They were hardly there for illegally dumped mattresses and car wrecks. So, what? A body? Drugs? Whatever it was it was something illegal, something serious enough to get eight gardaí with divers out here. What if Jack had seen something, seen someone? What if whatever the police were searching for was what had gotten Jack killed? She stopped walking. Thought about the Timeline map, about where Jack's phone had stopped recording his progress. It had been below the fork in the path, hadn't it? What if someone had been at the quarry that day, and Jack had seen them on the trail? She could almost see Jack greeting someone, giving a nod, a smile, a roll of the eyes that said, *Aren't we mad to be walking out here in winter*. Shit.

Aisling started running. She slipped twice, landing on her arse. The third time she twisted her ankle, but she ignored the pain and kept going.

She got to the fork before dark, but the sun was setting and the light was going. She cast about, but the narrow trail was floored with leaves and twigs and mud and she saw nothing. Breathing hard, she kept her head down, and walked slowly ahead. She pushed at clumps of leaves with the toe of her boot. Nothing. She kept going until she was twenty metres below the fork, then she stopped and turned back again, retracing her steps. She did that twice more, as the sun set, until she could barely see the ground in front of her. Then she dropped to her hands and knees and started feeling her way through the leaves. Wet soaked through the knees of her jeans. The ground was hard enough that there was no mud, but her hands froze in the cold, until she could barely feel anything. It was so quiet, so still. Had Jack been killed here? Was this the last place he saw?

She started to shake, from cold, and from fear. She heard a twig break, and looked up and around, her breath coming faster. An animal? A deer? She saw nothing, and returned to her search. She wanted to run, wanted to get out of there, but she couldn't leave. She searched again, and again, until the knees of her jeans were filthy and her hands were so cold they felt numb, like prosthetics attached at the wrist. And that was how she nearly missed it. Her right hand touched something, bumped against it under its blanket of leaves, but her hand was numb and she kept moving. Had that bump felt any different from the small stones she had picked up and discarded? She returned to where her hand had been, felt around, then again, and finally, her hand closed around something. Smooth plastic. She picked it up, and despite the dark, realised that she was holding Jack's phone.

CHAPTER THIRTY

Sunday afternoon saw Cormac take the coast road out to Strandhill. McSorley's bar was very close to the water, only three buildings back from the beach. The place was packed; cars were parked either side of the street and it took him some time to find a spot. When he got out of the car he looked around, taking in the smell of salt and vinegar chips, the tang of the ocean, the waves crashing in the distance. A voice came over a loud speaker, muffled from where Cormac stood, but he heard enough to realise that a surf competition was going on. The sun was going down. The competition would end soon, and the pub would be packed. Cormac crossed the road and walked to McSorley's, then walked around the back to the carpark. Fisher was already there, parked and waiting. Cormac walked to Fisher's car, opened the passenger door, got in.

'Why not Lanigan's?' he asked.

A beat. 'Pub was already named,' Fisher said. 'Guy called Tom McSorley sold it to him. Suppose Lanigan didn't see the point of making the change.'

Fisher had done his research, in fairness to him.

'What do we do now?' Fisher asked.

'How long since his last fag?' Cormac asked.

Fisher checked his watch. 'He's due one.'

'Then we wait,' Cormac said. 'I want a look at him.'

They were far enough back not to be noticeable, but it wasn't quite dark, and Cormac held his phone to his ear when Lanigan appeared at the back door. If Lanigan did see them he should assume that the two men were sitting in a car in his carpark because one of them was making a call. Lanigan had no reason to be suspicious; after all, no one had spoken to him about either murder in three decades.

Timothy Lanigan lit up, leaned against the wall to the right of the back door, and smoked. He took his time, and there was nothing unusual about him, except maybe that he looked at the sky as he smoked, instead of down into a mobile phone. When he was finished he stubbed the cigarette against the wall, dropped the butt on the ground, and went back into the pub. The door swung shut behind him.

'No one else comes out here?'

'I think it's the door to the storeroom,' Fisher said. 'The barmaid doesn't smoke. Or she didn't yesterday.'

'Come on so,' said Cormac. 'And bring your brush.'

The ground around the back door was littered with cigarette butts. There was an old planter to the left of the door, but whatever had once grown in it had long since died, and Lanigan had been using it as a bin until it started to overflow. At some point he had stopped pretending and started dropping the butts directly on the ground. There must have been a couple of hundred of them.

'Clean it up,' Cormac said. 'We need everything gone and the place photographed before he comes back.' He gestured for Fisher to hand over a bin bag, and when Fisher did, slowly, not yet understanding, Cormac took it from him and lifted the pot, putting it inside. Fisher caught on and started to clean up the cigarette butts that were littered all over the ground. When he'd gathered the lot, he stood and looked around.

'Good enough?' he asked.

'It'll do,' said Cormac. He gestured Fisher back, then using the evidence camera he'd slung around his neck, he took photographs, quickly but methodically. He wasn't a crime scene photographer, but these did not need to be technically perfect. It was getting dark as they returned to the car.

'Stay here,' Cormac said. 'Make a note of what time he comes out, what time he goes back in. How many cigarettes he smokes and how long it takes him. Make a note of everything and for God's sake do it in the dark.'

'Where'll you be?' Fisher asked.

'I'm going inside for dinner,' Cormac said. And he left Fisher to it.

Cormac thought about what might have attracted Lanigan to Strandhill as he walked around the pub to the front door. The reasons not to return to his last home were obvious – he'd basically been run out of the place. Was there something about this particular town that attracted him? Plenty of teenage girls taking surf lessons now. But what would the surf scene have been like when Lanigan came here? Had it existed at all? Maybe it was simply that the pub had come up for sale at the right time. Cormac reached the front door, pushed it open, and paused for long enough to see that the pub was a big space, contemporary not traditional. The kind of pub that served specialty brews and focaccia sandwiches. It wasn't full yet, but there was a happy buzz of conversation, and an atmosphere of anticipation for the night ahead. Cormac approached the bar, angling for the young woman serving pints. Lanigan was at the other end of the bar, no longer the handsome, open-faced young man of the photographs. He was in his sixties now, balding, and with the grey skin of a long-term smoker. The barmaid tilted an inquiring face in Cormac's direction, and he ordered a pint he had no intention of drinking and picked up a menu.

He took it to a corner table and sat at an angle that would allow him to keep an eye on Lanigan without being obvious about it. He was about to order food when he realised that he recognised someone sitting at the far end of the bar. Liam Hearne, reading a newspaper, a coffee cup on the table in front of him. Strandhill was his hometown, of course, but it hadn't occurred to Cormac that he would bump into him here.

When Danny had told him that Liam had turned to the drink, Cormac's first thought had been of an old mentor of his who'd gone exactly that way, bitter and broken and searching for solace in a bottle. His second thought had been surprise that it would happen to Liam. He'd never seemed the type. Liam was smart enough and hard enough to go as far as he wanted in the guards. The fact that he'd never wanted to be more than a garda working a small seaside town didn't take from the fact that he was one of the best Cormac had ever met.

Liam looked up from his newspaper, calmly caught Cormac's eye, and returned his attention to the paper. He took a sip from the coffee cup. Well, it didn't look like he was drinking tonight, unless that coffee was Irish.

Cormac glanced at Lanigan – still there, serving shots to a group of girls who were probably legal. He stood and went to Liam's table.

'Not talking to me, Liam?' said Cormac. He'd meant it as a sort of light-hearted opening, and it was only as he finished the sentence that it occurred to him Liam might have heard the rumours too. Liam, who knew everything that went on from Donegal to Cork.

But Liam folded his newspaper. 'I thought you might be on the job,' he said. 'You have that look about you.' He nodded to the seat opposite him.

Cormac grimaced as he took the seat. He was that obvious. Better then that he was chatting to Liam than sitting alone, if Lanigan happened to observe him. 'I hear you finally retired. What are you doing with yourself?'

Liam seemed mildly amused. 'A bit of this, a bit of that.'

'How's Cáit?' Cormac asked.

'She's grand. Busy. Sinéad has started in UCD so that's the last bird out of the nest, but they still manage to keep Cáit running.'

'Fair dues to her.'

Liam nodded, and glanced towards Cormac's left hand. 'No sign of you settling down? Not getting any younger, you know.'

'I'm seeing someone,' Cormac said. He felt awkward. He liked and respected Liam, and he wanted him to know that. 'You'll have to meet her. Will you and Cáit come out for a night in Galway, next time you're down?'

Liam was watching him with his cool, careful blue eyes. 'We'll do that, Cormac. If you give me your number, I'll call you next time we're coming down.'

Liam's coffee cup was empty. 'You're not drinking?' Cormac asked.

'Driving. Sinéad's home for the weekend. She's in the competition. I'll wait for her, drive her home. But I'm about to eat, if you'll join me? Or are you tied up?' Liam's eye turned to the bar.

They ordered food, waited, ate together. Lanigan showed no signs of leaving the bar. He brought their sandwiches, served them with professional indifference. Cormac and Liam ate and talked and Cormac found a collegial ease with Liam that he hadn't felt since he left Dublin. He finished his pint without meaning to, and found himself talking about the Blake case. He trusted Liam Hearne. He'd always been one of the good guys.

'There's someone pushing this thing, Liam. Maybe Murphy, maybe someone pulling his strings. The mother died twenty years ago, with a needle in her arm. Did Maude put it there? I don't know. Maybe she'd just had enough of the abuse, but if she'd taken it for fifteen years you'd think she could take it for a few more months. Then the kids would have been fostered and Maude wouldn't have had to run.' Cormac stopped for a second, but Liam was listening carefully. 'The thing is, even if Maude did kill her mother, I can't see how we can ever prove it. The nearest thing we have to evidence is a statement from a drug addict who wants to get out of prison. And even she doesn't claim to have seen it happen. So why was Maude Blake charged?'

'And you're asking me because you think I'll have some sort of blinding insight into your case?' The look Liam gave him left him nowhere to go.

'I'm asking you because I can't get a grasp of the politics. And I can't run my case if politics get in my way.'

'You think she's innocent?'

'I don't know.' He shook his head. Hesitated. 'I don't know.'

Liam studied him for a long moment. 'Go back to the last interview. That woman, Keane. She gave you a name?'

'Simon Schmidt, but I think that was bullshit. We ran a search, and got nothing.'

'Not Schmidt,' Liam said. 'Schiller. I think she's talking about Simon Schiller.'

Cormac said nothing, raised an eyebrow.

'This happened when? You said twenty years ago, so 1993?'

Cormac nodded.

'Simon Schiller was a teacher at An Ceathrach National School. That's only about twenty miles from Kilmore. He wasn't a priest, but he was a Minister of the Eucharist and was involved in some sort of children's group. They arranged holiday camps for children in care. Schiller was a paedophile. We got him in 2005. He died in prison two years ago.'

Cormac stared at him.

'Schiller went after little boys. The youngest victim that we know of was six years old. Schiller was very into his religion. That Keane one sounds like his sort of person. She may have given you a name because she thought you were close, and didn't want to be charged with obstruction. She could always claim she got the names mixed up. Blame it on old age.'

Cormac closed his eyes involuntarily. He saw little Jack again. Saw Maude with her hand pressed gently to his back as the squad car bounced over ruts and potholes. Saw the little boy's bruises.

'Jesus,' he said in the end. He felt an ache through his whole body. 'She did it. She did it to get Jack out. To get him away. Because her mother couldn't. Or wouldn't.'

Liam was watching him, his eyes unreadable. He didn't speak for a long time, and when he did he looked away. 'I've met a lot of victims, Cormac. A lot of families. Most of them had no idea, no clue what was happening to their children. They're broken by it, even decades later. But there are a few, a very few, who knew and turned a blind eye. If you talk to them now they will plead ignorance, claim that no one suspected anything in those days. If the bastard was a priest they'll claim shock at the very idea. But you can always see it in their eyes. The ones who knew, and did nothing because it was easier. Or maybe because they were afraid, or just couldn't accept it. If this girl was willing to do what it took to save her brother, when her mother gave him up, I say give her a fucking medal.'

'They're not giving her a medal, Liam. They're charging her with murder. They want her locked up.' And Danny had been right all along. Cormac had had blinkers on about this case, he'd wanted Maude to be innocent to the point where he hadn't accepted evidence that had been handed to him on a plate. She'd murdered her mother. And for twenty years he'd failed to see it.

Liam said nothing. Cormac tried to read his expression, then realised he was expecting Liam to deliver a solution, neatly wrapped up in a bow if possible. He felt a sinking depression.

'This Schiller thing,' Cormac said in the end. 'It's motive.'

'Is it though?' Liam said. He looked around the pub. 'I'm not a cop anymore. We're just a pair of old colleagues, catching up over a beer. And maybe I'm wrong. You were given a name. Maybe that's the name you put in your report.'

'Christ, Liam. You're not a cop anymore, but I am.' And if he'd been so wrong about Maude, could he have been wrong about everything? Could she have had something to do with Jack's death? No. Just no way. He didn't believe it, and there was still the question of why he'd been put on this case in the first place. Murphy hadn't known about Schiller. Hadn't even had Hannah Collins's statement when he'd set Cormac on the trail.

'Do you think Maude could know something?' he asked Liam. 'Could she have known something from those years that someone wants to keep a secret? Someone with the power to force a Garda investigation and a prosecution?'

But Liam was shaking his head. 'It's possible but I doubt it, Cormac. Schiller wasn't my case, but an old partner of mine was on it and I know the details. He wasn't alone, but we know his ... affiliates. I don't think we missed one. Then again ...' He shrugged. 'I can't say it's not possible.' Liam's eyes went to the door, then to his watch. It was dark outside; his daughter would be here soon.

Cormac watched him for a long moment before speaking. 'Danny said you had a drink problem.'

'What?' Liam looked bemused by the change of topic; he smiled as if waiting for a punchline.

But Cormac was suddenly absolutely sure that what Danny had told him was bullshit. 'Danny McIntyre told me a detailed story about you. He said that the last few years had taken their toll. That you'd retired, and hit the bottle, and that Cáit didn't want you spending time with cops.'

Liam's eyes had lost their amused glint. 'Did he now?' he said.

'What do you know, Liam?' Cormac said. 'What do you know that Danny wouldn't want me to know?'

'I don't know anything about your case, Cormac. Nothing more than I've told you.'

'But there is something. Something you haven't told me. Something he knows you know.'

For the first time in the conversation Liam looked less than comfortable. He put a hand to his mouth, rubbed his jaw. 'There're things Danny might not want you to know that have nothing to do with what you're working on. Secrets he'd keep for personal reasons. Professional too.'

'Secrets you've been keeping for him?' Cormac asked, and the question was more pointed than he'd intended. Liam shrugged. 'I have to ask you to tell me, Liam,' Cormac said. 'There's something not right here. It's been off from the beginning. And I don't know if Danny's part of it, but I need to know if I can trust him.'

'You're asking me to trust you too, Cormac,' Liam said. He rubbed his jaw again, apparently reached a decision. 'You might not know that Danny has a sister. Much younger than him – she'd be about eighteen now.'

'Yes.' Cormac thought Liam was about to tell him about Lorna's disappearance, and he was distracted, trying to work out how there could possibly be a link between that and secrets Danny might be keeping. It took him a moment to realise that Liam was telling him a very different story.

'Lorna's a nice girl. Quiet. She went out one night with friends to Westies – you know it? A nightclub in one of the villages. It has buses that collect kids from around the countryside. She got the bus there with friends, but came home alone the next morning, off her head on something or other. She'd had her drink spiked. Someone brought her into a back room to sober up. After the club closed, two men came into that room and raped her.'

'Jesus Christ.'

'One of them drove her home afterwards and dropped her at the gate like nothing had happened. Anyway, Lorna pressed charges, and two men were arrested. One of them was Aengus Barton, a local farmer. Owns a hundred hectares out near Lough Mask. The other was Jim Kavanagh, owner of the club.'

'Big Jim,' Cormac said. 'The man Danny arrested for drug dealing.'

Liam nodded. 'Jim Kavanagh and his mate were charged all right, but Lorna dropped the charges less than a week later. The rumour was that they'd taken photographs, posted one on the internet. The message Lorna took from that was unless she wanted a lot more published for the world to see, she would drop the charges. So that's what she did. Can't blame the girl. She would have known too that the chances of conviction were small.'

'And Danny goes on to arrest her rapist for drug dealing. Did no one think there might be a conflict of interest?'

Liam gave a shrug. Clearly no one had given a shit either way.

Cormac rubbed his eyes. 'Jesus, Liam, do you think he did it?'

'The rape or the drug dealing?' Liam asked.

'The drugs. That was Danny setting Kavanagh up, wasn't it? To get revenge?' And could he even blame him? Cormac thought about Emma. If he'd been there the day she was attacked he would have ripped the fucker's head off his shoulders. But this felt different. This was half the police force in the west of Ireland knowing what Danny was about and turning a blind eye. And everyone who did that had a smudge on their record. What would they do the next time a colleague asked for a small favour, a colleague who knew after all that they'd known about Danny McIntyre? And what would they do when that small favour turned into a big favour? The line was there for a reason. It mattered. It had to be respected, no matter how hard that was.

Liam was watching him.

'She's missing,' Cormac said.

'What?'

'Danny's sister. She's been missing for two weeks.'

'That's not good.'

'No.'

They sat in silence while Cormac thought it all through. How many officers would have known? Did Murphy know? Was this why Danny was promoted?

'They wanted him out of the village, didn't they? Wanted him in Galway where they could keep an eye on him?'

Liam shrugged.

'But why let him away with it?' Was it sympathy, a brothers-in-arms wish to take a rapist down, no matter the method? He could believe that of some, but not Brian Murphy. He wasn't the type. There was something more going on here. 'Where did Danny get the drugs, Liam?'

'I don't know.'

'I'd say you can guess.'

Liam met his eye, but said nothing. Liam knew, or at least had a theory he wasn't willing to share. The drugs had to have come from a bust. Danny must have taken them from evidence. But could he have managed that alone? There were evidence logs that would have to be changed; too many people would have had to be actively complicit. Did Healy know? Was that where the strain came from, between Danny and the rest of the drugs team? Cormac tried again with Liam but Liam either didn't know the answers, or wasn't willing to provide them.

Cormac remembered why he was there in the first place and looked around for Lanigan. There was no sign of him. There were two girls behind the bar, serving the growing crowd, but no sign of Lanigan.

'He's gone out the back,' said Liam.

'What?'

'Your man you're here to keep an eye on. He's gone out the back for a fag. He'll be back in a minute.' Liam stood. 'My daughter's here,' he said. He opened his wallet and took out twenty euro, left it on the table. 'Give that to the young one behind the bar for me, will you?' A quick handshake, and he was gone.

Cormac paid for the meal, ordered coffee, and waited for Lanigan to return. He was back before the coffee had cooled enough to drink. Cormac abandoned it on the bar, left through the front door and walked around to the carpark.

Cormac wasn't in the mood to wait. He opened the passenger door to Fisher's car. 'We'll have to be quick,' he said.

They walked to the back door of the pub. Fisher had a torch at the ready. Two cigarette butts, smoked down to the filter, lay on the ground by the door.

'He didn't even blink,' Fisher said. 'Didn't even notice that the pot was gone, that the place was cleaned up.'

'It was dark,' Cormac said. 'Or dark enough. And Lanigan's a creature of habit. He's not thinking when he comes out here, just going through the motions.' He took two quick photographs as Fisher pulled on a pair of gloves, then bagged the butts. They walked back to Fisher's car.

'Send it to Dublin,' Cormac said. 'This one shouldn't need to go to the UK. I'll have the American profile sent over for comparison, then we'll see. You understand that we won't be able to get him for the Hughes case, not unless something unexpected turns up?'

'But her family will know, right? If we get him for the American murder. You'll go to Maura Hughes's family and let them know?'

'Yes,' Cormac said. It would be a kind of closure for them. And once Lanigan was jailed there was always a possibility that he would give up the location of Maura's body.

Fisher nodded. 'I'd like to be with you, for that conversation, if it's all right.'

Cormac nodded.

'Thanks,' said Fisher. 'The DNA. It'll take a few months, do you think?'

Cormac shrugged. Fisher knew the answer to that as well as he did. No one skipped the queue at the state lab, not unless you had a politically significant case or a lot more pull than Cormac had. This case was too old, the connections they'd drawn too tenuous. They would have to wait. In the meantime, there was other work to be done.

The drive back to Galway was a sombre one. Cormac hadn't needed to be there for the Lanigan DNA collection. It was something he could easily have left to Fisher and another uniform. He'd gone because he wanted the distraction, wanted time away from Galway to think. But now that it was done and there was nothing between him and Monday morning except a bad night's sleep, he felt tired and defeated.

What the fuck was he going to do about Danny? The line that Danny had crossed; it was sacrosanct for Cormac. Never to be crossed, mostly because once crossed, how would you stop yourself from crossing it again, and again? And then maybe the threshold for crossing it would drop, until you found yourself justifying every corrupt step you took in the name of some nebulous greater good. But Danny'd been protecting his sister. Or avenging her. And if Cormac went after Danny, what then? Half the gardaí in the country – probably more – would condemn him for it. He'd have a target on his back for the rest of his career, which would probably be considerably shortened.

He thought about Maude Blake. He'd found her motive and it was compelling. Motive was not relevant to a criminal offence. Not under the law. Intent was what mattered. And yet juries needed a motive if they were to convict – and judges weren't immune from wanting one either. He should give Hackett the motive. It might be what was needed to push the case over the line, and he believed it now. Maude had killed her mother. He felt sick at the thought. What could he do? He was a policeman to his bones, but he couldn't give Maude up for this.

Despite his racing thoughts, Cormac felt his eyelids grow heavy, and he opened his window to let in some chilly air. Turned on the radio. News bulletins in Irish. Switched again. Heard the opening riff of AC/DC's 'Whole Lotta Rosie'. He had a sudden flashback to Templemore, to their graduation dance. He'd joined the guards straight out of school, and had been twenty when he graduated from Templemore. They'd all ended up in Thurles afterward, at a nightclub that still played slow dances. God, they'd been so young. Glad to get out of their ill-fitting uniforms, put on jeans and a T-shirt, sink a few – far too many – pints. It hadn't been about the girls, that night. So many nights were about finding a girl, but not that one. He remembered the opening riffs of 'Whole Lotta Rosie' had played and almost every one of them had hit the dance floor and gone mad in a sudden, testosterone-laden mosh pit. There had been female trainees; they'd either joined in, or stayed at the bar, watching the scene, amused by it maybe. Danny hadn't joined in, Cormac remembered now. He'd stayed at the bar too. When Cormac had asked him about it, he'd said he didn't like the song. Curled a lip.

The song on the radio came to an end and news headlines started again. There was more talk about austerity politics, more talk of protests about home and water taxes. Same old same old. He was reaching for the dial when he heard it. The body of a young woman had been found inside a car submerged in a flooded quarry near Lough Mask in County Mayo. She had not yet been identified. A man, the owner of the land on which the quarry was located, had been taken into custody on suspicion of murder and was being questioned at Castlebar Garda Station. Lough Mask. Christ. Lorna McIntyre, it had to be.

CHAPTER THIRTY-ONE

Aisling drove straight home. She turned the heat up to maximum but it was twenty minutes before she stopped shivering. Jack's phone sat on the passenger seat. She glanced at it every now and again, as if it was a live thing that might jump up and bite her. Her hands left brown and red smears on the steering wheel. She wiped them on her jeans. She should have waited for the police at the main road. Should have found out what they were searching for, made sure that they knew about the connection to Jack. But she'd been so afraid. That fear should have seemed stupid as she drove into Galway, down well-lit streets busy with traffic, but the taste of it was still with her, sour and curdled on her tongue, as she pulled in outside the house.

She went to their bedroom first. Jack's charger was still plugged in on his side of the bed. She connected it to the phone, waited, tried switching it on. Nothing. Aisling checked her watch and could have screamed in frustration. She was due at the hospital in less than two hours. With an enormous effort of will she left Jack's phone plugged in and headed for the shower. She dropped her dirty clothes in a heap onto the bathroom floor, and was climbing into the shower before the water had had a chance to warm up. It took far longer than she had patience for, to scrub the dirt from her hands and nails, to wash her hair, but when she got out of the shower and returned to the phone, it still wouldn't switch on. Damnit. Maybe it had gotten wet. Or the fall that had cracked the screen had broken something more fundamental.

Aisling pulled a pair of jeans from her drawer, a T-shirt, an old jumper. She would get a set of scrubs at work. She'd told them she was coming in for this shift. She couldn't change her mind again, or be late, or they'd think she'd turned into a total flake. But first she had to get to the garda station. She paused long enough to send a message to Maude, telling her that she'd found the phone and was bringing it to the police. Aisling felt she owed her that much. Would she even get the message? Not if she was still in custody.

Aisling got to the station just after seven, went straight to reception and asked for Cormac Reilly. Not available. Ceri Walsh too was off duty. In desperation, she asked for Rodgers, and was met with a polite suggestion that she return in the morning. That was when she raised her voice. Said that she wanted to make a formal complaint. Said that she had evidence her boyfriend had been murdered and the police weren't doing anything about it. Said that if she didn't get to speak to someone in the next ten minutes she was going straight to the newspapers. She felt sure that Maude would have been proud of her performance.

Unfortunately shouting got her nowhere. She was told, reasonably politely, by a now harried-looking young garda, that he couldn't produce officers who weren't in the building, and as they had a lot on at that moment there was no one who could see her. If she'd like to take a seat, and wait, he would see what he could do. Or alternatively she could come back in the morning.

She left, feeling like she was letting both Jack and Maude down, and was halfway to her car when she heard her name called.

'Miss Conroy.'

She turned. The man who'd arrested Maude, looking much less police-like now, was standing in front of her dressed in jeans and a ratty jacket, open over a Grateful Dead T-shirt.

'Daniel McIntyre,' he said, holding out a hand to be shaken. 'You wanted to speak to someone about Jack's death?' he said.

'I ... yes.' She checked her watch. 'I was hoping to speak with Detective Sergeant Reilly. But he's not there.'

'Is there something I can help you with?' His eyes dropped to Jack's phone, which she still held in one hand. He glanced over his shoulder towards the station.

'I don't think so,' said Aisling. She could come back. One more day couldn't make much difference.

'You told the duty officer that you had evidence Jack was murdered. If you do, I'd like to hear about it.'

Aisling hesitated. This was the man who had arrested Maude, after all. It didn't feel right to hand Jack's phone over to him. But he had the kind of face you could trust, the kind that looked like it could break into laughter at any moment.

He looked back over his shoulder again. He must be in the middle of something, whatever it was that was taking so much garda attention that evening. And she was going to be late for work. So Aisling talked, quickly. She said that she'd been wrong to ever even consider that Jack killed himself. That he would never, ever have done so. She talked about the CCTV footage. Standing there, in the carpark, she talked about the postmortem results.

'And that?' he said in the end, nodding towards the phone.

'It's Jack's phone,' she said. 'I tracked it. Jack went to Lough Mask on the day he died. To hike. I found his phone there, in the mud at the bottom of the trail. Something happened to him there. What if someone hurt him, then drove him to Galway and dropped him in the river, to make it look like a suicide?' She got it all out in one fast sentence, afraid that she might sound hysterical, but desperate to be taken seriously. Something flashed in McIntyre's eyes, but it was gone too fast for her to read.

'Lough Mask,' he said.

'Yes. Jack liked to hike there. I have his email password. I tracked his phone – that's where he went, that last day. I drove there myself this morning, to see if I could find his phone, and I did. It was just sitting there, at the bottom of the trail, half-covered in mud.' She didn't say anything about her desperate search on her hands and knees. Didn't say anything about her fear.

'Okay,' McIntyre said. He shivered, a little reflexive shake against the cold. 'Do you think Jack was meeting someone?'

'I don't know. He liked to hike alone. But when I was up there I saw gardaí, at the quarry. Do you know what's going on out there? What if Jack saw something, saw someone, while he was out there, and that's what got him killed?'

McIntyre frowned and shook his head. 'I haven't heard, but I can find out.' He held his hand out for the phone, and when she didn't react, he took it from her hand. He pressed a button, waited. 'You haven't turned it on? Have you checked his messages?'

'I can't,' she said. 'I've tried charging it but I think it's broken. I hoped maybe the gardaí could examine it. Or if you can't get it working, maybe you could get his messages from the phone company?'

McIntyre nodded. 'And you wanted to speak to Sergeant Reilly about this?'

'Yes. I've spoken with him before. I thought he might be helpful.'

'Not Garda Rodgers?'

Aisling flushed. 'No.'

He nodded slowly again, like he understood.

'Rodgers is an old-style garda. He's not always as pro-active as he should be.'

'Yes.' If ever there was an understatement.

'From the information you've given to me today, well, I was aware on the periphery of some of it, but your brother's death was not my case. Put together like this ...' He shook his head. 'Look, if you won't repeat this, it's obvious that a shitty job has been done on this case so far. No offence, Aisling, but it shouldn't have come down to you to find this. It should have been traced from the beginning.'

'Will Garda Rodgers ...' Aisling let her voice trail off. She wanted to know if this would finally get Rodgers kicked off the investigation.

'This is still his case, for now. But if you can leave this information with me for a few days, I'll see if we can make new arrangements.' His smile was a little warmer, as if they were friends and he was going to do her a special favour. And Aisling felt a little internal reaction – the smallest glimmer of dislike.

'Someone needs to go to the trail-head and look for evidence. There are rocks there. Tree branches. Someone could have hit Jack on the head, and the rock could still be there,' she said.

'As I said, if you give me a few days, we can move this forward,' he said.

'And you'll keep me informed?'

'Certainly. If you give me your contact numbers, where you can be reached.'

She gave him her details again, her address and how she could be reached at the hospital, her mobile number. He took a step closer to her and she caught a sour hint of stale sweat.

'You're heading home now?' he asked.

'To work,' she said shortly. 'Night shift.' She hesitated. 'Look, Jack's sister Maude. You arrested her. Do you know if she has a lawyer? Is it possible to visit her?' She tried to read his face as he shook his head.

'I'm sorry, no visitors until after her bail hearing. She can see her lawyer, but that's it,' he said.

She noticed a little crust of sleep in the corner of his left eye; his skin had the thin papery look of someone who wasn't getting a lot of rest.

'Did something new come to light? New evidence I mean? It just seems ... after all these years ...' she faltered.

'I can't discuss the investigation with you, Aisling,' he said, looking grave. He hesitated. 'I'd like to say more.' But he just shook his head.

He walked her to her car, almost shepherding her, with his hand at the small of her back, a gesture that made her uncomfortable, and left her with the distinct impression that he was in a hurry. He waited for her to get into her seat, put on her seatbelt, all the time holding the car door. Then he leaned in, a little too close.

'One thing,' he said. 'Maude Blake. I can see that you're worried about her. And I will look into this matter of the phone. But there's something I want you to think about.' He leaned a little closer. 'Did you ever wonder that it might be too much of a coincidence that your boyfriend, her brother, the only witness to what happened that night twenty years ago by the way – that Jack died in suspicious circumstances just after his sister returns to this country for the first time in twenty years?'

Aisling opened her mouth to speak, but no words came out. He put a hand on her shoulder and squeezed gently. Her stomach turned.

'Just think about it,' he said. 'Think about it, and stay away from her.'

Aisling nodded. She turned the keys in the ignition. He stepped back, and she closed the car door. Through the rear-view mirror she saw him watching her as she drove away. The taste of fear returned, and stayed with her until she reached the bright, welcoming lights of the hospital.

Monday 1 April 2013

———————————————

CHAPTER THIRTY-TWO

'Judge, the accused is a clear flight risk. She has lived outside this country for the past twenty years. She has no family and no property in this jurisdiction. It is our contention that she has already run to escape this charge – she disappeared on the night she murdered her mother, has been living abroad, and only returned three weeks ago, around the time of her brother's death, which took place in equally suspicious circumstances. The evidence against Ms Blake is strong – we have a statement from a woman who says that Ms Blake procured the heroin, with the intention of injecting it at overdose levels when her mother was under the influence of alcohol.'

'Judge, I have to object to that.' Tom Collins stood as he spoke. His manner was relaxed and his tone was measured, in contrast to the prosecutor's excited delivery.

'Yes, Mr Collins.' The judge, his wig slightly askew but his white collar pristine, was reading the papers, holding them up and slightly away as if his glasses weren't quite addressing his long-sightedness.

'I have a copy of the statement my friend refers to. The statement does not speak to Ms Blake's intent. In fact, the witness says very clearly that she had no knowledge of Ms Blake's intent at the time and that Ms Blake did not say what she intended to use the heroin for.'

'Is this the case, Mr Conway?'

'Uh ... I believe so, Judge. I apologise if I misspoke. But I would argue that the evidence is very compelling. I am also told that there are further witnesses speaking with the guards, although written statements have not yet been taken. These witnesses still live in the local area, and there is a risk that the accused would seek to influence their testimony if she were released.'

'Judge?' Tom didn't stand this time.

'Yes. Mr Conway, you have appeared in my court on enough occasions to know that I am not interested in potential witnesses who have not given statements, and I am not interested in allegations of potential interference where there is no evidence that the accused has any intention or history of interfering with witnesses. If you wish me to consider potential interference, you will have to give me more to go on than that.' The judge didn't even look up. He was turning the pages of the statements that had been given to him, his manner casual, but the tone of his voice was steely.

'Yes Judge.' Conway's head was down now, as he shuffled through the papers in front of him. He looked towards the back of the courtroom. Hackett was there, standing against the back wall, frustration evident on her face. She nodded her head firmly at Conway, who turned back to the judge. 'Judge, there is an active garda investigation into the death of Ms Blake's brother, whose death was originally thought to be a suicide, but in the past number of weeks evidence has come to light to suggest that his death may have been … uh … due to a third party. In the circumstances the gardaí are concerned that Ms Blake will again flee the jurisdiction, as she did when a family member last died in suspicious circumstances.'

Tom stood quickly. 'Judge, I hesitate to suggest that any colleague would intentionally mislead the court but the implications made here are really quite outrageous. Ms Blake has been tireless in her efforts to prompt the gardaí to properly investigate her brother's death. The gardaí have closed their investigation into Jack Blake's death. They believe that Jack committed suicide. My client does not. She has gone so far as to independently investigate his death, and has provided gardaí with evidence to prove that the garda theory was entirely wrong.' Tom looked at the prosecutor, his expression disapproving. He was very good at this, Maude thought. She wanted to applaud. Instead she sat stiffly, hands folded on her lap like a choir girl.

'If my client was in any way involved in the death of her brother she would have accepted the garda decision that it was suicide, not sought to overturn it.'

'Mr Conway?' the judge said.

The prosecutor didn't turn around this time. 'I have no instructions on that matter, Judge.' That felt to Maude like an attempt to put distance between the prosecutor and the gardaí, and the judge was having none of it.

'Well, perhaps you should take them,' he said.

The prosecutor gave a jerk of the head to Hackett; she came forward and they had a hurried, whispered discussion. There was another man standing at the back of the courtroom. He looked back at Maude solemnly. There was something familiar about him.

The judge had run out of patience. 'Well, Mr Conway?'

'Judge, I am instructed that the defendant did provide the gardaí with some evidence, but they do not accept that evidence as proof that Jack Blake's death was not a suicide.'

Tom opened his mouth to speak but the judge forestalled him. 'Mr Conway, the gardaí must pick a position. If you maintain it was suicide how can you argue that Ms Blake was responsible for his death?'

Conway tried to speak but the judge raised his hand. 'This is not a full trial of the action gentlemen, and there are other applicants waiting to have their applications heard. I am not prepared to deny bail in this case, as the evidence before me has not satisfied the criteria I am required to consider. However, I am concerned about the accused's lack of connection with Ireland and her resources outside of the country, as well as her history of leaving this jurisdiction ... precipitously. Bail is therefore set at one hundred thousand euro. If your client cannot provide a bond or surety, Mr Collins, I will remand her into custody pending the next trial date.' The judge held his gavel above the block, and raised his eyebrow in Tom's direction, the first time, Maude realised, that he had looked up from his papers since she had been called to the courtroom. Tom turned to her, his face pale.

'It's more than I expected,' he said, 'but it's bail.'

Maude shook her head. 'It's fine, I'll pay it.'

Tom nodded, turned to pass that information to the judge.

'Mr Collins, Ms Blake is to surrender her passport to the court. Bailiff, kindly take Ms Blake into custody and make arrangements for her to contact her bank.' The judge struck the block with the gavel and a bailiff called the next case.

Maude smiled at Tom, who seemed a little dazed. 'What happens next?' she asked. The bailiff was waiting beside her.

'I'll meet you out there,' said Tom. 'We'll make bail arrangements, which might take a while. Once the money comes through you'll be released, but I suppose given it has to come from Australia it may take some time, worst case scenario.' Maude shook her head, but they didn't have time to say more.

It took a little time to get the payment sorted, to sign the paperwork, to collect her personal belongings. They walked out of the courthouse two hours after the bail hearing. Tom took her arm as they left court, steering her away from the only journalist who regularly haunted the steps of Galway Courthouse.

'Where did the money come from?' he asked.

Maude looked away, avoiding his gaze. Lawton had paid her well enough, and she'd had little to spend it on. 'I moved my money over after the station was sold. I had my savings, and John left me something. Once the station was sold I didn't really have a place in Australia anymore. I thought I might come back to Ireland.'

Tom reached out and squeezed her hand. She found herself staring down at his hand on hers. How easy it seemed for him now to touch her, how impossible it had been when they were young. She wondered if time had healed that part of him, or if it had been a relationship, and if so, where that person was now. Tom withdrew his hand as they crossed the road.

'It fell apart pretty quickly for them, didn't it?' Maude said.

Tom shook his head. 'Faster than I expected, that's for sure. But it's not over yet, Maude.'

'Hannah?'

'Should be released this afternoon. I have to go back to the office, make a call, just to be sure. Then I'd like to go to Dublin, be there to collect her.' He stopped walking, reached out, and turned Maude towards him. 'What they said in there, about Jack, was appalling. Are you all right?'

'I'm fine,' she said, 'I knew it was coming.' She shook her head. 'Actually, I'm absolutely starving. Have you time for a late breakfast?'

Tom started to laugh.

CHAPTER THIRTY-THREE

After the bail hearing Cormac left the courtroom, crossed the street, and entered the Town Hall Theatre. The box office was just inside the entrance. It was quiet, staffed by a young girl who showed a profound lack of interest in his presence – she was reading a magazine with Emma Watson on the cover, and barely looked up at his arrival. The room had a large window that offered a perfect view of the courthouse exit, with the added benefits of making him a little less conspicuous, and keeping him out of the cold. He watched Hackett and the prosecutor confer outside, the prosecutor gesticulating, very obviously angry, before they separated and Hackett turned in the direction of Mill Street. Hackett had fucked up, had sent the prosecutor in there with air for evidence, had actively misled him even. There would likely be repercussions.

It was a long time before Maude and Tom Collins appeared, leaving from the custody exit. They stood outside the courthouse and talked for a few minutes. The way Tom bent his head towards her when he spoke, the look he gave her when she laughed; there was such intimacy between them that he almost expected them to kiss. They crossed the road, then parted, Tom walking back towards his office, Maude crossing the street at the pedestrian lights and walking up Eglinton Street. Cormac took two quick steps down the theatre steps, crossed the street, and followed.

She walked quickly, and when she reached the corner at St. Anthony's Place she turned down towards Woodquay.

Cormac picked up his pace, but very nearly missed her – she had opened the door to a pub by the time he reached the corner. He followed her, a few beats behind. It was a maze of a place, with interconnecting rooms spread over two floors. He found Maude at the back, sitting at a table. She held a menu in one hand, but her attention was focused on her phone. She looked up as he approached.

'Do you know who I am?' he asked.

Up close she looked different. More attractive than he had expected. He'd remembered a child, and now there were fine lines around her dark eyes. She had freckles, and a light tan where she'd been pale before. And though she was still slight she looked much stronger.

'Yes,' she said.

'I was at the bail hearing,' he said, then stopped. He didn't know where he wanted to bring this conversation.

'I would never have hurt Jack,' she said.

'I know that,' said Cormac. 'I wanted to tell you that I'm sorry. I'm sorry for what just happened in there, and for any part I played in it. And I'm sorry for what I didn't do twenty years ago, when you were only a kid.'

She gave him a smile then, an echo of that sad smile that he'd never quite forgotten, despite all the cases and all the years. 'You've nothing to be sorry for, detective. Nothing at all. You took us away from that house. There was nothing else for you to do.'

'I'm sorry then that no one stepped in before that night. That you felt you had to do what you did.'

Her smile faded, and her face grew shuttered.

'I know about Schiller,' he said. And he had the only confirmation he needed in the look in her eyes. 'I know why you did it. Your mother was a monster. She beat you. She beat your little brother. And then she handed him over to a paedophile. You had no way out. Social services were useless, you already knew that. There was nowhere for you to turn. So you did what you had to do.'

Her face had lost colour. She closed her eyes for a long moment, then opened them. 'My mother never touched us,' she said, her voice faint.

'You don't have to lie about it. There's no one left to protect Maude, except yourself. Look, this is your defence. If you did this to defend yourself, or your brother, you need to tell the truth.' It was the sort of thing he said to suspects. He'd give them something that looked like a way out, so that they'd bolt for it, only to find themselves in a noose. Was that what he was doing now? Maybe, maybe not. He'd never felt so conflicted.

'My mother never touched us,' she said, again.

He shook his head, gripped the back of the chair in front of him. He opened his mouth to speak but she cut across him.

'It was Domenica Keane,' she said.

He stared back at her.

'My mother was an alcoholic. She was sick. She tried to get a job at the school. But the nuns wouldn't hire an unmarried mother. We had to rely on the allowance Mother got from the state. And with the cost of the drink there wasn't much left. Miss Keane offered me a job working on her farm, helping with milking. She didn't pay much but we needed the money.'

Cormac pulled the seat out and sat. A waitress came towards them, but veered away at a shake of his head. 'She hit you,' he said flatly.

Maude inclined her head. 'She liked to hit. She liked to hurt. But in the beginning it was just me, and I could handle it.' She raised her chin, as if expecting him to contradict her.

'Your mother didn't do anything about it?'

'We didn't talk about it. We needed the money. No one else would give me a job.'

'And Schiller?'

She took a deep breath. 'He was a friend of Miss Keane's.'

'You were afraid of him.'

Maude was very still now.

'Did he hurt you? Hurt Jack?' His voice was very gentle.

But she shook her head. 'I only met him once. He never touched me, or Jack either.'

'Because you stopped it. You knew what was coming and you stopped it, didn't you Maude? You killed your mother because that was the only option. It was the only way to get you and Jack out of that house.'

Her eyes were far away, and very sad. Then Cormac felt a hand clasp his shoulder. He looked up to see Tom Collins, breathing fast and looking agitated.

'Interviewing my client without my presence, detective?' he asked. 'Did you caution her?'

'No caution, Mr Collins, this is just a conversation.'

Tom pulled another seat over to the table, sat, and picked up a menu. 'This is not the time or the place, detective. If you want to interview my client I suggest you make an appointment at my office.' He was making a valiant attempt at his usual professional poise, but he was nervous, afraid of what Maude might have said, or what Cormac might know.

'That's not what this is about. I'm not your enemy. I'm not saying what you did was right, but I understand why you felt you had no choice.'

But Maude and Tom were silent, unified now and unyielding.

Cormac stood. 'Your sister, Hannah, she got early release?'

Tom gave a grim smile. 'Yes.'

Maude's phone buzzed where it lay on the table.

Tom looked at Cormac. 'You're going to lose this case, you know. Hannah's statement is not enough to convict Maude of anything. Hannah claims she gave heroin to Maude, but that's it. Even if you accept that evidence, all it proves is that Maude possessed heroin around the time her mother died. That's the very definition of circumstantial evidence, detective. If you don't have anything else then you have no case.'

Cormac looked at Maude as he spoke. 'Then it seems you have nothing to worry about.'

Tom stared at him, trying to read him. When he spoke again, it was slowly and deliberately. 'I'm not worried about the case. I'm worried about what your lot are going to do next.'

Maude's phone buzzed again, and she picked it up, her eyes caught by whatever was on the screen, despite the conversation going on around her.

Cormac concentrated on Tom.

'Someone in the gardaí wants Maude out of the way. Your Sergeant McIntyre went to my sister and pressured her into giving a statement. Do you hear what I'm telling you, detective? He made up a story, went to my sister, and put it in her ear. Why did he do that? And why was Maude charged and arrested when you have nowhere near enough evidence for a conviction?'

Cormac shook his head, not in denial, but because he didn't have an answer yet.

'I don't know,' he said in the end. Christ. It was one thing to acknowledge his doubts, his questions, in the privacy of his own mind. It was another to make them known to a lawyer, a defence attorney who could twist them, use them against the force. But Cormac's eyes went to Maude involuntarily, and he found himself saying, 'I'm going to try to find out.'

'You do that,' Tom said, then turned to Maude himself, concern in his eyes, but she was looking at her phone.

'Maude?' Tom asked.

'It's a message. From Aisling.' She looked up. 'She found Jack's phone. On a hiking trail at Lough Mask.'

'What, just now?' Tom asked.

'Last night,' said Maude. 'She sent the message last night, after she'd dropped the phone to the police station.'

It took Cormac a moment to process the words, and when he did he left without another word.

CHAPTER THIRTY-FOUR

Cormac stalked back to the station. Mother*fuck*. Everything came back to Danny. He was the one who had appeared with the heroin evidence. Danny and Mel Hackett had arrested Maude. And now there was a connection between Danny and Jack's death. Lorna McIntyre's body had been pulled out of a quarry near Lough Mask; the last place, apparently, that Jack Blake had been alive. This was where Cormac ran into a brick wall. He saw the whole thing as a puzzle, every piece fit together, interlocking, with a single gaping hole. And the one piece he had in his hand didn't fit.

Cormac was halfway down Shop Street when it started to rain. It was almost a relief – the street was pedestrianised, and always busy, but in the rain shoppers tried to walk under shop awnings, leaving a centre aisle that was unobstructed. He picked up his pace, ignoring the rain that soon plastered his hair to his skull and soaked through his shoes. Danny was knee-deep in the Maude Blake case, had been pushing it along behind the scenes, probably from the beginning. And the rumour about him sleeping with Maude, Danny was the obvious source for that. He was the only person in Galway who Cormac had spoken to about Emma.

Still he had no *why*. In their first week in Templemore they had attended a lecture on court procedure. The class had been taught by a retired lawyer who liked an audience. He'd told them that motive was the least thing in any case, because it need not be proven – it was not a legal element of a crime. 'Intent, or *mens rea*, that is the thing,' he'd said. But he'd immediately countered his own argument by telling them that a garda who prepared a file for prosecution without regard for motive was bound for disappointment. Juries, ultimately, needed a reason.

Cormac reached the steps of Mill Street and ran up them, slowing to a slightly more decorous pace as he moved through the halls and up the inner stairs. He didn't want to draw attention to himself. The squad room was busy. Cormac took his seat quietly and logged on. First things first. The slow warm-up of his computer was infuriating. He tapped his finger on the mouse, the small movement nowhere near enough to release his increasing tension. He forced himself to calm down. Focus was what was needed now.

He logged in. Found the Lorna McIntyre case and confirmed what he already knew. Her body had been found at Lough Mask. Identity had been confirmed that morning through dental records; no date or time of death had yet been determined. But there had been an arrest. Cormac scrolled down and clicked on the arrest report. Name of suspect arrested: *Aengus Barton*. An anonymous call had been made to Mill Street on Saturday, prompting the search of the quarry. Barton owned the surrounding farmland and, according to the arrest report, had a prior connection with the victim. He'd been arrested and charged with her rape in December 2011, though charges had later been dropped. Cormac stared at the screen, willing the words to make sense.

Fisher appeared at his shoulder, cleared his throat.

'Yeah?'

'I've sent the sample off,' Fisher said. 'And I've started looking at the process for extradition warrants, if it is positive.'

'Right,' said Cormac.

Fisher paused, then dropped his voice. 'Murphy was looking for you earlier. Said if I was to see you, to tell you to call up to his office.'

Rodgers was crossing the room, heading for the door. Cormac looked at Fisher, who waited a beat, then shrugged. 'Haven't seen you, have I?' And he left Cormac to it.

Cormac caught Rodgers before he reached the stairs.

'I want that phone,' Cormac said. 'Jack Blake's phone. If it hasn't gone to the lab yet, I want it going under my name.'

Rodgers looked back at him, surprise quickly turning to indignation. 'There's no new evidence in the Blake case. And if there was, that case hasn't been assigned to you, as far as I know.'

Cormac was wearing plain clothes, but he pointed to his shoulder, where the epaulettes of his uniform would be if he was wearing one. He took two quick steps towards Rodgers, loomed over him. 'I'm not in the mood for bullshit, Rodgers. Get the phone to my desk, and get it there now.'

Cormac was barely back at his desk before the next interruption came, in the form of loud voices, laughing, joking, as Healy, Trevor Murphy and all the rest of them entered the room as a troop. Healy gave Cormac an ironic salute as he walked to the other end of the room. And there was Carrie O'Halloran, her back towards him, head bent over her work.

Jesus. The answers were right here. They were in this room. He was sure of it. Could feel them tapping at the inside of his brain, begging for his attention. Everything came back to Danny.

Danny had set Kavanagh up for drug dealing, which meant he had to get his hands on drugs. The obvious source of drugs for a policeman was the evidence locker, but a stash the size that Danny had used on Kavanagh would not be easy to get hold of. Cormac's eyes dropped to his phone. He thought of the video Matt had sent him, of Healy standing over plastic-wrapped bales of drugs as they were pushed into the incinerator. Except if Healy was involved, maybe what was in those bales wasn't drugs. Maybe the drugs had already been diverted elsewhere. Stored and sold on by Healy, Trevor Murphy, and whoever else he had in his dirty little network. Maybe even Danny. Why the fuck hadn't he thought of this before? Danny didn't take the drugs directly from evidence storage himself. He hadn't needed to. He'd known about Healy's stash and had helped himself. If Danny had stolen from Healy, that would explain the obvious tension and animosity between the two men.

It would also explain why Superintendent Brian Murphy had let Danny get away with so much. Setting up Kavanagh, for example, and that was just for starters. If Danny had proof that Trevor Murphy had been involved in drug running, or stealing drugs evidence for resale or whatever the fuck they were up to, what were the chances that Murphy senior would have looked the other way rather than risk his son's future?

Everything fell into place in Cormac's head. He had no proof, but he was convinced, although he still needed the *why*. He stood, and walked to O'Halloran's desk.

'I need to speak to you,' he said. 'It's important and it has to be now.'

He made his way downstairs and waited for her in the carpark. She appeared a few minutes later, stood on the top step. Stopped there. When she didn't take another step Cormac walked back towards her, stopping at the base of the steps. Even with that, she was just barely taller than him. She looked exhausted.

'You found her,' Cormac said. 'You found Lorna.'

'Yes.'

'Another anonymous tip.'

'Another?'

'Jack Blake's death was called in the same way. We got nothing useful about the caller.'

Carrie's face was very still. 'Nothing useful this time either. Call was from a burner phone to a Mill Street extension. A male who made a clumsy effort to disguise his voice said that Barton had confessed to him that he had killed Lorna, and dumped her body in the quarry. Claimed Barton had run into her and Lorna had gotten angry, had said she was going to file the charges again. Barton is supposed to have killed her in a fit of rage, dumped her body in the flooded quarry on his land.'

'You've arrested him?'

'No choice. Her body was in the quarry, on his land. We searched his place. There was bloodstained clothing hidden at the back of one of his wardrobes. We've sent it for testing but I think we both know that it will be her blood.'

The wind whipped Carrie's hair across her face, and she pushed it back with one hand, looking past Cormac to the street beyond. 'Everything leads to Barton. A great big neon sign, pointing his way.'

'You don't think he did it,' Cormac said flatly.

Her eyes returned to his. 'I know he didn't do it.'

He knew it too, knew it to his bones, but that didn't mean he understood. 'Why would he kill her? His own sister.'

A look of intense relief crossed Carrie's face, and was gone. 'He's not the person he pretends to be. Lorna was afraid of him. More afraid of him than she was of anything else. She was raped a year and a half ago. She came to Galway to report it and I met with her. She came alone, and her biggest concern was that Danny would hear of it.' Her eyes took his measure, trying to read how he was reacting to her words. 'I've just come from the house. Danny's not there. He took compassionate leave, but he hasn't been near the parents.'

Shit. 'Jack Blake was there that day. At the lake.'

'Your dead boy?' she asked.

'Danny's been all over the case from the beginning. Pushing for the sister to be charged. Coming up with evidence.'

There was a noise from the station behind them. A pair of uniforms came down the steps, throwing curious looks in their direction. And then her phone rang.

Carrie answered it, pressing the mobile to her ear, her eyes still on Cormac in a way that let him know that whatever this was, he needed to hear about it.

'Stay where you are,' she said into the phone. 'I'll be there in five minutes.'

She hung up, sliding the phone back into her pocket, her eyes still locked with his. 'I need you with me,' she said. 'She might talk this time.' She waited only for his nod, and then she was running, Cormac two steps behind her.

CHAPTER THIRTY-FIVE

The handover with Cummins hadn't exactly gone to plan. Aisling was there, ready and waiting, at 8 p.m. At first she was relieved he was late, it gave her a chance to pull herself together after her scare at the quarry and her conversation with McIntyre. When he still hadn't appeared by nine she assumed he was in a surgery that ran over. But when she went looking half an hour later she found that he'd changed his plans and wasn't coming in until ten. By the time he finally showed up she'd been exhausted, and furious, and incapable of holding it all in. For the first time in her life she told a consultant exactly what she thought of him: unprofessional, self-involved, with completely unrealistic expectations. She got it all out, then stood there, hyperventilating, and waiting for her career to disappear down the tubes. He'd looked her up and down for a long moment, laughed, said that maybe she had what it took to be a surgeon after all, and invited her to join him in an emergency surgery that had just come in. Asshole, she'd thought, but hadn't said. She'd taken a deep breath, and thanked him.

The aortic aneurysm repair started at ten thirty, and took nearly eight hours. She finally left the hospital just after 9 a.m. the following morning. Tired, but with her leave approved, and maybe an improvement in her relationship with Cummins. He'd let her run the procedure, only stepping in at her request for a pivotal section she had seen done only once before. Sometime in the night she'd made her decision. She was going home to sleep. Would take Monday and Tuesday to rest. Then, on Tuesday night, she would take those little white pills, go to bed, and wait. Aisling drove home feeling sad, and tired, but sure all the same that it was the right decision. Now was not the time for her to have a baby. Someday, maybe, if she was very lucky. She would do this, and she would forgive herself, and she would try, very hard, to move on with her life.

For now what she wanted was food in front of the TV, then bed. And she would try not to think about anything. Not about Jack, not about Maude, not about work, and definitely not about Wednesday. But she couldn't help turning it all over in her mind as she drove home. McIntyre was wrong. Maude hadn't killed Jack. She had done everything possible to force a police investigation into his death. If she'd killed Jack, why on earth would she set about trying to prove his death was murder, and not suicide? But something had happened to Jack at Lough Mask, and whatever was going on out there, it must be bigger than Jack and Maude. On Tuesday she would find a way to see Maude, talk to her. If she could find out who her lawyer was, maybe she would be able to arrange a visit.

Aisling pulled up outside the house and parked, mentally cataloguing the contents of the fridge, and how long it would take for the living room to warm up once she got the fire on. But when she opened the door she found that the house was pleasantly warm. Odd. The timer on the boiler must be behaving itself. But there was light too, coming from the living room, and the sound of the television. She went to the living room and pushed the door open. And her stomach turned and looped and her heart was in her mouth. Because there was a man, the same size and shape as Jack, sitting in his chair, wearing his jumper – the same one she had worn the morning before. And there was a fire on. And that was their programme even – a repeat of *Ant and Dec's Saturday Night Takeaway* – the same stupid programme she'd been planning to watch with Jack the night he never came home. Except it wasn't Jack sitting in the chair. It was Daniel McIntyre. And he was holding a gun.

CHAPTER THIRTY-SIX

Carrie drove. She'd had keys for an unmarked in her pocket and that was what they took, driving fast and controlled through busy streets. The car had lights they could have thrown onto the roof, and a siren, but she didn't use either and he assumed she had her reasons.

'Who was it, Carrie? Who called you?'

She didn't take her eyes from the road. 'Sarah McIntyre. Danny's wife. I gave her my number months ago, but she's never called me before.'

'Your domestic violence case,' Cormac said slowly. 'The one you talked about the other night. Married woman, two kids. That's who you were talking about, right? You were talking about Sarah.'

Carrie slowed, shifting down a gear as she took a corner, accelerated out of it. 'It's not a case. There's never been a formal investigation. Lorna told me about the abuse. I tried to talk to Sarah about it, more than once. She's always denied it.'

There was no time for more. Moments later Carrie pulled up outside a semi-d in Salthill. It had the slightly shabby look of a long-term rental. They got out of the car, Cormac loosening his gun in its holster. A little boy stood in the garden, a football in his hands. What would he be – five, six? He was wearing only a T-shirt over his tracksuit bottoms, and his arms were red with cold.

'My daddy plays football with me,' he said, as Cormac approached.

'Does he?'

'He's a garda.'

Cormac glanced at Carrie.

'Is your daddy inside, Luke?' Carrie asked.

The little boy shook his head, pushed at the ground with one foot. 'I'm not allowed to talk to strangers,' he said. Then, after a beat, 'Do you want to play football?'

'I do,' said Cormac, 'but I need to talk to your mummy.' He gave the boy the best smile he could manage, and turned towards the house. The front door was open. They could hear a child crying. Cormac didn't knock, just stepped inside. Terracotta floor tiles, magnolia walls. There were unpacked boxes in the hall, but otherwise it was very clean. There was a faint smell of bleach. Cormac followed the sound of crying. It led him to the kitchen. The room was exceptionally clean, but washed out. Nothing on the counters, nothing personal. No colour anywhere, except for the woman sitting on a kitchen chair. She was very overweight, her hair was blonde and long, and it hung unwashed and loose on her shoulders. She wore a black, long-sleeved T-shirt and a floor-length skirt. Blood ran from a cut above one eye, drying in a scarlet swathe down one cheek and shoulder. A little girl, no more than two years old, sat at her feet, pulling at her legs and crying for attention. The woman sat, unmoving, staring into the distance. She held a mobile phone limply in one hand.

'Sarah,' Carrie said. She took a step towards her. The woman – Sarah – didn't react, but their presence shocked the little one into momentary silence. She looked at Cormac and hiccupped.

'Sarah,' Carrie said again. She crouched at her side and picked up Sarah's hands, held them in her own. 'Is Danny here?'

Cormac knew he wasn't. The house held the aftermath of something. Something that had passed. The action had moved elsewhere.

'Where is he, Sarah?' Carrie asked. She put her hand to Sarah's forehead, checking her temperature as if she were a small child. Something in that gesture woke her. She turned broken eyes to Carrie.

'You're too late,' she said. Her voice was husky, little more than a rasp. Cormac's eyes dropped to her neck, to the smudge of dark bruises, the red marks that promised more bruising to come. This was Danny's wife. Christ. Had he done this to her?

'Tell me Sarah,' Carrie was saying. 'Tell me, and I can help you.'

'I think Danny killed her,' she said. 'He killed her, and God help me, I think I helped him.'

Carrie flicked her eyes to Cormac's. He could tell she was thinking about cautioning Sarah, was worried that anything they heard now wouldn't be admissible. Cormac shook his head.

'Talk to me Sarah,' Carrie said, her voice gentle, soothing. 'Tell me what happened.'

'He came home from work on St. Patrick's Day. Told me I had to drive him out to Lough Mask, to collect his car. He didn't tell me *why*. I had to bring the children, they couldn't be left. I didn't *know*, he didn't tell me what it was all about.'

Carrie nodded at her reassuringly.

'He'd left his car at the quarry. It was well hidden, off the road, but he wanted it home before anyone saw it. I drove him out there to collect it, and I didn't ask any questions. I never ask any questions. But she was already dead by then, wasn't she? That's what I keep telling myself. That what I did didn't make any difference.'

The toddler started crying again, and Cormac picked her up, shushed her, jigged her gently up and down. She put her thumb in her mouth and looked at him solemnly.

'Tell me who you're talking about, Sarah. Who was dead?' Carrie had to know of course, but it was better that Sarah say it without prompting.

'I didn't know,' Sarah said again. 'You have to believe me. But it was too late anyway, wasn't it? There was nothing I could have done to help her.'

'Did Danny tell you that he killed Lorna?' Cormac asked. None of this was admissible anyway, and he had such a sense of urgency. This wasn't over. The child in his arms was too young to understand the conversation, surely.

Sarah stared at him as if she'd just now realised he was in the room, then shook her head slowly. Then she closed her eyes, bent forward, and started to rock.

Carrie squeezed her hand again but the rocking continued, and she closed her eyes.

'Where is he, Sarah, do you know?' Carrie asked. She'd raised her voice, and the little girl in Cormac's arms started to cry again. But Sarah had withdrawn completely, wasn't reacting. Before Cormac could respond, Carrie stood and took the little girl from his arms, put her into Sarah's lap, forcing Sarah to take her. Cormac put out a hand to stop the child from falling, but Carrie supported the child herself, then took one of Sarah's arms and unfolded it from Sarah's body, helped the child cuddle in to her mother. For a moment Sarah didn't reach, then her arm tightened around her little one, and she opened her eyes.

'He'll find me,' she said. 'He always finds me.'

'Not this time,' Carrie said. 'You'll come to mine until we can find a better place. Danny McIntyre won't come near my house, I can promise you that. But I need to speak to Detective Reilly for a moment, all right? We'll just be over there,' she pointed to the far corner of the room, 'and when we're finished, you and I, we're going to get packing, all right?'

Carrie didn't wait for Sarah to respond, but took the few steps away, and Cormac followed. They spoke quietly.

'Christ,' said Cormac. 'I had no idea.'

'He's very good at pretending,' Carrie said. 'You aren't the only one to miss it.'

'Christ,' Cormac said again. He looked back at Sarah.

'Do you think he's done a runner?' Carrie asked.

Cormac thought about Danny, thought about his absolute sincerity when he'd apologised for not coming to Cormac with the Hannah Collins statement.

'He's not running. He's too fucking arrogant to run.' Something was nagging at him. That look on Rodgers' face when he'd asked about Jack's phone. *There is no new evidence in the Blake enquiry.* Pompous. Officious. Probably he would have been obstructive just for the sake of it. But hadn't there been surprise in his face when Cormac asked the question? Which meant Rodgers hadn't seen her, hadn't met Aisling. The phone had never reached him.

Cormac dialled Fisher directly on his mobile, cut through his greeting.

'I need to know if Daniel McIntyre was in the station yesterday evening. Find out who was on the desk. Patch me through.'

A minute later he was talking to Garda Stephen Moore, who hesitatingly confessed that yes, Aisling Conroy had asked for Reilly the evening before, and had been told to come back the next day.

'Danny McIntyre, did he talk to her?' Cormac asked.

'No ... uh ... no, I was the only one to talk to her, as far as I know,' Stephen Moore said.

'But McIntyre was in the station when she came in?'

'He came in because he heard his sister had been found. He wanted to know what we'd found out so far, you know, about the arrest. Someone sent him home.'

'Could he have overheard your conversation with Aisling?'
Silence at the other end of the phone gave him his answer.
'Did he leave at the same time as her?'
There was a pause. 'A minute or two after, I think.'
Christ. Cormac hung up.
'What?' asked Carrie. 'What is it, Cormac?'
'The keys,' he said. 'Give me the keys.'
They were in his hand before he had to ask a second time.
He hesitated, looking back at Sarah.
'I'll look after her,' said Carrie.
He nodded and made for the door. 'Call backup,' he said
over his shoulder. 'Tell them the house in the Claddagh. Jack
Blake's place. Right now.'

CHAPTER THIRTY-SEVEN

There was a car parked outside the house – a little grey Mazda that did not belong to Danny. Lights glowed behind curtains in every window and from the road he could hear music playing. Cormac ran for the door, knocked, rang the bell, waited a fraction of a second but no longer. He threw his weight at the door. Once. Again. A third time and the lock gave, the wood splintered, and he was in. Oh Jesus.

'Danny. Stop, Danny.' He pulled the gun as he stepped into the hall, aiming it but knowing he couldn't shoot.

'Stop. Or she goes over,' said Danny, almost shouting to be heard above the music. There was no emotion in his voice. No fear.

And Cormac stopped. Because above him, on the half-landing, Aisling Conroy stood, balanced in her stockinged feet but only just, on the banister. Her hands were tied behind her back, and a noose hung around her neck, the rope snaking upwards and tied high above her. Danny was hidden, almost entirely shielded, by Aisling.

'Jesus, Danny. What the fuck?'

'Cormac. Terrible start. You'd think you'd never read the manual.' If anything, there was a laugh in Danny's voice, hysteria.

Cormac adjusted his grip on the weapon. He had no shot. He locked eyes with Aisling. 'Talk to me, Dan. Come on. Nothing can be worth this. I know you have your reasons. Talk to me.'

'There we go. See, Aisling? That was much better. Open questions. Active listening. But you should have made it personal, Cormac, should have said something about our friendship, for example.' The music stopped as he spoke, the silence abrupt and shocking.

Aisling swayed slightly on the banister; she bent her knees and found her balance, but her eyes never left his. Slowly, she mouthed one word, carefully enough that he couldn't miss it. *Gun.*

'We're friends, Dan. Of course we're friends. Take her down from the stairs now, just lift her down, and we can talk. We can sort all of this out.'

Danny started to laugh, the sound relaxed and horribly natural. It was an imitation of a laugh, Cormac realised. A perfect parody. 'Beautiful, Cormac. Make it personal. Downplay the consequences of my actions. Excellent. Except if you're here, you know about Lorna, don't you? You know about Jack. How did you find out?'

The music started playing again. Was it on a loop? The heartbreaking sound of Sia singing that she was bulletproof. Danny's idea of humour, perhaps.

'I don't care about any of that, Dan. You know that. We can work this out.'

'I want to know how you know. It can't be to do with Barton, or that bitch O'Halloran would be here with you. It was the phone, wasn't it? Jack Blake's phone?'

Christ. Danny was holding back only to find out what Cormac knew. He still thought he could get out of the situation.

'Other people know about this Danny. Backup is on the way. You need to take her down.' Cormac's palms were sweating. If backup didn't arrive there was only one way this could end. If Danny thought Cormac was truly alone, that no one else suspected him, he would kill them both and try to cover it up. On the other hand, if he thought that other people knew, what was to stop him from trying to kill them both and making a run for it?

Danny said nothing. Cormac adjusted his grip on the gun. Tracked left, then right, looking for a shot. There was no cover here at the bottom of the stairs. He could try for Danny's legs through the banister, but if he did Aisling would surely go over. How long did it take to die, when hung by the neck? He couldn't look away from Aisling, not even for a moment. Their eyes were locked together and it felt as if that connection might be the only thing holding her. He could see pain etched on her face. How long had Danny had her standing there? The music soared again and then, horribly, her expression changed, slackened, and her gaze lost its focus. She closed her eyes.

Aisling couldn't hold her position. He'd had her standing there for twenty minutes, was entertained by her efforts to hang on, to balance. Her muscles were cramping. The pain was all she could feel now, and she had barely recovered from her last slip, her muscles refusing to obey her. Her hands were tied, a tight rope around soft fabric. To stop bruising, she supposed, so that this could be made to look like suicide. There was no way out. Which would be worse, death by hanging or by gunshot? The pain welled again and with it came the music, enveloping her, overwhelming her. She closed her eyes and let it come. She thought of Jack, called her memories to her and then he was with her in the void. She felt the warmth of his hand on hers. Saw his face. Oh, the everlasting dearness of him. She wanted him now with a physical ache that overwhelmed every other sensation. The gun in her back. The hardness of the banister under her feet. The screaming pain of her cramping calf muscles. Her eyes were still closed, and if she kept them closed maybe this moment would last forever.

No. No. Jack was dead. He was gone and he would want her to live. And if she wanted to live she had to fight.

Aisling's eyes snapped open and she was back in the moment with a jerking violence that made her gasp hard air into her lungs. Her feet slipped, and her eyes locked again with Cormac Reilly's. He took another step towards her, mouth open and breathing hard. She saw her fate in his eyes, felt it in the pressure of the gun in the small of her back. Had known it almost from the moment she saw Danny McIntyre sitting in her armchair wearing Jack's clothes. Now there was nothing Reilly could do. Danny was shielded behind her body. When he was ready he could shoot around her and take Reilly out. What could Reilly do to defend himself, with her body between them? He was totally vulnerable, standing in the hall before her, gun raised and eyes desperate. And yet he hadn't left her. She felt the pressure of the gun leave her back, heard Danny take a long slow breath in, watched Reilly's face crease with anxiety. She knew what she had to do. Her eyes still locked with Reilly's, willing him to understand, she mouthed one word at him, and stepped forward into the void.

Reilly watched as she mouthed something. One word. Unmistakable. *Now.* Then Aisling Conroy took a single deliberate step forward, and fell.

He had no time, no time to think. His gun hand was already up and instinct took over. There was surprise on Danny's face, a moment of hesitation, before he brought his gun around. Adrenaline heightened Cormac's senses. He saw Danny's finger tighten on the trigger, braced himself for the impact of a bullet, even as he felt the shock of the recoil from his own gun. Oh Jesus. Danny was falling backwards. And Aisling Conroy was hanging from the end of a rope, her feet less than a metre from the floor. Cormac dropped his gun and ran, lifted her weight so that she was no longer pulling against the rope. He held her with one arm and used his other hand to loosen the noose around her neck. It was too tight to get over her head. He tried to feel for a pulse, felt her weight slip, so he held her in both arms, as high as he could. It felt like hours that he was standing there, but it could only have been seconds, minutes, before he heard the sirens, and moments more before other gardaí were pouring through the door. Her weight was taken from him, the rope cut, and then the paramedics were there, checking her airway, her pulse, whisking her out of the door and into an ambulance. Another paramedic had run up the stairs to where Danny lay. Cormac took two steps to follow them, then stopped, breathing heavily, and waited for them to come back down.

They didn't come. A uniform found his way down the stairs and to Cormac.

'Sergeant?'

It was Fisher, looking shocked and questioning.

'Danny?' Cormac asked.

Fisher shook his head, his lips bloodless.

'Fuck, fuck.' Cormac couldn't seem to slow his breathing. Blood was roaring in his ears. It was all he could hear now that someone had finally, finally turned off that bloody music. Cormac turned away and leaned his forehead against the wall, breathing slow deep breaths until he was in control again. When he turned around Fisher was still standing there, hands loose at his sides.

'He's dead.'

'Yes.'

'He would have killed her, but this wasn't what I wanted.' Cormac leaned against the wall, let his head fall back against it and looked up. 'Danny killed his own sister, just to set up her rapist. I don't fucking get it.'

'Why did he come here? How did you know?'

Cormac shook his head. Some of it he thought he knew, but he needed time, needed time to put it all together. Danny had killed Lorna, inexplicable though that act was. Then

Jack had stumbled across his path as he disposed of her body, that had to be it. Even if Jack hadn't seen him with Lorna's body, letting him live would have been too much of a risk, wouldn't it? Once Lorna's body was found, and he'd always intended that it be found, there would be publicity. What if Jack Blake had come forward to say that he had seen a man at Lough Mask, a man who matched Danny's description?

So he'd killed Jack too, and would have killed Aisling, to keep it all from coming out. Christ, she'd come so close to dying, right there in front of him. She might be dying right now, for all of that. Cormac thought back to their conversation at the hospital. If he'd done a better job, if he'd built some sort of rapport with Aisling, would she have come to him earlier? Could he have prevented this? He thought about her stepping off the banister. It had been deliberate, that step. She'd been trying to give him a chance.

Another uniform stepped out of the living room, looked in his direction. 'You'll want a look at this,' he said.

The room was a shrine. A fire was burning low in the hearth, and every other surface was covered in candles. There were photographs on the coffee table, on the floor; photographs of Jack, photographs of Jack and Aisling together. There was a half-empty bottle of wine and a stained wineglass and Cormac wondered if Danny had made her drink it. If he'd sat and watched and forced her to drink while he held the gun on her. How long had he given her? Had he wanted it done fast, or had he enjoyed it? Had he wanted to toy with her, to watch her, and make her talk? There was a sheet of paper on the coffee table too, covered in writing. A suicide note. No. A suicide letter. Long and detailed. So it had been slow then.

'He was waiting for her, wasn't he?' Fisher asked. 'When she got in?' He looked like he was going to be sick. 'I always thought he was a bit of a dick, but fucking hell.'

Cormac stepped forward, picked up a photo. It was of Maude and Jack, taken when they were children.

'Reilly.'

Cormac turned. It was Brian Murphy, looking, if anything, more officious than ever. It was the first time Cormac had ever seen him out of uniform, but the navy slacks and jumper were as close as he could have gotten to Garda uniform in civvies.

'I'll need the gun.' He held out a hand, and Cormac gave it over. 'Fisher will bring you to the station. I want a full statement, straight away.'

Cormac nodded, and turned towards the door. He'd killed a fellow officer. But Danny would have killed him if he hadn't. He saw again the gun in Danny's hand as it turned towards him. Saw Aisling's face as she fell.

'The photograph,' Murphy said from behind him.

Cormac looked down at the photograph he still held, and Murphy's gaze followed. Murphy held his hand out for it. 'Let's keep it to the facts, Reilly. Your statement. No theories.'

Cormac met and held his gaze. How much had Murphy known? 'Yes sir. Just the facts.' There were more than enough of those, after all.

Friday 5 April 2013

CHAPTER THIRTY-EIGHT

They kept Aisling in hospital for four nights. Mary was with her a lot. David Murray came every day. She didn't want to talk, but they seemed to understand that. She slept. She wasn't medicated, but it felt like it. Sleep reached up and enveloped her, dragged her into a welcoming darkness from which she emerged, muggy and disoriented, just long enough to eat and use the bathroom, before falling again. Mary said it was healthy, her body doing what it needed to do to heal after everything she had been through. She was a good friend. Better than Aisling deserved. It seemed that Mary and Declan had broken up – that had been going on too over the past few weeks, though Aisling had been oblivious. Mary was going to move out of the student house, and she and Aisling were going to rent a new place together. Somewhere new and modern, with no memories attached. Maude had come to see her too, but Aisling had kept her eyes closed, feigning sleep, until Maude left. She hadn't been ready for that conversation. But when Aisling emerged from the hospital on shaky legs, seeing Maude was the first thing she wanted to do. She sent her a message, got an immediate reply. Maude was having lunch, but she'd be happy to meet, whenever Aisling wanted.

She found her at the café in Salthill. Maude, sitting at a table with a tall dark-haired man Aisling didn't recognise. There was a woman with them, a little tired-looking, but the baby she held in her lap was an obvious explanation for that. The debris of a good meal lay on the table. The baby held a chunk of apple in one hand, and gnawed at it with gummy enthusiasm, while the adults watched, enthralled.

'Maude.'

They all looked up at her voice.

Maude's smile was warm with genuine welcome, genuine concern. She seemed softer somehow. 'Aisling, are you okay? Sit down, will you join us? Tom, move over one.'

'No. Thanks, Maude. I've been lying down so much, what I really need is a bit of fresh air. Would you come outside with me for a minute? If I'm not disturbing you?'

They walked the prom together, silent for the first few minutes. It was a sunny, blustery day, the water a bright reflection of the blue sky.

'I'm so sorry, Aisling, for what happened. I never wanted you to be at risk. I should have thought.'

Aisling shook her head. 'Not your fault, Maude. There's no way you could have known.'

There was a long pause.

'If you'd like to talk about it, I'd like to listen, but please don't feel ...'

'I had a miscarriage,' Aisling cut her off. She stopped, turned to face Maude. 'Maybe because of the trauma of everything, but I ... wasn't going to ... You should know that I was going to ...' She couldn't finish the sentence, and Maude reached out and held her arm.

'Stop, Aisling. You don't owe me an explanation. You don't owe me anything.' There was endless compassion in her eyes.

Aisling wanted to weep then, but she didn't. She had had enough of tears. She looked away and they walked again for a time.

'What will you do?' Aisling asked.

'I'm going to stay,' Maude said. She glanced back towards the café. 'I have a family after all, it seems.'

Aisling nodded. She wanted to be pleased. If Maude was staying they could meet from time to time, get to know each other in a normal way. But Maude was on bail. The trial was still going ahead, though Danny McIntyre had been the one pushing for it, surely, and he was dead. She wanted to ask Maude if she had done it, if she had really killed her mother, but couldn't bring herself to say the words.

'And you?' Maude asked.

Aisling felt the corners of her mouth lift, an involuntary movement. 'I got a place. I heard yesterday. A training place. Paediatric surgery.'

'I'm glad for you.'

'I wanted to tell you too that I'm sorry, for the things I said to you. I'm sure you had good reason to leave Ireland. And I'm so very sorry that you never got to see Jack again.'

'I had reasons. They seemed like good ones to me then. Maybe there was another way, if I'd been a different kind of person. But I thought it was all down to me, you see?'

Aisling nodded, though she didn't really understand. 'What's happening with the police?' she asked instead. It was the closest she could get to the question she really needed to ask.

Maude took a seat at one of the benches facing the sea, and gestured for Aisling to join her. 'I don't know,' she said. 'It's all up in the air. My lawyer – Tom – he says it might be too difficult for the police to move forward now, with everything that's happened.'

'I'm glad,' said Aisling. And she realised that that was the truth. Whatever had happened in the past, she would be happy to let it stay there.

'I did see Jack again, you know,' said Maude.

'What?'

'I got to Galway on Thursday of the week that Jack died. The place where I lived had been sold. I didn't have it in me to build another life for myself. I didn't even know if I wanted to try. So I came home. I wanted to see Jack, at least once, then decide. I found out where he worked, and waited outside for him. I watched him come out with his friends.'

'Why didn't you talk to him?' Aisling asked.

Maude shook her head. 'I left him so that he would have a chance at happiness. Leaving him, and staying away … it nearly broke me. When I saw him he looked so happy, so perfect. I suppose I was afraid. That if I came back into his life it might bring back memories that he was better off without.'

'And when he died?'

'I waited for him again the following Monday, and didn't see him. Tried again on Tuesday. I wondered if maybe he'd gone on holiday. Then on Wednesday I saw it in the paper and I fell apart. Locked myself in my hotel room. Didn't eat, didn't sleep. I might have stayed there except that the newspaper article wouldn't leave me alone. I couldn't accept that Jack had killed himself. If he had, it would have meant that he was never really free. That it followed him all those years, that everything I did … that it was all for nothing.'

'So you pulled yourself together so you could fight for Jack.'

'I don't know if it was for Jack, really. It was for myself. I needed it all to have been for something.'

'It was for something, Maude. Jack was so good. He cared for me. Protected me. Loved me. Made me feel worth loving.' There were tears in her eyes but she wanted to get the words out. 'He was such a special person. And that was thanks to you. You gave him love and he gave it to other people. Not just me. Lots of people. So I don't want you to feel that Jack's life was wasted. That everything was for nothing. I'm different because of him. Better. And I wanted to thank you.' Her words stumbled to a close, and she took a deep breath.

'I'll always miss him, Maude. Always remember him.'

Maude blinked back tears as she looked out towards the water. She thought of the little boy she had left behind twenty years before, and wished hard for a moment that she could have every year back. 'I will too, Aisling. Always.' And she let it go.

Thursday 11 April 2013

CHAPTER THIRTY-NINE

It was a 1950s bungalow, built to the side of a country road. Outside the air was fresh and clean, and birds sang. The occasional passing car did not so much disturb the silence as punctuate it.

James McIntyre opened the door to Carrie, and led her to the living room, Fisher trailing behind. The house was much too warm. They passed a hall table, on which sat an old dial-up telephone, still plugged into the wall, and framed family photographs. There was one of Danny, young and uniformed and fresh out of Templemore. The others were all of Lorna. As a baby, pink and smiling. A little girl, standing with a new bike. And older, bright and pretty, teeth in braces, long hair loose, the smile of a girl who is well loved and knows it.

The living room was small and awkwardly proportioned. There was a faded green couch, a little too large for the room, a single armchair, and someone had placed a kitchen chair so that the couch and the chairs formed a circle. It might have been welcoming, that room, if it wasn't for the oppressive heat, and the grieving, dead-eyed woman who waited for them there.

Anne McIntyre sat at one end of the couch, and James sat at the other. Anne's face was raw from crying, and she scrubbed her hands together over and over again. Carrie resisted the urge to reach out and stop her. The tidiness, the neatness and pride with which everything had been arranged, all of it together with the heat made Carrie feel claustrophobic. Fisher shifted uncomfortably on his seat. He had looked in every direction but at Anne McIntyre since they had come into the room.

'I don't understand,' Anne said, not for the first time. 'You're telling us that Aengus Barton has been released. But he killed her. He killed our Lorna. Her body was found on his land. Her blood was on his clothes. You told us that.'

'Mr Barton was released because other evidence came to light. I'm so sorry, but Danny confessed to killing Lorna. He was responsible for her death.' The McIntyres knew this. They'd been told two days before by the family liaison officer assigned to them.

'He didn't do that. My boy would never hurt anyone. You must be mad. You're saying that he murdered his own sister.' Anne's lips were so dry that they were cracked and painful looking. Her grey hair was loose around her shoulders, and her eyes were red rimmed and wild.

'I'm very sorry, Mrs McIntyre,' Carrie said again. 'But you know Danny admitted what he did. He told a witness that he placed Lorna's body in the quarry, that he put the bloody clothes in Mr Barton's wardrobe.' Danny had told Aisling Conroy almost everything. He had killed Lorna sometime on the night of the fifteenth of March, had brought her body to the woods beside the quarry, to a spot where he could observe the Barton house. He'd waited for Barton to leave before dumping Lorna's body in the water, then entered the house to plant the trace evidence.

'That's just one person's word,' Anne said. 'You didn't hear Danny say those things.'

'Someone came across Danny after he had killed Lorna and placed her body in the quarry. Danny murdered that person also, to try to avoid detection. I'm sorry. I know this is very hard.'

Anne looked down at the newspapers that lay on the coffee table, at the lurid headlines. At the photograph of her son in uniform that took up half the front page. 'You killed him,' she said, raising her voice. 'He was murdered by one of his own, by a man he should have been able to trust.'

'Sergeant Reilly had no choice. He shot Danny only to save the life of a witness.'

'This says he's been suspended,' Anne gestured sharply at the papers. 'He wouldn't have been suspended unless he did something wrong.'

Carrie looked at James McIntyre. His eyes had been focused on the carpet since they all sat down. He hadn't looked up once during the interview that followed. Didn't reach out to his wife as her distress grew. He didn't react now either, his head hung so low that Carrie couldn't read the expression on his face.

'That is standard procedure for an officer-involved shooting,' Carrie said. 'Sergeant Reilly is on administrative leave, on full pay, until the investigation into Danny's death is completed, but it's my expectation that he will shortly return to active duty.'

Anne stood. 'If you're right, if that man goes back to duty ... if he's never charged for Danny's death, then ... This is all a cover-up, isn't it? What did he find out, our Danny, that you killed him for?' She spat the words out.

'Stop it.' James spoke softly, so softly that his single utterance might have gone unheard, but Anne reacted as if a gun had just gone off in the room. She turned to look at him, almost staggering in her haste.

'Stop it, Anne.'

'James,' is all she said, her voice a broken whisper. He finally raised his eyes to her face and whatever she saw in them caused her to turn and leave the room. Fisher, Carrie and James sat in silence in the cloying heat, then James walked to the window, and a moment later a welcome blast of cold air released some of the tension in the room.

'She has never been able to accept what Danny was,' James said, as he returned to his place on the couch.

Carrie opened her mouth to ask a question and shut it again. He had a story he wanted to tell. Better to give him the space he needed to do that.

'He's not mine,' James said.

'I'm sorry?'

'Danny was born in 1973. Anne was only sixteen. She had him in a Mother and Baby home, in Bessborough. She stayed there for six months, then she left to find work, and Danny went to an orphanage. It wasn't her fault. She wasn't much more than a child. Her family didn't want to know her. If she'd taken Danny with her she wouldn't have been able to rent anywhere, wouldn't have been able to get a job. She stayed as long as they would let her, and she refused to sign adoption papers because she was always going to go back and get him.'

'I see,' Carrie said. 'When did she go back?'

'I met Anne in London in 1982, we got married and she told me about Danny.' James's voice was gruff, his words cut off. Had Anne told him before or after the marriage, and would it have made any difference either way? Would they have moved back to Ireland if it hadn't been for Danny? Ireland in the early eighties would have been a difficult place to get a job.

'You came to get him once you were married.'

James shrugged. 'He was always a difficult child, but we should have expected that. We did expect it. Those places ... they were brutal. Well we've all heard about what went on in them, haven't we? And he was only a baby.'

'He found it difficult to adjust to living with you.' It wasn't quite a question.

'He used to go out at night. He would get up and wander the fields, the village. I don't know how long it went on, but

Anne woke one night and found him gone. We were on the point of calling the police in when he walked back in the door, cool as a cucumber.'

'Where had he been?'

'He never told us. Just gave us some story about needing to see the night's sky. Anne was terrified but she would have done anything for that child. She made him promise never to do it again, but I don't think he ever stopped. And that was the least of it. You have to understand the way it was with him.' James took a breath, leaned forward. He still looked exhausted but something was animating him, maybe the relief of telling a story too long kept to himself.

'Danny stole from other children at school, just random stuff. School books, pencils, whatever. We talked to him, the school talked to him, he just didn't care. Getting upset with Danny never worked. The only thing that stopped him was threatening to take the T.V. away. That worked for about a month. Danny behaved himself or he lost T.V. time. Then one day Anne was making dinner in the kitchen and she heard a crash. She went running, thought he'd hurt himself. When she got to the living room she found he'd taken a hurley to the television. Destroyed it. Anne said he didn't even look at her, just walked past her as if nothing had happened.'

'That must have been very distressing for you.'

James snorted, shook his head. 'I wasn't even there. It was poor Anne who had to try to deal with it, and with what came after.'

'He started stealing again?' asked Fisher.

'No. He never stole anything again after that day, as far as I know, but less than a week later he used that hurley on another kid's head.'

Carrie said nothing, waited.

'They were only ten, but the other kid was something else, just a natural athlete. I suppose he got a lot of attention for it, and Danny wouldn't have liked that. Danny just walked up to this kid one day, after school, they weren't even playing hurling or anything that day. Danny just walked up to him and cracked him across the head with it as hard as he could. The other boy had to get eight stitches.'

'What happened after that?'

'Danny was suspended for a month. The other family took their kid out of school, moved him to another one. We were lucky they didn't sue us, but people didn't, in those days. After that the other kids stayed away from Danny. The parents stayed away from us too.'

'Did things ever get better?'

'He would go through phases where things were almost normal, then something would happen and he would go backwards again. Stop eating, refuse to go to school. But as he grew older he learned how to imitate other people. How to pretend. Anne couldn't see it. She was just happy that Danny was getting better. She thought he was recovering from the trauma of his childhood. But I could see the truth. He watched us, watched other kids, and he practised. He finished school, went on to join the guards.'

'You waited until Danny left before you had another baby,' Fisher said. His eyes were on James McIntyre, focused, understanding.

James turned to face him, nodded slowly. 'I couldn't have brought a baby into this house while Danny was here. Anne didn't understand. She desperately wanted another, but in time she accepted it and she put all of her energy into Danny. When he left to join the guards, Anne was only thirty-four. It wasn't too late for us.'

'How did Danny feel about Lorna?' Fisher asked.

James snorted. 'He played it perfectly. Came home with a little soft teddy for her. Laughed and teased his mother a bit, about this late baby. About what we got up to, as soon as he left the house. By then he could be very charming. He waited for Anne to leave the room, then right in front of me he reached out and pinched Lorna's little toe so hard, just held it between his finger and thumb and right in front of me he pressed and pressed, as she screamed, until I shoved him away.'

James buried his face in his hands and stayed there for a long moment, until Carrie began to think he wouldn't say anymore. When he raised his head again, he was crying.

'He hated her. Anne refuses to see it, but that's the truth of it. He was a grown man, and she was only a little baby, but he hated her from the moment she was born. I could see it in his eyes, hear it in his voice when he spoke to her. I never left her alone with him, never once. I told the school he was not to be allowed to collect her or see her there, and as soon as she was old enough I explained to her that she wasn't allowed to see him. I kept her safe for eighteen years, but he got her in the end.' And he started to weep, great wracking, raw sobs, his pain too much to hold in. Carrie let him cry, bowing her head in the face of his grief, but unable to leave. And eventually, slowly, he came back to himself.

'Why did he kill her, do you think?' Carrie asked softly.

James shook his head. 'Maybe just because he hated her. Or maybe it amused him to hurt his mother so deeply. That was always a game of his. It would be easy to say it was all because he was angry that Anne left him, because he resented Lorna for her happy childhood. I can't say for sure that wasn't the case, but you're asking me what I think. And I think Danny never felt that strongly about anyone, even Anne. He was just a wrong one from the beginning.'

Carrie wondered about that, wondered where Danny had gone after Bessborough, what had happened to him there. Maybe Danny was a product of his childhood.

'Can you tell us about the rape?' she asked.

James took a breath, then let it slowly out. He was aging here in this room, right in front of them. 'Lorna went out with friends to a nightclub. It's a country sort of place, not somewhere she could get into too much trouble, we thought. But she caught the eye of that man Kavanagh, and he put something in her drink, and her friends just *left* her there. She came home the next morning, and she barely knew where she was but she knew what had happened to her.'

'She went to the police.'

'She did. Her mother and I didn't want her to.'

Yes. When Lorna came in to report the rape, she had come alone. Some of what Carrie felt must have shown in her face, because James grew defensive.

'How many rape cases result in convictions? If she brought the thing to court they would pull her apart, destroy her, and she'd still have to deal with those men walking down the streets of her own village.'

'And Danny?'

'He wasn't happy. Said that Lorna had embarrassed him in front of his colleagues. He said she should have come to him if she had a problem and he would sort it out in his own way.'

'Why did she withdraw the charges?' Fisher asked.

James swallowed. 'They took photographs. She got an anonymous email with a link to a pornography site, where they'd put up one of the photographs. There was no message, no threat, but it was clear all the same what they were telling her. If she went ahead with the case more of those photographs would have ended up on the internet. She couldn't bear that, and she didn't believe anymore that the case would result in a conviction.'

Carrie had known it, known that Lorna had lost confidence in her, hadn't believed that she could get the job done, but it hurt to hear it said all the same. Lorna had never told her why she wouldn't proceed with the case. She'd called and left a message and after that refused to talk about it.

'But that was what Danny wanted,' Fisher said. 'He never wanted her to press charges.'

'Meaning he should have left her alone after that? She should have been safe?' James said.

Fisher nodded dumbly.

'We sent her to Dublin to keep her away from him. He wasn't happy that she'd withdrawn the charges. He was furious. He said she'd made it worse. Made him look ineffectual, because any failure of the police would be seen by the village as his personal failure.'

Fisher made no attempt to hide his incomprehension, his revulsion, and James turned back to Carrie. 'That's what he said.'

And Carrie wondered if that's what this had all been about. A childhood trauma. Some sort of festering sibling jealousy. Or maybe Danny had seen an opportunity to advance his career. The Kavanagh drug bust worked so well for him, maybe he'd decided to go again with Lorna's murder. Would he have tried to make the Barton arrest himself, if things hadn't become so complicated? If Jack hadn't seen him that morning. If Reilly hadn't been there in the background, asking questions and getting closer. It seemed to Carrie that killing Jack had thrown his whole plan out. He'd had to hide Lorna's disappearance for a week, to try to make sure that no one connected the two deaths. The longer Lorna spent in the water the harder it would be for the pathologist to determine her time of death. But despite his efforts at obfuscation, Carrie had suspected him from the beginning. Lorna had told her just enough. And so she'd been on him from the start, pushing for the missing person's case to be taken seriously, pushing for search parties and posters and a full investigation. All that pressure had had its effect on Danny. Had it pushed him over the edge? Was that why he had taken the enormous risk with Aisling Conroy? Carrie forced that thought away. She wasn't to blame for Danny's actions, for who he was. How many people were now blaming themselves, questioning every step they had taken, when really the fault lay only with him? She refused to be one of them.

Monday 15 April 2013

EPILOGUE

On Monday morning, Cormac drove back to Kilmore. On Friday he'd had a call from O'Halloran, to tell him the internal affairs investigation was closed. He was to return to active duty. He'd hung up the phone without saying a word. The investigation had been closed without a single question asked about how Danny had gotten away with the Kavanagh set up, how he'd gotten his hands on the drugs. It was a cover up, and Cormac wanted no part of it.

He'd thought briefly about going to the papers but there was too much he didn't know, and as going public would mean losing his job, too much he would have had to leave undone. Twenty years before, he'd walked away from the Blake case, and it had come back to haunt him. He was older now, and wiser, and there were some things he was unwilling to let go. Charging Domenica Keane for her abuse of the children, or for her deliberate introduction of Simon Schiller into their lives, would be extremely difficult. They'd never be able to prove intent when it came to Schiller. For the abuse, they had the medical records for both children, and Maude's statement, if she could be induced to give it formally. But Keane's lawyer would argue that the twenty-year delay in prosecution was prejudicial, and that was an argument he would likely win. Case law was against them. The High Court had thrown out simple assault cases where prosecution had been delayed by less than three years. But Cormac wasn't giving up. In the Blake–Keane case there might be something they could do. Maude and Jack had been children when the abuse occurred, and in a position of dependence on Keane. Reporting the assaults hadn't been an option. And there might be something in the new legislation he could use – new offences for child abuse or procuring a child for sexual exploitation. Cormac had a meeting scheduled with a friend at the Office of the Director of Public Prosecutions, and he had a list of questions he wanted to ask.

In the meantime he was going to interview Keane again. She was sitting, spiderlike, in her house in Kilmore, thinking herself immune from consequence. He wanted to rattle her confidence, unsettle her. At the very least it might give the old bitch a few sleepless nights, at best it might provoke her into making a mistake.

But he pulled up outside the house to a flurry of activity. There was an ambulance in the drive, a local squad car, and a car he recognised as Caoimhe O'Neill's. Caoimhe and two uniforms were standing outside the front door. As Cormac approached, paramedics rolled a gurney from the house. There was a body on the gurney, and a sheet had been drawn up over its head. Cormac kept walking towards Caoimhe.

'What happened?' Cormac asked. He flashed his badge at one of the uniforms, who showed signs of becoming officious.

'Probably carbon monoxide poisoning sir,' the uniform said. 'Accidental death, unless you're here to tell us otherwise.'

'It was that shitty old heater,' Caoimhe said, wringing her hands. 'I warned her ten times. The bloody thing was recalled about fifteen years ago. But she wouldn't listen.'

Cormac turned and watched the paramedics load the gurney into the ambulance.

'You found her?' Cormac asked.

'I haven't been here for two days,' Caoimhe said. 'I had a day's holiday yesterday, and none of the other girls would see her. If I'd been here, maybe it wouldn't have been too late.'

Christ. 'She didn't deserve your care, Caoimhe, and she doesn't deserve your regrets.' He walked away, back to his car. He had nothing else to say.

'What did she do?' Caoimhe called after him, but Cormac shook his head, got into his car, and drove away.

He didn't drive far. It took him a few minutes to find the driveway – he wasn't sure which direction it was from the Keane house. But he found it in the end, drove the car up as far as the drive was passable, then got out and walked the rest of the way. The house had been derelict twenty years before, and it was rotting now. The roof had collapsed inwards. The front door was missing, and the doorway gaped, dark and threatening. He was glad to see the place in ruins. Glad that no young Celtic Tiger couple had come here with their dreams and their temporary money, to turn the place around and give it new timbers, new sheen. This house deserved to die.

Maude had killed her mother. Hilaria had been dying, certainly, and perhaps it had been an act of euthanasia as much as it was an act of defence. Would Maude now go to prison when Domenica Keane, the root of it all, escaped what she would have hated most – exposure, and public ruin? He couldn't do it. He'd sat on his knowledge of Maude's motive since Danny had died, had fallen one way, then another every day since. But now he was sure. He would tell no one. Fuck. Fuck. Cormac picked up the remains of a slate roof tile that had fallen to the ground, and threw it as hard as he could against the house, where it shattered. Fuck.

He drove to Galway. Drove straight home. Carrie O'Halloran's car was parked in his street. As he pulled in, she got out and walked towards him.

'You didn't come in to the station,' she said.

'No.'

'Thought you'd like to know. Murphy's made the call. Charges against Maude Blake are to be dropped. Insufficient evidence.'

Cormac let out a breath. 'He doesn't want to take the chance that all the Danny shit will come out at trial.'

'Maybe.' Carrie nodded. 'Or maybe he just agrees with you that there was no case to begin with.' She looked away, towards the canal. 'It's good the charges have been dropped. The case would never have gone anywhere. Our time is better spent elsewhere.'

Her expression was set, closed. How much did she know? And how much would she tell him? When he spoke, he did so slowly, deliberately. 'I think Brian Murphy knew about Danny. Knew, at the very least, that he'd set up Kavanagh. Knew about the drugs. Maybe even about Lorna.'

Carrie said nothing for a long time, so long that he began to think she wouldn't respond at all.

'He put you on the Maude Blake case,' she said at last, her voice quiet. 'If he knew as much as you think he did, then he had to have known that would put you on a collision course with Rodgers. That you would ask questions that would lead you to Danny.'

'What are you saying, that he wanted me to stop him?'

Carrie shrugged. 'I'm just suggesting that it might not be as black and white as you think it is.'

She turned her eyes to his and they were hooded, opaque. He couldn't read her.

'We've a good team,' she said. 'You've not seen the best of it.'

'Right,' said Cormac. Maybe.

As they spoke a squad car pulled up and double-parked. Fisher jumped out of the driver's seat.

'How ya,' he said. Both detectives stared back at him.

'You weren't answering your phone,' he said, unembarrassed. 'I wanted to let you know. Murphy made a call to the lab and got the DNA fast-tracked. It came back positive. A match with the sample taken from the body in America. Lanigan's definitely our man. I've a warrant here.' He gestured with a thumb towards the car. 'Thought you might like to come along for the ride.'

Cheeky fucker. 'Murphy fast-tracked it?'

A nod.

Cormac looked towards the little house. The lights were off. Emma was at work. 'Get in the car,' said Cormac. 'I'll be with you in a minute.'

Fisher climbed back into the squad car, cheery and unfazed.

'He's one of the better ones,' said Carrie, nodding towards the car where Fisher waited.

'I'm not letting it go, Carrie,' Cormac said.

'I know,' she said again.

They looked at each other for a long tense moment. Then she nodded, and walked away.

Cormac got in the car beside Fisher. 'Feel like arresting a murderous fucker who thought he'd gotten away with it?'

'Always,' Fisher said.

'Right,' said Cormac. He reclined the passenger seat a little, closed his eyes. 'You're driving,' he said. 'Wake me when we get there.'

AUTHOR'S NOTE

Thank you so much for reading *The Ruin*. Maude, Aisling and Cormac feel so very real to me, and I hope they came to mean something to you. I'd love to hear your thoughts on *The Ruin* ... or on any other books you've read this year that you've loved (always looking for good book recommendations!). You can find me on Twitter @dervlamctiernan, or on my Facebook page DervlaMcTiernan. You can also sign up for my newsletter on my website, www.dervlamctiernan.com, for news, book chat, and information on the next book in the series (coming March 2019!).

I hope very much that you enjoyed *The Ruin*. If you did and if you have a little time, I would be so grateful if you could leave a short review online.

Thanks again for reading.

*

A confession: I cheated, just a tiny bit, in the writing of this book. Last year, when I was writing the umpteenth draft, I researched methods by which Aisling could have traced Jack's phone. I had some rules about the solution I was looking for – it had to be something she could do without recourse to some sort of spy-ware, and without access to an overly convenient friend at the phone company. I also didn't want the solution to require Jack to have pre-installed something on his phone, which meant Find-My-iPhone or something similar was out. I wanted something that would work for someone as clueless about technology as I am, starting with nothing in hand.

Then I stumbled onto Google Timeline. I use Google maps, and I have a Gmail account, both of which I access through my phone. I didn't know it (I'm sure I would have if I had read the fine print) but because I had both apps on my phone, Google had been tracking everywhere I went, and had been recording that data at least since 2015. I looked up my Timeline and found a record of everywhere I had been, and how long I had been there, the routes I had taken, *everything*, without my knowing it and without me having to download or install anything more unusual than Google maps and Gmail (both apps have over one billion users worldwide and I couldn't think of anyone I knew who didn't have both).

A perfect solution. Perfect. All Aisling would need is Jack's Google password, and all that information was sitting there waiting for her. Only one problem. Timeline wasn't introduced until 2015, and the book is set in March 2013. I looked for other solutions, I really did. But nothing was as elegant, as perfect, as *simple and dramatic* as that perfectly plotted and timed route, sitting in Jack's Google account.

So I cheated. Sorry sorry. But it is fiction, after all. (Sorry.)

ACKNOWLEDGEMENTS

Thank you Mum and Dad. Impossible to capture in a few words all you have done for me. I love you both very much. Thank you to my siblings, Conor, Fíona, Cormac, Fearghal, Odharnait and Aoibhinn – for reading the early drafts and for your encouragement and support. Love you guys. Thank you to Kevin Shinners, Rob Moore, and Lorraine Lewis for the early reads.

Thank you to my agents, Tara Wynne, Sheila Crowley and Faye Bender for brilliant agenting and for being such a joy to work with. Thank you to my editors, Anna Valdinger, Nicola Robinson, Lucy Dauman and Laura Tisdel, for having such faith in me, and for your editorial genius. Thank you too to Jaki Arthur, Kimberley Allsopp, Sarah Barrett, Theresa Anns and Shannon Kelly. You've been so generous, so supportive, and so much fun to work with.

Thank you to Libby Mathews, for letting me bend her ear on our early morning walks. Thank you to the Australia Day camping team (43°... who needs a citizenship ceremony!?) – Libby and Tim Mathews, Claire and Grey Properjohn, and Sara and Michael Pearson. Thank you for your friendship, your humour, your support and encouragement.

Thank you to everyone who stepped in when things were rotten, with such generosity and thoughtfulness – Libby, Claire and Sara, and of course Helen Pelusey, Kate Francesca, Katherine Kalaf, Lisa Whiteley, Jess Sharp, Lisa Eastwood, Maja Bajin, and Kylie Walford. Your kindness meant so much to us.

Thank you to Hampers by HRP – Carly Dolinski, Katherine Davis, Louise Southalan, Carol Low, Kat Naude, and Tim Owen (I still have Ted with the Bandaged Head); and to Elaine Paterson and Michael Moltoni for your support and generosity.

There is a garda sergeant out there who was very generous with his time but who shall remain nameless as I am sure is his preference. I took wild liberties with what I was told when it suited the story – all errors and omissions are mine.

Thank you to Sara Foster, a wonderful writer and friend who was generous with her time beyond the call of friendship. Thank you too to Natasha Lester, for her fantastic teaching.

Thank you to Mary and Mick Callan, for your hospitality and support ... and for providing the world's loveliest writer's retreat!

Thank you to Orla McGowan, for picking us up and putting us up! You were so lovely Orla, and we've never forgotten it. Thank you to Lorna Quinn, for your support and general all-round loveliness.

Thank you to my quality control department, Kathleen and Seamus McTiernan, for all your love and kindness. Looking forward already to Perth 2018!

Thank you to Freya and Oisín, for sometimes letting Daddy do bedtime so I could write. I love you both so very, very much.

And thank you Kenny, for everything. For your unending support. For believing in me long before I believed in myself. Five-year plans are the best!

Read on for an exclusive
preview of Cormac Reilly's
next compelling case,
to be released in 2019.

CHAPTER ONE

Carrie O'Halloran's phone was stubbornly silent. She'd expected a call from Ciarán so the girls could say goodnight. When that hadn't happened she'd held out for a post-bedtime update. Eight o'clock came and went and her phone screen remained dark. She could have called him, she knew that, but she didn't have the energy for another one of those conversations. Instead she put her phone in the drawer, and turned again to the mound of paper on her desk.

The case she was working on needed all her attention. It should have been a slam dunk – Rob Henderson had been caught red-handed after all – but the case showed distressing signs of slipping out of her control. She couldn't allow that to happen. Carrie had interviewed Lucy Henderson herself, but now she was reviewing the statements of colleagues and extended family members, looking for the lever she could use to open Lucy up to the fact that her husband was a murderous bastard. Half an hour passed before Carrie put her pen down and sat back from her desk. She took her phone from the drawer and woke the screen. No messages, no missed calls. Damnit. She didn't want to go home. The girls would be asleep, the kitchen in a tip, and Ciarán would be pissed off and sulking. It would be easier to just go down to the basement, find an empty cell, and sleep there. She'd have to be back by six the next day anyway if she was going to finish her Henderson prep on time.

Carrie shut her computer down, stood, and took her jacket from the back of her chair. She looked around. She wasn't the only one working, but she was the only one in the room who had started her shift at seven that morning. Fuck's sake. It would be one thing if it was a once off, but it had been like this for months. When she'd made sergeant she'd been thrilled at the thought of managing her own time. She would report to Murphy, yes, but looked forward to the broad autonomy sergeants had to run their own cases, and the gardaí reporting to them. The reality was nowadays she had less control than ever. As a uniformed garda she'd been able to go in, work her shift, and go home. There was always someone to take her place. Yes, she'd worked overtime, but that had only been as needed, and in this day and age of budget cuts, as needed was a rare thing. Now she was one of only three sergeants working out of Mill Street Garda Station, and she never went home because if she did the work would never get done.

Carrie walked out of the room, along the corridor to the stairs, started down. She was still holding her mobile phone in one hand and it buzzed, finally. A text message flashed up on the screen and she read it in a glance. *I'm golfing on Saturday. Girls are going to my mother's.* Fuck. No way. Carrie stared at her phone, thought about Mel Hackett on holiday in the south of France, about Cormac Reilly walking out of the station at six o'clock, as he had every day this week. She turned on her heel and made for the superintendent's office. She knocked on the door, waited, then opened it and leaned into the room.

'A moment, sir?'

Brian Murphy was engrossed in whatever was on his computer screen. His mouse hand clicked twice before he looked up. It was after hours; he was probably posting on triathletenow.com again. Not for the first time Carrie tried to think of a way to drop a hint that Murphy's posting on the site wasn't as anonymous as he thought. Somehow, someone in vice had found out his user handle, and it was now known across the station. The night that *TopCopTriGuy* had engaged in a detailed discussion of haemorrhoid problems in older cyclists had resulted in station-wide hilarity, and the placing of cushions on meeting room chairs whenever Murphy was likely to appear. He couldn't possibly be as oblivious as he seemed, could he?

He gestured to her to take a seat. 'So Henderson is catatonic. Is he faking?'

Carrie shrugged. 'The doctor says not, but I've my doubts.'

'And the wife?'

'Still in denial. I've a meeting with her again tomorrow. I'm going to push her. I think she might be hiding something.'

'Update me afterwards,' Murphy said. 'Let me know if you make any progress.'

Carrie nodded. She would have done so without the request. The case was high profile, and Murphy had been all over it from the beginning. He looked at her expectantly, waiting for more.

'Sir, I've got too much on,' she blurted. 'Too many cases, I mean.'

He raised an eyebrow.

'I've six active cases. Seven more that will go to court within the next few months.' Meanwhile Mel Hackett had what, two? Three max. And Reilly nothing current at all. 'It's not sustainable. If I keep working like this I'll make mistakes.'

'It's not a nine-to-five job, Carrie. I made that clear to you when I offered you the promotion.'

She ignored that. Went straight to what she knew would motivate him. 'I've had a look at the stats. Our timeframe to clearance is running long. And we've two missing persons not yet traced. I know the Commissioner was looking for a zero rate this year from Galway.'

Murphy leaned back in his chair. 'Hackett is due back next week,' he said. 'We'll sit down then and do a case review, see what can be redistributed.'

'Sir, I talked to Mel before she went on holiday. She's positive she doesn't have the capacity to take on anything more.' Which was bollox, but beside the point.

Murphy rubbed his jaw, compressed his lips, and said nothing.

'Cormac Reilly …' Carrie started to say.

'Reilly is fully engaged,' Murphy said. 'He's caught up in a cold case review that takes all of his time.'

Carrie made no attempt to hide her frustration. 'Christ sir, when do you want me to get it done? In my sleep?'

'This is the job, Carrie.'

'Sir, what I'm telling you is that you've got three sergeants working for you, and the least experienced of them is doing seventy per cent of the work load.' Because Hackett was an old hand at managing the system, and Cormac Reilly wasn't let near anything that looked like a real case. 'Reilly is a bloody good detective,' Carrie continued. 'I've heard about some of the cases he's run and won. We're lucky to have him. And it is madness to keep him working pissy cold cases that aren't going to go anywhere. You need to put him on active cases, or replace him with someone you can use.' Carrie stopped. She'd gone too far. She waited for Murphy to show her the door.

'One of those pissy little cold cases, as you so colourfully call them, has resulted in a major arrest.'

'That's one case,' Carrie said quickly, hiding her relief. 'And the doer's been extradited. He'll be tried in the U.S., not here.'

There was a long pause, during which voices from the last few police in the building could be heard loudly talking about pints and weekend plans. It was all so bloody stupid. Did he really think that Reilly would just throw in the towel if he was frozen out for long enough? He was a career cop, it was in his DNA. Reilly was going nowhere, unless of course he transferred back to Dublin. He might already have done that if it wasn't for the girlfriend. Partner. Whatever.

'It wasn't his fault, sir. The shooting.'

'I never suggested it was.'

Carrie hesitated. The part of her that was interested in self-preservation and possible future career advancement wanted her to shut up. The part of her that was desperate for a weekend off, some time with her kids, and at least a chance of saving her marriage, said to press on. The little bit of her that believed Cormac Reilly had been treated unfairly tipped the balance.

'It's not going to work,' Carrie said quietly. 'He's not going to go anywhere, and people are starting to talk. The uniforms aren't stupid. They know about his experience, his previous success rate. Internal affairs cleared him in the shooting case, on paper he's back on active duty, but in practice he gets nothing. They're asking why. They're saying there's no smoke without fire. Sooner or later Reilly will have to do something. What if he calls in the union? Or worse, a lawyer?'

'If you're suggesting that Cormac Reilly has been treated unfavourably because of what happened in April, O'Halloran, you're out of line. Reilly gets his cases in rotation like everyone else.'

Carrie said nothing more, waited. Let the lie hang in the air between them. She looked at Murphy, caught his gaze and held it.

He was the first to look away. When he spoke it was very quietly. 'You're sure about this, Carrie? There's no going back.'

She hesitated. 'I'm sure.'

Without looking at her he turned to his computer screen, moved and clicked his mouse. Read something that Carrie couldn't see.

'Give Reilly the Durkan case.' Another click of the keys. 'Nesbitt too.' A pause. 'And the Henderson case.'

Carrie had been on the point of smiling in relief, but at the last she froze, opened her mouth to protest. 'Sir, I …'

'I read the transcript of your last interview with Lucy Henderson. You're not getting anywhere with her. Let Reilly see where he can take it. She strikes me as the type who'd respond better to a man.'

His tone made it clear that the meeting was at an end.

Shit.

'Thank you, sir.' She waited, but he didn't react. She had reached the door when he spoke again.

'O'Halloran. I hope this isn't a mistake.' His expression was distant and the message was clear. Carrie had been granted a favour and that favour had been noted in his little book of favours owed and given. He would call it in too, he always did.

'Yes sir.'

Cormac was surprised, but not unpleasantly so, to get a text message from Carrie O'Halloran asking if he was free for a quick drink on a Friday evening. He was in town anyway, as it happened, having a pint and waiting for Emma to finish work. They had a booking for a late dinner. He texted Carrie back, and ordered himself another drink and a glass of red for her while he waited.

He liked Carrie. She was a good cop, a good sergeant, and he trusted her. Three months before, when an investigation Cormac was working led him to a violent confrontation with a colleague, Carrie had done what she could to ensure that the powers that be didn't scapegoat him. Since then they'd had coffee or lunch together a handful of times, but they weren't on the kind of terms that included Friday night drinks. Something must be up.

She arrived five minutes later, made her way through the bar and found him in his corner booth. He watched her as she approached, noted the signs of tiredness around her eyes. She was still wearing the tailored pants and jacket he'd seen her in earlier that day. She clocked the wine as soon as she sat down.

'Thanks,' she said. 'But I should probably have coffee.' She still reached out and picked up the glass, took a sip. 'I haven't been home before ten o'clock any night this week. I worked the last two weekends, and worked three last month. I'm overloaded. I've spoken to Murphy and he's told me to transfer some cases to you.'

Cormac nodded slowly. 'That makes sense,' he said. He couldn't quite get a read of her – had she wanted this? 'Which cases?'

'Durkan. Nesbitt. And Henderson.'

'Right.' The first two he'd heard nothing about, assumed were standard fare. But the Henderson case. He'd heard enough about it to know that it was a case she'd been working passionately. It was almost certainly the case that had kept her at the station all hours for the past week.

'Henderson,' Cormac said. 'Are you all right about that?'

'No,' she said baldly. She sipped her wine, then turned to him. 'Murphy wasn't too pleased with me putting him under pressure. I gave him an earful about you working cold cases. Said he needed to shit or get off the pot. Well, not in so many words.'

'And Henderson was his way of saying …'

'His way of saying thank you, yes.' She put her glass down on the table. 'It's an important case to get right,' she said, and he could tell that she was picking her words carefully. 'Lucy Henderson is a hard read.'

'Right,' Cormac said. He drank from his pint, buying time. He didn't want the case, didn't want to pick something up that had someone else's fingerprints, someone else's method all over it. Particularly when that someone else resented handing it over. Christ, was he ever going to have a clean case to work again? Something that he could run from the beginning, something that wasn't lousy with station politics.

'Let's talk to Murphy on Monday. Decide which cases are at a good stage to unload. You keep Henderson. I'll take whatever you think is at a good stage to pass over. If we present Murphy with a fait accompli he'll have to take it.'

She looked surprised, then considering, then reluctantly shook her head. Took a longer sip from her glass of wine. 'He's right, though I hate to admit it. I've made no progress with the wife. She might respond better to you. And the hearing will almost certainly clash with one of my other cases. I think you're going to have to take it.' She still looked tired but some of the tension had gone out of her voice.

Cormac leaned forward. 'Carrie, I've no wish to be at outs with you.'

She waived him off. 'No. Sorry. It's me. I was a bit pissed off, but that's just the tiredness speaking. I should go home. Get some sleep.' But she made no move to stand.

A phone vibrated against the table and they both looked down. Cormac picked it up.

'That's Emma. Come with us for dinner. Have a bite before you drive home.' Before Carrie could respond Cormac answered the call.

'Em? You finished? I'm in Buskers. The back bar.' The relaxed look on Cormac's face faded quickly, and he stood, putting a hand to his ear to block noise so he could concentrate on the call. He locked eyes with Carrie.

'Where are you? Emma. Stop. Take a breath.' Cormac's face was tense but his tone was very controlled. 'Tell me where you are.'

And then he was moving.